Ex Libris

Elizabeth Hascin

Merry Christmas
2005

Love,

Nana

Marele Day is the author of the bestselling literary novel, *Lambs of God* (1997), which was published to acclaim in Australia and overseas, and the Claudia Valentine mysteries, including *The Last Tango of Dolores Delgado* (1992), winner of the American Shamus Crime Fiction Award.

Mrs Cook

MARELE DAY

Mrs Cook

The Real and Imagined Life of the Captain's Wife

ALLEN&UNWIN

First published in 2002

This edition first published in 2003

Copyright © Marele Day 2002, 2003

Allen & Unwin
83 Alexander Street
Crows Nest NSW 2065
Australia
Phone: (61 2) 8425 0100
Fax: (61 2) 9906 2218
Email: info@allenandunwin.com
Web: www.allenandunwin.com

National Library of Australia
Cataloguing-in-Publication entry:

Day, Marele.
    Mrs Cook: the real and imagined life of the captain's wife.

    ISBN 1 74114 121 4.

    1. Cook, Elizabeth, 1742–1835. 2. Explorers' spouses—Fiction.
    I. Title.

A823.3

Illustrations by James P. Gilmour
Internal design by Nada Backovic

Set in 10.5/13.5 pt Sabon (Old Style Figures) by Bookhouse, Sydney
Printed in Australia by McPherson's Printing Group

10 9 8 7 6 5 4 3 2

ACKNOWLEDGEMENTS

I would like to acknowledge all those who helped with research, in particular Ian Stubbs of the Captain Cook Birthplace Museum, Julia Rae of the Stepney Historical Trust, Chris Pryke and staff at the State Library of New South Wales, the National Library of Australia, the British Library, and other libraries in London and Barking. Special gratitude goes to Clifford Thornton, President of the Captain Cook Society, for his willingness to answer questions large and small, his attention to detail, and for rectifying historical inaccuracies in the text. Any that remain are my own.

I would like to thank George Mannix who read an early draft; my agents, Rachel Calder (UK) and Elaine Markson (US) for their encouragement and ability to see the potential of Elizabeth Cook's story; Patrick Gallagher, Christa Munns, Karen Penning and the team at Allen & Unwin for realising that potential; Julia Stiles for her understanding and inspired suggestions; Jo Jarrah for judicial editiorial cuts; Susie Burge for her steadfastness and ability to see the whole picture as well as the detail, and James Gilmour for his delightful illustrations.

Mrs Cook

Thirteenth of May, 1835. In Clapham High Street on the outskirts of London is a large Georgian house 'crowded and crammed in every room with relics, curiosities, drawings, maps, and collections'. There are tapa cloths from Tahiti, oars from a Maori canoe, a fur cloak from the Nookta people of Canada. Embroideries, boxes, sets of fine china, shoe buckles, books and a Bible. A coat of arms bestowed by King George III hangs by the bed, as well as the Copley Medal from the Royal Society. In cupboards and on shelves can be found quadrants, telescopes and other scientific instruments from the previous century.

The lady who lived in this house died today, aged ninety-three. Her portrait shows a dignified woman with fine skin, an aquiline nose and startling blue eyes. Though the face is that of an old woman, the eyes remain young. She is dressed in black satin, with a large goffered cap, a ruff around her neck, the fashions of an earlier time. Her hands, edged in white cuffs, are folded over each other and she is wearing rings. One of these is decorated with a motif made of her husband's hair. He died when she was thirty-seven, leaving her a widow for her remaining fifty-six years. She outlived all of her six children—a daughter who died aged four, and five sons, two of whom died as babies, one at age sixteen, one seventeen, and the eldest at thirty-one. So many deaths. But there was also a life.

THE FROST FAIR PRINT

Elizabeth came in the stillness of winter, on 24 January 1741 by the old Julian calendar. The ice-cold stars and the moon gleam stroking the masts of ships etched lines and shadows on the baby's papery thin eyelids. Sounds came in through the large-lobed ears, smells through the fine baby nostrils, ripples upon the air that were yet to be named. She was born in the middle of everything, in the Bell alehouse on the corner of Wapping High Street and Brewhouse Lane, opposite Execution Dock.

Two years earlier to the day, Samuel Batts and his new wife Mary set off from their alehouse and went to the Frost Fair. So much excitement—it had been years, more than twenty or so, since the coldness had dropped low enough to freeze the Thames.

'I'll tell you a story as true as 'tis rare, of a river turned into a Bartlemy Fair,' sang the balladeer circling round the couple for money as they stepped onto the ice noisy with all the trade of a solid-ground fair—bull-baiting, horse and coach racing, sleds, puppet shows, cooks and pancakes, ducks and geese, makeshift taverns, and drunks who had business on both sides of the street. There were jugglers, whores, pickpockets and cheats. The Frost Fair had all the attractions of St Bartholemew's except the prices were higher, and the booths were made of blankets. The frost froze the ships into the river and their masts rose out of it like a forest of bleak trees.

It was a welcome outing for Sam Batts, proprietor of the Bell alehouse. Men still drank when the river froze over but the trade was less with the ships stuck in one place with no cargoes to deliver and no gatherings in the alehouse when the colliers and the hands were paid off and passed the money straight over the counter.

Mary, the second wife of widower Batts, was a great deal younger than her husband, and as they were donning scarves and muffs and cloaks, he told her about the 1716 Frost Fair that he'd attended as a youth. 'I'd never seen the like,' he said. 'That big white thoroughfare. It went for miles.' During the Frost Fair of 1565, amid the archery and football and dancing on the Thames, Queen Elizabeth herself had descended on the fair, Sam said, and manoeuvred her wide skirts between the booths and stalls to witness an ox roasting on the spit.

'Did everybody curtsy?' Mary asked her husband, the question coming out as a puff of warmth into the frozen air. Sam pursed his lips, his chin folding into his collar. 'Them that could see her, I imagine,' he answered with his own puff of breath. 'Them that were in sight of her,' he added.

What a world marriage to Sam opened up, thought Mary, her cheeks tingling. It was almost as if he had arranged the Frost Fair himself, presenting it to her as a wedding gift. Mary was proud to be on her husband's arm. He was an important man on the riverside and everyone seemed to know him. He moved with ease through the fair, with as much self-assurance as a nobleman perusing his estates.

Samuel Batts was a freeborn Englishman, as good as any other. He had a nice little business going with his dockside alehouse, and a few other properties with tenants. His collar was trimmed with fur and although a merchant, and a publican to boot, he was as good as any man. Especially at the fair. The entertainments of the fair, its sports and pleasures, were there for all to see, whether you were a lord or a beggar.

The blanket of ice did little to muffle the noise but added instead to the excitement as boys skidded along on it, with no mind as to whom they collided with on the way. Galloping sleighs sent people scattering as well, with much shaking of fists, shouts of indignation and curses.

Wherever there was a cluster of people, even more gathered to see what the attraction was. Sam and Mary were heading towards such a cluster. As they made their way over ice pink with the rays of the winter sun slanting between the horizon and the swathes of grey clouds, they could make out above the milling crowds the sign pegged onto the opening of the booth—'Names Printed in Here'.

As they pushed through the crowd to the printer's booth, Mary and Sam could see a gent, forearm resting on the table to show off his cuffs, face in three-quarter profile and framed by a handsome grey powdered wig, having his portrait sketched.

'I'll wager some scamp will have that wig off and sold to the highest bidder by the end of the day,' Sam said out of the side of his mouth.

'Perhaps,' said Mary. It certainly happened in the streets, thieves robbing wigs straight off gents' heads, and the Frost Fair produced high spirits.

A pair of boats lay side by side in the ice, like the twin halves of a pea pod. Close by, a ball trundled its way up an ice alley to knock over a set of skittles. Sam and Mary saw a boy scrambling to retrieve the hat that had flown off his head during a fall. His companions were pushing and shoving each other to see who would be next to the ground. A flock of seagulls squawked overhead, wondering where their river had gone. On the horizon, behind the street of booths, were the buildings of the city, the dome of St Paul's.

The printing was done directly on the ice, with portable presses the enterprising printers had brought down to the river. For sixpence you could have your name done, for a shilling a personalised souvenir. Sam paid the shilling. When the work was done he presented it to his wife and she read: 'Mr and Mrs Samuel Batts, printed on the river Thames when frozen over, 24 January 1739'.

On 24 January two years later, the room above the Bell alehouse where Mary was giving birth grew fuggy with heat from the fire and candles, from the press of the midwife and the other women in attendance. As the hot pain of the coming child convulsed her, Mary stretched out to the print on the wall and the coolness of the Frost Fair.

THE QUILL

James shook the snow from his jacket and entered the Postgate school. As he hung the jacket on a peg he heard Mr Rowland giving the news that in London the Thames had turned to ice, freezing the boats into the river. 'No doubt those enterprising Londoners will find a way of turning it to their advantage,' said the Yorkshire schoolmaster.

The eleven year old took his seat at the table with the other children, at the end of the bench because he was tall and had to stretch out his gangling legs in that small room with its upstairs loft where the teacher retired at the end of his day. 'You're late,' said Mr Rowland, putting a mark against James's name. Small wonder when he had farm chores to do before trudging a mile through thick snow to school. But James had come. He would not be marked absent with an A, like Anne Clark or Joseph Webster, Pc for playing in church like John Grayson or Mary Mease, or the Curs for cursing marked against Nicholas Skottowe.

It was Mr Skottowe, Nicholas's father, who paid for James to attend the school in Great Ayton. James's father said they had a lot to be grateful for with Mr Skottowe and, aye, the boy knew it all right and he would come to school better late than never. Except for mathematics he was an average pupil. He came to school because it was an honour bestowed. None of the rest of them, not even his elder brother John, had Mr Skottowe paying for their education. This is what his father told him in quiet moments between the two of them. 'He knows you, James,' his father said. 'He sees that you have a good head on you and that you don't shirk from hard work. If you do right by him he'll do right by you.' It was Mr Skottowe who had advanced James's father from labourer to bailiff, with a measure of responsibility in running Aireyholme Farm. James hated being cooped up in that small schoolroom but he did not want to spend the rest of his days mucking out stables. When he passed through the doorway of the schoolhouse he was entering into a different world from cows and manure.

He had caught a glimpse of that world where the moors rolled towards the sea, when he was little and they still lived in Marton and he climbed the great tree outside the clay biggin where he had been born. The cottage was so small the tree was the only place to stretch out. He was high above everything. The wind was different up there. It was the wind made by the turning of the earth.

'What is the value of 58 361 hogsheads of tobacco at £48 12s 9d per hogshead?' Mr Rowland had shown James how to do such sums and as James worked the problem, a space for the answer at the top and the workings beneath, he could hear the teacher's questions and the droning answer of Christopher Maisterman. 'How many syllables are there in the word pupil?' 'Two.' 'How prove you that?' 'Because it hath two vowels.' 'How divide you them?'

James had already finished his problem, the figures neatly under each other in columns. As he made sure that his calculations were correct, his mind automatically formed the division 'pu-pil' before he heard Christopher say it, in the same droning tone that they used to repeat the catechism. James had learnt reading and spelling two years earlier. Then came writing. He liked that the best. Especially writing arithmetic. He looked to the next problem: 'If 5 shipwrights can build a vessel in 4 weeks, how long would it take 7 to do so?'

Mr Rowland had supplied James with the copybook and showed him how to make a quill. James had chosen a flight feather from one of the Canada geese that wintered in these parts, had found the grey feather with its white underside in the place where the geese preened themselves. He loved watching the great flocks of them flying in, loved to hear that honking sound fill the air. He'd hardened the feather by putting it in hot ashes and then, with a knife, scraped the skin off the end. 'Two inches will do,' said Mr Rowland. James observed how Mr Rowland's quill was shaped and made the same diagonal cut, then scooped out a section and made a small slit in the tip. Finally he removed a few more filaments of the feather to make the quill comfortable to hold.

It was a fine quill and James was careful with the ink so as not to drop blobs of it on the precious paper. How long would it take the seven shipwrights? He had already done the calculations in his head but Mr Rowland would want to see the workings. James dipped the quill in the inkwell and made marks on the paper. Then he wiped the quill clean and put it down.

The droning had stopped. 'If you've finished there, James, there's weights and measures to go on with. We won't have idle minds in this schoolroom.'

THE BELL ALEHOUSE

Elizabeth's first death was her father's, barely six months after she was born. It came to her in the souring of her mother's milk. The baby's insistent mouth searched for succour in that life-stream, and with no words or language to separate one thing from another, Elizabeth took in with life's sweetness also its sorrow.

The will of Sam Batts, victualler, was proved on the twenty-first day of July 1742, by the oath of Mary Batts, widow. He had left his wife the alehouse, the tenanted properties and a fatherless baby. When she had married Sam, Mary had hoped for a few more years than this. At least he had lived long enough to see the baby christened Elizabeth, quickly, seven days after her birth, for one never knew with babies.

Mary and Sam had carried their child, blanketed against the falling snow, across the marshy grounds to St John's Church. *Memento mori*. Death was always the uninvited guest, but at the christening Mary said prayers and burnt herbs to keep death away. She had not thought, on that last day of January, that so joyous an occasion would be followed so soon by the slab of death. On the hot July day of Sam's funeral, Mary carried the baby alone.

She knew what Sam wanted—for her to keep the business going. Her father, Charles Smith, agreed. Truth be told, it was one of the reasons he had assented to the transaction of marriage between his daughter and the businessman. Unlike other publicans on the waterfront, who gave it a try and lasted a year at the most, Batts had run his alehouse for more than fourteen years.

Mary hadn't reckoned on this, she told her father, as she walked the baby up and down. It was the only thing she could do to stop Elizabeth crying. 'You mustn't pamper the child,' her father advised her. Mary swallowed a hard lump in her throat. She would not succumb to tears in front of him. But didn't he see that the whole thing was upsetting Elizabeth? She could feel the bristled air.

'For the future of the child you must carry on,' her father said more softly. Mary nodded. She knew it already, knew there was no choice. In the swirl of life on the waterfront you couldn't stop. The tide would lap over you and eventually engulf you.

Mary held the baby to her after her father had returned home to Bermondsey across the river. She kept pacing. Sam had left her with two children to look after—sweet little Elizabeth and a big boisterous alehouse that would run into trouble if it wasn't watched carefully. If she let the alehouse go she would be in ruin. The poorhouse or worse. 'I will never let that happen,' Mary whispered into the baby's ear. She had worked by her husband's side, she would imagine him still there, as indeed the ghost of him was, though a ghost could not serve customers or keep order, employ men to unload cargoes, conduct meetings or undertake any of the other business that dockside publicans engaged in.

Mary sighed. Working alongside Sam was one thing, taking his place was another.

The tide was out and the river stank. The muddy iodine smell of it blended with everything else—the buckets of coal, stacks of timber, rope, beer and gin. Above all, the smell of men. Would the men respect Mary the way they did Sam? There were plenty who would seek to take advantage of a young widow.

The baby was fitful and wouldn't sleep. Mary held her at the window and looked out at the night. It was rarely clear in London, there was always a haze, and coal dust settling on everything like black snow. The hubbub of the streets had died down somewhat, though Mary knew there were those who had business in the dark of night. Like the two small shadows moving across the shine of mud towards one of the ships. She'd seen the cargo come in from that one—tobacco from the colonies—all of it now safely behind the high brick walls of a warehouse, protected by watchmen peering out between slits in the brickwork. Behind those walls the riches of the world were amassed. Bolts of cloth, tobacco, spirits and tea, spices. Coal and alum.

Mary identified the shadows now—two boys, no more than seven years old, slipping across the mud, wading into the shallows and climbing on board the ship, ready to pilfer whatever came to hand, or perhaps, Mary thought more kindly, looking for somewhere to sleep for the night.

'For the future of the child . . .' Mary had to prepare herself for the daunting task ahead. She wrapped Elizabeth warmly in a blanket, and took out Sam's ledger.

In the following year the Bell alehouse was thriving but the baby was not, one perhaps the result of the other. Mary had servants and employees to help, of course, but as Sam always said, the best way to run a business was to keep an eye on everything yourself. Mary was afraid she'd been keeping an eye on the alehouse at the expense of her daughter. The child remained small, despite Mary's attempts to feed her, and had a dry cough, but thankfully no blood with it. Elizabeth seemed happy enough, and at least the cough got no worse, even in the spring when the winds blew in all kinds of sudden calamities.

It had been hard for Mary, especially at the beginning during those busy summer months. She'd spent night after night going over Sam's ledger, forcing herself to do the calculations and to do them quickly. She had to keep her eye on everything, make sure that the servants and lodgers weren't stealing from her or taking advantage. Mary was especially grateful for the support of the Quakers with whom she conducted business. She had heard that at Quaker prayer meetings women sometimes got up to speak and that what they said was accepted with the same gravity accorded to a man. Perhaps that was the reason the Quaker merchants readily accepted her in place of Sam. Mr Sheppard, part-owner of John Walker's ships from Whitby, had helped her organise the gangs of coal heavers, and showed her how to keep a tally of what they drank.

The winter, with its slower trade, had brought Mary some respite and a little more time with Elizabeth, but now it was spring and the ships were starting up again and there were cargoes to unload. The alehouse was full of heavers turning money into ale, and ale into money, slaking their thirst only to sweat it out again over the next lot of cargo. An alehouse was not the best place for a child as young as Elizabeth, but there were plenty worse off. Mary tried to keep her daughter upstairs, but the little one had begun to walk and despite a barrier of servants and closed doors, had found her way out.

Elizabeth stood at the top of the stairs, her hands on the balustrade, and looked through the bars to the world below. Such a sea of bodies, some sitting, some standing, but all seemed to her to be in motion like a slow-moving tide. She breathed in the smell of it, a soup of ale and sweat and coal.

'Mama.' Her eyes finally lit on her mother, in conversation at the end of the bar with a couple of men in tall black hats and cloaks. Elizabeth began making her way down, each step an operation that involved arms as well as legs, one hand on the bars before the other let go to find its new place further down.

'What do we have here? A fine looking morsel for my dinner.' A big coal-smeared face loomed up at her, tobacco-stained teeth visible in the grin. Elizabeth stood stock-still, watching the flicker of bloodshot, rheumy eyes. She felt the roughness of his hands on her and suddenly she was lifted into the air, her little face only inches away from a timber beam. In the corner of it was a grey patch of cobweb.

Then she felt herself flying backwards, and the world was upside down. 'Mama!'

Mary was already fighting her way through the crowd, ordering the drunk to put the baby down. 'You wouldn't miss a sippet like this, would you, missus, a tidy morsel no bigger than a rabbit? I've a mind to put her on the fire and roast her straight-away.' He flaunted the baby high over his head, as if she were a prize he had won. Mary held her tongue, more fearful that the drunk would slip and fall with the baby than that he intended any harm to her. The muscles at the sides of her cheeks stood out as she clenched her teeth.

Then a lodger appeared on the stairway. Mr Blackburn. Mary had no idea how long he had been there. Her eyes were fully fixed on Elizabeth, the baby's little hands swimming in the air, trying to right herself. Everyone in the alehouse was still, except for the drunk, who continued swaying with his prize, grinning in his glory. Mr Blackburn advanced one step then two, till he was right behind the drunk. The baby made a small sound as Mr Blackburn took the drunk's prize as easily as if he'd relieved him of his hat. Then, with a deft movement, he kicked the drunk into the crowd.

Mr Blackburn handed Elizabeth to her mother. The baby gurgled but seemed none the worse for wear. Mary hugged Elizabeth to her breast, the baby's little nose squashing against the bones in her mother's stays. She saw no more of the drunk except fists pounding down on him and the back of his heels as he was eventually kicked out the door.

Mary walked the short distance along the High Street to the Quaker house of the Sheppards, lifting her skirts to avoid the mud, manoeuvring her way through the crowds of mariners, street girls and urchins, around a pile of oars and timbers, stepping over the feet of a beggar who had taken up residence in the street.

Quakers helped those in need. Fire was a constant menace in the crowded dock area, and there had been some terrible fires, especially when the flames got into the warehouses where gunpowder was stored. The Quakers took in those made homeless by the fires, and other unfortunate families. Mary didn't think of herself as unfortunate, but the Sheppards had often expressed concern for Elizabeth.

When she came to the Sheppards' alleyway, a woman in a raggy shawl and bare feet tried to sell Mary her baby. 'A young'un for you, missus,' said the woman, showing gin-rotted teeth. Mary, her thoughts full of her own little Elizabeth, momentarily forgot the riverside practice of ignoring such offers. She gaped at the baby in the woman's arms. It was a scrawny little thing with a bluish tinge. Mary wasn't even sure it was alive. She faltered, almost turned back. Mary gave the woman a shilling, much more than she'd normally give a beggar, and made herself knock on the Sheppards' door.

A servant showed Mary in to the plainly furnished house. She sat rigidly on a chair and made the necessary arrangements with Mrs Sheppard. Elizabeth would be taken by boat to Barking, then on to the Sheppards' country house at Crowcher's Yard.

Mrs Sheppard suggested a monthly sum for lodging Elizabeth and Mary offered more, to make sure the child was well cared for.

'That will not be necessary,' said Mrs Sheppard gently. 'I'll look after Elizabeth as if she were my own. It will be a pleasure to have her,' she added. 'She'll be a friend for my own little Sarah. Friday fortnight, would that be suitable, Mrs Batts?' Mary slowly nodded her head. Mrs Sheppard could see that the conversation was not an easy one for her neighbour. She put her hand on Mary's knee. 'I'll bring Sarah with me, that might make the . . . ' she searched for the right word, ' . . . transition a little smoother.'

On the appointed day Mary packed Elizabeth's bag. 'You're going to stay in the country with Mrs Sheppard,' she said brightly as Elizabeth watched her clothes going into the bag. 'She has a little girl about the same age as you. Won't it be fun to have a playmate! There'll be bunny rabbits and lambs,' Mary went on. Nothing seemed to stop the toddler's little mouth from quivering. 'Oh, Elizabeth,' said Mary, trying to stop her own mouth from quivering. How could she explain?

Mary carried her child towards the wharf. She took out her handkerchief and wiped the little one's face. 'We don't want to greet Mrs Sheppard with tears, do we?' she said, biting her lip. 'Be a brave girl for Mama.' She spotted the distinctive black Quaker dress in the crowd. 'There's Mrs Sheppard and little Sarah.'

Elizabeth looked at Sarah, a strange yet familiar creature, just like herself. When their mothers brought them up close, Elizabeth stuck out her hand, and after initial surprise at the gesture, Sarah put hers out too. The mothers smiled with relief.

Mrs Sheppard handed Sarah down to a servant in the waiting boat then stepped aboard herself. It was time to pass Elizabeth over. 'Be a good girl,' Mary whispered, smothering Elizabeth in kisses. 'Do everything Mrs Sheppard tells you to.'

The boatman loosened the moorings. 'Mama!' cried Elizabeth when she saw that her mother wasn't coming with them. 'It's all right, Elizabeth,' said Mary, swallowing back her tears. 'Look, Mrs Sheppard has a banana for you.' But Elizabeth wasn't interested. 'Mama!' she cried, reaching out for her. Mary clenched her fists to stop herself from plucking Elizabeth out of the boat and taking her home. 'Be brave, my little one,' Mary called as the boat pulled her child away from her.

Mary could hardly bear to watch yet she could not let Elizabeth see her mother turn away from her. She was not trying to get rid of her child like the gin-rotted woman, she kept telling herself, it was only a temporary measure. She steadied herself against the mooring post and waved her handkerchief, held it up high for Elizabeth to see. As the boat became smaller and smaller Mary felt her heart being dragged out with it as if she were tied to the boat by an invisible rope. Tears streamed down her face. She stood on the wharf waving her handkerchief long after the boat taking Elizabeth away had disappeared in a loop of the river.

THE GREAT TREE

J ames stood on the edge, the wind from beyond the horizon howling in his face. He looked down to the sea far below, its churning waters, blue on this day of sun, and the white spray hitting the rocks. He was walking the twelve miles from Staithes to Whitby, along the cliff-tops, listening out for the boggles who were supposed to live in the nooks and crannies. The creatures had never been seen but on certain days, it was said, you could hear them doing their washing. James listened carefully. The sound was not caused by unseen creatures. It was the wind itself, scouring out the crevices. That would make the sound of a washboard.

James continued on his way, shirt off, the wind drying the sweat on his chest. He had seen this coast, or at least the ships that sailed it, from the great tree which grew outside the tiny clay biggin in Marton where he and his brother John had been born little more than a year apart.

James had been barely four years old when he'd first climbed the great tree. Even now as he walked along the coastal path he could recall the rough texture of bark, the needle-like leaves he grabbed hold of to haul himself up. It had been a windy day but that was nothing unusual in Yorkshire. He had climbed, one big step at a time, looking up after each for a foothold for the next. Higher and higher he went up the sturdy trunk and branches till he was in the billowing sky. He looked across the patchwork of fields, the pastures and the dark gorse dotted with yellow flowers. Saw tiny specks of cows grazing, farms and buildings. Then, far in the distance, where the sky came down to the land, something caught his eye. He climbed higher, to get a better look, and as he gazed at it, trying to determine what the thing was, he discovered that it was moving.

The wind ate up all the sound of the earth, swirled it around and spat it out somewhere else altogether. It was ages before the wind carried up the sound of his own name and he looked down to see his mother beckoning, waving oatcakes in her hand.

'What moves between the land and the sky?' James had asked while they were eating their dinner.

'A bird?' said his father, thinking it was a riddle. He smeared butter on an oatcake. James shook his head. It wasn't a bird. 'A cloud?' his father guessed again. James furrowed his brow, frustrated at not being able to explain. Then he got an idea. He excused himself from the table, went outside and came back with his kerchief tied to a twig. 'Like this, Da,' he said, showing his father. James senior was about to bite into the oatcake but stopped, impressed by the boy's ingenuity. 'Why, that looks like the sail of a ship.' He looked around the one-room cottage that was their home, wondering what had given his son the notion of a ship.

'Young James climbed the tree today,' said Grace, his mother.

James had been reluctant to share this news with his father, fearing trouble, but James Cook senior accepted it with a chuckle. 'No doubt a little bird whispered in his ear,' he said, winking at Grace. 'The coast must be twenty mile away. I doubt you can see it from here, lad, tree or no.'

'Perhaps a ship entering the mouth of the Tees?' suggested Grace, trying to help her son out. His father continued doubting. But James had seen what he had seen, whether his father believed him or no.

Later, when they moved to Aireyholme Farm, James saw the sea itself. He had climbed to the peak of Roseberry Topping behind the farm and there in the distance was the streak of blue, a precise line separating it from the sky.

He loved climbing that hill. He could see all the land around, Mr Skottowe's minuscule farms and the narrow cart-track leading to Great Ayton far below. Mr Skottowe may have been lord of the manor, might have owned all the land, but he did not own the wind and the sky and the sea. Up here James was the lord.

Though from the heights of Roseberry Topping the sea looked easy to get to, it was years before James found himself gazing at it up this close. He skirted Runswick Bay, saw boats down below. A couple of men in each, a haul of fish, though from his time in Staithes, James knew full well other cargo found its way into the coastal boats. James thought about the village he had left that morning. From the land you didn't see Staithes till you were almost upon it, the little houses built right into the cliffs either side of the deep narrow creek, the cliffs four hundred feet if they were an inch.

Sanderson's shop, where James had served these past eighteen months, was right down near the water, but James was not sorry to have left it. Though he was good at arithmetic, he did not see cut out for him the life of a shopkeeper. Eventually he had told Mr Sanderson.

'You want to go to sea?' said Mr Sanderson. 'Well, lad, it's a matter that needs to be discussed. Mr Skottowe and your father will have something to say about it, I'm sure.' Mr Sanderson could see that his apprentice was determined. 'Tell you what, lad,' he said finally, 'I'll be making a journey to Newcastle shortly, by way of Great Ayton. I'll have a word.'

Mr Sanderson liked the boy well enough, had taken him on when his wife was expecting their second child and indisposed. He was related to Mr Skottowe by marriage and Mr Skottowe being lord of the manor and all, Mr Sanderson had felt obliged. But now the obligation was at a likely end.

Also, there was another matter Mr Sanderson couldn't quite put his finger on. There was nothing disrespectful about the lad, and he was a good worker. It was the size of him. The seventeen year old towered over Mr Sanderson. The whole shop seemed like a doll's house when James was in attendance. A modest lad but Mr Sanderson felt that if he were there much longer, he'd be the one running the shop and not Mr Sanderson.

At night, after Mr Sanderson had left for Newcastle, James lay curled up on his mattress under the counter, willing himself into the discussion of his future Mr Sanderson would be having with his father and Mr Skottowe.

The shop was spick and span by the time Mr Sanderson returned, and James could tell by the look in his employer's eyes that the discussions had been favourable.

'Don't take off your apron just yet, lad, there are certain conditions.'

James didn't care. Anything, he would abide by whatever the conditions.

'Your father knows what goes on in these parts,' said Mr Sanderson, flicking at a speck on his coat sleeve. 'While there's not a man around who would say no to a gift of tobacco or a bottle of brandy, it's getting caught that is the problem.' Was that the condition, not to engage in smuggling? James could agree to that readily enough. There was plenty of legal trade up and down the coast. 'Your father doesn't want you stepping out my door and picking up with the first cobble that sails past. He is especially concerned that you remain a God-fearing young man of sober habits. He does not want you falling into bad company. Stack those bolts of cloth, lad, you're still in my employ.'

James knew that the cloth needed stacking but had thought it better to give Mr Sanderson his undivided attention while such an important matter was being discussed. Mr Sanderson stood with both hands stretched out on the counter, as if he were a vicar delivering a sermon from the pulpit, while his apprentice stacked the cloth. It was late in the evening. The fruit baskets had been brought in for the night and muslin placed over the sides of bacon. James was glad no customers came to disturb the discussion.

'So I have made enquiries in Whitby,' Mr Sanderson continued, full of his own importance. 'There's a Quaker shipowner, a Mr John Walker, an honest and fair man by all accounts. He's willing to have a look at you.'

Now James stood on the cliffs overlooking Whitby, on his way to meet Mr Walker. He put on his shirt. It was late afternoon and the sun was losing its warmth. He had eaten the bread and cheese Mrs Sanderson had packed for him, and the apple as well. On his approach to Whitby he had watched men shovelling alum, the precious substance that was used as a mordant for dyes. It had turned Whitby from a quiet little fishing village into a thriving port. The ancient abbey on the other side of the estuary loomed up, its ruins jutting into the sky. One of the alum workers had shown James a snakestone, a peculiar spiral shape that looked like the inside of certain molluscs. He told James that Hilda, the first abbess, had got rid of the snakes around Whitby by turning them into stone. How else could you account for such a thing? James felt sure that in the life that lay before him, other explanations existed.

Down below, the port was crowded with ships and boats. James had never seen such a mass of craft. Whitby was at least ten times as big as Staithes, and prosperous by the look of the brick and stone buildings, such a contrast to the poky little cottages of Staithes with their mouldy thatches. James filled his lungs with the air of the place and began his descent into the town.

A BOX OF LETTER TILES

It smelled, it was dark brown, and to make matters worse, there were no other children. A big rowdy place with grown-ups behaving in a way that Elizabeth had never seen. Shouting at each other, laughing very loudly, rolling around and sometimes falling off their chairs, playing games and betting. The alehouse was so full of tobacco smoke that Elizabeth could hardly breathe. Even some of the ladies were sucking away at pipes. But Quakers, who stood soberly to one side, conducted business here, so it must be all right.

Mrs Sheppard had said that Elizabeth was now a big girl, almost five, and it was time for her to go back to London. Even though Mama came to visit occasionally, she must be missing Elizabeth terribly. Mama had a new husband to help with the alehouse and now she could take care of Elizabeth properly.

Elizabeth wished Mama lived closer to Crowcher's Yard, then she would not feel so sad about leaving the Sheppards and not being able to play with Sarah, feed the lambs, and help Mrs Sheppard pick peas. Elizabeth loved eating peas straight from the garden, they were so juicy and sweet, though Mrs Sheppard told Elizabeth it was not a good idea to eat them raw because they might give her colic.

There was no water to drink at the alehouse, only wine or ale. When Elizabeth asked for water Mr Blackburn said it would make her toes curl up and everyone laughed. It had not made her toes curl up at the Sheppards'. Wine left a sour taste in Elizabeth's mouth but she quite liked the fizz of ale, although that posed a problem too. Barrels of ale were stored in the cellar, under the ground, where dead people went. Perhaps, Elizabeth thought, the barrels of ale, the cheeses and bacon down there were food and drink for dead people. When she asked her mother about this she laughed gently and said: 'Nonsense, Elizabeth. We have enough lodgers to look after without victualling the dead.' Elizabeth bit the inside of her lip. 'The dead have no bodies,' Mama comforted her. 'They don't need to eat or drink.'

Though they lacked bodies, they might drink the essence, the fizz, for their souls. Elizabeth tried to avoid those ales with not much fizz, in case the dead had been supping from them.

'What have you brought back from the country, apart from those apple cheeks?' asked Mr Blackburn. Elizabeth was playing with a set of small wooden tiles, a letter painted on each. They were in a special box with a lid that slid out. She did not remember Mr Blackburn, though she recalled the feeling of flailing her arms but grasping only handfuls of air.

'My name,' said Elizabeth, showing Mr Blackburn her special box. One of the farm boys had made it for her, and the tiles too, but it was Mrs Sheppard who had painted on the letters, and it wasn't till Elizabeth could name a letter that Mrs Sheppard gave it to her to put in the box.

'A big name like Elizabeth in that small box?' She wrinkled her nose and held her breath because every time Mr Blackburn opened his mouth an unpleasant smell came out.

Elizabeth thought the box was quite big but didn't say so. 'It's not in one piece,' she explained, 'it's broken up into letters.' She slid open the box, something she loved doing so much that she often spent her time just sliding the lid backwards and forwards.

The first letter she took out was a K. She put it to one side. The first useful one was the E. She remembered how it looked like a set of shelves. And the Z, like the piece of wood on the barn door at the Sheppards'. Soon she had her name assembled and put her finger under each letter to show Mr Blackburn.

'What about my name?' smiled Mr Blackburn. She started looking for a B. 'That will take too long,' he said. 'Let's try my given name.' He put his big fingers into the box and pulled out a J. It looked like the tail of a cat. 'Now, what next?' He found the O, the shape your mouth made when you said it. Then the H and the N to finish. 'Do you know what that name is?' he asked.

'John,' she read the letters he had placed on the cloth. But to Elizabeth he would always be Mr Blackburn.

It was December 1745. Mama said she had waited for Elizabeth to come back so that she could help with the decorations. Decorations? 'Holly and other greenery. Don't the Sheppards put up Christmas decorations?'

No, they didn't. Nowhere in the Bible, so Mr Sheppard said, did it say to celebrate Christmas. Why should they set one day aside for Him who should be kept in continual remembrance? It led to suspicion. No, superstition. Nevertheless the greenery smelled very nice and Elizabeth was glad that Mama had waited. Elizabeth, Mama and the servants put laurel and rosemary and sharp glossy holly leaves everywhere. When they came to the stairs, Mama held Elizabeth up so that she could tie a bunch of rosemary to the ceiling beam. Elizabeth stared for a long time at the grain in the timber. She remembered looking at it when she was swimming in the air. That was all she recalled of the alehouse.

On Christmas morning they walked to church. The ground was muddy and slippery, and especially squashy the closer they came to St John's. 'Wapping is built on a swamp,' commented Mama. 'Only the good Lord stops St John's from sinking into the ground.' The snow hadn't come yet and it had not rained for a good few weeks but still their footsteps squeezed moisture out of the grass.

Mama paused for a moment at the gravestone of one who was already under the ground, taking Elizabeth aside with her. 'Can you read the name?'

Elizabeth looked at the stone, which, only a few short years after having been placed there, was already growing patches of moss.

'Samuel Batts,' read Elizabeth.

'Your father,' said Mary.

'My father which art in heaven?' asked Elizabeth.

Her mother could not suppress a smile. 'Let's hope so.'

Elizabeth had the red and green bird with her. When you blew into its tail it made a lovely chirrup. Mama had wanted her to leave it at home but Elizabeth had insisted so much on bringing Sam Bird that finally Mama had relented. 'But you must look after it. And I don't want to hear it whistling in church.'

Mama had explained that it was a special gift from her father, Sam Batts, and she had shown Elizabeth his likeness. He was old like Mr Blackburn, but he looked very nice and smiled at her from out of the picture. 'Your papa died when you were a baby, and now you have a new papa, Mr Blackburn, whose name also begins with a B.' Mr Blackburn may have become Mama's new husband but he was never going to be Elizabeth's new papa.

They entered the church to find rosemary and laurel leaves strung over the doors and along the pews, holly and other greenery decorating the altar, and altogether so many leaves and berries that Elizabeth felt herself to be inside a huge generous tree. What a wonderful place for Sam Bird. Only the statues of saints and the appearance of the vicar reminded Elizabeth that she was in the house of God.

The sermon was very long and thinking about God took Elizabeth's mind off the cold rising from the stone floor, up through the soles of her shoes and into her stockings.

Unlike the Quaker gatherings where everybody was very quiet and spoke only one at a time, the people in St John's coughed and blew their noses, and even chatted to their neighbour. It was almost as noisy as the alehouse. Mrs Sheppard said that the quiet allowed the Holy Spirit to come, and you could speak when It moved you, whether you were a man, woman, or child. The Holy Spirit could come to anyone, not just Quakers. You didn't even have to be English. God created us all, and so loved us all. Animals, plants and everything.

'Even rats?' asked Elizabeth.

'Yes, even rats.'

'Why would He create such a nuisance?' asked Elizabeth, using a word she had heard Mrs Sheppard herself use.

'They are only a nuisance sometimes.'

Mama nudged Elizabeth. It was time to kneel on the little cushions and pray. Elizabeth put Sam under her skirts to keep him warm. After the prayer came the part Elizabeth liked best. Everyone stood up, the choir began to sing and those who knew the words joined in: 'Joy to the world, the Lord is come! Let earth receive her King.'

When they returned to the alehouse, Grandfather and Uncle, both of them called Charles, were walking up the steps from the river, carrying packets and a basket. Everyone said 'Merry

Christmas', and Grandfather Charles lifted Elizabeth up to kiss her. Through his face powder she saw tiny little black dots all around his chin and up to his ears and under his nose. They prickled her face when he held her close. He smelled of leather.

Grandfather Charles entered the parlour, looking around like an officer inspecting his men. 'You've done a good job of it, Mary.' Elizabeth thought he meant all the Christmas greenery but he went on: 'They tell me, on the other side of the river, that it's as well run a business as it ever was. And you've bought yourself a wharf, I hear. No doubt Mr Blackburn had a hand in that,' he added, looking in Mr Blackburn's direction.

Mary was glad of the companionship of her new husband. John was reliable and he knew how to deal with the men, but Mary had acquired the wharf before she married him, as her father well knew. But it was Christmas and not the time to beg to differ with him. 'Some mulled wine?' she suggested.

'Excellent idea, Mrs Blackburn,' said her husband.

While they waited for Rose to bring it, Grandfather Charles started undoing his packets—a fine collar of brawn, jellied pig's trotters and some damson pies. Uncle Charles stood with his back to the fire, lifting his coat-tails, rocking backwards and forwards from heel to toe.

Rose appeared with a jug and glasses on a tray. She placed it on the table and Mary served the wine. 'To our good health,' proposed Mr Blackburn. And everyone lifted their glasses into the air. Elizabeth did the same. The drink was the colour of mulberries, rich and sweet as honey, though when Elizabeth swallowed, a vinegary taste stayed in the back of her throat.

When Rose brought the food to the table, Elizabeth didn't start right away but instead bowed her head. She had already noticed that no-one said grace before eating, but she thought for this special Christmas dinner they might. 'C'mon, little Elizabeth,' said Mr Blackburn. 'What are you waiting for?'

'I am thanking God for what we are about to receive.'

'It's me, your mama and Grandfather Charles you should be thanking,' he teased.

Elizabeth knew that it was not the Almighty Himself who brought the pies and everything, but that's not what saying grace meant.

'Let the child do it if she wants to,' said Mama.

Elizabeth bowed her head again, feeling hot and prickly all over. She felt as if she was in a house full of strangers.

'Well then,' said Mr Blackburn, 'let's hear the Quaker grace.'

It wasn't fair of Mr Blackburn to mock the Quakers. Elizabeth's embarrassment started to wane and in its place rose indignation. 'They say it quietly,' she glared at him.

He was about to reply but Mama put her hand on his sleeve. 'Let that be an end to it,' she said firmly.

After dinner of beef, turnips and potatoes, then a raisin suet pudding which filled everyone up so much they said they couldn't move from the table, Uncle Charles suggested they play bullet pudding. 'A Christmas treat for Elizabeth,' he added. Bullet pudding didn't sound like a treat but everybody was so gleeful about it that Elizabeth held her tongue and instead made a little nest in her lap for Sam Bird.

When the dinner plates were cleared away Rose brought in a pile of flour and arranged it into a cone. Uncle Charles took some of the wrapping paper and shaped it into a tight little ball. When the 'bullet' was set on top of the cone of flour, Mama invited Rose to join in the game, and after a shy giggle, she sat at the table with the family.

'Who shall go first?' boomed Mr Blackburn.

'The youngest member of our party,' said Uncle Charles.

Elizabeth's big blue eyes were as wide as saucers.

'Perhaps the oldest,' suggested Mama, squeezing Elizabeth's hand under the table. 'To show her how it is done,' she added.

Elizabeth supposed that Grandfather Charles was not normally one for playing games but it was Christmas and he was full of wine and he did feel, as head of the family, it was his responsibility—nay, his duty—to set a good example. He rubbed his hands together, picked up the knife and carved away a section of the cone. Then he passed the knife to Uncle Charles. Next it was Elizabeth's turn. She looked very carefully at the bullet, then cut away a thin slice of the 'pudding', without disturbing it.

'Well done,' said Grandfather Charles, and everyone applauded.

They all had a go at cutting the pudding, including Rose, who had to be coaxed, which Uncle Charles took upon himself to do.

Elizabeth's second turn was successful but the bullet was teetering. 'This requires some strategy,' said Uncle Charles, pushing his chair away and bending down so that he was at eye level with the bullet. It wasn't his turn but no-one seemed to notice. Using his thumb and index finger Uncle Charles made measurements. He took another sip of wine. Rose was giggling rather a lot and everyone's face was red and glistening. It had grown dark outside, and lit by the firelight and candles, the shadow of the bullet fell across the diminishing pile of flour like a tower.

Finally Uncle Charles made a cut and everyone roared as the bullet fell. But that was not the end of the game. Uncle Charles had to retrieve the bullet. He began nuzzling into the flour and everyone laughed to see it all over his face. But he managed to get the bullet between his teeth and stood up, triumphant. Then he spat the bullet into the fire. 'A shame it would be to see a good pile of flour go to waste,' he said merrily. He walked around the table till he was behind Rose and lightly tipped her face into it. When she brought her head up again, giggling all the while and saying 'Mr Charles' in a playful way, she had a spot of flour on her nose like a snowman.

'Blind man's bluff!' said Grandfather Charles bringing out his kerchief.

So they played more games and drank more wine long into the Christmas night, and no-one mentioned that perhaps it was time for Elizabeth to go to bed. When she finally climbed the stairs, said her prayers and put her head upon the pillow, her eyes would not shut. On the ceiling she saw them all at Christmas dinner again, saw the pile of flour and the bullet and the fun, all spinning round and round.

A small ale-tasting burp escaped from Elizabeth. Though she felt a little bit sick, she had enjoyed Christmas. Perhaps the Holy Spirit could come to you in celebration as well as quietness. Did it come in with the fizz, or hover outside like a halo around the saints? Was it made of air, which you couldn't see but was everywhere? Did it blow with the breeze, like a ribbon or a leaf?

Elizabeth took a feather from her pillow, opened the window and blew the feather out. It descended a little and danced above a mooring post, before floating into the shadow of the watchman, the collar of his greatcoat turned up to meet his hat. She caught sight of the feather again, in the flickering orange light of his lantern. Then it flew away in the breeze. Elizabeth was glad that Sam Bird wasn't a real bird because she didn't want him disappearing like that.

She found her way over to Mama's bed and began tugging at her sleeve. 'Mama.' Eventually Mama woke up, with a little sigh. 'What is breeze?'

'It is what blows your hat off,' Mama said sleepily.

'And if I'm not wearing a hat?'

'Then it ruffles your hair.'

Mr Blackburn stirred, and let out a grunt. Elizabeth waited a moment. 'And the fizz in the ale?'

'Oh, not again. Go back to bed, Elizabeth. It has been a very long day.'

'Can I come in with you, Mama? I'm feeling a little sick.'

Mama groaned, as though she were feeling a little sick herself. 'Too much pudding, that's all,' she murmured. 'You're fortunate to have a bed of your own, many children don't. Off you go.'

Elizabeth did not feel fortunate. At the Sheppards' she slept with Sarah. They giggled under the blankets, and sometimes, if they were feeling sick, or if there was a bad storm and they were scared, Mrs Sheppard let them come in with her.

Elizabeth dawdled by the bed, hoping Mama would say, 'In you hop, little bunny.' But all that came out of Mama's mouth was sleep breath.

Elizabeth crept back to her bed. She wished Mama would explain about the breeze, the fizz and all the things that perplexed her. Water, for example. If you took a shovelful of soil out of the ground it left a hole, but if you took a cup of water out of a bucket, it didn't. Mama's Frost Fair picture was printed on the ice, and if ice was made of water, why couldn't you make a mark on water? Elizabeth had tried it with a letter tile, leaving it on for a very long time, but when she lifted it off again there was no E on the water, not even a trace.

Elizabeth felt herself sinking into sleep. Then she was floating down the river on a letter tile. She didn't find it at all odd that everyone else was in a boat. She was afraid that she might collide with one of them but she never did. In all the crowdedness of the riverside Elizabeth saw a little white bird. No, not a bird, a handkerchief, and it was Mama who was waving it. How wonderful to see Mama waiting for her. The tile floated towards the wharf, Elizabeth held her arms out ready for Mama to lift her off, but then, dismay. Mama wasn't waving but shooing her away.

When Elizabeth woke up the pillow was damp and her face wet. Why did Mama shoo her away? Why did she leave her on the letter tile? Was it because Mama had become a Blackburn? Elizabeth wanted to go to Mama's bed but she couldn't bear it if Mama shooed her away again. She felt so lonely, the only Batts in the alehouse. But she knew where the other one was.

Elizabeth put a coat on over her nightgown and tucked Sam Bird into the pocket. Mama had warned Elizabeth about going outside, said there were people who might try to take advantage of a little girl wandering about on her own. But Elizabeth would not be wandering. If anyone looked like they might cut off her hair to sell to the wigmaker, Elizabeth would run very fast, the way she and Sarah did one day when the bull got out of the pen.

Elizabeth crept downstairs. Although the alehouse was empty and quiet, it still had the same bad smell. She tried to open the front door but it was locked. She went to the back but it was locked too. She was trapped. Elizabeth started to panic, rattling at the bolt, trying to open the door.

'Who's there?'

Elizabeth jumped. She turned to see the looming figure of a man on the stairs, lantern in one hand and a big club in the other. She wanted to run but couldn't move.

'Elizabeth?' Mr Blackburn said, coming over to her. 'What are you doing out of bed? Are you off somewhere?' Her heart was thumping so much Elizabeth thought it was going to burst through her skin. 'We'll have to send you back to the Sheppards' if you won't stay put. You don't want that, do you?'

Yes, she did want that. She wanted very much to be back in Crowcher's Yard with Sarah and all the Sheppards. Mr Blackburn was still holding the club, waiting for Elizabeth's answer.

'No,' she said in a small voice.

JOHN WALKER'S HOUSE

Mr John Walker, shipowner of Whitby, had liked the look of the boy from Staithes and had agreed to take him on as an apprentice. The indenture of apprenticeship was the first legal document James had ever signed. He was careful not to get blots of ink on the page as he agreed 'not to play dice, cards or bowls, not to haunt taverns or playhouses, not to commit fornication, and not to contract matrimony'. For his part, John Walker was to instruct the apprentice in 'the trade, mystery, and occupation of a mariner; and for the period of apprenticeship find and provide meat, drink, washing and lodging'.

Now it was winter, the end of the twelve days of Christmas, and James was lodged, with the other apprentices, in Mr Walker's house in Grape Lane. The attic was a big room extending the length of the house, but crowded enough when all seventeen boys were in from the sea. James was eighteen and already six foot tall and although the attic was high-roofed in the middle, he soon learnt to pay attention to the rafters.

In a corner, away from the palliasses where the apprentices slept, James sat at the small table which Mrs Prowd, the house-keeper, had kindly provided after she'd found him sitting on the steps one night trying to study. Candlelight flickered over the book Mr Walker had lent him. 'You must be the master's pet,' called one of the apprentice boys from his palliasse. 'He ne'er gave nought of us a book.' James could feel his blood rise at the taunt. This particular boy had been trying to rile him all day. James was old for a new apprentice, older than the other boys, and he wearied of their childish games, but he did not want to put himself apart. He spent twenty-four hours of the day with them, splicing ropes, learning the rigging and running of the ship, and at night all of them sleeping side by side in the attic. Shipwork was teamwork.

'It's just a book of navigation.'

'Hole Haven, Shell Haven and Mucking Creek. Tilbury, Graves-end and Northfleet,' the boy started shouting out the rhyme. 'Gray's, Greenhithe and Purfleet,' the others joined in. 'Erith, Rainham and Bugby's Hole. Greenwich and Limehouse, and into the Pool.' That was all the navigation they needed to sail up the Thames to London. There were a few more chuckles then gradu-ally the banter died down.

Though Mr Walker's copy of *English Pilot* was old and well thumbed, it was full of mathematical instruction for navigation and surveying, pilotage for various English ports and harbours, and local winds. As James pored over the book, he did the mathematics in his head, remembering Mr Rowland and his hogsheads of tobacco. Mr Walker would not want to see the workings, he was happy enough that James showed interest and promise.

Surveying—that was something, how maps were made. He had never imagined at the Postgate school or even at Mr Sander-son's that mathematics could be used to trace the world. The sailors' rhymes were good enough to go where others had been, to places that had names. Aye, but to make a map! The old salts from Whitby were familiar with every inch of the coast, had the map in their heads, knew every course they should steer. But the tiller wasn't the only instrument; you could navigate with the quill. In James's small bag of belongings was the quill that he had made at school, wrapped in a cloth. That feather had felt the winds of the earth, had travelled across the Atlantic Ocean.

Through the creaks and sighs of the house, James heard the snores and snuffles of the other boys. Occasionally one would cry out in his dream and wake fitfully. Below them, Mr and Mrs Walker and their children were sleeping peacefully in their beds, and Mrs Prowd and the servants. Except for Mr Skottowe's, the house in Grape Lane was the biggest James had ever been in. There were all sorts of things that caught his attention. A writing desk in the office, with drawers and pigeonholes which held important documents and papers; straight-backed chairs, looking glasses in some of the rooms, not for vanity, but to reflect the light of the candles in the brass candlesticks either side. The timber floors of the house were devoid of carpets and scrubbed to a spotless white. In one room was a clock which stood taller than James himself. He was curious about it. It had only one hand. It was a twenty-four hour clock made by Robert Henderson from Scarborough, Mr Walker had told him when he had signed his indentures.

James leant toward the chimney in the attic which radiated warmth from the fireplaces below. He closed *English Pilot* and snuffed the candle between finger and thumb. He raised his arms and felt the rafters made from old ships' timbers. The Quakers wasted nothing. Then James quietly stepped down to the landing and looked out through the big round window to the shipyards across the river. He saw the stacks of timber, and the skeletons that would become flat-bottomed cats used in the coal trade.

In the night the river was black as treacle. James could hear the lap of the tide. He came back up the stairs and curled up on his palliasse, the rhyme that the boys had recited dancing in his head. The Pool of London—he could hardly wait to make the voyage.

EXECUTION DOCK STAIRS

James came to London in the evening of a lengthening spring day. The colliers, as many as two hundred, gathered in the wide mouth of the Thames estuary, waiting for the tide and a favourable wind that would take them upriver to the Pool of London. James was below deck while the colliers waited. He couldn't see but he could hear the lap of the tide against the timbers of the *Freelove*.

Along with the other apprentices, James had helped load the coal, shovelling it into the hold, breathing in its black dust. The weather was good and they'd done the journey in five days. He'd stood watch, a senior member of his team ringing a bell each time the half-hour sandglass emptied. They kept a count of them, waiting for the eighth bell that would signal the end of the watch. The journey had been hard work with little sleep, yet James was exhilarated by it.

James took every opportunity for learning. He observed the leadsman in the forechains swing the length of line with knots at regular intervals, and the leaden drogue at the end, watched the line being reeled in again and heard the shout: 'Six knots!'

They had barely left Whitby when James went aloft for the first time at sea, a topman called Ned climbing behind him. James looked up to the tip of the mast, a hundred feet or so in the air. He thought of the great tree at Marton, the way he had found one foothold after the other till he'd finally reached the top.

Those apprentices who were not working gathered around, watching and waiting. 'Mind you don't heave your dinner all over us,' one of them called as James grabbed hold of the ratlines, feeling the tar-covered rope under his grip and thinking about the rough texture of tree bark. He had hardly climbed two or three steps before he realised that this was an entirely different proposition to climbing a tree. The heavy rope seemed suddenly flimsy but James kept going, feeling the increasing sway of the ratlines the further he went.

About halfway up he stopped, overcome with dizziness. His friends below had their hands to their mouths shouting something he couldn't hear. 'Look at your hands,' he heard Ned's voice. He was gripping the ropes so hard his hands were almost welded to them. Beneath the grime of coal dust his knuckles stood out white.

'Keep going.' Ned was directly behind him. James swallowed the dizziness, prised one hand off the rope and reached up, thinking only of the way he had climbed at Marton, thinking only of the tree. Then his leg found the next foothold.

'That's it, all the way to the top.' Men had fallen from aloft, to their death, but James promised himself he would not be one of them. Up he went, into the sky.

He was almost to the yardarm. 'Now lean backwards and hoist yourself onto the platform.' James did as he was instructed, trusting the rope, trusting Ned's voice, trusting himself. 'That's it, lad. You're there.'

The ship pitched and rolled but Ned was with him now and the two of them bent over the spar and untied the knots holding the canvas. James saw the minuscule figures on deck looking up but he was in a different world. A gull passed not two feet from him. He heard its cry and saw the way its wings caught the wind and soared. Saw its legs tucked underneath its body. James was in the air with it, in the element of birds.

'All done, lad,' said Ned. 'I can see you've taken to life aloft. Aye, it's a fine day for it. It'll be a different matter in the squalls and rain. When it's freezing cold and you have to chip ice off the shrouds. C'mon, time to go back down.'

They descended backwards, James looking up at the mast pointing into the sky, wondering how to determine the arc of its sway. A mathematical problem Mr Rowland had never set for him.

James thought of that moment up in the spacious sky when the tide brought the convoy of colliers upriver. The Thames was so thick with ships and boats of every kind that its murky waters were only just visible. There were ships from across the Atlantic, from Jamaica and the West Indies, bringing tobacco, indigo, cotton and corn. Sugar, rum, coffee and ginger. There were North Sea cats like the *Freelove* bringing coal; lighters which took the coal from the ship to the wharf. Brigs, sloops, barges and all manner of small craft. Behind it all lay London, the river and its traffic part of the great city's fabric.

Through the grid of masts were labyrinths of narrow streets, beggars, thieves, and ladies of the town. Every second house on the waterfront seemed to be an alehouse or tavern. Beyond would be the fine buildings, wide thoroughfares carrying lords and ladies in carriages. In the distance, against the pale sky, James made out the dome of St Paul's. No-one else in James's family had ever travelled this far, had ever been to London, and now he was here.

He hadn't even set foot on solid ground yet he was swept up in the excitement of the metropolis. It buzzed in the very air.

Through all the busyness on shore, James's eyes settled on one thing. Near a set of steps that led up from the river, a hanged man was being taken down from the gibbet. 'Execution Dock,' said Ned. 'They hang there over the river till three tides have washed over them. An example should any of us seamen get a notion to go pirating or smuggling. Captain Kidd was hanged from that very gibbet.' James watched the body being dumped on a cart and wheeled away. 'But don't be dwelling on the dead,' his companion went on. 'There's plenty of life to be had in London. Once we come ashore. But the coal goes first.'

When the *Freelove* had called into Yarmouth, Captain Jefferson had forwarded by land the official papers to the agent in London, who then set wheels in motion—arranging a buyer for the coal and organising the unloading of it, so that everything was done with as much haste as possible to avoid delays that cost money. The delivery of coal was the object of the journey and that was uppermost in the mind of the captain, not furnishing a holiday in London or a tour of its fleshpots for the seamen. Not that you had to go on a tour to find ladies of the town, Ned told him. They came looking for you. Thronging like a pack of seagulls round the docks of the riverside, their beady eyes on the lookout for tasty morsels such as a seaman with a pocket full of wages. Pounce on him before he had a chance to do the alchemist's trick of turning silver into ale.

'Here's the lighter heading our way,' Ned pointed out.

The river was so full of traffic that James was surprised craft could move at all, but the vessels did inch their way along, accompanied by much cursing and shaking of fists and manoeuvring of oars. Eventually the lighter carrying a gang of coal heavers, bristling with shovels, made its way alongside the *Freelove*. The heavers came aboard, at least ten of them, men with faces as hard as their muscles, bringing with them, in the soup of smells, the strong stale odour of sweated ale.

They wasted no time erecting wooden platforms from the hold to the deck; nimble work it was, from the heavy-built men as well as those sinewy as scrawny chickens. Then they began shovelling. James heard the crunch, the impact of metal on coal, as he shovelled alongside them. The bracing salt-sprinkled air that had filled his lungs for the past five days was replaced by the grit of coal dust. He worked methodically, saying nothing, thinking he'd rather be back shovelling muck, at least that was softer, and though you breathed the smell, at least you didn't breathe in particles of it. As the heavers worked, grunting and cursing, the smell of their sweat grew so strong that James could taste it in the back of his throat.

A boat arrived with pints of ale, rowed across from the ale-house, the price of which would be taken out of the heavers' pay. It was thirsty work and they drank at the rate of a pint an hour. Sweat dripped onto the coal and into the men's boots, and onto each other as shovel-loads of coal flew through the air. James worked away, as hard as the heavers, figuring the quicker the job was done, the quicker ashore. He put his back into it, as he did with everything. Unlike this gang of heavers, in a year or so, when his apprenticeship was finished, he would no longer have to shovel coal. In the darkness of the hold he tasted his own salty sweat as it ran down his face, and saw drops of it glisten on the lumps of coal on the shovel. Where would that sweat be carried to? Would it find its way into the fires of a lord or a poor man? Would it be used to steam-power a pumping engine or sail away to the lands beyond the Atlantic? With these thoughts, and with his arms and his back, and the arms and the backs of all of them, the mountain of coal became a hillock, a small mound and eventually it was no more.

When James's feet landed on the slipperiness of Execution Dock Stairs, he felt like Gulliver dropped by a giant orc into the marketplace of a new and exotic land. An old woman with no teeth but a loud voice yelled, 'Cabbages, cabbages, fresh from the gardens.' They may have been fresh from the gardens some days ago but presently they wore the same film of coal dust as everything else.

A man with a tray of oysters was deftly opening six of them for a customer, holding the creatures in a leather-gloved hand and prising the shells apart with a knife that could cause trouble. 'Oi! I'll 'ave you,' he roared, bringing his knife down between the fingers of a small hand reaching up for an oyster. The hand disappeared immediately and a young boy scrambled his way through the crowd.

'Shine your shoes, mister?' offered a voice somewhere else. James kept his hands firmly in his pockets, so that other hands couldn't find their way in. It seemed the only place free of the crowd was the gibbet, not six feet away from the Stairs, empty now, waiting for its next lodger.

'Move along there, lad,' said Ned, coming up behind him. 'Push your way through and don't pay any mind to what's for sale,' he added as two ladies of the town appeared from nowhere, thrusting themselves at the newly arrived sailors, giving off a whiff of gin as they laughed saucily and made cow's eyes.

James and Ned sidestepped another pair of ladies whispering promised pleasures into the ears of two mariners newly arrived from Canada. The men were showing the ladies furred pouches and telling them that they were fashioned from the testicles of bears.

James and Ned waited for a carriage to pass then crossed the road, stepping over the flow of effluent in the middle of it. 'Here we are,' said Ned when they reached the corner of Wapping High Street and Brewhouse Lane. 'This is your lodgings.' James looked at the big brass bell above the entrance to the alehouse, then back to the river. It was only a short distance away, yet with the crowd and the noise and everything going on, it seemed to take an age. 'As good a house as any is the Bell,' said Ned.

James stooped as he entered the low doorway. He and Ned pushed through the heat and noise inside, making their way to the bar. Standing on the serving side of it was a man with grey hair and side whiskers, along with a couple of serving wenches, pouring ale into mugs and sliding them across the bar as fast as they were ordered.

'A new apprentice of Mr Walker's,' Ned introduced James to the man. 'This here is Mr Blackburn. He'll look after you all right.'

James thought of offering his hand to Mr Blackburn but let it drop to his side when he saw what a grimy paw he'd be offering his host. Instead, he merely nodded.

He looked around and recognised some of the coal heavers he'd worked with, pints of ale in front of them, well on the way to being drunk and without the benefit now of hard work to sweat it out of them. They'd come straight to the alehouse, spending more time here than they did in their humble abodes. If you wanted work, you stayed where the publican who organised it would notice you. The coal heavers were presented with more pints of ale and continued slaking a thirst that was bottomless.

There were a few landmen in the alehouse but most of the customers were seamen, judging by the loose-legged trousers and short jackets. Practical working clothes that wouldn't get caught in winches and ropes and all the other traps on board ship.

Mr Blackburn slid a pint of ale in front of James. 'A glass of London hospitality,' he said, although it would be Mr Walker paying for it.

James looked at his hands again. 'Much obliged to you. I'll wash some of this off first,' he said. 'Don't want to dirty your mug,' he added.

'No-one minds the coal around here,' said Mr Blackburn. 'It's the living of all of us, one way or the other.' James looked at the pint of proffered ale, wondering what to do. He was dog-tired from shovelling the coal and having had no more than four hours sleep at a spell during the voyage. But he was in London, and he didn't want to miss a minute of it. He looked around for Ned and found him renewing his acquaintance with a young woman whose bosoms rose out of her dress like two plump doves. Everyone, even the women, seemed to be covered in coal dust. That might be all right for the riverside, but James intended exploring every inch of London and he didn't want to go about looking like a coal heaver.

'I'll wash up first, if you don't mind.' James saw the ale go to someone else.

'Up the stairs, first room on the left for you apprentices. You'll find a pitcher of water. Mind you don't drink it though,' he joked. 'No-one drinks the water in London.'

James strode up the stairs, rising above the rollicking noise. He found the room Mr Blackburn had indicated, and inside it a bed, a jug of water on a stand and one straight-backed chair. Then he heard a trill, like the whistle of a bird, but not a seagull or a pigeon, which were the only birds he'd seen so far in London. He heard it again—a bird trapped inside perhaps, calling to its mate. He followed the sound down the corridor and identified the room.

It wasn't a bird but a little girl, five or six years old, about the same age as his sister Margaret. She was kneeling on the floor, her skirts neatly about her. James could see the soles of her house slippers, the beginnings of a hole in one of them. In front of her was a box and a set of tiles which spelled out ELIZABETH.

She sensed his presence and turned, looking up at him, twin pools of blue in a small pale face. 'I . . . I thought I heard a bird,'

THE FAN OF TIME

In the year of 1752 the calendar changed and there were riots in the streets over eleven lost days, or more precisely, the wages for those days. For more than two hundred years England had resisted the Popish Gregorian calendar, which kept time for Spain, Portugal, France and the rest of Catholic Europe. England, while considering herself far ahead of her continental papal neighbours, was in fact eleven days behind. In 1750 the Earl of Macclesfield addressed the Royal Society on the inaccuracies of the Julian Calendar, the matter was brought to the attention of the Secretary of State and in May the following year, the 'Act for regulating the commencement of the year, and for correcting the calendar now in use' became law.

In the coffee-house newspapers, on street notices, from church pulpits, in alehouses and wherever people gathered, news of the New Style calendar spread. The year would now commence on 1 January instead of 25 March. Easter Sunday would fall on the first full moon after the spring equinox. Centennial years would not be leap years unless divisible by 400, and the modification that caused the most talk in that year of change—2 September would be immediately followed by 14 September. That is, eleven days would go missing.

Elizabeth, eleven herself in that year, was putting the finishing touches to her calendar. She had given the making of it a lot of thought, especially how to accommodate those days that would go missing. Perhaps time was a large expanse of fabric, a shimmering silk that you could make narrower by pleating it. So in the fabric of the calendar, 2 September was pleated next to 14 September and the lost days disappeared from sight; but if need be, you could unfold the pleats and the missing days would reappear. The best way to do this was to make a folding fan.

She had used Mama's as a model, but instead of a painted pastoral scene, Elizabeth had embroidered numbers onto her fan. She had chosen golden silk so that when the fan was opened to its full extent it looked like the sun rising on the horizon. Mama had at first been reluctant to let Elizabeth use good silk for this project but Elizabeth assured her that it was not a plaything, that she would look after it and keep it forever. 'I can even use it to do arithmetic,' she said, presenting the argument she knew would most convince Mama. Finally Mama had consented. She'd even gone to the staymaker's to get bone for the struts.

Elizabeth was very proud of her fan of time. It could show days, months and even years. She could arrange the fan so that it revealed her year of birth—1741. She could even make the fan show years yet to come such as faraway 1800.

If the fan could show time yet to come perhaps it could also reveal where lost things were—mugs and other items that occasionally went missing from the alehouse. Sometimes things that disappeared turned up again. But not Sam Bird.

Sam Bird had disappeared in the earthquake, the sudden shaking as if a giant were rattling her bed like a plaything. It had happened two years ago, when she was only nine. The whole house shook, the whole of Wapping, and maybe the whole world. Doors and windows rattled, the candlesticks fell over, glass smashed. Outside, horses whinnied and reared, people screamed, and ships ground together with the thud of timber on timber. For the first time since it had been installed above the doorway of the alehouse, the Bell's bell rang.

In the aftermath, when they were sweeping up smashed glass and putting everything back in its place, Elizabeth could not find Sam Bird. She looked everywhere, under her bed, under the stairs, in the fireplace, in drawers and cupboards. She even took a candle and went down into the cellar. 'That's enough, Elizabeth,' Mama had chided. 'You're too old to be fretting over a plaything.'

But Sam Bird had been a gift from her father, and now he was gone.

Elizabeth was concerned that if man changed the calendar, something tumultuous like another earthquake might occur. 'No, no,' Mr Blackburn assured her. 'It is a simple matter of us adjusting our calendar to that of the Almighty,' he said with a little cough, as if he were embarrassed. The Old Style calendar year was longer than the time it took for the earth to travel around the sun—by eleven minutes, Mr Blackburn knew precisely. Over the centuries those minutes had grown into hours and then days.

'Dinner's ready,' called Mama.

'What happens to the birthdays?' enquired Elizabeth, putting aside her fan. 'The birthdays in the pleats.' It slipped out before she could stop it.

'In the what?' asked Mr Blackburn, the beginnings of a teasing smile on his face.

'The birthdays in between,' she amended.

'They can still be celebrated,' said her mother, sticking her fork into a piece of turnip. 'Say a person's birthday falls on 7 September. When it is 2 September, how many more days till their birthday?'

'Five.' She didn't really need the fan to work it out; after years of Mama using every possible occasion for instruction, Elizabeth had all the combinations in her head. Whatever it was, Mama made arithmetic out of it. When ale was delivered, Mama would ask, 'If there were six barrels on the cart, and now only two, how many barrels are in the cellar?'

At the school opposite St John's, the girls learnt their catechism and passages from the Bible. They embroidered numbers on their samplers and learnt to recognise them, but they did not learn arithmetic as such. What was the use of it for a girl? Mama had found it extremely useful. The century was rising, half over, and England prosperous, though Mary Blackburn had only to look outside her own door to see that prosperity was a fine word in the newspapers and the coffee houses but it wasn't an air that everybody breathed. For some it required hard work, she said, watching to see that none of those six barrels found itself 'accidentally' rolling down the street and being sold again, even though she had already paid for it.

Education improved the mind and prevented idleness, idleness being a playground for the devil's work. But there were those— mainly the high born—who were of the opinion that you did a boy no favour by educating him above his station. It could lead to riots and revolt. As for educating girls . . . Mary imagined the curled lips of those lords and gents. To be skilled in embroidery occupied a woman's hands and her thoughts, and didn't addle the brain as novel-reading did. A little instruction in music and dance, perhaps French. That could be considered part of a young woman's dowry and, along with an amiable disposition, make her an attractive prospect for marriage. But arithmetic? Well, thought Mary grimly, one did not always know what the Almighty had in store. A widow might well find herself running an alehouse where knowledge of arithmetic proved very useful indeed. Who knew what lay ahead for Elizabeth?

'So if, in the New Style calendar, the day after 2 September is the fourteenth, what will seven days after the second be?'

'Twentieth.'

'So the person can celebrate their birthday then.' Elizabeth's mother waved away Mr Blackburn's offer of wine.

Elizabeth took a sip of ale. 'But the person was really born on 7 September, and that day will disappear.'

'It is only for this year,' said her mother. 'Let that be the end of the matter.'

Elizabeth was silent for a moment, cutting the fat off the beef. She liked it hot and freshly off the fire, but when it grew cold and white and solid it had a rancid taste to it. 'Perhaps,' suggested Elizabeth's mother, 'if you use your mouth more for eating and less for asking questions, that would not be necessary.'

'Yes, Mama,' Elizabeth demurred.

Mr Blackburn, who hadn't yet finished eating, got up and went to the chamber pot to relieve himself. The sound of it was as loud as a horse. 'Mama,' Elizabeth said over the top of it, 'if the year now starts on 1 January, does it mean that I will be thirteen next birthday instead of twelve?' Thirteen sounded so much more grown up than twelve.

Mama was using her last piece of turnip to sop up gravy. 'You were born eleven years ago on 24 January. Next birthday you will be twelve.'

Elizabeth heard the chamber pot being slid back into the cupboard. 'It's the men grumbling about lost wages,' said Mr Blackburn, rejoining the conversation. Elizabeth watched him fill his glass with wine and spill a little of it on the table. 'But they'll get paid the same as ever—a good day's pay for a good day's work.'

'No doubt there will be a period of confusion,' said Mrs Blackburn. 'But we will grow accustomed to the New Style calendar as indeed we grow accustomed to everything.' She spread salt on the stain of wine.

Elizabeth arranged the scraps of fat in a neat pile then laid her knife and fork side by side, the way Mrs Sheppard in Essex had shown her. The calendar and dates were arithmetic. Man had made a mistake and the new calendar was for aligning man's time with God's time. Nevertheless it seemed odd to her that a year should start in the middle of winter and no longer at the beginning of spring. That seemed altogether better aligned with the calendar of the Creator.

In the six years he had been with Mr Walker, James had sailed into the Baltic, to Finland and St Petersburg. He also continued the Whitby to London run. By 1752 he had become mate on Mr Walker's ship the *Friendship*, with Captain Richard Ellerton in command. James was starting to rise. He learnt the ways of leadership from Mr Walker—to be firm but fair, to teach and encourage by example, to foster pride in work rather than using force and abusive language.

He was on the coastal run again, this time from Shields to Whitby, in that September when the calendar changed. Seamen went by a different system of time from landmen, their days beginning at noon although the sun had brought the natural day to them hours before. James was interested in time, not only in calendars that marked the passing of days, but as an instrument for pinpointing positions in space. A sailor could navigate using time.

Most of the old hands avowed that dead reckoning was good enough for them but in James's conversations with John Walker, now less master to employee than man to man, the problem of ascertaining longitude was discussed. It had been a subject of conversation, of wild schemes and ambitions, for as long as James could remember, if for no other reason than the king's ransom of £20 000, on offer since 1714, to whomever could find, and here Mr Walker quoted, a 'generally practicable and useful method' of calculating longitude. 'It will come,' said John Walker, 'if not in my lifetime, then certainly in yours. This is a century of revelations. Latin and Greek are fine studies with which to become acquainted with the knowledge of the ancients, but science, mathematics, they are the way of the future.'

It wasn't just a mathematical problem. Ships had been dashed upon rocks and the lives of thousands of seamen had been lost due to lack of a reliable method of calculating longitude. Though of more benefit to seamen than landmen, it was a subject that was in the air. On a trip to London James had seen, in the window of a shop near St Paul's, a print of Hogarth's *Rake's Progress*, depicting a madhouse in which one of the lunatics was working away on the problem. 'Certainly there are those who scoff at the idea,' said John Walker, 'but a solution will be found.'

James was in favour of a mathematical solution, although not every seaman was as adept at the discipline as he. The simpler solution was a watch-machine, but who could build such a machine that would keep time precisely, despite being subject to storms and waves and all the other vagaries of sea life?

Whether a solution was found or no, James enjoyed his conversations with John Walker on the matter, and felt that he was living in an age when anything was possible, even discussions of this kind with his employer. It stretched James's mind in the same way shovelling coal had stretched his muscles.

THE PORCELAIN TEAPOT

'Please, Elizabeth,' said Mama, 'you're eighteen now, you must think of the future. Take this opportunity to buy something for your own trousseau. Embroidered cushion covers aren't enough. Use your birthday money. And mind you hide it up your sleeve,' she warned. 'Oxford Street may be smart and elegant but that doesn't mean there won't be thieves around. Even more than on the riverside, with the pickings being so much better.'

Elizabeth loved going shopping, whether she made a purchase or not. She especially loved the windows—you never saw this much glass by the riverside. To visit those shops, where no end of trouble or expense had been gone to on decoration and lighting, was to enter into a world far removed from the riverside, though much of what could be bought there had come in to London through the docks. But at the docks the goods were still in boxes and pallets.

Everything about the shops was extravagant, the chandeliers, the columns and statues, the way great long falls of material were displayed — silks, muslins, striped dimmity, and chintzes, hanging in folds as they would when made into a dress, so that you had a perfect idea of the finished garment simply by looking at the cloth. Some shops even sold ready-made dresses.

When she went with Mama, they would examine everything on offer, and come away with a few buttons, or a small piece of ribbon, a kind of payment for the privilege of looking. But today she was shopping with her best friend Becky Southwood and they had money to spend.

'So much all in the one place!' Becky exclaimed when she and Elizabeth alighted from the coach. Rather than having mainly booksellers as in Little Britain or lace and milliners as in Paternoster Row, in Oxford Street were shops of every kind. Becky was shopping for her trousseau. She was marrying her father's apprentice. Not only that, she was with child. Becky wasn't the first riverside girl to put the cart before the horse, nor would she be the last.

Elizabeth knew how such things happened. Once she'd even come across a lady of the town in a darkened doorway with a customer. All that pushing and shoving, it looked like the customer was trying to cram a bolt of linen into a cupboard. Though she had seen it, she didn't know how it felt. She couldn't ask Mama, couldn't imagine Mama doing it with Mr Blackburn, although by the grunts she heard some nights, she guessed Mama must. It was part of wifely duties. But Becky had performed the duty even before she was a wife.

'What does it feel like?' Becky repeated Elizabeth's question. 'It feels . . .' she sighed dreamily, searching for words. 'It is very . . . pleasurable. Like your bones are melting.'

That did not sound at all pleasurable. Elizabeth wondered if Becky meant the giddy, pins-and-needles feeling she had had that day when she opened the door to a man — James Cook. Elizabeth remembered every detail of that summer afternoon though it was five years ago. She'd been lying on the sofa in the front parlour, fanning herself with the time fan. Mama and Mr Blackburn were next door, in the Ship and Crown. They'd moved from Wapping to nearby Shadwell, to one of the tenements inherited from Samuel Batts, Elizabeth's father, though of course on Mama's remarriage her fortunes had become Mr Blackburn's. Although the Bell had given them a good living, Mama maintained she was glad to be out of the alehouse but, having said that, she and Mr Blackburn seemed always to be in the Ship and Crown, its best customers.

Elizabeth was expecting Becky and, while waiting, she practised the art of fan fluttering used by ladies to convey thoughts. While not a lady, Becky knew how to flutter a fan. Fanning fast meant 'I am engaged', slow that 'I am married'. Drawing the fan across the cheek meant 'I love you', opening it wide was a signal to 'Wait for me'. Elizabeth wondered if the men that ladies addressed in this fashion understood, and where they learnt the language, not being ones to carry fans themselves.

Beside the sofa lay *The Governess* by Sarah Fielding, sister of Henry, a novelist himself and a Bow Street magistrate. Elizabeth had promised Becky not to delve too far into the novel on her own. They planned to read the story of Mrs Teachum's female academy aloud to each other. Elizabeth treated herself to a delicious slice of orange, savoured the sweet taste of sunshine. What a pleasurable way to idle away the afternoon—a fan, exotic fruit, and a good novel at hand.

She picked up the book and began. Into the warm furry afternoon, into the little female academy, came the sound of firm confident knocking. Finally. Elizabeth went to the door to greet her friend.

It was not Becky at all, but a man. Tall, over six foot, a wide face with a firm confident set to his chin, and a well-curved mouth. Dressed in dark blue with white silk lapels and neckcloth.

His eyes looked into Elizabeth's, further than her eyes. Something inside her, of which she had previously been unaware, a closed tight bud, opened into a flower.

'Elizabeth?' he said, filling her name with breeze.

'Yes,' she replied, wondering who he was.

She felt her cheeks redden and tried to will the blush away, bowed her head, hoping he hadn't noticed. But then it got worse, because in bowing her head she saw that she'd come to the door barefoot, her toes peeping out from the folds of her skirts.

He sensed her embarrassment and took a step back. 'It's James Cook, Miss Batts,' he addressed her more formally. She heard the North Country in his voice, the gentle roll of the moors. She knew the name James Cook, Mama and Mr Blackburn sometimes talked of him, a seaman on Mr Walker's ships. A man who would go far, according to Mr Blackburn.

'Are Mr and Mrs Blackburn at home?' he asked.

'They're next door, at the Ship and Crown.'

He stood there a minute longer in the doorway. Elizabeth waited. 'I . . .' he began, as if to tell her important news. 'I hope to see you again, Miss Batts. Good day.' He bowed deeply then was gone.

Elizabeth shut the door. She went back to the parlour. The novel was still there, the fan beside it. Everything looked the same except that James Cook's presence seemed to fill the house. Perhaps she had dozed off and dreamt the whole thing. She'd had dreams like that, in which she opened the door to the unexpected.

Most often the dreams were of the Bell. She recognised the alehouse but in the dream there were doors she had never noticed before. Sometimes the unexpected was pleasant, like finding her father on the other side. He had eyes the same deep blue as Elizabeth's, a handsome man in fine clothes smiling at her. When she woke from those dreams she always felt happy and snuggled down under the bedclothes hoping to dream some more.

Then there were the dreams in which the unexpected was monstrous, how she imagined Bedlam to be. She had never been there, but she knew it was an entertainment that people paid to see—lunatics writhing in their cells and doing all manner of things. Elizabeth did not like it when the door opened to such spectacles and would try to wake herself up.

'Elizabeth.' Recalling how he'd said her name gave her pins and needles all over. She felt dreamy, alert, feverish, all at the same time. She wanted to see him again, but at a distance, to observe him without the flurry of blushing he had evoked. To watch and see whether her feelings were the same.

She picked up *The Governess* once more, touching its smooth leather cover, the sharpness at the corners. As she opened it, her hand swept down the smooth texture of the paper, caressing it. She saw the hard black letters but was too distracted to read. Mrs Teachum and her little female academy seemed a long way away.

Elizabeth let the book rest in her lap. She picked up the fan and slowly fluttered it, felt the movement of air on her face. She smelled oranges, the exotic fragrance of faraway places where the sun shone every day, and in winter the lightest of frosts descended to sweeten the fruit. Elizabeth. Now sequins danced in the breeze of her name.

Though James Cook had asked for Mama and Mr Blackburn, he had noticed Elizabeth in a way that their other friends didn't, almost as if he'd been calling on her instead.

She heard noise and abruptly got out her embroidery. Fortunately the needle was still threaded, so it would not appear that she'd just started. It could only be Mama and Mr Blackburn returning. But what if James Cook was with them, what if they had invited him back for supper? Elizabeth felt a tingling in her chest, wanting and not wanting it to be so.

'Becky has left already?' asked Mama, giving Elizabeth a kiss on her cheek.

Elizabeth could smell the ale on her breath. She watched in case a guest trailed behind Mama, but there was no-one. 'She didn't come.'

'But you had a visitor,' said Mr Blackburn. Did he say it in a peculiar way? Elizabeth couldn't tell.

'Are you ill?' Mama enquired, putting the back of her hand on her daughter's cheek. 'You feel quite hot.'

'It's been a warm day,' Elizabeth replied. She made way for Mr Blackburn, who had deposited himself on the sofa to take off his shoes.

'Ah, that's better,' he said, releasing the odour of his feet into the room. 'You remember James Cook,' Mr Blackburn continued, loosening his waistcoat. 'He lodged with us at Wapping, when he was an apprentice on Mr Walker's colliers.'

Elizabeth said nothing, head bent over her embroidery. As a child she was often in Essex with the Sheppards during the busy time when seamen lodged at the Bell. Surely she would have remembered if she had seen him before? But James Cook knew who she was, addressed her familiarly as Elizabeth.

As she stitched with the red silk thread she did arithmetic in her head, so much a part of her upbringing that she did it even without Mama's prompting. She would count almost anything— the number of barrels on a cart, the number of masts she could see from the window. She even counted how many buttons Mr Blackburn had undone on his waistcoat. Four. Now the arithmetic was about James Cook. Making allowances for the weathering effect of sea and wind on his mariner's face, Elizabeth judged him to be about twenty-seven years of age, fourteen years older than herself.

He could even have known her as a baby. Thinking of this made her feel as naked as Eve and she wished for a fig leaf, though she could not see what sin had been committed. She felt the blush rise again and wondered whether Mama and Mr Blackburn were exchanging glances, but she did not want to look up and show her special interest while the discussion was of James Cook.

Perhaps she had missed some conversation because the next thing she knew, Mr Blackburn was saying: 'He has joined the Navy. I asked him why, of course, seeing as how Mr Walker had offered him captaincy of the *Friendship*, and you know what he said?'

Elizabeth felt compelled to look up, as if Mr Blackburn was expecting her to know the answer, but he appeared to be talking to the air. 'He said: "I have a mind to try my fortune that way". Well, I suppose it's better to volunteer than to be press-ganged.'

Elizabeth, like all riverside dwellers, knew about the press-gangs. Hired thugs, Mr Blackburn called them, who dragged seamen off lighters and barges, came into the alehouses where they drank and rounded them up when they were the worse for wear. Word spread quickly along the riverside, and those liable for impressment made themselves scarce if they were able. Some dressed as women to avoid the gangs. Sometimes even landmen were impressed. 'The worst of all,' said Mr Blackburn, 'they don't know the ways of the sea and they don't want to be there. A ship's company needs to be tight, you don't want a landman under your feet in a storm.'

Elizabeth continued with her work, the little cross-stitches forming into squares that would mark the edges of the eventual cushion. Mr Blackburn had now undone the buttons around the knees of his breeches and loosened his stockings. He was at home.

'Even so,' Elizabeth heard her mother say, 'they'll be looking for able-bodied men, what with the war coming.'

There was much talk of the war, a subject that ran through the riverside community like a rat, not always seen but ever present. England seemed to be perpetually at war with France. Whilst there were not yet battles in the Channel, fighting had already broken out with the French in the colonies, in Canada and in India.

'It is yet to be declared,' Elizabeth joined in the conversation, safe now that it was about generalities.

'War is not an egg and spoon race,' commented Mr Blackburn. 'It always starts before it is declared.' He helped himself to some wine from the decanter on the mantelpiece.

'There'll be prize money to be had,' said Elizabeth's mother, rubbing a spot on her cheek, 'if they capture a ship.'

Elizabeth started threading dark green silk, to contrast with the red.

Mr Blackburn was warming to his subject. 'I'd be volunteering myself if I was a few years younger and didn't have . . . responsibilities,' he said, looking fondly at his wife. 'An able-bodied seaman can earn himself £100, to say nothing of the share what comes to the captain and officers. And I'll warrant James Cook will be an officer before too long.' He sounded as if he had picked the winning horse in a race.

Elizabeth studied the cross-stitches. They looked like little kisses.

'He's had schooling, he's a hard worker,' Mr Blackburn went on. 'Even though he's not a gent, with gent's connections, he'll be noticed. With his own skills, and a good patron, he will rise quickly in the Navy.' Mr Blackburn had his legs stretched out in front of him, glass of wine the colour of mulberry juice in hand.

Elizabeth saw the black stain of his tongue when he spoke. She quietly moved her embroidery to avoid possible spills and bent her head to her work, wondering where James Cook was now. Why had he not come back with Mama and Mr Blackburn?

By the time she looked up again, Mr Blackburn was snoring happily on the sofa, Mama having removed his empty glass — though even in sleep, he had a firm grip on it.

After supper, Elizabeth climbed the stairs, undressed and put on her nightgown. She went to the window. It was only four days away from midsummer. Evening light still lingered in the sky, and the streets were busy. She hoped the press-gangs had finished for the day, though night, with the seamen drunk and off-guard, was a good time for them to do their work. Ladies of the town were after seamen too, and a drunken sailor often fell asleep before the deed was done, the ladies helping themselves to the fee nevertheless. Elizabeth watched one wench, a girl not much older than herself, making eyes at a sailor. He touched her breast, drew her close. She laughed saucily, her hands busy in his pockets. She hurried away on finding them empty and disappeared into the crowd.

Elizabeth got into bed. How cool and refreshing the bed linen was against her skin. It was the same bed linen she always slept in but tonight it felt different, almost as if it were waiting for her. She stretched out her arms and her legs, caressing every part of it. Her body seemed to be in motion, like the undulations of the river when a ship passed through. 'Elizabeth.' Once again she heard his voice, and took it into her dreams.

'Careful,' said Becky, veering Elizabeth away from a puddle on Oxford Street. Elizabeth had not seen James Cook since that day five years earlier but there had been news and that same giddy feeling rippled in Elizabeth every time she heard his name mentioned.

Not long after the official declaration of war in May 1756, Mr Blackburn had come in from the Ship and Crown to announce that James Cook had seen action. 'His first fight at sea, in the *Eagle*. They took prisoners but the French ship sank. To think of that prize lying on the bottom of the Bay of Biscay.' He shook his head at the pity of it.

It must have been a few months later that Mr Blackburn, knocking on his own door because he was too drunk to open it, fell into the house with more news of the *Eagle*. He had been celebrating and reeled around the parlour. 'The *Eagle* put a broadside into the *Duc d'Aquitaine*. A change of captain, a change of luck. Hugh Palliser's the new captain, a Yorkshireman like Cook, though a few steps further up the ladder. James Cook got his prize money this time.' Despite his groggy state, Mr Blackburn was able to describe the battle minutely, as if he'd been there himself. The *Eagle* had sustained damage—a shot through the foremast and the sails almost rent to rags.

'Is he safe?' Elizabeth had found herself asking.

'Safe? Of course he's safe,' said Mr Blackburn. 'The man's an oak. It'll take more than the French to cut him down.' The last Elizabeth heard of James Cook, he had gone to fight in Canada.

Now Elizabeth and Becky skirted around a lady and gentleman admiring prints in a shop window. A giddy feeling was a world away from the pushing and shoving Elizabeth had witnessed in the darkened doorway. Neither seemed an appropriate basis for marriage. Elizabeth saw from Mama and Mr Blackburn that marriage was a companionable, sober affair, though perhaps in their case, sober wasn't quite the right word.

Elizabeth did not fancy marrying any of the riverside boys who came calling on her. The only possibility was Frederick, son of Reverend George Downing, who lived near the Sheppards in Essex. Frederick was destined for the law. Reverend Downing said that a lawyer in the family was the only one you could trust, all the others were intent on 'wresting land from its owners and thieves from the gallows'. Elizabeth had known Frederick since she was a child and had let him play with her letter tiles. She could easily see herself setting up house with him. He was companionable, and she loved him as a brother. Perhaps if she married him, she would learn to love him as a husband.

Whoever she married, Elizabeth wanted children. Unlike Mama, she would have more than one and they would not be monsters like Becky's two young brothers—Elizabeth would see to that. They would be well behaved like Uncle Charles's two little boys, Isaac and another Charles. She remembered when they were babies, the way they softly smelled of milk when she cuddled them.

Elizabeth's thoughts of babies were abruptly interrupted by a couple of dandies sauntering along Oxford Street. 'A fine pair,' said one of them, veering close to the girls, practically forcing them onto the road. Elizabeth wasn't sure whether he meant the two of them, or Becky's bosoms, which wobbled like jellies as she walked. Although Becky knew as well as Elizabeth that such advances were best ignored, she said, 'For heaven's sake!', affecting a disgusted tone and giggling as she would have done at school, not like someone who was about to become a wife and a mother.

Elizabeth directed her closer to the shops, reminding her of the task at hand. Nevertheless, Becky dawdled, looking in every shop window at everything from prints to frivolous hats.

They inched their way towards the glass and crockery shop, sidestepping muddy puddles and the advances of even more young bucks. Finally, Elizabeth and Becky arrived at their destination. Such a dazzling display in the bow windows, with light bouncing off crystal wine glasses and decanters, and cups and plates gleaming. It was all so splendid.

Inside, an Aladdin's cavern awaited, lit by a magnificent chandelier from the high ceiling. The shop shelves were full of more sparkling glasses and decanters, and sets of crockery. There were pieces from the factories in Limehouse and Bow, as well as imports from China. English and imported alike bore the fashionable Chinese chrysanthemums.

'I'm going to buy huge glasses that will take a whole bottle of wine to fill. What about you?' Though Becky whispered, her voice carried to the woman behind the counter. So many of the shopkeepers were women nowadays, with the men away at war. She cast a quick glance at the two young women, on the lookout for shoplifters.

'A teapot,' said Elizabeth.

While Becky deliberated, going from one set of glasses to the next, Elizabeth fixed on a beautiful porcelain teapot from China. Its creamy whiteness was decorated with a central band of red diagonal lines filled in with green petals, the band punctuated by red flowers with yellow at their centres and around the edges. Smaller red flowers decorated the spout, which came up on the diagonal from the body of the pot. Near the top of the pot was a band in a more muted red, featuring the same small red flowers, this time with blue and green leaves. Red flowers bloomed on the lid, which had an elegant nob shaped like a thimble.

Elizabeth imagined the artist delicately applying the colour; a man with a very long pigtail leaning over his work, holding his brocaded sleeve out of the way. She saw the teapot being carefully packed in straw so that it could make its way across the seas to her without breaking.

As she released the sovereigns from her sleeve and handed them over the counter, Elizabeth heard Becky sniggering. Elizabeth turned and frowned, but that only seemed to make things worse. Eventually Becky had to leave the shop and wait outside.

'What's so amusing?' said Elizabeth, when the transaction was finished.

'The teapot.'

Elizabeth held the box containing the teapot protectively under her arm. 'What about it?'

'The way the spout sticks out.'

'They all stick out.'

'Not at that angle,' said Becky, giggling all the while. 'Your trousseau teapot has a spout exactly like a John Thomas.'

THE ORIENTAL BOX

In preparation for Frederick's arrival, Reverend Downing had brought out the best tea service, with a special tea caddie and good china with a flower design. The pot was not dissimilar to Elizabeth's, which had been tucked away in a special drawer, Mama saying it was bad luck to use trousseau items before the marriage. No-one had passed comment on the spout that had induced so much laughter from Becky, who was now married with a son. The three young Sheppards Elizabeth had in her charge were angels compared to Becky's little terror.

Although she missed Mama and even Mr Blackburn, Elizabeth was happy that the position of governess had brought her back to her 'sister' Sarah and family life with the Sheppards. She had been with them almost two years now. Elizabeth loved her little charges but was glad to have this time off from them, to enjoy a cup of tea in pleasant company and conversation a little more lively than 'A is for apple'. She was looking forward to Frederick's arrival. He always brought the latest news, what plays were showing, new shops that had opened, what the ladies in London were wearing this season. Of particular interest this time, in November 1762, was how the metropolis celebrated the end of the war.

Elizabeth imagined the great ports—Plymouth and Portsmouth—discharging their sailors, imagined Wapping, Shadwell and the riverside, the brave soldiers and sailors who had fought the French now drunk as lords and fighting each other. She imagined Mr Blackburn throwing his hat up into the air and buying drinks in the Ship and Crown as if it were his own alehouse.

The coach was late. Such a brisk wind whistling down the chimneys, the sky so dark and ominous. Horses became skittish in this weather. Elizabeth hoped everything was all right, that there hadn't been an accident. Frederick had recently finished his studies and had secured himself a position with good prospects at Temple Inn. Perhaps today he would put to her the proposal everyone, including Elizabeth, expected. She had imagined his proposal several times but was still not sure of her answer. Perhaps when she heard the proposal from Frederick himself, she would know.

'And what is your opinion, Elizabeth?'

She put down her cup. 'I'm sorry?'

'Reverend Downing was asking what we think of the fair,' Sarah said. 'The Fairlop Fair.'

On this grey November day the summer fair seemed a long way away. Yet there was talk of it because certain parties wanted to see an end to it. Not Elizabeth. She loved fairs as much as she loved shopping, especially Fairlop Fair, because old Mr Day, who owned the Fairlop estate near Hainault Forest, was from Wapping, well known on the riverside and so considerate to his block and pump workers that they called him Good Day.

The fair had started when Elizabeth was a child, and what a sight it was to see people arriving for it. Its beginnings were small, a summer picnic for the workers in the shade of the Fairlop oak, by far the greatest oak in Essex, its branches reaching over three hundred feet. Though Mr Day was generous, he also had a touch of impishness—he stipulated that the picnickers come to the very oak itself, which was not on a river, or even a creek, by boat! That did not stop the enterprising waterside workers of Wapping, though.

Elizabeth had thought she was dreaming that day when she and all the Sheppards, forgetting their natural Quaker reserve, ran outside to watch the boat coming along the road. It was drawn by horses and bedecked in extravagant bouquets of flowers. Mr Day's workers sang sea shanties into the Essex countryside as the boat transported merriment for the day in the form of a full barrel of beer, a barrel as stout as a rich man's stomach.

That was only the first of a procession of vehicles in the years to come—vans with awnings, carts, omnibuses, other horse-drawn boats, all of them gaily bedecked and as magnificent as their owners could make them. Add the bands of musicians and it was as grand a procession as the coronation of King George, but instead of royalty, it was the watermen of the East End and their wives who were the kings and queens. By midday there must have been over 100 000 people spread out around the wide girth of the oak tree, leaving the East End practically empty.

'Perhaps,' ventured Elizabeth, 'those who object to the fair should not attend. It's only one day, it's easy enough to stay indoors.' As far as she knew the fairgoers had not so far attempted to storm country houses.

'There are plenty of other fairs,' argued Reverend Downing. 'Let them attend those.'

'But Fairlop is the watermen's fair,' Elizabeth protested. 'And it does them the world of good to be breathing air that is not peppered with coal dust and all manner of unhealthiness.'

'I have no objection to them breathing our country air. It's the quantity of drink they bring with them that causes the trouble.'

But everyone in England drank large quantities, from lords to the humblest servant. The real trouble was the power of the mob, to those who were afraid of it. The mob owned the streets and public places, especially on the riverside, and those not wise to its ways ventured there at their own risk. Mr Blackburn said it was better to have a fair than a riot. 'Mark my words,' he said, wagging that finger of his, 'if they try to put a stop to the fair there will be a riot.' England was a land of liberty, and any attempt to put the least restriction on this highly prized virtue was actively resented. In 1750, when Mr Fielding created the Bow Street runners to apprehend thieves, there was fierce public outcry that such a thing would introduce a military state. And much as everyone hated impressment and the press-gangs, compulsory conscription into the Navy, which was occasionally muted in the Houses of Parliament, was seen as a tyranny of the same order as the Spanish Inquisition.

Reverend Downing's housekeeper, Mrs Bradshaw, who had been following the discourse, poured more hot water in the pot and said, 'There is much that goes on at these fairs that is not suitable for young ladies to know about. It's that what people are objecting to,' she muttered into the steam arising from the jug.

'Thank you, Mrs Bradshaw,' said the reverend. 'That will be enough.'

Elizabeth wasn't sure whether he meant the hot water or her comment, but Elizabeth already knew what Mrs Bradshaw was referring to—the goings-on in Hainault Forest during the evening on fair day.

James Cook stood at the bow of a small boat winding downriver towards Barking Quay. He had been discharged only days before, with the tidy sum of £291 19s 3d owing to him. Although the Treaty of Paris which officially ended the war was not signed till February 1763, the preliminary peace negotiations had brought the ships home in November 1762. James's peacetime prospects looked promising. Lord Colville had praised the surveying work he had undertaken in Canada during the war, and had told James that in his report to the Admiralty he would be informing their lordships of James's 'genius and capacity'.

James had survived seven years of war with the French, attacks by Indians and the hazards of the St Lawrence River. Nevertheless, apprehension and uncertainty gnawed at him now as he stepped ashore at Barking Quay, a square package under his arm. Would 'genius and capacity' see him through his present undertaking?

He paused before beginning the two mile walk. Though it was a cold November day, it was nothing compared to the winters in Canada, to the sleet and sea ice and howling winds that whipped straight through the cold weather clothing, the skin, flesh and bones, and chilled a man's very marrow.

An easterly wind had brought a dark grey sky but at least it wasn't raining. He did not want to arrive at the Sheppards' dripping with rain, or for the package to be spoiled in any way.

He had made the acquaintance of James Sheppard, part-owner of Mr Walker's ships, in Wapping, and in preparation for his visit, had learnt a little of Barking and its surroundings on his journey down the Thames. The boatman who had ferried him here from Sinart's Quay near Billingsgate had told him about the market house and gardens, the busy fishing industry and the local church, St Margaret's, an important abbey before Dissolution. But the first thing James noticed about Barking, and the least suitable subject of conversation with the Sheppards, was the muck. Indeed, as he disembarked, also disembarking from another boat was a load of muck from London—night soil, slaughter-house refuse and carcasses. Cartloads of it were being wheeled away from the quay through the streets of the town to eventually end up on the market gardens.

The easterly did little to abate the smell of it, and James waited a moment to put some distance between himself and the manure. Not that a Yorkshire farm boy was unfamiliar with such things, but today of all days he wanted to present well. He smiled to himself at the thought that the potatoes, cabbages, turnips and onions, to say nothing of the apples, plums and walnuts destined for the best tables in London, were nurtured in the city's muck.

James strode into the grey day. He passed the market house with its row of mullioned windows, the arcades of the ground floor which would be full of corn on market days. Then he passed the Green Man Inn, and the timber and brick houses of Barking. The flint and rag-stone tower of St Margaret's led him out of the town and into the fields, the stubble of corn, rye and wheat catching the last brown leaves the wind flurried off the trees.

Across the fields James found the bridle path, wide enough for a horse but not a coach. He passed the manors of Uphall and Rayhouse, and on the London–Colchester turnpike road finally came to Crowcher's Yard. Set back from the road he saw a large solid brick house and counted five attics jutting into the sky.

He took in a deep breath, summoned up his courage, and strode decisively towards the house, towards what he hoped would be his future. The pair of barking dogs which accompanied him up the path settled as soon as the door was opened.

'James Cook,' he announced himself. 'Come to see Miss Batts.'

The coach bearing Frederick had not arrived.

'I'm sure everything is all right,' said Sarah, as the girls walked back along the turnpike road. 'The driver is probably going slow to avoid accident.'

'The ideal pace for highwaymen,' Elizabeth pointed out.

'They wouldn't dare hold up a coach with a lawyer on board.'

Sarah's comment lightened the mood. It was pleasant to be in the crisp cold air after the warm fug of Reverend Downing's drawing room, though by the time they turned off the road and made their way to the house, escorted by Blacky and Spot, the girls were well and truly ready for another fire.

But Elizabeth was not prepared to see who was sitting beside it. James Cook. It had been more than seven years. Though the sound of his name still caused giddiness to ripple through her, when she had tried to recall his image it was blurred by her feelings for him. Yet she recognised him immediately, instinctively.

'Ah,' exclaimed Mr Sheppard, 'I see our fine Essex weather has brought colour to your cheeks,' he said, looking at Elizabeth, who herself didn't know where to look. 'Mr Cook, this is my daughter, Sarah. And of course you know Miss Batts.'

James Cook rose out of his seat and bowed. Elizabeth watched the flow of movement through his blue coat and the neat white breeches. He must be thirty-four—Elizabeth couldn't help but do the calculation—and the years of war, of harsh Canadian winters, were visible in his face, yet his eyes were the same. They swept over Sarah and came to rest on Elizabeth.

'How is Frederick?' Mrs Sheppard enquired.

Elizabeth left it to Sarah to answer. 'Not yet arrived.'

'But we heard a coach.'

'Frederick wasn't on it,' Sarah said.

'How disappointing for you, Elizabeth,' Mrs Sheppard sympathised.

Sarah glanced at Elizabeth. Why had she suddenly gone quiet?

'Mr Cook and I have been exchanging news of our mutual friend, Mr Walker,' Mr Sheppard broke the silence.

Elizabeth felt she must say something. After all these years. Was James Cook here to see her or the Sheppards? 'Will you be returning to Whitby?' she finally asked.

'To see Mr Walker, and my family. Then back to London. I've taken up lodgings in Shadwell. Near your mama and Mr Blackburn.'

Elizabeth knew now that she, not the Sheppards, was the object of his visit.

'The wind appears to have dropped,' James Cook said. 'I was hoping Miss Batts, and Miss Sheppard,' he added, 'might show me a little of the countryside.'

Nobody commented on the fact that Mr Cook must have already seen something of it on his way from Barking.

Of all the Sheppards, only Sarah seemed to know what was going on. 'I'm feeling a little tired,' she said. 'If Elizabeth and Mr Cook will excuse me, I'm sure they have much to discuss. Family news to catch up on,' she emphasised.

A moment of indecision hung in the room, Elizabeth could feel it like a wrinkle in an otherwise smooth fabric.

'Would you prefer to stay, Miss Batts?' asked James Cook.

'No, no,' Elizabeth replied, she hoped not too hastily.

'Mr Blackburn tells me you are living with the Sheppards now,' he began as they made their way down the yard and onto the road. Though the wind had dropped it was still the same low grey sky, but with James Cook by her side, Elizabeth felt she was walking in brisk sunshine.

'I am helping with the little ones.'

'Their governess?' suggested James Cook.

'Yes.' Elizabeth couldn't help but smile as she remembered that *The Governess* was the novel she had been reading when James Cook first strode into her life.

In the natural motion of their walking she felt his hand brush hers. A precious thing, like a bird coming to rest on her hand. Though it was only the slight brush of skin on skin, the feeling quivered up her arm and through her entire body. In the time since they'd first met Elizabeth had grown from a girl into a young woman, yet now the years fell away and she felt the same as she had when she'd opened the door to him.

'Are you cold, Miss Batts? Do you wish to return to Crowcher's Yard?'

No, she didn't. 'You've hardly seen anything of the countryside yet.' They relaxed into an easy pace.

They passed Reverend Downing's. Elizabeth hoped the reverend, or worse, Mrs Bradshaw with her clucking tongue, wasn't peering out the window, because up ahead was the Fairlop oak and, looming behind it, Hainault Forest, the place of the 'goings-on'. Here she was, walking towards it, unchaperoned, with a man she had met only once before.

As they approached the tree, a great flock of crows rose up, screeching and mawking into the sky. 'When I was a little girl,' said Elizabeth, 'I would stretch out my arms and try to encircle the trunk. I did it each time I returned to the Sheppards', sure that my arms must have grown long enough, but they never reached even a quarter of the way around.' She had a desire to do it right now, to enfold the tree in her arms, but it seemed too intimate a gesture.

'A magnificent tree,' James remarked. 'And it continues growing, despite the abuses to it,' he added, referring to the burnt-out lower section, remnants of fires from the fair.

They leant against the amplitude of the trunk and watched the crows settle in the forest.

'Boys climb right to the uppermost branches of this tree,' said Elizabeth. 'They swear they can see London.'

'There's a tree outside the cottage where I was born. An evergreen, with dark green bristly leaves. It was from that tree that I first saw a ship,' he told Elizabeth.

'And you decided to become a seaman?' How easy it was to be in James Cook's company, to talk with him as if he and Elizabeth had been friends for life.

'It piqued my curiosity. A determined curiosity. My father doubted I could see a ship from Marton — "tree or no," I remember him saying. I saw the sea itself later, when we moved to Great Ayton.' He gazed into the distance. 'It was the horizon as much as the sea that intrigued me. I'd never seen such a straight line. The schoolmaster said it was an apparent line, that you could never reach it. But I wanted to see for myself, wanted to know what lay beyond.' His voice softened. 'Are you not curious about what lies beyond the horizon, Elizabeth?'

There it was again, breeze rustling sequins through her name. Elizabeth felt as though she were being edged into the forest, into its dark enticing promise.

'I don't need to go to sea to find out,' said Elizabeth decisively. 'Much of what lies beyond the horizon ends up in London anyway.'

'Indeed it does,' laughed James, a low chuckle that seemed to spread out in his chest and rise into his throat.

'Do you have brothers and sisters, Mr Cook?'

'Two sisters. Christiana and Margaret. All that survive from eight births. My mother and father are still living. In Yorkshire, in a house built by my father with help from Mr Skottowe, his employer.' He turned and gazed directly at her. 'Perhaps you will see the house one day.'

Elizabeth did not look away, instead matching his gaze with her own. She took in every detail of him. The strong nose, the turn of the chin, the soft curve of his mouth. She saw his greatness, his ability to master any task he set his mind to, yet with his eyes he humbled himself before her. It was Elizabeth who felt as tall as a tree, her feet planted solidly on the ground, her branches rustled by the winds of the earth.

Before anything could be said, those same winds brought the sound of galloping hoofs. A coach. 'Perhaps we should be heading back,' suggested Elizabeth, aware of what their situation must look like. As the coach flew by, Elizabeth saw Frederick waving, his face full of confusion.

'A friend?' enquired James.

Elizabeth nodded.

'The Frederick spoken of at the Sheppards'?'

'Yes.'

The walk back continued in silence, the only sound the wind starting to whip up again.

They arrived at Crowcher's Yard. 'It was a pleasure to renew your acquaintance, Miss Batts.' His formal tone was a long way from the shared intimacy of Fairlop oak. 'I must get back to Barking, I'll be late for the boat. Please give my regards to the Sheppards.' And he was off, without a word of any future meeting.

Elizabeth was dismayed. Surely it wasn't the sight of Frederick that had sent him off? Would it be another seven years before she saw him again? She couldn't bear it. Why had he bothered showing up at all if he was going to disappear so quickly? Was he trifling with her? She walked slowly up to the house.

It wasn't till later, when the dogs were let in for the night, that Mrs Sheppard remembered the package. 'Perhaps treats sent from Mr and Mrs Blackburn. Sonya,' she addressed the servant, 'where did you put Mr Cook's package?'

'In Miss Sarah and Miss Elizabeth's room, marm.'

He hadn't mentioned a package, not even when he was leaving.

'Go up and see what it is,' said Mrs Sheppard. 'If it's food it might spoil. Sarah, take a candle.'

Elizabeth followed Sarah up the stairs, Sarah holding her hand in front of the candle's flame to protect it from the breeze her movement made. She seemed a lot more enthusiastic about possible treats from the Blackburns than Elizabeth was.

The package was lying on Elizabeth's bed, wrapped in brown paper and firmly tied with string in a series of knots. Elizabeth picked it up—not as heavy as it looked. She gently shook it but heard nothing rattle. There were none of Mama's puddings or pies inside.

'Open it, open it,' begged Sarah. Elizabeth fiddled with the knots, looking for the piece of string that would unravel all of them.

'I'll get scissors,' said Sarah. She returned in time to see Elizabeth loosen the last knot and unwrap the sturdy brown paper to reveal . . .

A box. An oriental box of black lacquer that gleamed in the candlelight. Around its edges were gilt flowers—chrysan-themums—and in the centre an oriental scene: bridges, steps, houses with curled roofs, all floating in the air, as if detached from the earth. This was not Mama and Mr Blackburn's doing. It was a gift from beyond the horizon.

'Oh,' said Sarah, 'it is beautiful.'

Despite the fact that there appeared to be nothing inside, or at least nothing that rattled, Elizabeth couldn't resist the invitation the box—all boxes—extended, to open it. She held the clasp, as small and delicate as an earring, between thumb and forefinger, and released it.

There was nothing in the box except its rich red velvety lining and a piece of rice paper on the inside of the lid that had squares drawn on it in neat lines. Inside each of those squares was a letter. Elizabeth held the candle to it and read: 'Elizabeth, marry me. James Cook.'

THE MARRIAGE CERTIFICATE

James Cook *of the Parish of St Paul, Shadwell, in the County of Middlesex, Batchelor and Elizabeth Batts of the Parish of Barking in the County of Essex, Spinster were married in this Church by Archbishop of Canterbury. Licence this twenty first day of December one Thousand Seven Hundred and Sixty two by George Downing, Vicar of Little Wakering, Essex.*

This marriage was Solemnized between us James Cook, *Elizabeth Cook nee Batts in the Presence of John Richardson, Sarah Brown, William Everrest.*

The square battlemented tower of St Margaret's rose above the row of yew trees with their lumps of dark evergreen foliage that was cut to wave Hosanna on Palm Sunday, but which all the year round provided protection from the winds, the dense foliage forming a large hedge separating the gravestones from the church. An old woman of the district, who some said was a witch, had told Elizabeth one day, as Elizabeth was feeling the furrows in the reddish yew trunks, that centuries ago, before even the abbey existed, yew trees were worshipped and venerated for their strength and endurance. As the wedding party skirted the hedge and entered through the arch of the tower, Elizabeth made a wish for a long life and a marriage as strong and enduring as a yew tree.

In the weeks that followed the proposal, when Elizabeth came to London to give her answer, and the couple declared their sentiments for each other, James said it was all Elizabeth's doing, that she had called to him, through the red and green bird, and he had come. James said he dreamt of her in the long Canadian nights, of that moment on the Blackburns' threshold, and knew that when he knocked on the door of home it was Elizabeth he wanted to find waiting there. He said that he loved her, and that he wanted to grow old with her. Elizabeth thrilled to hear him say such things and nodded yes, it is the same for me.

Not knowing when he might be at sea again, James thought they should be married as soon as possible, with no time for the posting of banns, and was granted a special licence from the Archbishop of Canterbury. Elizabeth was impressed with the way James had organised such a thing. Meanwhile, Elizabeth and Mama had gone to the grand shops and purchased cream silk for the wedding dress. There was much stitching and sewing, fitting and refitting, Mama with pins in her mouth making adjustments here and there, pleating the fabric in at the waist, to finally produce a beautiful gown with a lace tucker and stiffened cap to match.

Now James and Elizabeth entered the church, with its ceiling constructed of crown-post timbers that made it look like an upside-down boat. The stained-glass St Margaret held a palm leaf cradled in one hand, a staff in the other. She was standing on a dragon, her symbol, representing the dragon that had swelled and split in two when St Margaret made the sign of the cross. When women prayed for ease in childbirth it was to St Margaret that they looked, at her lovely gentle face, surrounded by a halo.

Ahead, at the altar, stood Reverend Downing. Reverend Musgrave, vicar of St Margaret's, had given permission for him to officiate on this occasion. Reverend Downing had strong connections to the parish. He lived here, was chaplain at Ilford Hospital, before taking up his present position of vicar at Little Wakering, and his sons John and Frederick had been christened at St Margaret's.

Frederick. Elizabeth had not relished the task of telling either him or his father. But better to get it over and done with as quickly as possible. When Elizabeth returned to Essex and went to make her announcement to the Downings, both father and son were dismayed at her news.

'Yes,' she said. 'On St Thomas's Day.'

'So soon?' commented Reverend Downing.

'He's a navy man, we want to get married before he goes to sea again,' Elizabeth explained, in case the reverend thought there was another reason.

'Congratulations,' he declared, not knowing what else to say.

Elizabeth did not have the courage to look directly at Frederick. When she got up to leave, as blithely as if she'd just brought a present of eggs from Mrs Sheppard, Frederick followed her. 'Elizabeth,' he began, 'I thought, well . . .' The new lawyer was lost for words. 'I had hoped . . .' Her heart went out to him. Elizabeth was as fond of Frederick as she'd ever been and hated seeing him like this. But even if right there and then Frederick, or any other man, had asked for her hand, she would have said no.

Elizabeth did not know where the path of her life would lead, only that she must take it with James. It may not be the settled life Elizabeth would have had with Frederick, in which so much was already familiar. James had to go where the Navy sent him, be away for weeks, months. There were dangers at sea that a husband like Frederick would never be exposed to. Financially, James was able to provide for her. He had a small fortune in pay awaiting him, and prize money as well. Although navy men were universally loved and admired in these heady days after the war, marrying a navy man was not the same as marrying a vicar's son. James was not born to respectability as was Frederick. He had earned it. As master, he'd reached the top rank of warrant officer. It would be unusual for a man of James's background to rise further in the Navy, despite Mr Blackburn's extravagant claims. But James was an unusual man.

There were a few days of silence after her visit to the Downings, then Reverend Downing came to see Elizabeth. 'You know I've always considered you as one of my own.' Elizabeth thought of the reverend's little daughter, Elizabeth, buried in Ilford chapel at the age of ten. 'I was hoping to perform the ceremony,' he said. 'Whomever you marry,' he added, smoothing relations between her and the Downings.

As the couple walked down the aisle, Elizabeth felt the prayers of all those who had worshipped here across the centuries, the prayers for a long life, for ease in childbirth, for strength to have the Lord's will be done. She glanced at the skull set in stone, a *memento mori*, reminding everyone who gazed upon it that in life there was always death.

James and Elizabeth stood at the altar. Reverend Downing beamed a smile of welcome, then cleared his throat, waiting till everyone was still and quiet. 'Dearly beloved,' he read from the Book of Common Prayer, 'we are gathered together here in the sight of God and in the face of this congregation, to join together this man and this woman in holy matrimony . . .'

When the time came, James took Elizabeth's right hand and repeated the words: 'I take thee Elizabeth, to my wedded wife, to have and to hold from this day forward, for better, for worse, for richer for poorer, in sickness and in health, to love and cherish, till death us do part, according to God's holy ordinances; and thereto I plight thee my troth.' James delivered them solemnly from his heart, and as a man of his word, thus it would be.

Now it was Elizabeth's turn. Reverend Downing pronounced the words repeated by so many who had stood before this altar and others. The posy in Elizabeth's hand was quivering, her whole body trembling under the weight of the occasion, the gravity of the undertaking. It was one thing to declare her love for James in private, another to make this lifelong promise before witnesses, before God. Although her body was trembling, when she made her vows Elizabeth's voice rose up into the church as clear and bright as birdsong.

They started with long, succulent kisses, a soft searching of the other's mouth. Elizabeth could have continued like this forever. Eventually James brought her to the bed and laid her down, undid her nightdress and ran his hand over her breasts, cradled them as if they were precious fruit and finally put his mouth to them. Elizabeth's back arched, offering her breasts more fully to him. She was surprised that her body knew what to do. It was as if she and James were partners in a dance, the movements of which had been etched into her bones, like the courtship dance of birds, movements that she knew instinctively. Elizabeth could feel love streaming out of her breasts. She wanted to give and give, as if her supply of love was endless. But when it came time for the ultimate intimacy, she gasped, overwhelmed by the sheer size of him. Were the members of all men like this? James pulled back. 'Are you all right, my dear?'

'It is a little uncomfortable,' Elizabeth replied. He tried again but could not get past the threshold. 'I'm sorry, James,' she whispered.

'It is of no consequence,' said James, rolling onto his side. 'We will wait until you are ready.'

Elizabeth lay with her head on his chest and eventually went to sleep, lulled by the steady rhythm of his heart.

In the following weeks James and Elizabeth Cook set up house in Mr Blackburn's tenement at 126 Upper Shadwell northside. Elizabeth brought out all her trousseau items, put the cushions with embroidered covers on the sofa, the new kettle by the fire. The trousseau teapot seemed to be in constant use. There were visits from friends, from Mama and Mr Blackburn, who had now removed to Starr Street, Uncle Charles with his two growing boys, Isaac, aged nine, and Charles, aged eight, and a baby daughter, Ursula; Christmas celebrations, New Year fireworks. The newly-weds barely had a moment to themselves, let alone a honeymoon, yet in the spring James would be sailing to Canada. He would be away for five or six months at a time, he said.

Elizabeth would rather have James half the time than any other man all of the time, she thought as she moved her pieces around the board. She and Isaac were playing backgammon—with a variation. Elizabeth was Montcalm, and Isaac General Wolfe, trying to beat the French general. Uncle Charles had dropped in, bringing young Charles and Isaac, and had been disappointed to find that James was not at home. When they discovered the reason for his absence—that he'd gone to the Ordnance Office to purchase surveying instruments—the boys had begged to stay. Isaac could stay if he wanted, but Charles had a cold and his father had said it was best to get him home before the night air settled on him.

Elizabeth looked across the board at 'General Wolfe'. Isaac had the same Smith features that Elizabeth shared with her mother: angular lines to the face, aquiline nose and heavy eyelids. Charles was more like his mother, having a round face with apple cheeks. Even at the age of eight he resembled a portly little merchant, standing in front of the fire with his coat-tails lifted to warm his backside, just like his father.

Elizabeth had just scooped the dice back into the container for her turn when she heard her husband come in. She hadn't realised it but she'd been listening for his return. The house seemed still and empty without him in it, even though she had Isaac to keep her company. James deposited his packages on the table, kissed Elizabeth, and said: 'Hello there, young Isaac.' He looked around for the other Smiths.

'Papa's coming to collect me in the morning,' said Isaac, who was peering hard at the packages, as if his very eyes might penetrate the wrappings to the treasures that lay beneath.

James stretched the moment out. 'Well,' he said thoughtfully when he saw that Isaac was on the point of bursting. 'Let's see what we have.' It seemed to Elizabeth that Isaac wasn't the only one wanting the packages opened. James would have chosen carefully at the Tower, looked over each item, but there was nothing like examining them at one's own leisure.

Elizabeth sensed his excitement, anticipation, and did her best to share it, but the purchase of the instruments brought his departure one step closer. It was all very well thinking she'd rather have James half the time than any other man all of the time but living it was a different matter. She missed him even when he went to town for a few hours.

'In Canada,' James said to Isaac in the same man-to-man way in which Mr Walker had discussed scientific matters with him, 'I was privileged to learn land surveying techniques from General Wolfe's own engineer.' James recalled his chance meeting with Mr Holland in the summer of 1758, a meeting that had had a great impact on him, that would stay with him after the war and into the peace. 'It was the day after the capture of Louisbourg.' James started undoing the first package. 'I saw a man walking about with a small square table, but instead of legs, it was mounted on a tripod. A plane table, similar to this one,' he said, revealing the contents of the package. 'The man would set it down at regular intervals along the shoreline, bend to get his eye aligned and look across the tabletop in various directions. After each reading he took a little book out of his pocket and made notes. I was very curious to know what he was doing.'

Isaac watched as James set the table up, as if he were a magician about to perform a trick.

'Eventually we struck up a conversation. He introduced himself, explained how the plane table worked, and told me he was making a plan of Kennington Cove and the encampment. We talked so much about our mutual interests that he invited me to accompany him the next day.' James told Isaac how in the months that followed, between the fighting, he found time to survey Gaspé bay and harbour, using the very techniques learnt from Mr Holland. It was a small piece of work but good enough to be published in London by Mount and Page of Tower Hill the following year.

'I am convinced,' James continued in his man-to-man tone, 'that combining those land methods with marine techniques will produce precise and accurate charts of coastlines.' He recalled again the soaring realisation at the Postgate school, when the sea was still far away across the moors, and Canada a type of goose, that the quill was an instrument of flight. Drawing an accurate picture of the world, a map that others could follow, while it was work with pen and paper, was not the same as sitting in lawyers' rooms on a high stool, copying wills and other documents, or being a draughtsman.

James would be venturing into new territory and outlining its contours with the feather of a bird which, in flight, saw every detail. Putting onto paper that bird's-eye view, as if its feather quill still held the memory of coves and inlets, and every other feature. A representation that, in Lord Colville's words, 'may be the means of directing many in the right way'. So accurate that it would show the way not just for a few months but for centuries to come.

He undid the second package. A quadrant. Elizabeth saw the brass quarter-disc in its green baize casing. It reminded her of a lady's fan.

'What's the quadrant for?'

'First we measure a baseline and place marker flags either end. Then we fix the latitude of the line by using the quadrant to take sightings of the sun. Work is continued with the next package. Perhaps you would like to cut the string.'

Isaac glanced at Elizabeth before taking the scissors, remembering her warning that instruments were not playthings and he wasn't to touch anything without express permission. Elizabeth made a gesture indicating he should go ahead. Isaac cut the string, enjoying the crisp snip the scissors made, wound the string off the package, and put it into his pocket. There were a thousand and one things a boy could do with string. James removed the wrapping with a flourish, as if revealing a dove that had supposedly vanished.

This was the most mysterious instrument of all. 'It's called a theodolite. For determining the angles between each end of the line and a more distant object, like a tree, or the mast of a ship. These three instruments give us a pattern of triangles. All you have to do then is plot points onto paper and join up the dots.'

Elizabeth smiled at how easy her husband made it sound, as simple as a child's puzzle rather than the painstaking work it was. It might be dangerous too—attacks from Indians, wild animals, to say nothing of the hidden rocks and shoals of the coastline itself. Elizabeth took in a breath. She must rein in thoughts of what might or might not happen while he was away. He was here now.

She moved in for a closer look at this theodolite, an instrument which James had talked of but she had never seen. It was made of brass, including the screws, a tube set upon a toothed wheel, a tube that would be released from its clasps and brought up to the vertical to do its work.

'I'd wager this is the only house in Shadwell to have a . . . thee . . . theodite,' Isaac struggled with the word.

'The-od-o-lite,' said James, separating the word out into its syllables. 'And you're too young to wager, Isaac.'

The instruments were examined and re-examined late into the night. It was only when Elizabeth noticed that Isaac was beginning to resemble an owl that she suggested it was time for bed. As Elizabeth and James made their way upstairs they heard young Isaac say: 'Theodolite.'

'What was that?' James asked.

'Goodnight,' murmured Isaac from beneath his blanket by the fire. 'I said goodnight.'

A Plan of St John's

Newfoundland was a great inkblot piece of land facing the Atlantic on one side and the Gulf of St Lawrence on the other, a big doorstop of rock on the threshold of Quebec, Labrador and the rest of Canada. The edges of the inkblot, where they drizzled into the sea, formed a fringe of harbours and bays, cliffs, rocks and shoals, the indentations adding up to a total of 6000 miles of coastline. Icebergs travelled on the currents to Newfoundland from the glaciers of Greenland, amassing in the spring like a gathering of huge white clouds. Fog descended so thickly that a man almost lost sight of himself. The fog diminished his senses and left him disoriented. It took more than quadrants and theodolites to get your bearings, and it seemed that your companion had vanished off the face of the earth, even though he might be only two feet away. In summer there was rain. It was not a place for a settlement, yet the British government was investing ten shillings a day, to say nothing of other expenses, to have it surveyed, because Newfoundland had its riches—cod, cod and more cod, with which the offshore banks were teeming. The surveyor's season was the fisherman's season. James had to be ready to start work at the beginning of June and not linger later than the end of October.

That first year as the king's surveyor, James had a special reason for returning to Elizabeth as soon as possible. With his instruments and books, he had departed for his first season in Newfoundland on 4 May 1763, taking the coach to Plymouth then joining HMS *Antelope*, which sailed with the tide ten days later. James had left Elizabeth for the summer but he had not left her alone.

She had wondered whether to tell him before his departure. It was early days, though, and much could happen in the months before his return. A pregnancy did not always mean a living child at the end of it. If that were God's will, perhaps it would be better that she bore the burden of it alone. But she remembered the words she had so recently and solemnly repeated—for better or worse, in sickness and in health. It was not only honouring this promise. Her happiness was so great that it spilled out of her, and on the eve of his departure she told him that she was with child, knowledge that would buoy and warm him during the cool Canadian summer.

That night, when they had snuffed out the candles and all was quiet, James drew himself down in the bed and lifted Elizabeth's nightgown inch by inch, the slowest, surest thing he had ever done in his life. When the garment was level with her breasts, he touched the small mound of her stomach, which was as round and as smooth as a globe. First with his hands, then with his lips. He buried himself in Elizabeth and surrendered to her completely.

Scientific instruments might be well and good for measuring and mapping the world, but when it came to childbirth, Mama's advice prevailed. Elizabeth was young and healthy, and Mama saw no reason why a man-midwife with his newfangled instruments should be present. 'He might know the ins and outs of anatomy,' Mama said, 'but he's never given birth himself, has he? I've heard of more than one bungle with those forceps.' So Elizabeth was attended by old Mrs Sutton, who had delivered many a riverside babe.

Though the Bible taught that women were to bring forth in pain, nothing had prepared Elizabeth for it. Mama said she could not remember the pain, only the Frost Fair. On 13 October 1763, in the upstairs room where Elizabeth had slept so many months alone, the walls seemed to cave in around her and she was overtaken with searing, shuddering pain; eviscerated, drawn and quartered.

When she felt the first pains she sent a message to Mama, who arrived with Mrs Sutton and a birthing stool. Elizabeth looked at the horseshoe-shaped seat, which still held a mystery, even though Mama had explained that you squatted over it, the gap providing a space for hands to safely catch the baby. At first Elizabeth had no desire to squat, instead spending her time ranging around the room. She felt extremely uncomfortable, and the only thing that seemed to relieve the discomfort was walking. 'That's good,' Mrs Sutton encouraged her. 'It makes the baby press downwards.'

Eventually, though, the pains came more frequently and Elizabeth's legs turned to jelly. Now she was grateful for the stool. Through the lather of sweat, her hair clinging to her face, she could hear Mrs Sutton say 'Push' or 'Breathe easy' and though the midwife was right beside her, the voice sounded as if it were coming from a long way away. The pain was hot. Red and raw. Elizabeth gasped and screamed, but like Mrs Sutton's voice, those sounds also seemed to be coming from afar, from another woman, not Elizabeth.

Perhaps Elizabeth had ice in her blood, passed on from Mama's Frost Fair, because she found her haven in the frozen reaches of Canada. 'Sometimes an iceberg breaks up in a storm, rolls over like a giant in his sleep, dragging those nearby down with him. Ice floes are scattered on the sea like great pieces of a jigsaw puzzle.' James's words drifted back to her. 'On the horizon icebergs are difficult to distinguish from clouds bright with light.' His voice mapped the shoals and the rocks till Elizabeth's head was filled with the great jagged edges of Newfoundland. 'Night is the most dangerous time—you cannot see the ice till you are upon it.' His voice dipped in and out of her pain. 'Howling gales, the wind whisking words right out of your mouth.'

The ice and the pain melted as the baby was born, in a great flood of water that gushed out of his mother. A son. He took his first gulp of air and bellowed it out to the world.

Although she had eschewed the services of a man-midwife, Elizabeth was not a follower of every traditional practice, and did not swaddle the babe as countless mothers before her had done. Apart from the growing body of opinion that held swaddling to be unnatural, Elizabeth's time with the Sheppards in Essex had taught her the benefits of fresh air and loose clothing for newborns. It strengthened the bones and allowed the child to grow strong and sturdy. The Quakers believed that babies were born innocent, not in original sin. Control and restraint could come later. A well-applied rod would lead a child on the path of righteousness if he showed signs of straying. Likewise, she did not give the baby over to a wet-nurse but suckled him herself, watching the wee infant take to the pink nipple as naturally as a newborn calf to its mother's teat. The baby drank deeply of the milk that filled his mother's breast, and the love in her heart beneath it.

Elizabeth marvelled at the child, could not stop gazing at him. She examined his every detail—the miniature toenails, the creases at his wrists, the delicately etched eyebrows. His slightest movement—the flicker of an eyelid, the furrowing of his brow—made Elizabeth's heart melt. How could such a small creature draw forth such an immense outpouring of love?

On the first of November, Elizabeth brought the baby to St Paul's to be christened James. A month later, his father returned.

When James saw his son he gently laid a finger on the baby's wide face and determined little chin. 'Aye, that's a Yorkshire lad,' he commented. 'But with his mother's blue eyes.'

'They all start blue,' said the new mother. Elizabeth did not mind whose chin or eyes the baby had. It was enough that he was healthy.

Elizabeth's happiness was complete. Tears welled in her eyes as she watched James hold the baby in his arms, and she saw the look of rapture on her husband's face as he bent to kiss his son. That first night in bed the baby slept between mother and father, each parent a curve, two halves which joined together to provide a sphere of love and protection.

Before the end of the winter Elizabeth determined it was time for the Cooks to find a nest of their own. Mr Blackburn had been most charitable in offering them the Upper Shadwell tenement for a peppercorn rent, but she did not want to be beholden to him forever, and proper tenants would provide him and Mama with more income.

She broached the subject one day when James was busy refining his charts and maps. While Elizabeth sat, her straight back parallel with the back of the chair, head bent over her embroidery, James, in unbuttoned waistcoat and billowing sleeves rolled up out of the way of inks and quills and instruments, moved around the table on which his work was spread out. Baby James, asleep in his new crib, a christening gift from Uncle Charles, murmured and Elizabeth looked in his direction, listening to the sounds, hoping they would stay small and not develop into full-blown cries.

The sounds did not fold back into sleep but grew louder. Little fingers started groping the air and the tiniest frown developed on the forehead before the eyes squeezed tightly and the mouth opened into a cry.

James heard it. His head came up from his work. Was it a scowl on his face or merely a look of concentration? Elizabeth tried rocking the crib but it did not lull the baby back to sleep. He was hungry and only one thing would fix that. She undid her laces and freed a breast, the nipple already weeping milk, and put the baby to it.

James left his work table and came over, stopping short of the two. James stood there awkwardly, as if the mother and child had around them an aura he could not penetrate.

He went back to his work. Although the curtains were open, the day outside was dull and dark, and he sometimes needed to hold a candlestick over the work. He replaced it in its holder on the wall directly afterwards, bringing into the house his shipboard habits of a place for everything and everything in its place. He could not afford to have wax spatter on the charts, or worse, the documents go up in flames.

Though Elizabeth had seemed entirely absorbed in her task, she was not oblivious to the cramped conditions of their accommodation, and the difficulty it must cause her husband. If it were not such an unpleasant day outside, Elizabeth might have taken baby James to visit Mama and Mr Blackburn, but instead she decided to take him upstairs, out of his father's way.

She bent down to lift the crib, which was made of heavy oak.

'There is no need to move him, ' James said softly. 'Perhaps I've done enough for one day.'

But Elizabeth knew her husband. He did not do a 'day's work'. He carried on till the job was done, with a look of fierce concentration on his face.

'I'll take him up.'

'If you are determined, my dear, let me do it,' offered James.

Elizabeth watched him go up the stairs, carrying the crib as lightly as if it were a basket of fruit. She let him have this moment alone with his son, and tiptoed over to the table where James's work was laid out, taking care that her large skirts did not brush against anything.

'Plan of Harbour of St John's in Newfoundland by James Cook, 1763'. Towards the bottom left-hand corner were the cardinal points that James had filled in and shaded so that it looked like a star. Around the curve of shoreline, and looping into the harbour, were hatchings of penstrokes which, together with a gouache of pale green, denoted scrub. Elizabeth could see the faint pencil lines from one reference point to another, and the numbers in the water which measured the depth of the channel. It was very pretty work indeed. Several features were marked with letters of the alphabet and at the top of the plan was a key to the references:

A   Kings Wharfe
B   Navy Brew House
C   Six Gun Battery
D   Rosses Rock
E   Chain Rock
F   Battreys of Two Guns
G   Sigd Hill
H   Cuckolds Head

Elizabeth wondered how H got to be named.

When James came back down Elizabeth broached the subject of purchasing a house. She knew they could afford it because she was the one who managed the accounts, carefully noting the income and the outgoings in her ledger. They had saved quite a bit through Mr Blackburn's generosity and Elizabeth's own careful household management. 'A house bigger than these two rooms,' she said. 'A place where you can work, with a little garden for James, and his future brothers and sisters,' she added. 'Not too far from Mama and Mr Blackburn,' she said, thinking of the months when James would be away.

A few weeks later James announced that he'd found something. 'Remember Mr Curtis, the distiller from Wapping?'

'The Curtises who removed to Mile End?'

James nodded. 'There is a house next door to them, newly built. Number 8 Assembly Row.' James added to its attractions by telling Elizabeth that, yes, Assembly Row did have assembly rooms where the important families of the area gave balls and routs. 'But that's only during the season. Otherwise it's quiet.' He omitted telling her it was also the site of less frivolous but equally spirited political meetings.

Mile End was a mile, as its name implied, from Aldgate. Though it was still the East End, it was just far enough from Wapping to be genteel. Merchant seamen went to live there when they could afford it, and with improving coach services it was not at all far from the river.

The next day Elizabeth left baby James — Jamie they had taken to calling him — in the safekeeping of Mama, and went with James to view the house. The coach passed an impressive block of conjoined houses on Mile End Road, well-laid brick, the whole having gables adorned with model ships. 'Ships?' exclaimed Elizabeth. 'Is that what decided you?'

'It's Trinity Almshouse,' James laughed. 'For retired seamen. I'm not yet ready to set up house in there.'

The sweet sickly smell of gin reached Elizabeth's nose even before they alighted from the coach, and it got stronger as they walked towards Assembly Row. By the time they got to number 8, the smell of fermenting juniper berries was so obvious that James felt he had to account for it. 'Mr Curtis's distillery.'

Elizabeth hadn't realised that in the move to Mile End, Mr Curtis had continued in the same line of business. Could she never get away from it? She was born in an alehouse, grew up, between interludes in Essex, next to one, and now James was proposing a house joined by an archway to a distillery. Still, that wasn't the same as an alehouse. There wouldn't be drunks congregating to menace baby Jamie. And the house itself was just what she had in mind. The same liver-coloured bricks as the grand almshouse, with two rooms up and two down, and though hardly a manor, it was double the size of the Shadwell tenement. It had a garden back and front, and fields behind. She was delighted. After they'd inspected the interior, they spent the rest of the day familiarising themselves with the surroundings, laughing at the names of nearby passageways such as Ducking Pond Row, Red Cow, Mutton Lane. They sounded positively rural compared to Gravel Lane, Cut Throat Lane, Rope Walk, and the rest of the streets in Shadwell.

Though there was the cluster of buildings of Mile End Old Town, and the neighbouring houses, they did not crowd the vista. The air was not so thick as the coal-laden air of the riverside, and there were pastures and meadows and market gardens. Elizabeth found it all most pleasing. By the end of the day she barely noticed the smell of gin at all.

So it was agreed, and in the last days of winter 1764, James Cook signed the deed by which he purchased the lease on the house.

The plot of ground—15 feet from east to west, and 139 feet deep—lay south of the road from Whitechapel to Bow. The term of the lease was sixty-one years, long enough, God willing, to see Elizabeth and James out for the rest of their days.

THE TELESCOPIC QUADRANT

James loved Elizabeth's back, a violin of creamy skin. It smelled of milk and nutmeg, and something that James could not define; it smelled of Elizabeth. At night, when the house was quiet and a square of stars appeared at the window, he would move the covers—gently, slowly—and murmur: 'Are you cold?'

'No,' whispered Elizabeth, lifting her buttocks so that the covers fell down and she was naked before him.

The candlelight cast shadows, bringing into relief the ridges and furrows of her back. How strange and wonderful that there was a furrow along the line of her spine. He would slowly run his finger down the accepting groove, feeling the little cotton reels of vertebrae beneath. Sometimes Elizabeth sighed under her husband's touch and he felt the quivering of skin. 'Does it please you?' he asked and asked a thousand times, and she would sigh, 'Yes, my dear, yes.'

He would start at the nape of her neck, gently blowing aside the wisps of her hair, and making a place for his lips. He began the journey south, each vertebra rising to the moist warmth of his mouth. The long channel under which lay the reef of her backbone descended to her buttocks, two plump hillocks with a dimple either side. Elizabeth lay with her arms by her sides, and when she shifted, bent her elbows to make a pillow of her hands, James saw the shoulder blades rise up like the beginnings of angel wings.

How often he thought of this when he was away, he told her, in the small cramped cot that was so short his legs hung over the edges. In the Canadian summer nights, in that long northern twilight after his work was done, in the gentle lull of the ship and the rain falling down, he imagined the larger bed he shared with her. As he snuffed out his lantern, the candle of home would flicker beneath his eyelids and he was with her again, the warm mist of his breath settling on her back. When she was ready, she turned to face him and their desires would meet.

Elizabeth now knew what Becky had meant when she said it was like your bones melting, but it had not always been so. At first it was uncomfortable, more like the bolt of linen. Gradually, James's gentle perseverance awakened Elizabeth's pleasure. How wonderful that her body opened to him, moistening the pathway he would take. Then he lifted her into rapture and Elizabeth became a wave.

While James was away in Canada Elizabeth's longing for him was intense. Sometimes she felt it as an ache, like a breast heavy with milk. As she went about her tasks, she carried it inside her like a secret, but as autumn approached and the days grew shorter, yearning turned into anticipation.

It seemed this would be the pattern of their lives, James being away for the summers and returning like a migratory bird, for the season of nesting. Each spring, when he spread his great wings and flew across the Atlantic, he left a fertilised egg in the nest. By the end of James's fifth season in Newfoundland, there were two more little birds—Nathaniel, aged three, and, joy of joys, a baby daughter, Elizabeth.

Their mother had settled very nicely into her new home, bought furniture, and arranged her treasures—china, embroideries, the oriental box, her cream silk wedding dress. Into the Chippendale chest of drawers she placed the marriage certificate, and the licence from the Archbishop of Canterbury.

Elizabeth made the acquaintance of neighbours, Mr and Mrs Honeychurch, the Shanks, the Knights and Mr and Mrs Blade. The Witherspoons on one side and the Curtises on the other. Mama and Mr Blackburn were frequent visitors, as Elizabeth was to them, although it wasn't easy travelling with two small boys and a baby.

For better or worse, the boys adored Mr Blackburn, or Grandpapa as he preferred. He played roughhouse games with them, pillow fights which knocked them over. They simply got up with shrill delight and yelled: 'More!' When they visited Shadwell, Elizabeth even tolerated Mr Blackburn's occasional 'damn' or 'blast' in front of the boys, although back home, when she came across them standing squarely on their bed, hands on hips, having a shouting match of 'damn and blast' she took to the rod. 'We'll have no more of that below-deck language in this house, thank you very much.' She'd even had to admonish her husband when the occasional 'damn', or worse, 'bloody' slipped out.

Of more concern was the fact that the boys considered Mr Blackburn and James to be interchangeable, and even called Mr Blackburn 'Papa', though daily she showed them James's likeness, or read parts of his letters, and told them their papa would be home soon, in the autumn, when the leaves fell off the trees. Otherwise, little ruffled the smooth waters of their domestic life. Elizabeth lived with her yearning for James, and the worry that something might happen.

Something did happen, in the summer of 1764, an accident that James had written of, to prepare Elizabeth for the scar. A powder horn had blown up in his hand, almost severing his thumb. James had to wait hours in Noddy's Harbour for a surgeon to arrive, watching his kerchief fill with blood. Finally a surgeon from a French fishing boat had arrived and attended to it, sewing it with stitches as neat as any seamstress's. It was almost a month before James was recovered enough to work. 'Still, a quicker recovery in Canada's clean air and water than I could expect in London,' he said when he returned home that year. The scar was long and raw, running between his thumb and forefinger, right up to the wrist.

'The fairground gypsies would say you had a long life ahead of you,' Elizabeth said as she traced her finger along the length of the scar, feeling the tensile strength of the shiny pink tissue.

It was unusual that such an accident should occur. Elizabeth knew her husband to be a careful man, careful of himself and the men on board. He carried with him for life the habits taught by John Walker. The *Grenville*, compared to other ships, had fewer accidents or illnesses aboard, fewer incidents of crimes and therefore punishments. Among the seamen James had gained followers, men who would remain loyal to him, their life in his hands. And his in theirs.

Still, whilst he was away Elizabeth tossed and turned on nights of high winds and during storms, even though she told herself the weather conditions London was experiencing couldn't possibly stretch across the ocean to Canada. But there was one storm, in 1767, where reason agreed with sentiments.

It was almost mid-November, the month James normally returned. He would already have left Canada, sailing into the storm, and must be nearly home. Elizabeth expected him daily.

If the squalls and gales and thundering rain were this bad over their roof, she imagined them ten times worse at sea.

Lightning cracked so hard across the sky and down to the ground that it was like a flash of broad daylight. Then followed thunder booming like a cannon, so loud Elizabeth jumped with fright. Everything shook as it had during the earthquake of 1750. Even the boys, who normally revelled in a storm and wanted to go outside and play in it, came running to the safe haven of Elizabeth's bed.

A day or two later there was a knock on the door. Elizabeth dreaded opening it to what, in all likelihood, was bad news. She was even more alarmed to find that it was indeed the postman, and she only finally let out breath when she saw it was a letter from James, sent from Sheerness.

He had indeed been caught up in the storm that had swept the entire south-east coast of England. He wrote that he was all right, would be home soon, once he'd seen the *Grenville* safely to Deptford for repairs. What an introduction to the sea it had been for fifteen year old Isaac, James added, who had joined the navy and sailed on the *Grenville* this season.

When James walked in on the fifteenth of November, Elizabeth was entertaining the Blackburns and the Curtises to Sunday dinner. The mood was high, Elizabeth full of relief and anticipation. Mr Curtis had brought to the table not gin, but bottles of good French wine. Baby Eliza lay gurgling in the crib, and Mr Blackburn dandled the boys on his knee, showing them a trick with a coin which disappeared and was then miraculously found behind the ear of first Jamie, then Nat. They paid no attention to the thicket of hair growing out of Mr Blackburn's ears, nor did they enquire why so much should be growing there while the hair on his head grew thinner and thinner.

Above the general merriment at the table, Elizabeth heard James enter and deposit his luggage. She broke into a smile, taking the sight of him in through every pore of her body. She rose and they greeted each other politely, with their eyes promising more in private. 'Jamie, Nat,' Elizabeth invited. The boys didn't move from Mr Blackburn's knee. 'Boys,' she said brightly. 'Look, it's Papa.'

Mr Blackburn nudged the two off his knee.

'Hello,' said Jamie.

'Papa,' said Nat, although Elizabeth couldn't be sure whether it was query or acknowledgment. Nevertheless, the ice was broken. James bent down level with his sons and they accepted the invitation of his open arms. 'I believe you have a little sister Elizabeth. Would you like to show me?'

'We call her Eliza,' Jamie corrected him.

Nat knew exactly who his father meant, and skipped over to the crib. 'Here!' he said proudly, as if he'd produced the baby himself.

James lifted his daughter out of the crib. The child took to him immediately, much to Elizabeth's relief, and gave him one of her heart-melting smiles, with two small teeth in the middle of it. He held her carefully, so that his brass buttons wouldn't press into her, and looked across to Elizabeth, his eyes brimming with tenderness.

'Sit yourself down, James,' Mr Blackburn interrupted, as if he were the host and James the guest instead of the other way around. He also took it upon himself to offer James some of Mr Curtis's wine. 'Our former enemy, but they still make a blessed good drop.' At least he didn't say 'bloody'. James joined the table, taking a quaff of the proffered wine. 'Yes, John, a blessed good drop.'

Everyone wanted to hear about the storm. Elizabeth could see the tiredness in James's eyes, the strain of exhaustion on his face, but now that he had weathered the storm and was home safe, it had become a story to tell. Her husband rallied and began.

It had been a remarkably speedy sail, James aboard the *Grenville*, with Hugh Palliser leading in the *Guernsey*. They had departed St John's on 23 October, and reached the Channel by 8 November. Then, on their way up the Thames, the great brooding wing of disaster touched the *Grenville*, descending in a hard storm of wind and squalls, with rain as 'leaden as bullets', James said. The men spent the afternoon trying to curtail the damage but by six in the evening, with darkness already fallen, the best bower parted, the ship tailed into shoalwater and struck hard. Jamie and Nat listened, eyes wide as saucers, not understanding all of it but remembering the storm and enthralled by the tale.

The men battled fiercely but it appeared that the storm was winning, with the ship striking hard again, despite the topsail yards and cross-jack yards having been got down on deck. The ship lay down 'upon her larboard bilge'. Elizabeth recalled the storm that night, how frightening it had seemed even from the safety of her bed. She imagined the rain beating down on James, his orders shouted into the howl of the wind.

James continued. The gale showing no signs of abating, and to lighten the schooner, the men hove everything overboard from the deck and secured the hatchways. By midnight, with no end to the gale in sight, the crew were rowed ashore. The gale lasted through the night but by mid-morning the next day it had softened enough for assistance from Sheerness Yard to come aboard. By the afternoon the *Grenville* was afloat once again.

After everyone had drunk a toast to James's health, Nat asked: 'What's larboard bilge?' James explained. Not to be outdone by his little brother, Jamie then enquired: 'What got hoved overboard?'

'Everything dispensable, including,' James remembered, 'an Indian canoe that Palliser was sending back to a gentleman botanist. Who knows, it may be floating up the Thames this very minute.' Jamie and Nat looked out the back window, but of course they couldn't even see the river from the house, let alone what might be floating on it.

'Hear about our coal strike?' asked Mr Blackburn. 'Over wages. The price of bread soaring like a bird and the wages staying on the ground. By God, the heavers deserve a rise. Not one lump of coal unloaded in the Port of London, and to top it all off, the attorney in charge of the funds for widows and orphans helped himself to £600 of it. In debtors' prison for his troubles. There were parades in the streets of Shadwell, four hundred odd coal heavers marching along with their shamrocks, and beating their drums.'

'James doesn't want to hear about the strike,' said Mama.

'Of course he does,' Mr Blackburn went on. 'There was a time when James heaved coal himself. Or shouldn't I be mentioning it?' Elizabeth glared at him. He had mentioned it, so why bother saying that he shouldn't? The uncomfortable silence at the table was broken by Mr Curtis.

'Wilkes threatens to return from exile in France,' he said, obviously happy at the news. 'He published a statement in the newspaper last month. Says he is going to put up his parliamentary candidature in the general election next spring.'

Elizabeth glanced at her husband. They had been amused by John Wilkes's witty attacks on the government in his weekly paper, the *North Briton,* and of course supported his cry for 'liberty not joined with licentiousness'. He had a great following in Shadwell and along the riverside, but was too rakish for James's liking, and his anti-Scottish sentiments offended James's heritage. James knew that David Curtis was pro-Wilkes, Mr Blackburn too. Whenever James returned home he was avid for news, to catch up with what was going on in London, but Elizabeth felt the tenor of the present discussion was more suited to the coffee house than her Sunday dinner. She did not want arguments spilling over their daughter's crib.

Mrs Curtis and Mama must have been of the same mind because almost in unison they said it was time to get going, to leave James to his family.

In that winter of 1767–68 James produced more than thirty charts, with sailing directions, and was glad of the extra room at Mile End devoted to his work. The trigonometrical survey of the Newfoundland west coast, for instance, was 10 feet long, on the scale of one inch to a mile. The charts were precise and scientific and, as well as coastline, showed rivers, lakes and other topographical features. In addition to the detail of pen-lines, there was blue wash, and green and brown brushwork, and the charts were as impressive and lifelike in their way as any portrait.

While Elizabeth was busy with the children, James worked on his charts, making fair copies and preparing them for publication, consulting with Mr Larken, the engraver. His skill and confidence were ever growing and he had started giving the Newfoundland topography nomenclature. Grenville Rock was named for his ship. He transported the names of English rivers—Humber and Thames—to Newfoundland, leaving his signature on the landscape.

James had also left his signature with the Royal Society. In Newfoundland he'd observed an eclipse of the sun, using a telescopic quadrant made by Mr John Bird, and applied his knowledge of astronomical mathematics to determine the longitude of his place of observation. On 30 April 1767, James's account of it was delivered by Dr John Bevis to the Royal Society back in London. The account, though brief, had been tabled.

James Cook had come to the notice of the Royal Society, that illustrious body devoted to scientific enquiry. The name if not yet the man.

On the first warm day of spring the boys were out in the garden seeing who could jump the furthest, Jamie marking the position with a stick, and Nat moving it to wherever took his whim. Exasperated, Jamie introduced a new element into the game. 'Nat, this stick is England and this stick,' he said, placing the second one at what he thought was an appropriate distance, 'is New-foundland. You have to jump right over without falling into the ocean.'

'It's grass, not ocean,' Nat pointed out.

Jamie ignored him and prepared to jump. 'Watch me, Nat, watch.' Finally he got his brother's attention. 'England then . . . Newfoundland!' he said when he had completed his jump, landing well over the stick coastline. 'Now you.' He made sure his younger brother had his feet behind the stick of England. 'When I say. One, two, three—jump!' Nathaniel bent his knees, stuck out his elbows and jumped for all he was worth. But not far enough to land in Newfoundland. 'You fell in the ocean,' taunted his elder brother.

'Did not.'

'Did.'

While the game dissolved in a chorus of dids and did nots, Elizabeth watched her husband gazing from the window at the now abandoned sticks. It was time for him to make the jump too.

In preparation for the next season in Newfoundland, and with his powder horn accident in mind, James had applied to the Admiralty for a surgeon's mate, and also for £28 for stationery, and repairs to instruments. In its meeting that April, the Board had resolved to appoint a surgeon's mate to the *Grenville* and to reimburse Master Cook his expenses. But a larger, much larger, matter was discussed at the same meeting and though he did not yet know it, the name of James Cook was inextricably linked to those discussions. The minutes of the meeting were tabled — Master Cook was not to sail in the *Grenville* that year, the Admiralty making the temporary appointment of James's assistant, Mr Lane, to the position. In the dry perfunctory style of minutes, lacking any portent, was noted the resolve to fit out a vessel for a voyage 'to the Southward'. The sea lords had altogether different plans for James Cook.

The Endeavour

The *Endeavour* was not fast, she was not sleek, but she had what was deemed suitable for a voyage to the South Seas— strength and capacity. She was a cat-built vessel, an ex-collier from the yards of Messrs Fishburn of Whitby, the kind of barque on which James had learnt his seacraft. Master and ship accorded perfectly.

James had written to John Walker as soon as he had been appointed, telling John how he was to sail to the South Seas to observe the transit of Venus in a Whitby-built cat. She was 106 feet long, 29 feet 3 inches at her broadest. She'd be refitted of course, including an extra layer on the hull of boards lined with tarred felt, protection against the potentially devastating effects of the teredo worm which lived in tropical seas.

At the beginning of May, James wrote to Joseph Banks:

I received a note today from Mr March of the Victualling Office, wherein he desires that we will call on him on Friday morning,

*as he is obliged to attend at the Admiralty on Thursday. I left a
line at your house yesterday, desiring to know your sentiments
concerning a stove for the cabin, it being necessary the officers
of Deptford Board should know how to act. If you approve of
a green baize floor cloth for the great cabin, I will demand as
much cloth from the Yard as will make one. As you mean to
furnish the cabin well, I think you should have brass locks, and
hinges to the doors, etc., this, however, will be a private affair of
your own, as nothing of this kind is allowed. ——Thus far I had
got with this letter when your note arrived. I think it is a good
thought to take Mr Buzagio's stove with you, as it may be very
useful on many occasions. I shall go to Deptford tomorrow to
give directions about the other. Whenever it is certain Dr Lynd
goes with us, I beg you will let me know by the penny post.
My respects to the Dr, and am, Dear Sir*

Your very humble servant

James Cook

The dockyard work dragged on, sometimes coming to a complete
standstill, even though the Navy required that the barque should
be refitted 'with the greatest dispatch'. It was not only landmen
and coal heavers who were striking, but seamen and dockyard
workers as well. Bills were posted all along the riverside—men
would not return to work until they had a fair wage. It was
late May by the time the *Endeavour* was out of dry dock and in
the water.

'Only one ship?' said Elizabeth. 'All that way, and only one
ship? Wallis and Byron had two, didn't they?'

'Don't worry yourself,' James tried to assure her. 'I'd stake
my life on Mrs *Endeavour*. A Whitby-built collier, sturdy as they
come. As you shall see for yourself.'

They'd left baby Eliza with Frances Wardale, a cousin of James's who had come to live with them. Jamie and Nat were told to be on their best behaviour but it was an unnecessary warning, for as soon as they boarded the vessel they were awed by the size of it, not large by navy standards but huge to two small boys.

'Can you manage, my dear?' James asked his wife as they prepared to descend the companion to the afterdeck. She felt queasy every time she boarded a boat, and this time, to make matters worse, she was again with child. But she was determined to come. She wanted to see where her husband would sleep, to know every inch of the barque, so that when he sailed, she could imagine him there. 'Yes,' she said, turning to descend the ladder backwards. The boys followed, clambering down like a couple of monkeys.

They came into the great cabin, as large as the living room at Mile End, but much more elegantly furnished. Sash windows fitted with heavy shutters for bad weather, with lockers below. A stove for heating, a serving table with cutlery drawers, and a large table surrounded by chairs taking pride of place in the middle of the cabin. James had requested for the floor the same green baize that covered the table, but the Navy Board would only run to painted floorcloth.

Though James was the Admiralty's chosen man, recommended by their secretary, Mr Stephens, and by Hugh Palliser, he was not a commodore like Byron, or post-captain like Wallis, just returned from the South Seas, and James Cook's wish was not yet the Navy's command. The matter of floor covering was one thing. Another was the selection of crew. The ship's cook they had assigned him was lame and infirm and, as James wrote to the Navy Board, 'incapable of doing his Duty without the assistance of others'. The Navy Board took note of the complaint but three days later, James found himself writing to the board yet again.

John Thompson, the first cook's replacement, 'hath the misfortune to loose his right hand'. The one-handed cook remained.

While James sat the boys on the chairs, their legs dangling down, chins barely level with the tabletop, Elizabeth fingered the edge of the green baize on the table where her husband would sit with his officers. At the moment the baize was as neat as a bowling green, not even as much as one speck of dust on it, but during the course of the voyage it would be covered in charts.

'Specimens and drawings as well, no doubt,' said James. 'I am sharing the great cabin with the naturalists. I only hope they don't take over completely. Banks has had extra storage cupboards fitted to his cabin.' James escorted the family to it. 'For specimens and botanising equipment. Also, I dare say, for his creature comforts. Four servants are coming along to take care of him.'

Elizabeth raised her eyebrows. She knew the ways of gentlemen but thought that on a ship of limited proportions even a gentleman might consider paring his entourage to a minimum. But that wasn't the end of it. 'Two artists—Sydney Parkinson to draw natural history specimens, and Alexander Buchan to do figures and landscapes. Then there is his secretary, Mr Sporing, a Swede. So Dr Solander will have a countryman aboard. Banks also intends bringing two greyhounds—for hunting, he says, though I suspect they are pets that he cannot bear to leave behind.'

James paused for a moment, a memory floating back to him. 'Banks came to Newfoundland,' he told Elizabeth.

'You knew him there?'

'We were never introduced, but I saw him briefly. At the time of the anniversary ball.' He related the episode to Elizabeth.

The ball was held one Saturday in late October 1766, to celebrate the anniversary of King George III's coronation, but James was away surveying La Poile Bay and didn't arrive back at St John's till the Monday. He greeted Commodore Palliser, then made a courtesy call to Sir Thomas Adams, captain of the

Niger. With a day in between to nurse headaches, there was much talk on that Monday of the ball and celebrations. Plenty of gentlemen had attended but the paucity of ladies in St John's was so great that even humble washerwomen had received formal invitations. Despite the uneven numbers, everyone had danced and worked up a hearty appetite for an elegant supper, followed by fine wines and Italian liqueurs.

As he was accompanied to Sir Thomas's quarters, James noticed in one of the nearby cabins a young man, a gentleman judging by the cut of his clothes, and a botanist if the specimen box was anything to go by. As James waited to be received by the captain, he perused the specimens—meadow rue, Newfoundland mosses, a kind of cuckoo flower, and moon wort, all of which James had observed in their native state during his onshore surveying. In a cage on the young gentleman's cot was a porcupine, as large as an English hare, with black and white quills.

But the most memorable trophy hung above the escritoire. A scalp, so well preserved that James immediately recognised it as Sam Frye, a fisherman who had been shot by the Indians the summer before. He was able to identify it so precisely because it had been taken by the Indians of Labrador who, unlike the other Canadians, removed not just the hair but skinned the upper face as well, almost down to the mouth. James wondered how the young gentleman had come by the scalp.

Busy writing, he had his back to James, but was not so absorbed that he didn't, from time to time, stop to scratch his earlobe or the back of his hand. James recognised the telltale angry red spots of mosquito bites. Welcome to Canada, he thought to himself. James had experienced those mosquitoes first-hand. The only place that provided some relief from the swarm of them was on board ship. He had grown accustomed to them after the first year, although it was reported that they were capable of bringing down large animals—caribou and deer.

As James waited for the captain to finish his business, the young man turned to feed the porcupine—ants perhaps, or hopefully mosquitoes themselves. He nodded and smiled at James with largesse, not at all concerned that he was being observed. James would like to have struck up a conversation but before any words could be exchanged the door of the captain's cabin opened and James was ushered in. Next day the *Niger* sailed for Lisbon, taking the young botanist with it.

'The canoe that went overboard last year in the storm,' James reminded Elizabeth, 'that was destined for Banks, along with some Indian costumes.'

'A pity,' mused Elizabeth. 'Otherwise he and his suite could have trailed along behind the *Endeavour* in it.'

James chuckled. Nevertheless, he could not dismiss Banks so lightly. He was a Fellow of the Royal Society, and though only twenty-five, had a great deal of influence—and was a friend to men of influence such as Lord Sandwich. He would have known about the proposed voyage before even James himself, and with the opportunities for adventuring and botanising it promised, would have made sure he was going. Influence was one thing, authority another. The Admiralty had made it clear that James was to receive 'Joseph Banks Esq. and his suite consisting of eight persons with their baggage, bearing them as supernumeraries for victuals only'. Anything else Banks required he could supply himself. He did. Machines for catching and preserving insects, nets, trawls, a library of natural history, a type of telescope which, when put into the water, allowed you to see the bottom even at a great depth. The estimated cost of the expedition for Banks was in the region of £10 000. The Cooks counted their income in hundreds, not thousands of pounds. Ten thousand pounds was more than the salary of an admiral or post-captain.

'It sounds as if he's trying to make this *his* voyage,' Elizabeth commented.

'I'll accommodate him as much as I can but our first priority is arriving in Tahiti in time for the transit. He won't be doing a skerrick of botanising without my say so. I'll not jeopardise my ship or the lives of those on board for botanising, Mr Banks's included. But I'm glad to have him aboard, Elizabeth. He promises to be entertaining company. A charming fellow with a zeal for adventure. He was considering a trip to Sweden, to pay homage to his hero, Linnaeus, perhaps to continue on to Lapland. "But the South Seas," he told me, "that will truly be a voyage of discovery". The next is my cabin,' James said as they moved away from Banks's.

He pushed open the door and Elizabeth caught a whiff of fresh paint. She breathed away a wave of nausea, and focused on the narrow cot on which her husband would sleep. The mattress was in place but it still lacked bed linen. A lantern hung above the area where the folding table of Spanish mahogany would go, the one still at home at Mile End, on which he would write letters to her. James would have to rely on passing ships, if any, to deliver them. The voyage was to the other side of the globe. How long would it be before her husband shared her bed again? How would her heart know when to turn longing into anticipation? Elizabeth looked at the red curtain on a door. It was pulled aside to reveal panes of glass looking into the officers' mess. The other entrance led into the great cabin.

'Where's Isaac sleeping?' asked Jamie.

'On the lower deck,' James answered. 'Can you manage another set of steps, Elizabeth?'

The sea chests in which the crew, or 'the people' as they were called, would store their belongings sat in neat rows either side, with mess tables suspended by thick ropes above them. Each rope was furnished with a set of tassels.

'Very decorative,' commented Elizabeth.

'Table napkins,' said James, running his hand down one of them to demonstrate. Elizabeth imagined how greasy and grimy those clean new tassels would become.

'What's in the red bag?' asked Jamie, pointing to a bag hanging from the ceiling.

'That's where we keep the cat-o'-nine-tails,' his father said.

'For when they are mischievous and have to be punished?' said Jamie.

'Precisely,' grinned his father. 'But there's not enough room to swing a cat down here so the punishment takes place on deck.'

'And that noose,' piped up Nathaniel, 'is that for when they are very naughty?'

James smiled. 'The noose has an entirely benign use. When the people store their hammocks, they must be rolled up tight enough to fit through the noose.'

'Why?' asked Nat.

James and Elizabeth exchanged glances, hoping this was not the beginning of another of Nathaniel's series of 'whys'. 'To make room,' James said. 'There'll be more than one hundred men on board, to say nothing of the stores, the hens, cattle and other livestock.' He thought it better not to summon up clouds on the sunny horizon of the voyage by mentioning also that a tightly rolled-up canvas hammock gave a shipwrecked man a few hours flotation. 'Wallis has offered me his milch goat, to provide fresh milk for the officers,' James told his wife.

'Imagine that,' Elizabeth said to the boys, 'a goat that has circumnavigated the globe.'

'Why?' asked Nathaniel.

'Why not?' replied his father.

THE FOLDING TABLE

On 25 May 1768, as befitting a man who was to command a ship taking a scientific party to the faraway South Seas, James Cook was made lieutenant. It was a rare honour for a man of his background, as both he and Elizabeth knew, but the momentum of voyage preparations was so great that James did not have time to stand still and fully savour it. Even at home he was busy, firing off letters to the Navy Board, the Victualling Board, and every other board concerned with the voyage.

In a quiet moment, with James at Deptford for the day, the boys on an outing with Cousin Frances, and Eliza asleep in the crib, Elizabeth polished the folding table. Being the neat and tidy seaman that he was, James had cleared its surface of writing paper before leaving, and arranged his pens and ink. The soft cloth caressed the slim, straight legs of the table, from top to bottom. It reminded Elizabeth of washing her children, except that when she reached the feet of the table, there were no little wriggling toes.

The table was made of Spanish mahogany, more resistant to worm and damp than any other timber. Some of Elizabeth's neighbours recommended a linseed rub but Mrs Curtis maintained that such oil would darken the wood and make the piece unfashionable. Besides, the cabinet-maker's finish seemed to provide adequate protection. Elizabeth kept it so polished in between James's letter writing that she could see her own reflection in it. There were places she touched with her hands and did not rub away, so that her touch would voyage with him, and be present when he wrote his letters home.

The folding table straddled their lives. At home he wrote letters upon it that would take him away from her, and when he was in the faraway places he would write letters back home. 'Every week,' she had insisted.

Though he had told her that the further the *Endeavour* went the less chance there was of coming across a ship that might convey the letters back to her, he had agreed. 'I am sailing into the blue,' he said, 'do not fret if there is no word. I doubt they have the penny post in the South Seas,' he said with a smile. There would be months, perhaps years, with no word.

'I will watch the stars,' Elizabeth said, 'the same stars by which you will navigate.'

As she polished the table, Elizabeth recalled letters to the Victualling Board that James had written on it. 'Provisions for a year?' she'd asked. What with fish to catch, seabirds to shoot and fresh food to be had when they made landfall, she immediately understood that the anticipated voyage might be much longer. Though she did not say so to her husband, in her heart she wanted the voyage to be over and done with as quickly as possible, and for him to resume his post in Newfoundland, or better, somewhere closer to home.

Newfoundland was far enough away for Elizabeth. At least it was the same ocean lapping its shores and England's. Now

James was sailing to the other side of the world. Though she yearned for him when he was in Newfoundland, at least she knew he'd be home every autumn. 'When the leaves fall off the trees,' as she told the boys. But not this year, or perhaps even the year after.

She'd accepted the migratory pattern, and though she was reluctant to admit it, things were easier in the household without James there. She had a routine for the boys and made sure they stuck to it. James did his best to keep the boys to the habits Elizabeth had established, but on his return each year, after their initial reticence, the boys wanted to spend every minute with him. He filled their heads with tales of adventuring. They even wanted to voyage to the South Seas with him. 'Isaac is going, why can't we?'

'When you're big boys, like Cousin Isaac, you can come,' James promised them.

The routine would resume but the pattern was broken. When the leaves fell off the trees this year he would not be coming home. Their wedding anniversary, Christmas, New Year, would be spent without him. How great would her yearning be then?

Elizabeth stood up to straighten the crick in her back. At least with James away for so long she'd have a year free of pregnancy. As she massaged the small of her back she caught sight of the celestial globe on the mantelpiece. The purpose of the voyage was twofold. The first was to observe the transit. James had explained what he and Mr Green hoped to see: on 3 June 1769, Venus would be in exact alignment with the earth and the sun. With their instruments, they would observe the planet make its passage across the disc of the sun. 'How long will it take?' she'd asked.

'Approximately six hours. But in astronomy, approximate is not good enough, we need to know precisely. Such a transit will not occur again in our lifetimes, Elizabeth, not till 1874, according to Edmond Halley. When we are all dead and buried. It is a rare opportunity. There will be observers in other parts of the globe as well. If the weather is favourable and we get a good sighting, we will be able to determine the distance of the earth from Venus, and Venus from the sun. We are measuring the universe, my dear, using the same methods of parallax—working out angles and distances—that I employ in my surveying work.'

'Will we be able to see it in London?'

'Possibly, in the evening, for half an hour or so before sunset. If it's not cloudy. Let's hope June third is not overcast in Tahiti, otherwise that part of the voyage will be for nought.'

Elizabeth was silent for a moment, then she asked James to repeat what he had said, so that when he was away she could explain to the boys. 'Don't let them look directly at the sun or it will burn out their eyes.' He told her how to look at the image of the sun on a piece of card.

Elizabeth bent down and resumed polishing the table. The second purpose of the voyage was secret, and James was to open the Admiralty's instructions regarding it only when he was at sea. However, the nature of those instructions was so breathtaking that they had spilt through the bonds of true secrecy. 'I am to investigate the existence, or no, of the Great South Land.'

The Great South Land. It had fired men's imaginations since antiquity. A great continent at the southern end of the world to balance the land mass of the northern hemisphere. The earliest maps showed it stretching from the equator to the South Pole. Yet these maps were based on an imagined world; in the absence of fact, the Great South Land became whatever men wanted it to be. A rich fertile land whose civilised, welcoming inhabitants built cities of gold. Some saw unicorns and fabled animals grazing in lush verdant meadows. Marco Polo imagined it as 'overflowing with spices'. Though the explorations—by the Portuguese, Spanish, French, Dutch and English—over the last two centuries had reduced the size of the Great South Land, and although no ship that had set sail for it had yet found the continent, it still obsessed the minds of men. Some of the crew aboard the recently returned *Dolphin* swore that they had seen the mountaintops of a continent.

'Sailors' talk,' said James. 'I will believe in the Great South Land when I see it.'

'Why didn't Wallis sail closer?' asked Elizabeth, fearing dangers her husband might also encounter.

'Wallis and his first lieutenant were ill and, having been separated from the other ship, thought it imprudent to investigate further. Nevertheless, Wallis discovered the island on which we will observe the transit. Such a place is discovery enough for any man.'

King George's Island, which the natives called Otaheite. A paradise, so it seemed, or at least a sailor's paradise. Elizabeth recalled words of the song that echoed in the riverside alehouses.

We've found it, my boys, and with joy be it told
For beauty such islands you ne'er did behold.
We've the pleasure ourselves the tidings to bring
As may welcome us home to our country and king
For wood, water, fruit, and provisions well stor'd
Such an isle as King George's the world can't afford.

Then there were the women, not mentioned in the song but on every sailor's lips nevertheless. Compliant women, exotic flowers in their hair, who would entice a man as easily as a siren for the price of a ship's nail. Wallis joked that he made haste to leave before the ship fell apart.

The women of the South Seas were only a small part of Elizabeth's fears. Her husband was an upright man and would remain so no matter upon what shore fate landed him. Besides, it would not do for the captain of the vessel to stoop to fornication. There had been no stain of that nature upon his behaviour in Newfoundland. But then sailors did not grow misty-eyed when they spoke of the Canadian women the way they did when talk turned to the Tahitians.

Elizabeth brought her mind back to more immediate matters as she realised she'd been polishing the same table leg over and over. She would pray, of course, that he be guided in the path of righteousness. She knew James intended to do his utmost to establish peaceable relations with the people of the South Seas, particularly on Tahiti, where the observation facility was to be set up. She hoped that he would have no trouble, either from the men or the natives.

James had shown her the 'hints' suggested by Lord Morton, the President of the Royal Society: 'To exercise the utmost patience and forbearance with respect to the natives of the several lands where the ship may touch. To check the petulance of the sailors, and restrain the wanton use of fire arms. To have it in view that shedding the blood of those people is a crime of the highest nature . . . They are the natural, and in the strictest sense of the word, the legal possessors of the several regions they inhabit.' Lord Morton pointed out that the natives might, understandably, consider their visitors to be intruders, and act accordingly. He stressed that violence should be avoided if at all possible, but if inevitable, then 'the natives when brought under should be treated with distinguished humanity, and made sensible that the crew still considers them lords of the country'. Before they reached Tahiti, James would issue rules based on these principles, to be observed by the people of the *Endeavour* in order to establish friendly relations and regularise trade with the natives.

Someone was knocking at the door. 'Butcher boy!' Elizabeth heard him call. She put down her polishing cloth and went to answer the door. The butcher boy handed her the leg of pork which Elizabeth placed in her wire meat-safe. She wondered how the supervision of deliveries was going in Deptford, and tried to imagine the *Endeavour*, empty when she visited, filling with provisions—eight tons of iron ballast, coal, beer and brandy, salt, cork jackets, one hundred gallons of arak, stationery, dried pease, oil, vinegar and a machine for sweetening foul water, to say nothing of 7280 pounds of sauerkraut.

'They'll not take to it,' Elizabeth asserted. 'You know their ways—beef and bacon every meal if they could have it.'

'They will eat it,' James said, 'one way or the other. A long voyage like this needs every man able-bodied, not dying of scurvy. I might try the method of serving it out to the officers, as a special dish, and leave it up to the men to take it or not. I warrant that once they see the officers set a value on it, the people will think sauerkraut the finest stuff in the world.'

As there would be no chaplain on board, James was taking their own Bible to read from on the Sabbath. On the grand title page the light of heaven shone down onto figures in biblical dress, Negroes, all the peoples of the world.

Before dusting the Bible with a goose's wing in the recommended manner, Elizabeth leafed through it, folding her prayers for James's safety into the Bible, stopping at all the beautiful engravings, from the Garden of Eden, Eve with her hair draped modestly about her private parts, to the last engraving at Revelations, showing the Great Dragon being cast out.

Elizabeth had already dusted the other books on their library shelf and was about to apply the rub. Once a year she boiled up wool fat, beeswax and cedarwood oil to produce a rub to feed the leather bindings. She was doing it sooner this year so that the leather of the Bible James was taking aboard would be well fed. As with the table, there were parts of the Bible she touched and did not rub away. James was not the only one preparing for this voyage.

'Mama, Papa, look. Look at Eliza!' It was just after supper. James and Elizabeth were sitting at the table discussing the accounts, Elizabeth showing him how his pay would be divided up between land tax and rates, as well as daily expenses such as the butcher's and grocer's, when they heard Nat's cry. They turned to see their daughter inching her way along, one hand on the sofa to steady herself.

'C'mon, Eliza, come on,' Elizabeth coaxed.

Eliza realised that she was the centre of attention. Whatever she was doing was a great feat, but she was reluctant to leave the support of the sofa and cross that large void to the table.

James held out his hand to her, but Elizabeth said: 'See if she can do it on her own.'

Eliza hesitated.

'C'mon, Eliza,' repeated James, 'come to Papa.' He offered his hand again but not so close that she could reach it without leaving the sofa.

Eliza came, one step then two, into his arms. James stood her on the table and paraded her around. 'What a fine going-away present you've given me, Eliza.' He lifted her into the air so that those hard-working little legs dangled freely. He had missed seeing his sons' first steps but he was here to see his daughter's. Elizabeth hoped that James would be back in time to see the coming baby — Grace if a girl or Joseph if a boy — take its first steps.

She said her farewells to James, tenderly, in private. Elizabeth wanted that last bitter-sweet night to go on forever. She thought of her calendar fan tucked away in a drawer. In the quietness of the Mile End house she heard the inexorable tick of the clock, each tick pleating time more narrow. How she wanted to open the fan out, for her and James to be enveloped this night in the full extent of time.

After their intimacies she lay in James's arms, with James lovingly caressing her hair, softly, slowly, he too wanting to stretch out each moment. Elizabeth saw every hair of his chest, tasted the salt in his sweat, felt his every movement. When pre-dawn light began to lift the veil of night, Elizabeth closed her eyes. The message of the open fan was 'wait for me', but now she wanted to close the fan up tightly, for the imminent voyage to disappear in the pleats of time's fabric so that when she opened her eyes again she would see James standing before her saying, 'Hello, my dear. I have returned.'

It was Cousin Frances who took the boys to Gallions Reach on 30 July 1768 to see the *Endeavour* set off for Plymouth. Elizabeth stayed at home that Saturday, not wishing to see the barque carrying her husband pull away. She busied herself with needlework while Eliza toddled about the room, abandoning her playthings and trying to explore the grown-up treasures of the oriental box that held the sewing equipment. Elizabeth would have liked to give her daughter an item from the box to play with, but all were so dangerous — sharp scissors, thread she might swallow and choke on. Eventually she gave Eliza a square of silk which the toddler put on her head as a hat, stood on, blew up into the air, and found a dozen uses for.

Frances was exhausted when she returned from Gallions Reach, but the boys were full of the adventure of it all. 'There were pipers, Mama,' said Jamie, 'and pennants flying, and the sailors danced and sang. Papa looked so grand walking up the gangway, Mama. I wish I was going with him.'

'And me,' echoed Nat.

In a way, James and Nathaniel Cook would be on board the *Endeavour*. Elizabeth knew that their father, as was common but not lawful practice amongst officers, would enter his sons on the ship's listing, to earn the boys sea time. Elizabeth smiled at the thought that while their names sailed with her husband, the boys themselves would be safely at home with her.

Jamie and Nat pranced about like mad things, despite Elizabeth's admonitions not to wake Eliza upstairs in the crib. It was difficult getting the little ones off to sleep in summer when it stayed light for so long, and Elizabeth had to draw the curtains, which darkened the room but did not quite muffle the sound of the occasional coach rumbling by.

There was quite a bit of traffic inside the house as well, with the boys trying to show Mama exactly how the sailors had danced. 'Enough,' she said sternly. 'To bed before I reach ten or I'll be taking the rod to you.' Elizabeth started counting.

She had got to seven and was heading for the rod on the mantelpiece before the boys took any notice. 'Eight,' Elizabeth said, the rod now in hand. Jamie and Nat paused a moment to ascertain the degree of menace. It was high. Jamie gave Elizabeth a wide berth and scampered towards the stairs, Nat hot on his heels.

Quietness reigned. Elizabeth looked at Frances, cheerily arranging crockery for a cup of tea, tired though she was. A big healthy girl with unruly curls that would just not stay in place. Dear Frances. She was such a boon, happily applying herself to any task, noticing what needed doing without Elizabeth having to point it out. And when the tasks were done, the breath of fresh country air she brought to the house carried with it stories of James's family. 'His Da is very proud of him,' said Frances. 'Uncle James is a man of few words but what he does say is worth the listening. And poor Grace, so many bairns now dead, yet she does not complain.'

Elizabeth instinctively placed her hands on her belly, to protect the coming child. Daily she gave prayers of gratitude that none of her little ones had perished. So many did. 'It's the sturdy York-shire stock in them,' commented Frances, quite forgetting in that moment the passing away of Grace's children. Elizabeth hoped that some of the sturdiness came from her side of the family. She knew that as a child Mama had sent her to the Sheppards in Essex on account of her cough. She had survived and her children would too, God willing.

The sound of sniggering wafted downstairs, despite attempts by its authors to muffle it in pillows. Elizabeth could never seriously be cross with her children, though she did her best to give them quite a different impression. She tapped the rod on the banister. 'I am coming.' Up she went and found her angels kneeling beside the bed, ready for prayer. Elizabeth kneeled beside them, feeling the weight of the child within her. 'God bless Papa,' she prayed. Jamie and Nat joined in the familiar prayer, hands together, their eyelashes brushing their cheeks. 'Preserve and protect him, and keep him safe from harm.' When the time came they all said 'Amen'. Elizabeth felt the baby inside her quicken.

It was a boy, baptised Joseph on 5 September 1768 at St Dunstan's Church, and within the month he was dead. He had come early, a thin little thing that did not thrive. Elizabeth felt herself withering away as he did, as if the umbilical cord was still attached and the life was bleeding out of her. She held the dear baby in bed with her, and gently blew into his tiny nostrils even after she knew it was too late. The warm rain of her tears fell on him but he did not respond. 'Oh James,' she cried, wanting so much for him to be by her side. She kept hold of the baby, kissing and nuzzling him, pressing him against her beating heart, against the breast heavy with milk that trickled out of her like tears, willing the baby back to life long after his inert little body had grown cold.

When Joseph Cook was buried and a little headstone placed over his mortal remains, Elizabeth went about her tasks as normal but it was not the same. She was in a belljar of grief. 'I know it must be hard,' sympathised Frances, 'but the little one is with the Almighty. Try to accept His will.'

'Yes,' Elizabeth nodded dully, but her heart was not ready.

It wasn't till almost Christmas, after Elizabeth and James's sixth wedding anniversary had passed, that Frances tried again. There had been letters from James, and Elizabeth read parts of them to Frances and the children. The letters had been sent from Madeira, the last dated 14 September. They were having an easy passage, carried along by the north-east trade winds. James reported that he and everyone were in excellent health, although Mr Banks was suffering from the seasickness but did his best to appear jovial. The letters lifted Elizabeth momentarily, then, on the day of Christmas Eve, she fell into a slump again.

'James would not have you feeling this way,' said Frances. 'It would break his heart to see you suffer.'

'James does not know,' Elizabeth pointed out, slowly stirring flour, almonds, sugar and eggs into a pudding. 'He even wrote that we must be enjoying the company of our new arrival, a little Grace or Joseph.' As she spoke the dead baby's name Elizabeth broke into heart-rending sobs, her whole body convulsing with them. Frances came over, gently removed the spoon Elizabeth was still holding, and enfolded Elizabeth in her comforting arms. 'I'm sorry, Frances,' Elizabeth apologised.

'Better to have the tears out than store them up inside,' said Frances, rubbing Elizabeth's back as if she were a baby.

'The grief weighs me down so. Everything is so difficult. It takes all my strength to rise from my bed each morning,' she cried into Frances's shoulder.

'Mama?'

Elizabeth looked down to find Eliza at her knee, tears in her eyes at her mother's distress. Elizabeth wiped her own eyes and found a smile for her daughter. 'Eliza,' she welcomed the child into her arms. 'Show me how many teeth you have,' she said brightly, eliciting a big teeth-revealing smile from the child. She hugged Eliza to her breast. 'I feel I am to blame,' Elizabeth whispered to Frances. 'I had the thought that with James away it would be a year when I wasn't with child. I was grateful for it. But little Joseph was already inside me. It was such an easy birth, him being so small. And then he slipped away after such a short time, as if he didn't want to be a trouble to me.'

'It's not your doing,' Frances said gently. 'Nobody's thoughts are greater than the will of the Almighty, are they?' asked Frances. She took out of her pocket the Book of Common Prayer that Cousin James had given her. Elizabeth recognised its maroon leather binding, and though thick, the small volume fitted neatly into the palm of Frances's hand. The book contained psalms and catechisms, the order for the burial of the dead, baptism, matrimony, the calendar with the table of lessons, hymns, and prayers for all occasions.

Frances began reading while Elizabeth listened, Eliza on her hip, freeing her hand to begin stirring the pudding again. 'We bless thee for our creation, preservation, and all the blessings of this life.' Frances held the Book of Common Prayer out so that Elizabeth too could read. They continued together, not kneeling, but standing by the table with the flour, almonds and raisins. 'But above all, for thine inestimable love in the redemption of the world by our Lord Jesus Christ; for the means of grace, and for the hope of glory.' Eliza gurgled contentedly and neither her mother nor Frances made any attempt to quieten her. 'And we beseech thee, give us that due sense of all thy mercies, that our hearts may be unfeignedly thankful, and that we show forth their praise, not only with our lips, but in our lives.'

That night, when all the house was sleeping, Elizabeth quietly went to the window. It was a cold December night with the stars like chips of ice. On many nights great banks of cloud covered the sky, with not a star to be seen. Elizabeth took it as a sign of God's divine grace that tonight He revealed them to her.

She often took the boys outside to look at the night sky. 'If you join the stars up in your mind, the way Papa joins the markings on his charts, you can see shapes in the heavens.' She bent down, an arm around each of her boys, nestling them in her voluminous skirts. 'Can you see the Great Bear? Look, with its neck stretched out.'

Jamie peered, trying to see a bear in the sky. Elizabeth held up his finger and went from star to star, tracing the invisible outline of the bear.

'Me too,' piped up Nathaniel.

So Elizabeth held his finger and repeated the process. Then she turned them eastwards and found in the sky the great box of Pegasus. 'Can you see the corners of the box?' Both boys nodded yes, though Elizabeth had her doubts. 'That is Pegasus, a winged horse.' Jamie's eyes and mouth were open wide, as if drinking in the night.

'Is it God's horse?' he asked. Elizabeth imagined the great winged horse carrying the messages of her heart across the Atlantic.

It was James who had traced Elizabeth's finger over the configurations in the night sky and told her the names of the celestial bodies. 'Can you see the same stars in Newfoundland?' she'd asked. 'We could beam messages to each other. Much more expedient than letters.'

'Then the whole world would be able to read them,' James pointed out in his practical manner. Elizabeth knew that her husband gazed at the stars with a more scientific and navigational frame of mind, but they were still the same stars that she saw.

She looked into the great canopy of night and found the smatter of the Milky Way. So many stars, visible and invisible. There must be thousands and thousands of them. She pinpointed a small star at the edge of the formation, winking brightly. She named it Joseph, his eternal soul shining in God's firmament.

Elizabeth stood there gazing at the night sky, at the little star of Joseph, one amongst so many. She imagined James, too, gazing at this sky, recalled her thought about beaming messages. In her mind she joined up stars to form words, making of them a letter to her husband.

'My dearest James,' she began. 'Little Joseph survived but a month in this world but he will be a part of our family for as long as his star shines. I feel as if a limb has been severed. Although scar tissue has folded over the rupture it still aches in the place the limb should be. I now know the measure of grief at losing one who is our own flesh and blood. It is exactly equal to the love a mother feels for her newborn and that love is immense. How I wished for you to be with me during that terrible time, for you to be with me now. During the day your unseen presence is my constant companion and at night I sleep in the curve of your body. In my dreams you are so real that I can taste you, feel you so much that I am sure they are visitations not dreams, that the stars upon which I write this letter have guided you back to me.'

THE TELESCOPE

Elizabeth and Frances were taking great pains to prepare a supper that appeared as if no pains had been taken at all. Frances had suggested toasted cheese but Elizabeth pointed out that it would entail careful supervision at the fire right at the moment of eating, and if Frances wanted to look her best, that would not do. They had decided instead on individual pigeon pies, along with cheese and bread, and coffee. Apples from the tree in the back garden, and a few precious spears of asparagus that Elizabeth had succeeded in growing.

When James was in Newfoundland Elizabeth made sure there was always garden produce waiting for him when he returned. She buried carrots in sand to keep them fresh, and stored apples high up in a basket on top of their bed, which gave a pleasant aroma to the room. Hens inhabited the garden too and Elizabeth had a way of keeping eggs for two or three months by dipping them in boiling water for twenty seconds then packing them away in sawdust.

As well as the neighbours, a Mr Lieber was coming to the transit of Venus party. There had been frequent letters delivered by the penny post, with Frances rushing to the door whenever she heard the bell. When Frances took Jamie and Nat for walks along the green and played cricket with them, 'a man', as the boys described him, always seemed to be there too. Eventually Frances had sought permission to invite Mr Lieber to the house.

Elizabeth had asked Mama to come for this special evening but despite all her entreaties, Mama would not leave Shadwell. Mr Blackburn had passed away a few months before the transit, and Elizabeth regretted so much. Regretted glaring at him when she was a child, not extending more Christian love to him. She regretted that the children had lost their grandpapa. Most of all, she regretted what was happening to Mama. She seemed to love Mr Blackburn more in death than she ever had in life, and was drinking enough for both of them. Sprawled out along the sofa, the site of many memories, she resembled the woman on the steps in Hogarth's *Gin Lane*: hair unkempt, stockings that needed darning, grinning benignly as her baby toppled to the ground. Elizabeth felt like that baby, understood the dismay, even horror, on its face, the baby's hands reaching out as it toppled but finding nothing to hold on to. The only strength left in Mama was her determination to keep drinking.

Elizabeth kneaded the dough for the pies. She was not going to let dark clouds spoil the evening. She wondered if James was observing the transit at this very minute. His last letter had been from Rio de Janeiro. The people had taken to the sauerkraut so well that James had had to ration it. Not one life had been lost to scurvy. But he had met his first real challenge of the voyage, and it had come not from the men or the natives, or even the sea, but from the Portuguese officials.

When Elizabeth heard the name Rio she saw a big mountain shaped like a loaf of sugar behind a city that stretched into heat haze. Ornate Catholic churches, Benedictine convents, and statues of the Virgin on every street corner. Men with moustaches and pointy beards and ladies gliding along, their faces shrouded in black lace mantillas. She saw Portuguese, natives, Negro slaves, creoles. Black boys carried baskets of lemons yellow as plump pointy suns, bristling pineapples and curves of bananas. The markets were full of coffee beans, sugar, dark blue indigo and bright red pimiento.

Elizabeth pictured James, in full dress uniform, walking those streets, stopping at the markets, smelling the rich aroma of coffee, the fragrance of lemons, but he wrote none of these things. 'You want a silk purse, and when it comes to writing, I am a sow's ear,' he'd said when she'd asked for vivid descriptions, for the smell and the taste, so that she could imagine herself in the places he visited. Nevertheless, Elizabeth was convinced that gentle persuasion would eventually produce a silk purse.

What James wrote in his letter was that the viceroy in Rio de Janeiro would allow James and no-one else off the *Endeavour*. Provisions must be purchased through an agent at five per cent, and there would be no 'illicit trade'. When he came ashore he would be accompanied by an officer, as a 'compliment' he was told, but in reality as a guard. James was so frustrated by the viceroy and his restrictions that he finally elected to stay on board with the others, and engage the viceroy in a 'paper war'. What reams of paper were wasted, what a barrier of polite phrases was erected, what obedience to the king of Portugal's commands Don Antonio Rolim de Moura showed. The man could simply not understand that 'His Britannick Majesty's vessel' was on a scientific expedition, thought they must be smugglers or spies. 'When I explained the transit of Venus to him,' wrote James, 'he could form no other Idea of that Phenomenon than the North Star passing thro the South Pole.' Elizabeth was amused by this; even Jamie and Nat seemed to have a better grasp of the transit than the viceroy. At the risk of being thrown into prison, Banks and the gentlemen had snuck ashore under cover of darkness, climbing out of the cabin window and lowering themselves by rope to a boat, then rowed to an unguarded part of the shore. They botanised all day and came back at night, Banks even purchasing from the friendly inhabitants a pig and muscovy duck for dinner.

Elizabeth was concerned that James's difficulties with the Portuguese would reflect badly on his authority. His was the ultimate on the *Endeavour* but the men had seen it thwarted. If it was like this with a friendly European power, how would it be when he sailed to parts unknown?

'Is it time yet?' Nat was tugging at Elizabeth's skirts, impatient for the transit to begin. She put the pies on to cook. 'Time for you to get ready, young scallywag.'

'It's not just Papa and the astronomers, is it, Mama?' said Jamie as Frances and Elizabeth helped the children dress. 'There are men all over the world watching. In Siberia and India even.'

'And England,' added Nat. 'We are too.'

'Where is Papa watching from?' asked Elizabeth.

'Tahiti!' said Eliza.

'Yes,' said Elizabeth, hugging the little one.

'And where is Tahiti?'

'Yorkshire!' said Eliza.

Frances laughed. 'Tahiti is in the South Seas, much further away than Yorkshire.'

Elizabeth went to check the pies, which were filling the house with a delicious aroma. At least if they didn't see the transit they would have a good supper. But they were hoping to see something.

The boys had their own little telescope. James had told them how to care for it, stressing that it was not a plaything but an important instrument. They were not to fight over it, and above all they were not to look directly at the sun through it. Elizabeth recalled watching James polish his telescope till the brass shone like burnished gold. How long ago that seemed, yet this evening, imagining her husband taking the instrument out of its case, she felt so close to James it was as if he had left only yesterday.

At least they would be watching the same star, or rather, planet, as James had corrected her. 'Stars twinkle but the light of planets remains constant.' Be that as it may, Elizabeth preferred to think of Venus as the evening star, the consort of the moon.

Mr Lieber was the first guest to arrive. From Frances's glowing description, Elizabeth had expected a swashbuckling adventurer like Captain Kidd, and was surprised to find a short dark-haired man hidden behind an enormous bunch of flowers.

The house hummed with anticipation, and after the pigeon pies and asparagus had been polished off, Elizabeth announced that it was time to draw the curtains. Then she hesitated, not quite sure what was supposed to happen next, although she knew it involved shining the sun's image onto the piece of card she had ready.

'Here,' said Mr Curtis, coming to the rescue. 'We'll poke the telescope out through the curtains and then,' he said, looking around at the guests, 'perhaps Mr Lieber would like to hold the card behind the eyepiece.'

'Don't crowd them,' Elizabeth whispered, holding the boys back. 'We'll all be able to see.'

While Mr Curtis tried to get this little telescope to find the sun, Elizabeth thought of the barrage of instruments that James and Mr Green, the astronomer, had at their disposal. The Royal Society had supplied two reflecting telescopes and wooden stands for them with polar axes suited to the equator; also an astronomical quadrant made by Mr Bird, a brass Hadley's sextant, barometer, journeyman clock, thermometer, and a dipping needle. Added to this were James's own instruments—telescope, theodolite, plane table, a brass scale, a double concave glass, parallel ruler, a pair of proportional compasses, stationery and markers to the value of £48 10 s. He had sent the account to the Admiralty.

'Look, there it is!' shouted Jamie.

'No, it's a fly spot,' said Mrs Curtis.

In the darkness of the room, Elizabeth made out the hands of the clock. It was getting late, the sun almost on the point of setting.

'That's right, Mr Curtis, you have it now. Keep it steady,' cried Mr Lieber, adjusting the position of the card. Then everyone went silent, looking at the reflected image of the sun, and the small smudge of Venus. It lasted about a minute, then the card went blank.

'Where did it go?' cried Nat.

Mr Curtis took a peek out the curtains. The sun has set,' he announced. 'That's the end of it.' But they had seen the transit, if only a minute of it, here in the living room with the boys' telescope and a piece of card.

Gradually the party dispersed. 'I'll see Mr Lieber to the door,' said Frances.

'Me too,' offered Nat.

'It's bedtime for little boys,' Elizabeth told him, leaving Frances and Mr Lieber a moment to themselves.

Frances must have gone further than the door because when Elizabeth came downstairs there was no-one about. She put muslin over the remains of the cheese, then began clearing up.

Frances's face was flushed when she finally came in. 'He asked me to marry him,' she announced, sinking contentedly onto the sofa.

'I think I can guess the reply.'

'Yes,' Frances sighed.

Elizabeth hugged her cousin. 'I am so pleased.'

'I'll not leave you alone, Elizabeth. We're taking lodgings nearby, we can see each other every day.'

'Of course,' said Elizabeth. She was genuinely pleased for Frances but number 8 Assembly Row would not be the same without her. She so cheerily went about everything she did. When baby Joseph died it was Frances who eased Elizabeth out of her grief. And she was James's cousin. Having a member of James's family living here was some consolation for James's absence. Now she was going.

'Then we plan to try our fortunes in America.' It was a good time to go. The new Prime Minister, Lord North, had repealed all taxes, save the tax on tea, and relations between England and the colonies were improving. 'In a year or two,' added Frances. 'After James has returned.'

There'd been no news for months. After the transit James was to sail in search of the Great South Land. It was as extraordinary as setting sail for the moon, thought Elizabeth, as she went upstairs to bed. She wasn't even sure he had found Tahiti, such a small island on the other side of the world. Still, there were men aboard who had travelled the South Seas before—midshipman Charles Clerke, from Essex, an adventurous fellow with a roving eye. He had become famous along the riverside during the war with France for having been on the mizzen-top when the *Bellona*'s mast was shot away by the *Courageux* and having crawled up the chains almost dead from drowning. Beneath his derring-do he had mathematical ability and shared James's interest in scientific navigation. The American-born Lieutenant John Gore had sailed with both Wallis and Lord Byron, and had more experience of the South Seas than anyone else on the *Endeavour*.

'What does Gore say of Tahiti?' Elizabeth had asked one night, when the rest of the house was sleeping.

'Paradise,' her husband answered.

'That's what they all say. I want more, James, a word-picture, so that I can imagine you in Tahiti when you are away.' He said nothing. 'Perhaps you will find it easier with the candle out.' She snuffed the candle. It wasn't easy, but eventually she coaxed it out of him.

He told her that in Tahiti the air was always warm, even in winter. The colours were brighter than any Englishman had seen, the ocean a blue as deep as her eyes. Closer in, the water became turquoise as the blue washed over yellow coral. A volcanic upthrust, green and wooded, jutted into the sky, and sometimes it wore a necklace of mist. With his fingers James drew the picture on her body, tracing a line to the upthrust of her breast. 'There are beaches of black sand and supple coconut trees that lean windward over the water. When the breeze moves through them the fronds rustle like straw,' he said, blowing gentle tropical breezes onto her belly.

'And what did Mr Gore say about the women?' she had asked drawing him closer.

'I don't recall.'

Elizabeth was alert to a small coughing sound coming from Eliza's crib. She tiptoed over to the child, who thankfully had not woken. Elizabeth got back into bed, her arm resting on the side where James slept, and imagined him on the tiny cot in his cabin. She saw the folding table of Spanish mahogany, his pens and inks, a sheet of paper which might have written on it: 'Dear Elizabeth'. He said he would write every week. Almost a year's worth of letters now.

She could not sleep. She took the telescope and found Venus. Six hours of transit. Perhaps James was watching now. She beamed her loving thoughts into the stars. God keep and preserve you, my darling, and may you soon be home.

'Mama?' Elizabeth saw the small silhouette of Nat beside her. 'Won't your eyes burn out?'

'What are you looking at?' Jamie had joined them. She gave him the telescope and helped him find Venus. 'It's so bright,' he said.

'Let me see,' begged Nat, trying to wrestle the telescope away from his brother.

'What did Papa tell you? It's not a plaything.' Eliza began to stir. 'You can both have a turn. Venus is not going to disappear in a minute like its image did.'

Elizabeth went to the crib, gently lifted Eliza out, wrapped a blanket around her, and brought her to the window with the boys.

The family took turns at the telescope, seeing the same planet that James was watching half a world away. Eventually, when the eastern sky was paling and the stars fading, the children fell asleep. Elizabeth kept watch, till all the stars had disappeared.

BINGLEY'S JOURNAL,
FRIDAY 28 SEPTEMBER 1770

> It is surmised, that one grou
> present preparations for war
> secret intelligence received
> Ministry, that the Endeavour n
> which was sent into the Soutl
> the astronomers, to make ob
> and afterwards to go into a ne
> make discoveries, has been sun
> her people, by order of a jealc
> who has committed other
> against us in the Southern h
> Mr Banks, and the famous Di

Elizabeth's mother died two months after the transit of Venus, surviving Mr Blackburn by less than a year. No amount of cajoling on Elizabeth's part had been able to deter Mama from her path. She would not return from mourning. Nothing worked, not even little Eliza's soft caresses or her invitations to Grandmama to play dolls with her. Mama had closed the door and would not let Elizabeth, or anyone else, in.

'What a pale little child that is,' Mama said, staring at Eliza as if she were a stranger. When she spoke, Mama's breath smelled like Mr Blackburn's. 'Almost blue. Send her to the country at once!' Eliza ran and hid in the safety of her mother's skirts.

Though Mama refused to come and live with them in Mile End, Elizabeth persevered, visiting her mother almost daily, leaving Eliza and the boys with Frances. Sometimes Mama consented to a little soup or bread, but Elizabeth suspected it was only to give her strength to go for the next drink. Elizabeth prayed, an imploring prayer that Mama would see the sin of what she was doing, that as long as there was breath she must keep living, and accept God's will.

On the last day Elizabeth came to her mother's house, she had trouble getting in. 'Mama, it's me.' But the door remained unanswered. It was pointless looking in the windows because Mama always kept the curtains drawn, even when Elizabeth suggested she should let some light into the house. She went around to the back and found a way in.

The cat immediately started meowing around Elizabeth's feet, and there was a terrible, acrid smell.

Mama was lying on the sofa in the parlour, from which she'd barely shifted over the last few months, face down in vomit. Elizabeth felt the sobs wrenching out of her. She had come too late.

They interred Mary Blackburn at St Paul's. As Elizabeth threw soil onto the coffin, she thought of that day they'd walked to St Paul's for Jamie's christening, Mama helping her carry the baby. She felt betrayed. Mama had left her and now she was an orphan. It did not matter that Elizabeth was a grown woman. Mama's death made her feel as helpless as a little child. It was so unnecessary. Couldn't Mama see the wake of grief her passing would leave?

James may have lost no lives to scurvy but nothing Elizabeth did prevented her people from dying—baby Joseph, Mr Blackburn, and now Mama. It was as if in the break to the pattern of her life with James, death had found its way in. She wanted the old life back, for him to resume the work in Newfoundland and come home every winter.

But another winter passed and still James did not come. The voyage had now gone on longer than both Lord Byron's and Wallis's. Elizabeth watched the stars that guided her husband, she felt the winds that carried him on their great arcs around the globe. She sniffed the air for signs of him, and breathed her love back out, long gentle waves of it. He was still living, she told herself. She could not bear it if anything had happened to him.

So she grew stiff-lipped with disapproval of the wagers that were going around London as to the loss or not of the *Endeavour*. Englishmen would bet on anything, but this was not the bearpit or the cockfighting ring. The boys brought home tales from school—even children were making wagers—and Jamie and Nat had to defend their absent father with fisticuffs.

It was more than disapproval; Elizabeth felt as if they were burying James alive, and she with him. When the children were sleeping, Elizabeth wrote to the Admiralty, begging pardon for her humble letter but asking for news of the barque *Endeavour*.

Worse, much worse than the games of chance was the account in *Bingley's Journal*. The rumours were in print:

> *It is surmised, that one ground of the present preparations for war, is some secret intelligence received by the Ministry, that the Endeavour man of war, which was sent into the South Sea with the astronomers, to make observations, and afterwards to go into a new track to make discoveries, has been sunk, with all her people, by order of a jealous Court, who has committed other hostilities against us in the Southern hemisphere. Mr Banks, and the famous Dr Solander, were on board the above vessel, and are feared to have shared the common fate with the rest of the ship's company.*

'Scurrilous,' announced Cousin Charles, who at eighteen sported a grey wig and had the air of someone much older. Now that his father had passed away Charles had taken it upon himself to be head of the family. 'It is surmised,' he began reading. 'That is all.'

'They do not mention James, or Isaac,' Elizabeth pointed out. 'Only Mr Banks and Dr Solander. Do they think the vessel is sailing itself? Is my husband only a coach driver?' Elizabeth and her cousin looked at each other. Of course the newspaper would only mention Mr Banks and Dr Solander. They were gentlemen.

'Perhaps a letter to the Admiralty,' suggested Charles.

'I have written,' said Elizabeth, 'but had no answer.'

Charles went in person to call on the board, but Mr Stephens said they'd received no intelligence concerning the matter.

'He is alive,' said Elizabeth with determination, 'I know he is. They have missed the trade winds, that is all. We shall see them in the spring.'

Their wedding anniversary passed, and another Christmas without James. Nevertheless Elizabeth made an occasion of it, with presents for James beneath the tree. He may have found the Great South Land, he may even be back in the Atlantic, on his way home, Elizabeth didn't know, but in her mind he was always in the South Seas. 'It is warm where Papa is, and perhaps he has a coconut tree instead of a fir, but he is celebrating Christmas nevertheless.'

Jamie was growing so quickly that Elizabeth seemed to spend much of her time either making new clothes for him or altering the old. He looked so much like James that she almost cried to see it. Nat was a big boy too, but with the angular features of Mama's family. Eliza remained tiny, despite Elizabeth's attempts to feed her, but she was a pretty little girl with such dainty features that she resembled a doll.

'Will they have fireworks?' asked Nat.

'Of course,' said Elizabeth. 'And all manner of things to eat, which Papa will tell you about when he comes home.'

'Bullet pudding?' asked Eliza.

Elizabeth was hard-pressed to imagine James playing bullet pudding with Mr Banks, Mr Green and Dr Solander and the others, but 'Yes,' she said. 'Of course they will play bullet pudding.'

'And Papa will win!' exclaimed Eliza.

Though Elizabeth regularly showed Eliza and the boys James's likeness, she wondered if their daughter remembered him in person. One day Eliza had asked: 'Is Papa like the Almighty?'

'What do you mean?'

'He is our father but we never see him.'

'We will see Papa soon,' said Elizabeth, hugging her daughter to her. 'In spring.'

'Spring?'

'After the snow is gone. When the leaves come back on the trees, and the daffodils appear in the grass. Then we will see Papa.'

On Christmas night Elizabeth took her husband to bed. Not the real one, thousands of miles away, but her imagined husband. She saw his dark hair flowing over his shoulders, the brightness of his eyes when he looked at her, his strong shoulders and the muscles flexing in his arms when he reached down for her. She heard the voice that could thunder orders to his crew, murmur her name. Elizabeth. In her mind she travelled over every inch of his body, caressed his chest and felt the heart beating there. She even imagined the ultimate intimacy and found herself sighing for want of him. If her imagined husband produced such a response, the real one must surely live.

Eliza saw the trees bud with leaves, and the first daffodils of spring appear in the grass, but she never again saw her Papa. In the blustery March winds she caught cold, and despite lemon juice and infusions of thyme, and even the physician's letting of her blood, she got worse and worse. Her little chest was racked with coughs, her forehead drenched with sweat, but the malady was tenacious and would not let go.

'Preserve her, oh Lord, let her father see her once again.' It was a wish prayed for with all Elizabeth's heart and soul, a prayer she gave out through every pore of her body. When she looked up from prayer she saw Eliza, still smiling, almost bemused to find this thing, this evil disease, living inside her. The boys were sent to stay down the street with Frances and Mr Lieber so that Elizabeth could give her full attention to Eliza. She sat by the bed, wiping her brow, arranging cushions to make the little girl more comfortable.

She brought in daffodils, and hens' eggs for Eliza to feel the smooth brown shells. Eliza's favourite doll grew sticky with sweat but still she would not let go of it. Elizabeth told her stories of the South Seas, and Papa soon returning, although she had not one shred of news herself. Her stories were buoyant with hope. 'Papa is drinking milk from coconuts. They are fruit as big as your head and they have rough brown fur on them like a monkey.' Elizabeth showed her daughter a picture of a monkey from a book of animals. 'When you are better, Eliza, we will go to Regent's Park and see all the animals.' 'Yes, Mama,' answered Eliza hoarsely.

At the start of the second week of April, Elizabeth had spent the night beside her daughter, wiping her brow, crushing lavender leaves in her hands to release fragrance that might ease the child's laboured breathing.

When the sky grew pink with dawn Elizabeth whispered, 'The sun is coming, Eliza.'

'Sun.' Eliza opened her eyes and smiled.

Elizabeth grew frantic with hope that daylight had brought the answer to her prayers. But Eliza's breath grew softer and softer till it was no more.

Frances brought the boys back, and Elizabeth stood vigil, a candle flickering in its brace on the wall. The candle continued burning well into the day, Elizabeth not having the heart to snuff it out, wondering why the Lord giveth if only to take away again in such a short time. The boys had already been in to see Eliza. 'She has gone to God,' Elizabeth had explained. They had stood there watching, as if Eliza might simply wake up and smile at them, Nat with eyes wide to stop tears pouring down his cheeks, Jamie staunch and serious, the man of the family.

Elizabeth looked out the window, dry-eyed, at the birds darting among the apple blossoms, the hens scratching on the ground. One of them drew a worm from the soil; Elizabeth saw its struggling body hanging from the hen's beak before it disappeared down her gullet.

She felt a hand on her shoulder. Frances. 'I know what must be done,' said Elizabeth grimly. 'I am not yet ready.'

Why did the world keep on turning, the sun rise inexorably on to a new day? For Eliza to die in the spring when everything was coming alive again . . . Elizabeth wanted it all to stop. She did not want to be swept along in the current of life. There should be a time for standing still, for everything to come to a halt as it had in her heart. It was worse than baby Joseph. To have little Eliza for four years, then never ever have her again. Not to see her nose wrinkle with delight when she chased the hens, to hear her sweet little voice tell the neighbours: 'Papa is in the South Seas. He will be home in spring.'

Elizabeth was aware of an aroma and the sound of footsteps. When she finally turned from the window she saw a thick slice of cheese toast, grown cold. There was no room inside Elizabeth for food, it was entirely taken up with a greyness as vast as a dirty sky. She looked once again at the blue sky outside. Perhaps it was better that James was lost at sea, as the newspaper said. Better than coming home to two dead children.

Eliza was buried beside Joseph in St Dunstan's. The vicar had met the funeral procession at the entrance to the churchyard, and stopped before the small coffin. Elizabeth was dressed in black,

PORTRAIT OF SIR HUGH PALLISER
BY GEORGE DANCE

Elizabeth, dressed in mourning black, was cleaning out the fire. It was a dirty job, coal dust rising into her nose, but she cared not a jot for her own discomfort. Apart from the interment, Elizabeth had not left the house since Eliza's death. The curtains were still drawn, though by the noise outside she could tell it was a fine day. Elizabeth did not want to go out into the sunshine, it was too much at odds with the darkness inside her.

It pleased her to be doing the dirty work of cleaning out the fire. She was on her knees, no apron, her black satin dress smudged. She swept and swept at the fireplace, filling the cinder box with ash. Some of it flurried up to her face, settling on her cheeks and stinging her eyes. She did nothing to try to stop it. Her insides felt as if they'd turned to ash anyway, so dry that she had not been able to shed even one tear for Eliza. She had stopped praying, severed her connection to the Lord. Perhaps if she were covered in ash He would think her dead and no longer seek her out.

Elizabeth began applying blacklead to the grate with a soft brush. It had an unpleasant smell that made her feel sick, but she did not waver from the chore. She used a harder brush to rub off the excess, vigorously working her arms into it till they ached. She wiped the back of her hand across her forehead, smudging it with ash, as someone knocked at the door.

The knocking persisted. Elizabeth took her time, arranging the brushes and making sure the cinder box did not tip its contents all over the floor. The sound at the door stopped. The person had finally gone away. But no, three final knocks, a light but firm hand.

Elizabeth got up off the floor. She took no care to fix her hair, or even wash her hands. The caller would see her just as she was.

A navy man. He looked familiar to Elizabeth but it was as if she were viewing him through a fog.

'Is Mrs Cook at home?' he asked.

She recognised him now his oval face with its kindly expression. Hugh Palliser. The fellow Yorkshireman was a friend of James's; he had first been his captain, then governor of Newfoundland, and recently, this year of 1771, Comptroller of the Navy Board. He was wearing a long jacket with wide lapels, similar to the one in the portrait James had taken her to see. She recalled Mr Palliser's casual pose in the portrait, his elbow resting on a column, elegant fingers hanging from a lace cuff, the vague outlines of a ship in the background.

The opened door threw light onto Elizabeth and her darkened house. She saw herself in the mirror of Mr Palliser's eyes. She looked like a chimneysweep. Be that as it may. For Mr Palliser to coming knocking on her door in person, it must be important. Had the Almighty not finished with her after all? Was Mr Palliser about to announce the news she dreaded most?

'May I come in, Mrs Cook?' he said, recognising her now. He showed no surprise at her forlorn state.

He came in and, although she offered him the sofa, waited till she sat before he did so. It made no difference to Elizabeth whether she sat or stood. Eventually she sat on the edge of a chair.

Mr Palliser sharpened the edge of his hat with long elegant fingers. 'My deepest sympathies for your recent loss,' he said.

Elizabeth bowed her head, accepting his condolences.

He paused, giving the dead their due. 'But I come on a happier matter. Intelligence which may lift your spirits. You may have heard reports that the *Endeavour* was lost—indeed, we feared so ourselves. But,' he said, placing the hat beside him on the sofa, 'we recently have advice from the India house that the *Endeavour* arrived in Batavia on the tenth of October, last. All well on board. We can expect them soon.'

All well, we can expect them soon. The words Elizabeth had so longed for had been spoken in her house. She slumped into the back of the chair, not giving one thought to the possible dirt she was spreading. She felt tears flood into her eyes. Tears of relief for James, and a well of sadness for Eliza. 'Oh, Mr Palliser, thank you, thank you,' she said, as if he himself were responsible for the glad tidings. 'I don't know . . . I . . .' She gave herself over completely to the flood of tears.

Though a bachelor, Mr Palliser seemed not the least embarrassed by her display of emotion. Instead, he reached into his pocket and offered her a white lace handkerchief. She buried her face in it, smelling its subtle perfume, drenching it with her tears. She did not realise she had such a flood of them inside her.

When they were finally spent, she lifted her face and saw how besmirched the handkerchief was. 'I am so sorry, Mr Palliser.'

He waved away her apologies, the handkerchief remaining in her lap, a bond between her and him. She was full of admiration for James's old friend. A man in his position could simply have sent a message, but he had come in person.

The lightness, the sea breeze that Hugh Palliser had brought into the house stayed, even after he had gone. It was mid-May, and high time for spring-cleaning. When the boys were at school, Elizabeth, Frances and Mrs Pore from down the street cleaned the house, literally from top to bottom.

Rugs were taken outside and beaten, blankets and bed linen washed and hung out in the spring sunshine to dry. All the upstairs furniture was covered with dusting sheets while the rooms were swept. Elizabeth cleaned the wallpapers, first by blowing the dust off with bellows, then with a section of white bread, holding onto the crust and wiping downwards in deft, light strokes. Mirrors were cleaned with a mixture of water and gin.

The three women together took down the curtain poles, and Mrs Pore cleaned them with vinegar, then rubbed them with furniture polish. Frances got down on her knees and cleaned the kitchen floor with sand and hot water. Elizabeth took the heavy velvet bed curtains down and replaced them with the linen ones, having first hung these outside for the breeze to disperse the smell of camphor. The hens in the yard scattered at the flurry of activity, clucking disapproval of the disturbance to their ways. When the wind flapped the curtains hanging on the line, the hens remembered they were birds and even managed, with a few fluttery wing movements, to become airborne. Elizabeth took hold of the bottom corners of one curtain, felt the pull as the wind filled it. 'Frances, look!' she cried with delight. 'I am sailing.'

Daily they waited for the return of the *Endeavour* and at night Elizabeth listened to the wind, judging its direction and speed, waiting for the wind that would bring her husband home. Batavia was half a world away, but it had been more than six months earlier that they were there.

A fortnight into July, on a day when the breeze was fresh and the weather fine, Elizabeth came inside with an apron full of eggs to find a message. She carefully placed the eggs in a dish, wiped her hands down the apron, picked up the letter and recognised Mr Palliser's handwriting. She broke open the seal. The *Endeavour* had been sighted off Dover. Elizabeth told herself to be calm, but she could not be. She was thirty, yet she skipped about with the same gaiety as a five year old.

On the evening of Wednesday 18 July, he came. He stood in the doorway, just as Elizabeth had first seen him when she was thirteen. She saw his beloved features, and the three hard years of waiting dissolved away. She felt waves rippling through her as they embraced, smelled the vestiges of the sea on him. She wanted to press against him like this forever. But forever would have to wait. The boys were here to greet their father. Jamie and Nat looked at him, as tall and strong in the flesh as he was in their memory. Elizabeth noticed a few grey hairs at James's temples, felt her heart miss a beat as she saw the scar on the hand that he extended to the boys.

She heard a bleating, and beyond him, beyond the trunks and paraphernalia from the voyage, saw a goat. It was so unexpected that she laughed.

'You have brought a goat?'

'*The* goat,' James stressed, 'that has now twice circumnavigated the globe. She deserves a well-earned rest. I can think of no better place than our garden.'

'Best we install her there then,' said Elizabeth, 'before she eats your sea chests.'

They brought her through the house and out to the back where they firmly tethered her, the hens clucking like disapproving old ladies at this creature with whom they were to share their domain.

'I think I need the aid of two strong lads to bring in the chests,' said James.

A small crowd of neighbours had gathered outside the front door. James nodded a greeting while he and the boys lugged the things inside. Time enough for friends and neighbours when he was once more in the bosom of his family.

That night the boys were allowed to stay up as long as they wanted, and it was after midnight when they finally laid their heads on their pillows.

Before James and Elizabeth followed, to enjoy the long-anticipated intimacy of their bed, James went to one of the sea chests and brought out a package wrapped in cloth with leather binding around it. 'My dear,' he said, presenting it to her. Elizabeth undid the deft sailor's knots and out tumbled letters, hundreds of them, one for each week that he had been away.

Elizabeth left them where they fell. She would savour each and every letter later. Right now there was an urgent need to reacquaint herself with their author, to share her bed with her real husband after so many nights with the imagined one.

She felt the softness of his lips on hers, the play of fingers, the trembling of their bodies as they recharted one another. Elizabeth thought that perhaps after so long the ultimate intimacy might be difficult, as it had been on their wedding night, but instead it was the greatest ecstasy. She felt her skin, her very boundaries, melt and she became the warm South Seas.

Afterwards, as they lay together, she asked, 'Did you find the Great South Land?'

'Of riches beyond compare? I have come home to it, Elizabeth.'

It was not till the first morning birds began twittering, after a night in which neither James nor Elizabeth slept, that the subject of the absent children was broached.

'Hugh told me about Eliza,' said James softly.

Elizabeth bowed her head, tears pricking her eyes. How quickly the sadness welled up, even in the midst of happiness.

James had never known the baby Joseph, but felt keenly the loss of little Eliza. 'I want to visit her grave. Will you come with me, Elizabeth?'

Elizabeth picked flowers from the garden and gave them to her husband. Together they walked in the fresh morning, towards St Dunstan's.

Elizabeth led James to the grave. He placed the flowers in front of the headstone, and stood quietly, his head bowed. Elizabeth took a step back, to allow her husband a moment alone with his daughter, but he reached his arm out and together they stood. 'Talk to me of her,' he asked.

Elizabeth took a deep breath, preparing her heart for this difficult task, for the sweet sadness of remembering the dead. As Elizabeth had told Eliza of her father, now she told the father of his daughter, how affectionate she was, kissing everyone and putting her little hands on their cheeks. When neighbours asked after her father, she would say, 'Papa is in Tahiti', rising up on her toes as if she couldn't pronounce the name of the place without doing so. Elizabeth told him how they had all witnessed the transit of Venus, how at Christmas Eliza asked if Papa was playing bullet pudding. Finally, Elizabeth told James that their daughter had died peacefully. She did not mention the racking coughs, the fever that consumed her, the terrible sound of her gurgling breath.

James looked at his wife, into her oceanic eyes, and found the etchings of lines around them that had not been there before. 'How difficult it must have been for you, both Eliza and the new baby.'

She nodded, but said nothing of the bleakness that had invaded her, how she'd wanted to bury herself in ashes to avoid God's will. How she now understood the nature of the darkness in which Mama drowned.

Slowly they walked back to Assembly Row, where the boys were already up, despite their late night, as if it were Christmas morning. They couldn't stop looking at their father, not wanting to miss a single word, a single movement, not even the blink of an eye.

After breakfast, the grand opening of the chests began. There were presents for Elizabeth and the boys, for friends and family, but most of the booty was bound for the Admiralty.

James presented Elizabeth with several pieces of tapa cloth from Tahiti, some with coloured designs and others plain. She felt its papery texture as James told her it was from the bark of a tree, and beaten rather than woven. Nevertheless, the fabric was fine and Elizabeth appreciated the workmanship of it. Also for Elizabeth was a ring made of turtleshell with the tooth of a shark attached. She slipped it onto her finger after the boys had closely examined it. The ring fitted perfectly. Elizabeth was amazed that the Tahitians' fingers were the same size as her own. 'When the women dance they move their fingers like this,' said James, making the motion of waves.

'The men too?' asked Nat.

James showed them how the men danced, legs apart, thighs thrust out in a suggestive manner, though fortunately the suggestion was lost on the boys.

The next item appeared to be some sort of mat. 'A mantle worn in wet weather,' said James, lifting it out of the chest. 'A gift from a Tahitian chief.' It was made of pandanus leaves, James explained, which repelled the rain, and it had a dark brown ornamental border.

'It rains in Tahiti?' That was not Elizabeth's idea of paradise.

'By the bucketload. Then it is over and done with. The sun comes out again.'

For Jamie there was a hatchet of jade from New Zealand. It was dark green, the colour of yew trees, and had a smooth, polished finish. For Nat, an adze, the head fashioned from dense black volcanic stone, and bound to the handle with coconut fibre. There were fish hooks made of shells, decorated paddles and clubs, cloaks made of feathers, a basket of coconut fibre with shells and beads decorating it. It seemed as though all of the South Seas was spread out in the Cooks' living room.

The quantity of items brought back by James was nothing compared to the bounty gathered by Dr Solander and, especially, Mr Banks. 'Is it true that Mr Banks brought back 17 000 plants we've never before seen in England?' Elizabeth asked.

The newspapers were full of the voyage, all of London ablaze with Mr Banks this and Mr Banks that, but little mention of James. Though James did not keep a house in fashionable New Burlington Street, as did the celebrated Mr Banks, with nobility dropping in to visit, he was high in the esteem of everyone at number 8 Assembly Row. To the boys it was as if King George had come to stay. The Admiralty, too, was obviously impressed. The minutes of their meeting for 1 August 1771 read: 'Resolved that [Lieutenant Cook] be acquainted the Board extremely well approve of the whole of his proceedings, and have great satisfaction in the account he gives of the good behaviour of his officers and men, and of the cheerfulness and alertness which they went through the fatigues and dangers of the Voyage . . . '

There was talk of a second voyage, hopefully not too soon, Elizabeth thought to herself. It looked as if James would never resume his post in Newfoundland. He was mapping the whole world now. Mr Banks would go again, and on a much larger scale.

While Mr Banks could not help but be puffed up by being the toast of the town, he did not forget his friend and fellow traveller, James Cook. It was Banks who had the pleasure of writing to James to tell him that he had been promoted to captain.

There was a family dinner to celebrate the promotion, with Charles, Isaac and their young sister Ursula present. Isaac must have grown six inches since he'd been away and, while not yet twenty, had developed a confident, smooth manner. '*Captain Cook*,' he said, striding into the room and shaking James's hand.

'Isaac had the honour of being first to step ashore at Botany Bay,' announced James. 'He's master's mate now.'

James had discovered the east coast of New Holland, which he re-named New South Wales. Elizabeth recalled James's letter about this 'capacious safe and commodious' bay, their first landing place. Mr Banks likened the coastline to a 'lean cow, covered in general with long hair but nevertheless where her scraggy hip bones have stuck out farther than they ought accidental rubbs and knocks have entirely bard them of their covering'. The natives, who went about naked, were a very dark brown with hair 'black and lank much like ours', James wrote. Unlike the South Seas people he had so far come across, the New Holland natives distanced themselves. Even the beads and nails left as gifts for them remained untouched.

'It was Stingray Harbour when I first stepped ashore,' Isaac began, 'on account of the stingrays. Then the captain renamed it Botanist Harbour because of the large number of new plants Banks and Solander collected.' Isaac's words almost tumbled over each other in his haste to get them out. Beneath his man-of-the-world veneer Elizabeth saw the excitement of the small boy who had once marvelled over James's instruments.

'And eventually,' added James, 'long after we'd left the place, it became Botany Bay.'

They had not found the Great South Land. Hopes of finding it had risen when they sighted New Zealand but were dispelled when the *Endeavour* skirted the coast of that country and discovered it to be two large islands. New Holland was not the fabled continent either. 'As far as we know,' said James, 'it does not produce anything that can become an article of trade to invite Europeans to fix a settlement upon it. However the eastern side is not that barren and miserable country that Dampier and others have described the western side to be. Everything flourishes and the natives think themselves provided with all the necessities of life.'

'Ahem,' Cousin Charles cleared his throat, finally finding a gap in the conversation. He unrolled his copy of the *Historical Chronicle* and proceeded to read:

> *An express arrived at the Admiralty, with the agreeable news of the arrival in the Downs of the* Endeavour, *Captain Cook from the East Indies. This ship sailed in August, 1768 with Mr Banks, Dr Solander, Mr Green, and other ingenious gentlemen on board for the South Seas to observe the transit of Venus; they have since made a voyage round the world, and touched at every coast and island, where it was possible to get on shore, to collect every species of plant, and other rare productions of Nature. Their voyage, upon the whole, has been as agreeable and successful as they could have expected, except the death of Mr Green, who died upon his passage from Batavia. Dr Solander has been a good deal indisposed, but it is hoped a few days refreshment will soon establish his health. Captain Cook and Mr Banks are perfectly well.*

Although it was old news, dated Saturday 13 July, everyone took great pleasure in hearing it. 'Ingenious gentlemen,' repeated Nat. 'Yes,' said Jamie, 'and we have two of them at the table with us.' They laughed, and every time either of them addressed James or Isaac they called them 'ingenious gentlemen' again.

'How's the goat faring?' asked Isaac.

'Eating her way through the garden,' said Elizabeth. 'We've had to tether her closer to the house. She's developed a taste for roses, thorns and all.' Elizabeth turned to Ursula, who had barely said a word. 'Perhaps after dinner we can feed her the scraps. Would you like to do that, Ursula?' The little girl nodded.

'A true *Endeavour* voyager is our goat, one who eats whatever is at hand,' said James. 'Banks maintains that he has eaten his way further into the animal kingdom than any man, but we were right there with him, eh, Isaac?'

Isaac started listing some of the beasts that had kept the voyagers alive. 'Penguin, kangaroo, dog. Everything that walks, crawls, hops, swims or flies. Banks has a recipe for albatross, if ever you happen to come across one at Billingsgate Market. "Skin them and soak their carcasses in salt water overnight, then par-boil them and throw away the water, then stew them well with very little water. When sufficiently tender, serve them up with a savoury sauce". But the albatross had its revenge on our botanist. He was sick for days afterwards.'

'Did you eat a man?' asked Jamie.

'Jamie!' admonished Elizabeth.

'The fellows at school say that the men of New Zealand are cannibals,' Jamie defended himself.

'Aye, that they are,' said his father. 'They eat the bodies of their enemies, to take in their strength.'

'Do they eat everything? The ears and eyes as well?' asked Nat, eager for gory detail.

'They preserve the heads for trophies,' said James. 'Banks bought a head from the Maoris, or rather, it seems he forced them to sell it to him, because they never showed us another afterwards.'

Ursula looked as if she were about to faint, and pushed her dinner plate away.

'I think we've had enough on that subject.' Elizabeth drew herself up. 'There are certain people at this table who are very impressionable.'

Elizabeth was sitting up in bed drinking a cup of tea and reading James's letters. The Tahitian ring was on the bedside table. To the image of a tropical paradise, with verdant mountains and coral seas, were now added turtles and sharks.

'There's much mention in your letters of thievery,' Elizabeth commented. She watched her husband shave, preparing himself for the day. How she treasured these moments, the everyday intimacies that for other wives were a common occurrence.

'There was much thievery,' James said. 'At one stage a native even made off with the quadrant, which was kept under heavy guard.'

'But it was retrieved,' Elizabeth pointed out.

'Thankfully, yes.'

Elizabeth thought of all the curiosities laid out in the living room downstairs, how the boys could hardly wait to touch and handle everything. She thought of the shops in London, with everything on enticing display. That's what the *Endeavour* must have looked like to the natives, a big shop full of curiosities, and so many of them that the sailors wouldn't miss one or two.

'I think it was not so much covetousness as a game of skill,' James said.

'Or in return for Banks taking so many of their plants,' Elizabeth suggested.

She went back to the letters. Canoes coming to greet the *Endeavour*, coconuts, breadfruit and fish in exchange for beads. 'Apart from the thievery, it sounds as if you had good relations with them.'

'Would that it was always so in the South Seas,' said James, putting on his shirt. 'We enter their ports and attempt to land in a peaceable manner. If we succeed, all is well. If not, we land nevertheless and maintain our footing by the superiority of our firearms. In what other light can they first look upon us but as invaders of their country?' James continued dressing, getting ready to take the boys to Stepney Green.

'The Tahitians didn't mind you cutting down their trees to make a fort on Point Venus?'

'I asked permission first, and offered gifts as payment. They seemed not to mind the construction at all. On the contrary, they pitched in and helped, digging trenches and carrying water, as if it were all a huge game. One of the chiefs even brought his family along and set up house near the site.' James buttoned up his waistcoat. He'd not be needing a jacket on this warm day, certainly not to play cricket.

After James and the boys left, Elizabeth continued reading. The fort became a little community, with a kitchen-dining tent, a forge for the blacksmith, and even a tent set up for Sunday service. For Divine Service 'as many of the principal natives were admitted as we conveniently could', wrote James, 'and there was a vast concourse of people without the fort. The whole thing was conducted very quietly, those in the tent doing as we did, kneeling, standing or sitting. They understood perfectly that we were speaking with our God, as they themselves worship an invisible and omnipotent being.'

Elizabeth thought of the Bible, now safely home again, which she'd lovingly prepared for the voyage, with its frontispiece showing the light of God shining down on all the peoples of the world. Eliza's death had made her want to hide from the Lord. Now she felt ready to stand in His sight, to feel the light which shone on all the peoples of the world also shine on her.

A Pair of Shoe Buckles

There was much ado in the Cook household leading up to 14 August. 'Go to the hatter to collect your father's hat,' Elizabeth instructed Jamie and Nat. 'Make sure he puts it into a proper hat box, and mind you take care with it on the way home.' She had not sent her husband's dress clothes to the washer-woman, preferring this time to take care of the laundry herself. She had soaked his stockings in lye to remove stains. He would have the whitest stockings in the whole of London. The same with the white kerchief and cuffs. On 14 August, Lord Sandwich was to take James to meet the king.

'You are fussing too much, Elizabeth,' James said as she got him to try on his coat and made small alterations at the back of the waist. 'I am to show the king my charts and recount the voyage, not impress him with my sartorial splendour.'

Elizabeth knew what a special honour it was to have an audience with the king. Ladies and gentlemen who were presented at court spent thousands of pounds on new attire. The least the Cooks could do was make the old look like the new.

'I feel like a marionette,' James grimaced.

'As well you might. You don't want your coat splitting when you bow to His Majesty. Have you practised your bowing?'

James smiled. Despite his protests, he was quite enjoying the fuss. An audience with the king would certainly be something to tell his father, and John Walker, when they went to Yorkshire at Christmas as planned.

Satisfied with the coat, Elizabeth made preparations for ironing, first securing a blanket on the table while the coals were getting nice and hot. Rather than using a flat-iron, which risked imparting rust and dirt to garments, she used a hollow box-iron into which she placed, with the aid of tongs, a glowing hot coal. When the ironing was done, she carefully placed the billowing shirt on a hanger. All that remained were the shoes.

'Elizabeth,' said James, 'I can do the shoes myself. Do not exhaust yourself.'

As a small concession, she let him black his own shoes and polish them to a mirror-like finish, inspecting the work to see that it was to her satisfaction. It was.

'To one who has brought so many presents to his family, I have a gift for you.'

James took the proffered package and opened it to find a pair of shoe buckles, the edges of which were trimmed with diamantés that glistened in the afternoon light like two perfect sets of teeth. 'They are beautiful,' he said, turning them this way and that. After they both had enjoyed the spangles of light the buckles threw into the room, he said, 'Let's see how they look in place.' He fastened them onto his newly polished shoes.

On the appointed day, Lord Sandwich came in his carriage. Elizabeth thought he'd send his footman to collect James, but

Lord Sandwich himself had alighted from the carriage and was standing at the door.

'Mrs Cook,' he greeted Elizabeth, bowing low. At least he hadn't brought Martha Ray with him, although Elizabeth was curious about the young woman who was Lord Sandwich's mistress. It seemed she accompanied him almost everywhere and even acted as hostess when he entertained guests at Hinchingbrooke, taking the place of his wife who was shut away in a madhouse in Windsor. Miss Ray was a collector of birds, and what an odd bird she'd collected in Lord Sandwich. Although he was a grand personage, he had a face like an old shoe. Elizabeth had heard the rumours of his debauchery and gambling, and knew that he had been a member of the infamous Hellfire Club, where all sorts of bacchanalian things had gone on. Elizabeth did not appreciate the leering look he gave her, though perhaps it was an expression he wore permanently. 'I have come to pay my respects to the goat, Mrs Cook,' he said grandly. 'Who has served her country, and is now in well-deserved retirement.' He wasn't joking, he really did want to see the goat. 'She's found her land legs, I presume?'

'Not only that. She's found everything which is edible and some which is not.'

The two men went out to the back garden. Elizabeth hung in the doorway, glad that the weather had been dry and there was no mud to dirty James's shoes. The diamanté buckles shone beautifully.

The goat did not look up from her eternal task of grazing. The hens seemed to have accepted the newcomer and pecked at the grass nearby. After greeting the goat and, it appeared, speaking to her, Lord Sandwich brought his gaze up to the fields beyond the house. The two men stood there squarely, gazing at the vista, hands behind their backs.

After a minute they turned and came back into the house. James gathered up his charts, all neatly rolled and tied with tape.

He was as handsome as she had ever seen him, and seemed not the least bit anxious about his pending audience with the king.

Elizabeth watched the carriage drive away from the house. She waited at the door, watching it grow smaller and smaller, till it became a tiny speck and was engulfed by the traffic on Mile End Road.

A DAMASK SERVIETTE

Yorkshire was hardly the South Seas but Elizabeth had never been further than Barking.

'All aboard that's going aboard,' shouted the coach driver. Excitement hovered about the coach station like a swarm of bees. Both those departing and those remaining behind were caught up in it. Rowdy boys chased each other and tipped the hats of unsuspecting passers-by. Street vendors plied their wares, trying to sell cakes and little dumplings to the voyagers. The horses snorted steam out of their nostrils and pawed the ground impatiently.

The Cooks had the most luggage of all. 'At least we will return lighter than we are leaving,' commented James. Earlier in the month he had written to the Admiralty applying for three weeks leave of absence. The Cooks were bearing gifts for their hosts the Wilsons, John Walker and his family, James's father and his sister Margaret.

A bell was rung to signal departure. Elizabeth bent down to Jamie and Nat. 'Now, you are to be on your best behaviour with Cousin Frances and Mr Lieber, do you understand?'

'Yes, Mama,' the boys chorused.

The coach driver helped aboard a fat woman who slapped away the hand placed on her behind. Another woman, grinning a toothless grin, was hoisted up into the basket at the back of the coach. Elizabeth hoped the old woman did not have too far to travel. The wind was brisk on that cold December day, and although it was cheaper to travel in the basket, it was not as comfortable as inside.

All the luggage was on top, but Elizabeth had kept aside a valise of her own to take with her in the coach. It contained some items of food, even though James had told her that they would be well victualled at the inns on the way.

It also contained the Book of Common Prayer that James had given to Frances. She had offered it as a travel companion to Elizabeth. 'You don't know who you might have in with you,' Frances said. 'You might prefer to bury your nose in a book.' It was a good choice. Novels, which Elizabeth was fond of reading, had to be selected carefully, otherwise they might elicit comments from her fellow travellers. The Book of Common Prayer would establish Elizabeth as a respectable woman.

Nevertheless, as the coach pulled away and the waving figures of Frances, Mr Lieber, Jamie and Nat got smaller and smaller, Elizabeth felt not the least bit respectable, despite the fact that she'd just celebrated her ninth wedding anniversary and that her thirty-first birthday was approaching.

She and James had never had a honeymoon, never been away on a holiday at all, and though they would not go as far as Gretna Green, she had such a heady feeling that they could almost have been eloping. Away from the children and the rest of the family, away from the neighbours in Assembly Row, away from everyone.

Even though they would be staying at inns and then with the Wilsons at Great Ayton, she felt that she and James would be alone together.

Elizabeth never imagined that the wheels would make so much noise on the road. Nevertheless, it was agreeable to be travelling. The coach went so fast she felt as if she were flying. As well as the fat woman, who took up the place of two, there was a couple— a man with ginger hair poking out beneath his wig, accompanying a much younger woman—and two gentlemen, thin and angular as spiders, dressed alike in black suits. James tried, as best he could, not to take up too much of the precious room. He'd welcome the stops, when he could stretch his long legs.

They hadn't even left the roads of London but already the ride was bumpy and the driver going at a cracking pace. Perhaps, mused Elizabeth, it was not so bumpy up there as it was inside.

At Highgate Hill, on the northern outskirts of London, the ride became smoother, and when they descended the hill, Elizabeth experienced a sliding sensation she thought would never end.

Though Elizabeth had a window seat and spent her time looking at the fields racing by, she was aware that she and James were under the scrutiny of the fat woman, who was no doubt trying to assess their station in life.

James was wearing landmen's clothes and looked as fine as any gentleman. Elizabeth wore a dark blue dress with a rich brown woollen cloak. When Elizabeth turned her gaze towards the fat woman, the woman looked away. What was the polite mode of behaviour in the close confines of a coach? Did you avert your gaze, as the woman had, or chat to each other? Elizabeth looked out the window again, at the heavy grey sky bearing down on the horizon.

She became aware that the two spidery men were talking about what they referred to as 'Mr Banks's voyage'. One of the men had a copy of *Gulliver's Travels* on his lap; perhaps that had led to the conversation. James was saying, 'Aye, what an exciting voyage it must have been.' Elizabeth smiled. He had obviously not announced himself.

'They came across a coral reef, more than a thousand miles long, which nearly did them in,' said one of the thin gentlemen, obviously well informed. Of course the newspapers had been full of it. 'All of a sudden the ship hit the coral, which sliced through the timbers as easily as a saw. The captain, I heard, came on deck in his drawers.' Elizabeth looked at her husband but he merely continued giving the man his polite attention. 'Well, they threw everything overboard, casks of water, tons of ballast. What a decision the captain had to make. If they stayed where they were, the ship would grind itself to pieces on the reef. If they waited for the tide and went to deep water, the ship would, in all likelihood, sink.'

Elizabeth wished the man had chosen a happier story to relate. It was the one time, James had said, that he'd truly feared he'd never see his loved ones again. Shipwrecked on a barren shore of New Holland, with no hope of rescue. He'd named the place Cape Tribulation.

'Anyway, the captain decided to go to the deep water. All hands pumped even faster to gain on the four feet of water that had found its way into the hold. In desperation they decided to fother her. That's coating a sail with tufts of wool and oakum, and wrapping it around the hull,' explained the man, leaning forward to the one person on the coach who knew full well what fothering involved. 'That was sufficient to get the ship close enough to land to assess the damage. And you know what they found? The biggest hole in the ship had a lump of coral wedged in it, blocking it up. What had caused the trouble had also saved them.' The storyteller stopped for breath.

While Cape Tribulation had been James's worst moment, it was also his proudest. In the panic produced by desperate situations crews often took to plundering, refusing to obey commands. But not on the *Endeavour*. Instead of 'every man for himself' it was 'every man exerted himself to the very utmost for the preservation of the ship'. Banks had reported that: 'The seamen worked with surprising cheerfulness and alacrity; no grumbling or growling was to be heard . . . not even an oath (though the ship in general was as well furnished with them as most in His Majesty's service).'

'I'd rather do my voyaging in this ship,' said the man, brandishing his book. 'I agree with Dr Johnson on that score—going to sea is like being in prison, with the chance of being drowned.'

The old woman in the basket alighted at Nottingham. Elizabeth noticed how ruddy her cheeks were from the journey, but she seemed otherwise in good repair. Two more passengers came aboard which made it very squashed inside the coach.

It was almost midnight when they arrived at an inn near Leeds. Elizabeth could not believe how tired she was, even though she'd done nothing all day but sit. James had secured them a bed to themselves. Elizabeth had no idea what arrangements had been made for the other passengers.

Despite the lateness of the hour, the yard was full of noisy men gaming and playing skittles. Though the window was closed and curtains drawn, still they could be heard, but Elizabeth was determined nothing was going to spoil her night with James. She did a quick inspection of the bed sheets. Passably clean.

By the time the couple disrobed, the yard had gone quiet, and all that could be heard was an occasional owl calling. Elizabeth watched her husband. First he took off his wig and loosened his hair so that it hung down around his shoulders like kelp floating on the tide. She kept pace with him, taking off her hat and unpinning her hair. They watched each other in the candlelight, the flame glittering in their eyes. When James was disrobed completely, she could see, as she had done on the first night of his return, where the South Seas wind and sun had burnished his skin. The South Seas sun still shone in him, he had brought it back, a gift for Elizabeth. His chest and back, his arms, everywhere save the paler skin which his breeches had covered.

Elizabeth's tiredness seemed to have been overtaken by a stronger force. To feel the warmth of the South Seas captured in his skin, to hold him close and feel his beating heart, to hear the quickness of his breath as his desire for her rose. So many times James had played his fingers on Elizabeth's skin, and now it was her turn. She felt the leathery texture of his arms, drew her fingers up to his shoulders and down the long soft curve of his back to the hard mounds of his buttocks, a body formed by farm work, heaving coal, climbing ropes. His eyes were closed, the lashes brushing his cheeks, the candlelight giving them an even greater sweep.

There were no murmured tales of the South Seas that night, of the voyage that rose like a tide from his chest and rode on his breath, the words gliding and forming into stories like a flock of birds rising into a sunlit sky. It was time for their bodies, their skin to tell stories of longing and desire finally fulfilled.

James and Elizabeth awoke to the sounds of the coach being made ready for the day's travel, and the horses whinnying. They dressed and ate a quick breakfast, staying inside the warmth of the inn till the driver called, 'All aboard that's coming aboard.'

The fat lady had been replaced by a vicar and an elderly couple who were going to Newcastle, although they appeared altogether too frail to make such a long journey. Elizabeth sat next to James, her skirts billowing over his lap no matter how much she tried to contain them.

After two hours travelling, the day rose and with it a wind. 'An easterly,' said James. 'It will bring rain, no doubt.'

It did. They'd hardly gone a mile when the wind really churned up, and brought squalls of rain.

Inside the coach it was atrocious, with Elizabeth being thrown into the lap of the vicar on more than one occasion. She felt nauseous and fearful as the wind threw them this way and that, the rain beating so hard on the windows, Elizabeth was sure they would shatter.

She felt as though she were in a barrel, a butter churn perhaps, being stirred round and round, her head hitting the ceiling one minute, then diving for the floor of the coach the next.

James seemed not the least bit perturbed for himself, and Elizabeth understood that he would have faced much worse at sea. His concern was for her and the other passengers, bringing his arm around his wife to cushion the blows, while bracing his other arm across the corner of the carriage so that the vicar could save himself from lurching forwards.

Elizabeth spared a thought for the driver and the horses that baulked against the wind and the rain, trying to run off the road, away from the weather. She could hear the driver cracking his whip and cursing at the animals.

But by nightfall the storm had abated and they reached the white-walled city of York without mishap. It was Christmas Eve. Elizabeth lay on the bed in the Black Swan Inn. It was hours before the movement of the coach left her bones.

Elizabeth caught her husband's quickening of interest the closer they got to their destination.

'You see how it changes? You see the roll of the moors?' James was like a young puppy sniffing the air, finding the familiar smells of home in it.

Elizabeth looked out the window at the gaunt trees, ploughed fields giving way to thick clumps of gorse.

It was mid-afternoon when the coach deposited Elizabeth and James outside the dark-timbered Royal Oak, Great Ayton. Word spread quickly that James Cook had returned to his boyhood village. Before long a small crowd had gathered. Elizabeth was thankful to see Commodore Wilson's footman come forward and show them to the carriage. They wouldn't have been able to carry all that luggage to the Wilsons'. Elizabeth was so tired she could barely even walk.

The carriage crossed the Leven River, and near All Saints Church turned up the yew-lined driveway, so smooth after miles of rutted roads, leading to Ayton Hall. Elizabeth wondered what the upkeep of such a grand residence might be. Tax on the front windows alone would amount to twenty-eight shillings, to say nothing of the rest of the ochre-washed building.

They came to a halt at the porticoed entrance to the manor which, up till a few months ago, had been home to Thomas Skottowe. Elizabeth caught the intent look on her husband's face as he alighted, the squaring of his shoulders. She saw in his expression the boy approaching the house, and now the man. It was only for an instant, in the pause before he helped Elizabeth out of the carriage and cast a look towards the driver taking care of their luggage.

To come to this house through the front door, as a guest and friend of the host, and not cap in hand at the back door, the boy ready to do his master's chores, he had circumnavigated the globe.

Commodore Wilson's brother-in-law, Ralph Jackson, the Admiralty secretary, was also visiting. There would be much talk of navy matters.

Tired though she was, Elizabeth found a second wind in the flurry of greetings. Great interest was shown in the Maori club that James had brought as a gift for the commodore. This led on to a discussion of cannibalism. Then the commodore, who on his final voyage with the East India Company had discovered the Pitt passage to China, turned to more nautical matters. How did the *Endeavour* handle herself? How did the collier compare to a sloop, say, or a frigate? Elizabeth and Mrs Wilson left the men to their port and tobacco.

Elizabeth smiled as snippets of their conversation wafted out of Commodore Wilson's library. It was the proposed second voyage that was the subject of conversation now.

Mrs Wilson bent over her embroidery hoop and Elizabeth to hers. Elizabeth's held a large damask serviette, part of a set into which she was working her initials, with a number on each serviette so that it could be easily identified at the laundry. She had other embroideries in progress at home, but had deemed the serviettes, with the small amount of work they required, to be most suitable for travelling.

She had already completed the 'E.C.' and was embroidering the number 9 in cross-stitch using grey-blue thread. She could hardly keep her eyes open, yet felt that she should at least keep Mrs Wilson company. Elizabeth noticed that she'd missed a square in her work and made a note to check the piece in the morning when she was refreshed.

'It's a lonely life being married to a man who is married to the sea,' said Mrs Wilson. 'But one day, like the commodore, Mr Cook will retire.'

Elizabeth could hear the excitement in her husband's voice as he discussed the second voyage. He sounded a long way from retirement.

Lonely was not the word Elizabeth would have chosen. Her husband's absences were many things—anxiousness, longing, frustration—but not lonely. She carefully pulled thread through a stitch.

Elizabeth had two husbands—the one who spent months at a time with her, with whom she had come to Yorkshire; and the imagined husband, the one who was by her side when the one in the next room was away. The one who was there in every breath she took, who inhabited her body as much as she did herself. The husband made of air, and memories and yearning, who nestled into the bed beside her at night.

'And then,' said Mrs Wilson, 'when they are at home, they are under your feet all the time.' She snipped at her thread with a dainty pair of scissors.

Elizabeth smiled. It did suddenly seem crowded when James returned, not only with his presence in the Mile End house but with the relics and curiosities, charts and maps, the very air of excitement he brought with him. Even at home he was often out, catching up with news and writing letters in Will's coffee house, visiting the Admiralty, the Navy Board, the docks. He was never under her feet enough.

COOK COTTAGE

The door opened a crack and Elizabeth saw an eye looking out, a dull watery eye, the centre of a ripple of wrinkles. 'It's James,' her husband announced. 'And Elizabeth.' The door opened fully and Elizabeth saw an older, stooped version of her husband. He had not come to meet them when they had alighted from the coach. 'He is almost eighty,' James had explained. Nevertheless, he greeted Elizabeth warmly and held her hand in his.

James Cook senior bid them come in and shuffled after them in his house slippers. 'Kettle's on the fire. I've got tea.' Elizabeth heard the roll of the moors in her father-in-law's voice, and a hint of the Scottish brogue he'd carried with him across the border.

They walked along a short hallway of red stone floor and whitewashed walls. There was a dark timber wall-stand from which hung tools—a shovel, two pitchforks, a mallet. All cleaned and well-oiled, in as perfect condition as the day they were made.

Elizabeth could see here the same pride and care for instruments and tools that James had.

They entered the main room of the house, where a thin fire licked the bottom of a cast-iron kettle hanging from a hook. 'Set yourself down, girl,' James senior said to his daughter-in-law, and patted a place on the bench built into the wall beside the fire. Its twin jutted out from the opposite wall.

Elizabeth sat down, taking care to tuck her skirts away from the fire, meagre though it was. The room was furnished with an oblong table, chairs, a sideboard with drawers, and a shelved display case, in which were arranged pewter plates. Elizabeth noticed one pewter plate by the fire, with a smear of hard gravy still visible although an attempt had been made at wiping it clean. At the end of the room were two tiny bedchambers, with a single bed in each. In one of the chambers Elizabeth could see a framed embroidery sampler but it was too far away for her to read the text.

'How are you, Father?' James asked.

'Father is it? Too big to call me Da, are yer?' said the old man.

Elizabeth felt anxiety knot in her chest. It's nothing, she told herself, just that father and son haven't seen each other for a long time, not since the Seven Year War, not since she and James married.

Elizabeth shivered. She wanted to put a few more lumps on the fire, but it was not her place to do so. James senior didn't seem to feel the cold. His woollen jacket must have provided enough warmth, even though there were buttons missing and his shirt poked out in those places.

'How are yer wee bairns?' At times his accent thickened so much Elizabeth could hardly understand him.

'Not so wee any more,' answered James. 'Jamie's just turned eight and Nat's not far behind.'

'Are yer hungry? Would yer like oatcakes? It were James's favourite when he were a lad.'

James looked away. It was less a question of oatcakes having been his favourite than that was all there was.

Elizabeth didn't want the old man going to any trouble. 'We've had breakfast,' she said. 'But we'd welcome a cup of tea, wouldn't we, James?'

The tea things were ready by the fire. It was as if in all the house, James senior had reduced his living to this small area beside the hearth. He picked up a thick cloth, lifted the great kettle off its hook, and started pouring steaming water into the pot. Both Elizabeth and James made a slight forward movement, as if to help, but the old man's pride stopped them short. James was about to say something, but didn't. Elizabeth looked at her husband. This was his father's house but James didn't appear to feel at home in it.

'I brought these clubs back from New Zealand, to give to Mr Skottowe,' James said suddenly, taking the items out of his bag. The polished clubs with carved nobs lay there inert, the old man paying them scant attention.

'Mr Skottowe be dead,' said James senior.

'Yes, I know,' said James quickly. He took the cup of tea offered by his father, a puddle of liquid spilling into the saucer as the old man's hands shook. 'We are staying in his house, Commodore Wilson lives there now.'

'Nineteen years I worked for Mr Skottowe,' the old man said into the air. 'He gave me this land, and I built this house. For Grace and the children. Our own proper house, built with my own hands.'

James looked at Elizabeth, then at his father. 'I'm sorry to have missed him,' he said in a low voice.

'You have a lot to be grateful to Mr Skottowe for,' the old man said to his son, as if finally noticing he was there.

'Yes, Da,' said James.

'He paid for your schooling, gave you a start.' The old man leant towards Elizabeth. 'It were my doing as well,' he said. He took a slurp of tea, wiping his chin on his sleeve afterwards. 'The hiring fair at Stokesley.'

Elizabeth of course knew of the hiring fairs, not particularly the one at Stokesley, but in the season, through Michaelmas to Martinmas at the end of the year, hiring fairs were held all over the country. Elizabeth loved fairs, but there was something about seeing farmhands and dairymaids, shepherds and grooms, all lined up, which reminded her of a slave market.

Those looking for work would come in their best clothes — for some reason Elizabeth always felt touched by the effort they'd made — and each wearing the badge of their occupation — the milkmaids a tuft of cow hair, the shepherds with their crook, maids with mops. Then the masters or, more often than not, someone sent by them, would trawl along the lines, looking them up and down — the fresh-faced young ones, and the older hands, who looked out anxiously from weather-beaten faces, hoping that they would be picked out again, hoping for another year's work, that the man would overlook the bent back and prefer experience to youthful strength.

'It was Mr Skottowe himself who chose me,' James senior told Elizabeth. 'I had the boys by my side, letting him know that he was getting not only myself but strong workers in them.' He took another slurp of tea, with no spillage this time. 'James was eight year old,' he said, glancing at his son, 'but a big strong boy who was never afraid of a day's work. Curious too, he was, always asking questions.'

James shifted uncomfortably in his seat.

'What sort of questions?'

'About the stars, about why the leaves came off the trees in the autumn.' Elizabeth remembered her own questions to Mama and Mr Blackburn. 'Perhaps you can tell me, son,' said James senior, 'now that you have circumnavigated the globe. In all your travels, did you find out why leaves come off the trees in autumn?'

'It might please Elizabeth to look over the house, to see what a good job you made of it,' said James, veering away.

'Aye, we did a good job of it. The first and only house that was ours. Built with my own hands,' he repeated, holding out big gnarled hands, displaying them like tools. When the old man saw how they trembled, he brought them down and gripped the bench he was sitting on to still them. 'You show Elizabeth. The stairs are a trouble to my legs.'

Upstairs the house seemed to be made of ice. It was so cold that when Elizabeth touched the white walls she felt her fingers sticking to them. Everything was neat and tidy, but covered in dust. Cobwebs were visible in the corners. It had been a long time since anyone had been up here. Directly at the top of the stairs was a tiny bedchamber, with a narrow bed and a wooden trunk beside it. A small window let in a square of the dark grey day.

'I used to sleep in here when I came to visit.'

'Such a tiny bed,' Elizabeth commented.

'Aye,' said James, 'but no smaller than a bunk in a ship's cabin.'

They came into the main upstairs room which appeared to be a living room and bedroom combined. There was a dark timber matrimonial bed, a round table and three chairs, all with a film of dust.

James picked up a carding brush which was lying beside a square spinning frame. 'My mother used this,' he said softly. 'She did the spinning. Margaret and Christiana too, even when they were little girls. This is the same brush, the same frame.'

Elizabeth came and gently placed her hand on James's arm. She remembered that day full of promise beneath the Fairlop oak, when he'd said, one day perhaps you'll see the house. She had no idea then how far from this house James would travel. How far he would now have to travel back to it.

'With me and my father, Margaret and Christiana are the only two that survive. John, my older brother, lived to be twenty-two. All the others, Jane, William and the two Marys, died as little bairns. Jane was the same age as our Eliza.' He gazed at something in the corner on the other side of the bed. It was a baby's cot, shaped like a boat with a little roof at the head. Its sad emptiness brought tears to Elizabeth's eyes, for the babies who had occupied such a place and gone to early graves.

Elizabeth and James went to the window and looked out at the barren winter landscape. Even in the midst of life there was death. Elizabeth had first heard the saying in church, then read it with Frances in the Book of Common Prayer. And she had lived it with her babies, when her own heart, her whole being, shattered like ice under a hammer. Yet it must be. And the sadness must be. That is what it was to be in the ebb and flow of life.

From the upstairs window they could see Roseberry Topping, its mound offering itself to the sky like a breast, with a darker aureole at its point.

'Many's the time I climbed the Topping,' said James, his voice brightening. 'All of us boys did. We raced to see who could get there first. I liked to go up alone too. Stand at the top, breathless from climbing, turning my face to the four winds. You could practically see the whole of Yorkshire from up there.'

'And the sea,' said Elizabeth.

'Yes,' said James. 'And the sea.'

On the Sunday they went to church. After prayers, after the reading and the singing, with the musicians playing in the back of the church, accompanied by the cooing pigeons who had taken refuge in the rafters, James, Elizabeth and James senior walked in the grounds of All Saints, along the path past the tombstones sticking up like teeth, till they found the one that marked the final resting place of Grace Cook, James's mother.

It had been icy cold in the stone church, and despite kneeling on a hassock, Elizabeth had felt the cold snaking its way into her bones. She had watched as her father-in-law struggled to kneel down, taking a grip so firm on the back of the pew in front of him that the candles spluttered in their holders. She kept her hands together in prayer and resisted her urge to help him.

They stood by the grave, flecks of snow silently falling from the sky onto their shoulders. 'Grace Cook, died 15 February, 1765, aged 63 years'.

It was the old man who spoke first, and then it was so quietly that Elizabeth couldn't be sure whether he was addressing them or the Almighty. 'When I came across the border,' he said, 'all those years ago, a keen young man, as keen as young James here, to try my fortune in a new place, my mother blessed me. "God send you grace," she said, holding my hands.' He paused for a moment, oblivious to the snow settling onto his hat like frozen tears. 'I did not know that the Almighty would send me Grace in the form of that beautiful young girl, and she graced my life till the day she died.'

The three of them bowed their heads before Grace, before the memory of her, and when Elizabeth finally looked up, her father-in-law was staring into the distance, his cheeks wet. Elizabeth could not tell whether they were tears or melting snow.

He made a noise in his throat, and looked in the direction of Ayton Hall just beyond the row of yew trees. 'I suppose you'll be going back to the big house now,' he addressed James and Elizabeth.

'We will see you home first, Da,' said James.

'You go on back to Mr Skottowe's,' said James senior. 'I can find my own way home.'

When James took a horse and rode across the moors to the coast, Elizabeth walked through the village, past the Postgate school where James had his schooling, until she found herself once again standing in front of the doorway of the two-storey brick and timber house. On the lintel above was engraved '1755' and the initials 'G' and 'J'. Grace and James. A thick mat of ivy adorned one wall. In the tangle of the garden Elizabeth identified medicinal herbs, onions that had gone to seed, a few meagre rosebushes. She could see the work that had been put into it once upon a time, but now it appeared as if the garden had been left to its own devices. No doubt it had been Grace's domain.

She invited herself in to sit by the thin fire with her father-in-law, and told him of Jamie and Nat, what big strong boys they had become. She could see the resemblance between James the grandfather, James the father and James the son, three links in a chain of being that stretched back for years and that would, God willing, stretch far into the future, after their individual lives were done.

The boys' grandfather nodded and smiled. Elizabeth placed another lump of coal on the fire.

'It were very small, the clay biggin at Marton,' said her father-in-law. 'Young James would be outside as much as he could, in all weathers. There were a big tree outside the cottage, and barely could the bairn walk than he was climbing it. He's climbed a long way now, hasn't he?'

Elizabeth smiled. While she nodded and encouraged his stories, she found herself with the little dustpan and broom, sweeping up the dust from the fire. Then she polished the table. He didn't seem to mind. ''Tis a long time since this house has felt a woman's touch,' he said, watching her. He spoke of Grace, the mother-in-law Elizabeth never knew, and the sisters, Margaret and Christiana, whom she'd never met. But most of all he talked of James. 'My boy has made his mark on the world, hasn't he?' he said.

'That he has,' answered Elizabeth.

'Our boy's done well, Grace,' said James.

James returned, hair streaming and cheeks ruddy from the horse-ride. Standing by the fire, rubbing his hands together, he told the Wilsons of the agreeable time he'd spent with the Walkers.

That night in their room, he turned to Elizabeth and said: 'I saw Mrs Prowd too. You remember, the Walkers' housekeeper who first gave me a little table and a candle to study by.' Elizabeth remembered. 'John had obviously instructed his servants in the etiquette of greeting a circumnavigator. They were all polished as new pennies, soberly dressed in Quaker black. But Mrs Prowd, ah dear old Mrs Prowd, stooped and shorter than I remember, she broke rank and I was the apprentice boy once again. She came forward, threw her arms around me and said: "Oh honey, James! How glad I is to see thee!" And I declare, Elizabeth, there was a tear in my eye at the sight of her.'

Elizabeth let her husband enjoy his memories, then asked: 'Did you speak to Margaret?'

James nodded. Now it was his turn to be quiet.

'Are you worried he won't take to it?'

'He's a proud man.'

'He's proud of you too.'

'That's as may be,' murmured James. 'He travelled, came across the border seeking a better life. I followed his example, but I fear I've gone too far for him. He'd be happier if I'd become a shopkeeper in Staithes, or kept up the Whitby–London run on the colliers, not sailed to the South Seas in one of them.'

Although it was already New Year by the time James returned from the coast, they celebrated Hogmanay with James's father, bringing food and Scotch whiskey. The old man was as animated as they had seen him, and though a sober man, proposed almost as many toasts as Mr Blackburn had in the old days. James stoked the fire up, and while his father said it was wasteful, he clearly enjoyed the warmth of the blaze and of their company. It seemed the right moment to bring up the subject of the old man's future.

James and Elizabeth had already discussed the matter. Elizabeth had said she did not mind bringing him back to Mile End, caring for him. 'The journey alone would probably kill him,' James had said. Now, having made the journey from London to Yorkshire, Elizabeth knew full well what he meant. 'Far better that he go to Redcar and live with Margaret and her husband.'

'What do you think, Da?' James said after he had put the idea forward.

The old man stirred sugar into his tea, circling round and round, long after the sugar was dissolved. 'With Margaret and Mr Fleck?' he said. He slowly nodded his head. 'You have all gone from here, there is no-one left. I can bring my tools. Chop wood for them.'

'And more,' said James, seeing the path his father wanted to take. 'There'll be lobster pots to mend for James Fleck.' He was going to add that the sea air would be good for him, but instead continued in the way of service. 'Plenty of other jobs as well. Three bairns already and no doubt more on the way, they could do with an extra set of strong hands.' And so it was agreed.

Elizabeth watched her husband writing to Captain William Hammond, from whom the Navy Board had purchased the two colliers destined for the second voyage.

Ayton, 3 January, 1772

Dear Sir,

I am sorry to acquaint you that it is now out of my power to meet you at Whitby nor will it be convenient to return by way of Hull as I had resolved upon but three days ago. Mrs Cook being but a bad traveller I was prevailed upon to lay that route aside on account of the reported bad state of the road and therefore took horse on Tuesday morning and road over to Whitby and returned yesterday. Your friends at that place expect to see you every day. There is only myself to blame for not having the pleasure of meeting you there. I am informed from Lieut. Cooper that the Admiralty have altered the names of the ships from Drake *to* Resolution *and* Raleigh *to* Adventure, *which in my opinion are much properer than the former. I set out for London tomorrow morning, shall only stop a day or two at York.*

I am with great regard
Dear Sir
Your Most Obliged
Humble Servant

James Cook

Already the great wheels were in motion, even during this holiday. Changing the names of the colliers was a matter of diplomacy. *Drake* and *Raleigh* would leave a sour taste with the Spanish, who were already piqued by the idea of British ships in the Pacific Ocean, which they seemed to think of as their domain.

James was sitting at Commodore Wilson's escritoire, quite at home. He had the ability to appear at home anywhere, except perhaps in his father's house. But there lay memories, ghosts that inhabited every corner of the cottage except the hearth, the place of the still living. Elizabeth remembered how she had felt when she saw Mama grow so quickly old, as if sands were shifting under her, she too being dragged out on the tide of Mama's life. But James did not talk of such things. Instead he said, when they were packing up to leave: 'I am proud to be his son. If I am the man I am today, it's his doing.' He sounded almost as if he were laying blame. 'He started as a farm labourer and ended by being Mr Skottowe's bailiff. He taught me the value of hard work, by God he did.'

Elizabeth could not face the thought of a journey to Hull, of spending even more time on those dreadful roads than was absolutely necessary. She was once again with child. It was early days but she could feel it in her bones.

When they were about to set off, she asked Mrs Wilson for some raisins to take on the voyage. 'To settle the stomach.' Mrs Wilson gave her a knowing look. Yes, smiled Elizabeth.

Mrs Wilson hugged her. 'God grant you an easy lying-in and a child in good health.'

Then the Cooks set out, on the long road back to London.

Mr Kendall's Clock

Now that they were back, Yorkshire seemed like a dream, a shared one but a dream nevertheless. Elizabeth had mementoes from the journey—some hand-tooled knick-knacks for the boys from their grandfather, and a tablecloth embroidered by Grace. 'Does your South Seas voyage seem like a dream?' Elizabeth asked her husband.

'A dream?'

'Now that you are returned home.'

'The house is full of things I have brought back; your tapa cloths, clubs, axes, fish hooks. They are solid, they are real. I will go again soon. What can I bring back to show you that it is not a dream?'

Elizabeth sighed. She knew that it had actually happened, that those places whence the relics came existed, and that they were peopled with men, women and children, plants and animals, all the Lord's creations. She knew, but that is not what she felt.

Yorkshire was always there, whether she was in it or not. But now back in London it had become a memory, with the same quality as a remembered dream or a story she had made up. The only difference being that the relics of dreams existed solely in her mind.

James was lying on his back, idly stroking her hair. 'Are you in the South Seas already, my dear?' she asked.

She felt his hand caress her forehead. 'In the icy high latitudes as well,' he replied. 'If a Great South Land exists, it will be towards the Pole.'

'Perhaps it exists only in the dreams of men,' Elizabeth said.

'In that case, it is a continent that ships won't find. Other vessels are necessary for travelling into men's dreams.'

As Elizabeth had a real and imagined husband, so James had a real and an imagined voyage—one he sailed by ship, and the other in his mind. Elizabeth turned towards her husband. He was looking at the ceiling, imagining the islands he had visited, mapping onto the ocean of ceiling the direction of the prevailing winds, the currents and tides, the route they would take, seeking out the stars that would guide him.

'Where are you at this very moment?' Elizabeth asked.

'With you, my dear. With you.'

Preparations for the second voyage had been proceeding, even when the Cooks were in Yorkshire: the colliers had been selected and were being fitted out. The latest scientific instruments would be on board, and there was particular interest in Mr Kendall's remarkable clock, which would also make the voyage.

Elizabeth recalled alehouse talk, Mr Blackburn saying that lack of a reliable method of ascertaining longitude was the greatest problem for a seafaring nation like Britain and, indeed, for the rest of the world. Many lives had been lost at sea, valuable cargoes too, because dead reckoning did not suffice.

Ascertaining longitude depended on a simple calculation in degrees, based on the time at a given point—say, Greenwich—and the time in the world where the ship was. A reliable clock was all that was needed. But what would it take to make a clock that would keep regular time, in blistering cold and blistering heat, through the vicissitudes of ship life and in all weathers? It took the inventive genius of a Yorkshireman, Mr John Harrison, and, according to the man himself, 'fifty years of self-denial, unremitting toil and ceaseless concentration'.

'I knew the mechanics would win out,' said Cousin Charles, unbuttoning his waistcoat to allow more room for Elizabeth's delicious roast beef. His watchmaking business had grown into quite an enterprise, and he had grown accordingly.

Though there had been many outlandish schemes put forward to ascertain longitude, in the end it basically came down to the astronomers versus the mechanics. The lunar method, practised by the astronomers, required mathematical skill and even then could not always be relied upon. There were several days in the monthly turning when the moon was so close to the sun that it wasn't visible at all, and measurements couldn't be made. James, although a master of the lunar method, was in favour of any solution to the longitude problem. But not everyone was. Not surprisingly, the royal astronomer, Nevil Maskelyne, was an advocate of the lunar method, and though Mr Harrison's various timepieces—there were four generations of them—proved in their trials to be astonishingly accurate, the Board of Longitude resisted giving him the prize money. 'That poor fellow, Harrison, has devoted his life to it,' said Charles. 'For years the board has denied him what's rightly his.'

'A delay due also to Harrison's own sense of perfection,' added James. 'But he has succeeded. The clock going aboard the *Resolution* is indeed a pretty piece of work.'

Mr Harrison's first three timepieces, beautiful and efficient in themselves, were large, boxy affairs, but H-4, or rather K-1 as James referred to it, a copy having been made by Mr Kendall of Furnical's Inn Court in London, resembled more a flat disc. Three other timepieces, designed and made by John Arnold of the Adelphi, would also be aboard but all the attention was on Mr Harrison's creations.

Charles, knowing that Elizabeth would be interested in the decorative aspects of the timepiece, said: 'Small enough to fit into your hand. On the back are engraved curlicues as fine as any of your embroideries, Cousin.'

Elizabeth smiled, acknowledging his compliment.

'Friction-free,' said James, 'and therefore requiring no cleaning or lubrication, rust-free, no pendulum. Steel and brass combined in such a way that each metal compensates for the expansion or contraction of the other.'

With James so successfully returned from the first voyage, no expense was spared for the second. Two ships this time, much to Elizabeth's relief. James would have all the latest inventions, including timepieces, and whatever else he wanted. However, in the mind of the public, and especially the newspapers, this was to be once again Mr Banks's voyage.

Mr Banks himself was of the same opinion. He had grand plans, and plenty of money to turn them into reality. Nevertheless, he still found time to have a collar engraved for the goat which had eaten its way through the back garden of the Cooks' home. The collar had a distich composed in Latin by Dr Johnson which ran: 'The globe twice circled, this the Goat, the second to the nurse of Jove, is thus rewarded for her never-failing milk.'

'The goat appears to be almost as celebrated as Banks himself,' commented Elizabeth when James told her that the gentleman was dropping around to deliver the collar.

Despite her expectations, Elizabeth was charmed. Joseph Banks's enthusiasm far outweighed his pomposity, great though the latter was.

'Oh, how glorious would it be to set my heel upon the Pole! And turn myself round 360 degrees in a second,' he declared.

He was young, the publicity had gone to his head, that was all.

Jamie and Nat laughed to see Mr Banks turn himself around. Of course, now they wanted to go to the Pole and turn themselves around. 'And what will your dear mother do, with all her men away?' Mr Banks said to them.

Though discussion of the *Resolution* itself was diplomatically avoided during the visit, Elizabeth knew that the alterations being done to accord with Mr Banks's wishes were straining the friendship as well as the ship. James had chosen the collier for a voyage of geographical discovery, and although larger than the *Endeavour*, it was never intended to be a passenger ship. But Mr Banks's entourage was growing daily. There were to be seventeen people in his party this time, including Dr Solander once again; the well-known physician and man of science from Edinburgh, Dr James Lind; painter Zoffany; and a host of others, including two horn players. Then there were the dogs, and a staggering amount of paraphernalia.

James was against the massive alterations, as was Hugh Palliser, but Mr Banks blithely bypassed the Navy Board and went directly to his friend, Lord Sandwich. The waist of the collier was heightened, an additional upper deck built, along with a raised poop to accommodate James, who had given over the great cabin, and that of the captain, to Mr Banks.

'You are prepared to do all this for the sake of his friendship?' Elizabeth asked.

'It matters not where I sleep,' said James. 'I have not grown so used to comfort that I've forgotten what it is to sleep on a mattress under a counter, as I did in Mr Sanderson's shop.'

'But the ship,' said Elizabeth, 'won't it be top-heavy?'

James sighed. 'Indeed. By my reckoning, and that of Hugh and other members of the Navy Board. But Sandwich has approved the alterations. We can only hope for the best. There will be a full trial of her, then we shall see what we shall see.'

When Elizabeth and the boys went to look over the *Resolution* she was astonished at the numbers of people coming aboard, milling around, gawping from the waterside. Not just workmen and people who had business on the ship but the whole of London, it seemed. Gentlemen and ladies, people of all ranks and walks of life.

To take best advantage of the season and the prevailing winds, James was hoping to set sail in March. Medals had already been struck by Matthew Boulton, for distribution throughout the islands of the South Seas, bearing the impression of the *Resolution* and the *Adventure*, and the words 'Sailed from England March MDCCLXXII', but by mid-March there was still no fixed departure date.

James started ranging around the house as he had after that last season in Newfoundland, getting tetchy at the slightest little thing, at the crowdedness of the house, till finally Elizabeth said: 'It will be considerably more crowded aboard the *Resolution*, with Mr Banks and his entourage, with the stores and the precious instruments. If you find the house crowded, perhaps you should go into the garden. The goat, the famous goat who has twice circumnavigated the globe, appears to be quite happy there. I do not see her scratching itchy feet.'

Husband and wife stood facing each other, a distance between them, as if they were engaged in a duel.

James was the first to drop his weapon. 'As you wish.' Before Elizabeth could say anything, he grabbed his jacket and walked out of the house, by the back door, heading into the fields.

Elizabeth watched his determined stride, the swing of his arms, felt the tug on her heartstrings as he walked away.

She busied herself by scouring a pot. Vigorously. What was said was said. She remembered the conversation with Mrs Wilson at Great Ayton, about her husband being under her feet. When James was away and Elizabeth's longing intense, she thought she could never have enough of him, that for him to be at home was all she wanted. Now, though she could hardly admit the thought even to herself, she also was waiting for a departure date.

Elizabeth had cleaned the surface dirt off the pot but kept on scrubbing. She felt somehow slighted by his restlessness, as if he could not bear to spend more than a few months at a time with her and the boys. She looked at the pot and sighed. Her scrubbing had been so vigorous that she'd scratched the brass. Now she would have to go over it again with a soft cloth.

The back door opened. James stood there, a silhouette against the low misty sky that flurried over the fields, obliterating all trace of where he had been. 'I am sorry, my dear.' Elizabeth put the pot aside, wiped her hands on her apron. She barely came up to her husband's shoulder, yet in this moment she felt much taller. 'I shouldn't be bringing my concerns about the *Resolution* into our home. This is my haven, my safe port, no place for the tempests that have nothing to do with you.' He came right in and sat at the table, wiped his hands over his face as if to erase his worries. 'I fear the ship will never sail with Joseph's alterations.'

Elizabeth put her irritation aside when she saw how weary James was. She gently laid her hand on his shoulder. 'There is still the trial. Your good judgment will win out.'

At the end of March, after a few days of looking poorly, the goat died. No-one knew what the problem was—perhaps an organism in the soil—but James said: 'She is a sea-goat, she fretted for the ocean. Our back garden, with plenty of land and the attention of all of London, is not what nourished her.'

He could well have been speaking about himself. He had the sea in his veins and he must return to it. Elizabeth thought of pelicans, albatrosses, of the great seabirds, how awkward they were on the land, how graceful in flight. She had grown up on the river, knew that seamen were of a different ilk to landmen, it showed in their clothes, in their gait, in everything about them. And she was wedded to such a man. He was a sea creature, he could only breathe for a certain time on land and then he must return.

Swayed by Mr Banks's charm, his enthusiasm, station in life, the great prestige he brought to this voyage, the fortune which he invested liberally in the undertaking and the high public esteem in which he was held, the Navy Board and the Admiralty, under Lord Sandwich, had momentarily forgotten their better judgment and been swept along in the gentleman's wake.

The consequences of it were brought home with a thud when, in May, the *Resolution* was finally trialled. She was top heavy, and on the point of capsizing a short way down the river. Mr Cooper, the first lieutenant, agreed with James, saying that in its present condition, the *Resolution* was 'an exceeding dangerous and unsafe ship'. Even Mr Clerke, ready as ever for adventure, wrote to Mr Banks: 'By God I'll go to Sea in a Grog Tub, if desir'd, or in the *Resolution* as soon as you please; but must say I think her by far the most unsafe Ship I ever saw or heard of.'

James had waited long enough. He stepped in and told the Admiralty secretary that all of Mr Banks's work would have to be undone. He thought of the storm they'd met with when sailing home from Newfoundland, and how the canoe he was carrying for Joseph was heaved overboard. 'By Jove, we are in a storm again and Mr Banks's things will have to be jettisoned,' James boomed.

'What will he say?' Elizabeth asked.

'We'll see what he has to say. The *Resolution* will be returned to the way it was, Banks or no.'

Whilst Mr Banks had had greatness bestowed upon him, he was yet to grow into the personage that matched it. He was not pleased, behaving like a wilful child who could not have his way. 'My young midshipman, John Elliott,' James reported, 'says that when Joseph came to Sheerness and saw the remedial work in progress, he stamped upon the Wharf like a mad man, and instantly ordered his servants and all his things out of the Ship.'

Mr Banks wrote a rather foolish letter of self-justification to Lord Sandwich, there were questions raised in the Parliament, but the upshot of it all was that Banks retired with his tail between his legs. Lord Sandwich made no counter offers to his young friend. He would not sail on this second voyage of discovery, nor Solander, Zoffany, the horn players or any of his entourage.

By the third week of June the *Resolution* was ready. A father and son duo—John Reinhold Forster and George Forster—had replaced Banks and Solander. The astronomers aboard were Mr William Bayly, and a Yorkshireman, Mr William Wales. On his return from the voyage, Mr Wales would go on to become master at the Mathematical School at Christ's Hospital, an inspiring teacher to his pupils, one of whom was a boy called Samuel Taylor Coleridge.

The Admiralty had given James their instructions, which were more or less a written version of what he had proposed to them in the first place. He was to call in at Madeira for wine, and the Cape of Good Hope for supplies. Elizabeth could expect letters from these places. Then there would be the years of waiting, as

James sailed beyond the horizon towards the South Pole. He would explore, survey, chart, and claim lands for England.

But he had not left yet. His preparations done, he devoted the last few days to his family, to Elizabeth. Though she was heavy with child in the second half of June, husband and wife embraced tenderly, lovingly, and found ways to fulfil their desire for each other. James stroked her breasts, traced his hand over the mound of her belly, felt the movement of the child within.

'We will call him George,' said Elizabeth. 'For the king.'

'And if a girl?' asked James.

'It will be a boy,' she smiled. 'I can feel it.'

She hated seeing James leave, watching the coach pull away. The neighbours were there, the Curtises and Witherspoons, the Blades and Honeychurches, all waving and calling out their goodbyes as James's luggage was loaded and he finally climbed aboard. In that crowd of well-wishers Elizabeth felt alone. She could not share their excitement, their anticipation for the voyage ahead, but she did her best to keep a smile on her face so that when James looked back, this is what he would see, would remember.

When the coach was finally out of view Jamie and Nat went to play with the Curtis boys. Mrs Curtis invited Elizabeth in for a cup of tea but Elizabeth made excuses, said the baby made her feel tired and she needed to rest. She entered her still and empty house. It was midsummer, the longest day of the year.

On the eve of the *Resolution* and *Adventure*'s departure from Plymouth, while the chronometers were being checked then started, James Cook received news that on 8 July, a day heavy with heat, his wife had given birth to a son. He wrote to her immediately, leaving the letter to be delivered, and early in the morning of 13 July 1772 set sail, once again, for the South Seas.

THE GLASS TUMBLER

As the leaves turned burnished gold and their hold on the trees was loosened by the autumn winds, the post brought letters from Madeira. Though Mr Banks had taken himself off to Iceland, that was not the end of him. Gone but certainly not forgotten. James reported that a person had been waiting on the island of Madeira for three months and had left but three days before the arrival of the *Resolution*. The person, purporting to be a gentleman, had spent the time botanising whilst waiting for Mr Banks. As it turned out, the gentleman was a woman, by the name of Mrs Burnett.

Elizabeth smiled as she read this part of her husband's letter. Mr Banks had thought of all his creature comforts, including a female companion. She wondered what decision James would have made concerning this extra passenger if things had turned out differently and Mr Banks had been aboard.

James also wrote apropos of Mr Banks that he missed his convivial company and would write thanking him for the dried salmon he left on board, and other words which might mend the friendship.

Jamie and Nat received a letter from Cousin Isaac. Elizabeth rocked the cradle of baby George, listening to Jamie read. All on board the *Resolution* were in excellent health, although Mr Banks's replacement, Mr Forster the elder, gave cause for many frayed tempers. Isaac found him a humourless, pretentious chap who complained endlessly and had no idea of shipboard life. The captain ended a particular meeting by turning the botanist out of his cabin, and on another occasion Mr Clerke threatened to arrest him. The son, George, was more amiable, went around forever apologising for a father who was, Isaac surmised, a great burden for any son to bear. Everyone laughed at the story, and Elizabeth reflected that if an exasperating botanist was the worst of their worries, life aboard the *Resolution* was not too bad. But these were early days, and they all had a long way to go yet.

With Cousin Frances and Mr Lieber making plans to go to America, optimistic for their future life despite strained relations between the colonists and the British government, Elizabeth engaged a servant, a spinster a little older than Mrs Cook herself, by the name of Elizabeth Gates. She was a steady, homely woman who became Elizabeth's companion as well as servant. The boys liked her as well, and she accepted their jokes about gates and fences with good humour.

Elizabeth delighted in baby George. He readily took to his mother's breast and gained weight. His healthy appearance after the first month alleviated Elizabeth's fears that he would go the way of little Joseph. Elizabeth did all she could to ensure he continued to thrive, caring for him in the recommended manner, which she now knew intuitively. She saw to it that the room where he slept was well-ventilated but not draughty. When she put him in the cradle she lay him on his side, never on his back. When she tucked him in she checked that the covers were neither too heavy nor tight. Though little ones had to be kept warm, too much heat excited perspiration and weakened them.

Despite all her vigilance, when Elizabeth went to fetch him from his cradle on the first day of October, she found him dead. She had not heard him cry during the night nor make any noise at all, nor were there any marks on him. It was as if he'd simply stopped breathing.

'Wake up, little one,' Elizabeth had implored, her cheek to his nose, waiting to feel even the faintest breath. But there was none.

Elizabeth was sitting on her bed, nursing his cold little body, when Gates knocked and entered. When she saw her mistress's tear-stained face she knew immediately what had happened. 'Oh, marm,' Gates said. 'The poor little thing.' She came as close as she could to her employer but resisted the natural urge to embrace her. Instead, Gates wrung the corners of her apron. ''Tis a pity your good husband is not here.'

Elizabeth looked up, the baby still resting against her chest. 'He was not here for Joseph or Eliza. I bore those on my own and no doubt I will bear this one too.' Not here to see the children born and not here to see them die. It seemed James was only home long enough to plant his seed and then he was off again. Why did Elizabeth have to bear this grief on her own when they were his children too?

She kissed the top of the dead baby's head, felt the membrane of skin above the fragile fontanelle, and gently brushed away the tears that fell onto his downy hair. 'You would think,' said Elizabeth, 'that the grief would lessen. But it does not.' She lay down on the bed, placing the little one beside her. 'I will stay here a moment.' She could hear Jamie and Nat running around downstairs. 'Please send the boys up.' The servant stood there, reluctant to leave her mistress alone. 'Thank you, Gates, that will be all.' Elizabeth gazed at little George. Once again death had waited till James was away, then snuck in like a thief.

Elizabeth wrote to Cape Town, informing James of their loss, but the news arrived after he'd left. His last letter from that place was dated 23 November. He was heading southwards, to the ice. All aboard were in good health, the only death aboard the *Resolution* being accidental—James Smock, a carpenter's mate, had fallen into the sea whilst fitting a scuttle. When they had commended his soul to Almighty God, James had read from the Bible: 'I am the resurrection and the life, saith the Lord: he that believeth in me, though he were dead, yet shall he live; and whosoever liveth and believeth in me shall never die.'

How often it seemed Elizabeth had heard these words. She felt like a piece of crazed china, the death of each baby adding more hairline cracks. How many more would it take before she shattered completely and the life-blood spilled out of her?

Elizabeth turned back to James's letter, the last precious letter for months that would turn into years. She must cast out these thoughts, must rid herself of the expectation of more deaths. Three dead babies. Surely that was the end of it.

At Christmas, when Elizabeth proposed a toast to their father, Jamie and Nat toasted him in watered-down wine from Elizabeth's good glasses, and each thought of what he might be doing.

'Drinking from a coconut,' suggested Nat.

'No,' said Jamie, 'he's in the ice. Perhaps even at the South Pole.'

'Do they have Christmas down there?' Nat asked.

'Wherever they are, they will celebrate Christmas,' Elizabeth said, and imagined her husband drinking whiskey from the glass tumbler he'd had engraved prior to departure. It was a sturdy, heavy-bottomed tumbler with 'Resolution, Capt. Cook, 1772' etched into the glass. Elizabeth had traced her fingers over the letters, reading them with her fingertips, feeling their sharp edges.

'In any road,' said Gates, 'if I know English tars, they will all be drunk as lords and boxing each other.'

'Not Papa,' Nat begged to differ.

Not Papa. James was the captain. He would be drinking with the gentlemen, measure for measure, but he could hold his drink well and did not get sloppy as Mr Blackburn used to, or any of the seamen Elizabeth had observed at the Bell. She hadn't thought about the alehouse for years. Such a hot steamy place, redolent with the smell of tobacco and ale, salt, hempen rope and the bodies of seamen, yet in the dark brown corridor of her memories, Elizabeth reflected on it fondly.

Nat was at the window. 'Mama,' he said, 'there's enough snow to make a snowman. Can we? Can we?'

The snow had come early that year, and indeed when they all went to the window they could see the blanket of white covering not only their garden but the fields as well. It shone bright on this Christmas night. The boys ran to the back door.

'Mittens and hats first,' said Elizabeth. 'I don't want you catching your death.'

The boys hurriedly obeyed.

Gates and Elizabeth sat inside, washing the plates in a bowl of hot water, Gates carefully drying them with a soft cloth. They heard a tapping on the window and turned to see the grinning face of Nat, his warm breath fogging up the pane. 'Come out,' he mouthed, beckoning with his finger.

The washing up was just about done. Gates wiped her hands on her apron. 'Gloves and hat, marm,' she smiled to Elizabeth. Servant and mistress put on gloves and hats, while Nat grew impatient at the window.

As they moved towards the door, Nat disappeared, only to reappear the moment they stepped outside, to lob a snowball at them. Gates shrieked as the snowball hit her skirts, more in the spirit of the game than at any harm done. Elizabeth saw the next one coming and deftly turned to avoid it. 'I thought you were making a snowman. Why don't we all build one together,' she suggested, before the horseplay turned too rough.

Under the icy stars, Elizabeth, Gates, Jamie and Nat scooped up snow in their gloved hands, packing it on and tamping it down, till finally they had a snowman. They stood back admiring their creation, but there was something wrong—it lacked a face.

'I know,' said Nat, disappearing inside and returning with the bullet they'd used for bullet pudding, even though Jamie thought it was a silly game. Still, he hadn't been able to suppress a grin at the sight of his brother's face covered in flour.

Nat placed the bullet in the centre of the snowman's face, for a nose. Jamie dug in the snow and found two pebbles for its eyes. 'It looks like Dr Johnson,' said Nat, 'who wrote the poem for our goat.' Elizabeth frowned, but not too severely because indeed the snowman did look like the good doctor. She was sure he wouldn't mind, because she'd heard tell that the tall lumbering man had done an imitation of a kangaroo, the strange animal from Botany Bay with a face like a deer but the rest of its body all out of proportion, which bounded on a big thick tail. Apparently Dr Johnson had gathered his coat-tails and arranged them in a fashion to resemble the animal's pouch, had put his hands up like paws, then taken two giant hops across the room. His audience hadn't known whether to laugh or clap.

It was icy cold outside, and Elizabeth felt it even if the boys didn't. 'All right,' she said, slapping the snow off her gloves, 'time for bed.'

'He needs a hat,' said Nat as if he hadn't heard.

Elizabeth was familiar with this ploy. 'Bed,' she said firmly.

'But Mama,' protested Jamie, 'it's Christmas.'

'And good use you've made of it too. I don't see any other boys in Mile End up at this hour, do you, Gates?'

'Certainly not,' said Gates.

Once prayers were said and the boys tucked up in bed, Elizabeth poured herself another glass of wine, went upstairs with it, then took out the letters that James had written from the *Endeavour*. There was a big pile of them and she had them in separate bundles, tied together with ribbon, a different colour for each year. She savoured these letters from the first voyage, taking no more than one a week and not reading the selected one too often so that the words would appear fresh and the pleasure of anticipation would always be present.

On this Christmas night, Elizabeth selected a letter from the icy latitudes 'When the sun shines and the sky is clear,' she read, 'icebergs are a fine light blue and transparent. In dirty weather they resemble land covered with snow, the lower part appearing black.' On calm days penguins cavorted at the edges of the floating ice mountains, but when the wind increased, the swells rapidly built up and dwarfed the sixty foot bergs, breaking 'quite over them, such was the force and height of the waves, which for a few moments is pleasing to the eye, but when one reflects on the danger this occasions, the mind is fill'd with horror, for was a ship to get against the weather side of one of these islands when the sea runs high, she would be dashed to pieces in a moment'.

Elizabeth prayed there were no such winds with James now, and that it was as still at sea on this Christmas night as it was in Mile End. She read his words of love, his yearning for her, closed her eyes and imagined him sitting at the Spanish mahogany folding table, dipping the nib into the ink, writing late at night, by the lamplight, hearing the sigh of the ocean, the lap of it against the ship. She saw his furrowed brow, the scarred hand holding the pen.

With these images in her mind, Elizabeth snuffed out the candle and went to the window, looking down on the newly made snowman which stood silent sentinel in their garden of white.

It was the dead of night yet Elizabeth found herself outside, no gloves, no hat, standing in the snow in her nightdress and slippers. She wanted to feel the cold that he felt in the icy latitudes, while the core of her was warmed by desire. She gazed upwards to the stars that guided him, and she imagined herself into his hemisphere, found the place on that great cold ocean where he was, boarded the ship and glided into his cabin. Did he stir as she lay down beside him on that narrow ship's cot? He was in the high latitudes of sleep, but sailed closer to the warmth and instinctively reached an arm out for its source.

Elizabeth asked the snowman: 'Do you not think it strange that they say high latitudes when they mean the lower reaches of the world?' The snowman said nothing, merely grinned with the mouth the boys had formed on his face. Elizabeth was disappointed in Dr Johnson, he usually had an opinion on everything. Elizabeth's mind told her that high, in the sense of latitude, meant high degrees. So the nearer to the poles, the higher the degrees. But degrees were temperature as well, and when Elizabeth thought of high latitudes, her feeling was of heat, of Tahiti, of languid nights, red hibiscus flowers, islands encircled by coral, turtles and sharks.

Elizabeth was awoken from her reverie by the sound of hooves clip-clopping along the road, careful of the ice. She was freezing. She hurried inside and buried herself under the bedcovers.

It seemed like only minutes later that a persistent knocking on the door drew her up. 'Marm.'

'Yes?' Elizabeth said, pulling herself out of the grasp of sleep.

'It's unusual for you to sleep so long. I wondered if everything is all right.'

Elizabeth opened her eyes. It was daylight outside her window. On this midwinter day that meant it must be nine o'clock at least. 'I will come down presently,' Elizabeth heard herself say. It was Christmas, Boxing Day, there was not the usual traffic on the road to wake her up. That is what she told herself. She slid her feet out of bed and felt the cold floor. She'd neglected to add coal to the fire before retiring.

She sat before the mirror, preparing herself for the day. As she put a comb through her hair, droplets of ice fell onto her shoulders like diamonds in a necklace. There was a moment of suspension, between the rhythms of the day and the rhythms of the night. She had been in the high latitudes and brought their iciness back in her hair, had caught it just in time, before it melted in the routine of daily life.

In 1773 Jamie entered the Royal Naval Academy at Portsmouth, with Nat to follow the year after. It was James's wish. The academy was an undisciplined place, but no more so than Eton or any other school, and it did provide good training for naval life. Elizabeth hoped that the master, Mr George Witchell, who had worked on the observations James had made of the eclipse in Newfoundland, would take James's son under his wing. She wanted him under someone's wing if it couldn't be her own.

Ten year old Jamie was as tall as his mother, and insisted on taking the coach by himself. 'The other fellows will not have their mothers accompanying them,' he said fiercely.

'You're not to know that.' So much could happen, a coach accident, highwaymen, anything. Elizabeth knew she fretted too much but couldn't help it.

Jamie's voice was croaking like a frog, and although he tried to keep it in the lower registers, the rumbling voice of a man, every now and then the child in him would squeak a protest. 'I am almost a man. I will go as a man does,' he said.

'You will not, I hope, deprive us of the pleasure of coming to the coach stop to see you off.'

'Of course not, Mama,' said Jamie. He wanted everyone to see him go off to Portsmouth to become an officer, to see how grown-up he was. However, though it was important to young Jamie, the rest of Assembly Row virtually ignored the event, except for the Curtis boys, who had come to see him depart.

Jamie took charge of his own bag, handing it to the driver himself, engaging him in banter about the conditions of the road as if he were a seasoned traveller. Elizabeth knew that his father would be proud of him, making his way in the world—with a little help from James himself, who had entered both boys not only on the ship's list of the *Endeavour* but also the *Resolution*.

Before the coach departed, Elizabeth found a moment to give the driver a shilling, to make sure her son was looked after on the trip. 'Don't you worry, missus.' Then, as the coach was about to pull away, the driver leant down and said to Elizabeth: 'Captain Cook's son, I'd have done it for nothing, but thanks for the shilling all the same.' With that he cracked his whip and the horses lurched into action. Elizabeth's eldest son waved from the window. Death had taken three children, now life was taking the eldest.

THE STAFFORDSHIRE CHINA

On 14 July 1774, Furneaux, captain of the *Adventure*, returned to London with an islander in tow, a Tahitian by the name of Omai.

Elizabeth's first concern was for James. Why had Furneaux returned and not her husband? It was Joseph Banks who explained, in the same letter in which he asked permission to bring Omai to Mile End to meet the wife of the great captain. The *Resolution* and the *Adventure* had parted company off the New Zealand coast in October 1773, not long after young Jamie had boarded the coach for Portsmouth. As far as Furneaux knew, Captain Cook was in good health. Furneaux had been late for the November rendezvous in Ship Cove, New Zealand. The *Resolution* had already left, but Furneaux found the bottle with Cook's message that he'd set a course south-east, towards the ice.

Elizabeth went to the bedside cabinet, took out *Endeavour* letters from New Zealand, and read James's description of a country 'with valleys and hills luxuriously clothed with woods and verdure. It abounds with a great number of plants and the woods with a great variety of very beautiful birds.' James sailed and charted the coast of it, each placename telling a story—Poverty Bay, which 'afforded us no one thing we wanted', neither provisions nor water; Hawke Bay, honouring Admiral Sir Edward Hawke; Cape Turnagain; Bay of Islands; and Cape Kidnappers, where the New Zealanders kidnapped one of the Tahitians aboard the *Endeavour*.

The natives of New Zealand were the fiercest James had come across. He described the war dance they did, poking their tongues out and rolling their eyes up into their heads. They brandished their weapons and made loud grunting noises designed to send fear into the enemy. When a shot was fired, even if it felled a man, the others just kept coming. Again and again James had to win their friendship.

Elizabeth was glad that James had safely left New Zealand, especially when the *Adventure* returned with tales of a massacre. The master's mate, John Rowe, and eight men of the *Adventure* had gone in the cutter to gather greens. The next morning, when they hadn't returned, a search party was sent, assuming the worst—that the cutter had been stove on the rocks. What they found was much worse than the worst. Evidence of slaughter and cannibalism—baskets of cooked flesh, scattered shoes and clothing, and the head of Furneaux's Negro servant. It was bad enough when the *Endeavour* brought back tales of South Sea cannibalism, but this news, of natives eating not just their own kind but the flesh of Englishmen, both shocked and titillated London.

Elizabeth wondered what James would have done had it been *Resolution* men. He admired the New Zealanders, and even knowing they were cannibals had found them 'no more wicked than other men'.

James had not given Furneaux an order to follow him, merely noted his own prescribed course. Furneaux made some attempt to join the *Resolution* but by latitude 61 degrees south, finding his to be the only ship, a tired ship at that, in the lonely ocean, had taken a course directly to the Cape of Good Hope, and after making another attempt, through the ice and the fog, to arrive at Cape Circumcision, had set a course back to England.

Elizabeth admonished herself for wishing that it were her husband who had returned instead of Furneaux. Captain Furneaux had loved ones at home too. They would be as desirous to see him as Elizabeth was to see her husband. She prayed that the Almighty, and the elements, were treating James kindly and that he would return home soon.

The house was spick and span, the best china ready. Elizabeth had made the usual preparations for receiving guests though she had little idea what to expect with the imminent visit of Omai. Mr Banks himself had taken the islander under his wing, dressed him, taught him to bow and how to handle a walking stick. All of London was talking of the exotic creature. The king had presented him with a sword.

Elizabeth was dressed in her Sunday best, as was Nat. She had the kettle at boiling point, ready to serve tea, as she would any English visitor. She and Nat waited, listening for the approach of Mr Banks's carriage. With everything at the ready, mother and son played backgammon.

'Is he the one that ate Captain Furneaux's servant?' asked Nat.

Elizabeth vigorously shook the dice. 'We must not tar all islanders with the same brush. He is from Tahiti, not New Zealand. As for what happened to Captain Furneaux's servant and the others, your father would not make a judgment on the matter till he knew all the facts,' Elizabeth reminded their son.

'The South Sea islanders aren't all the same?' Nat queried. 'They speak the same language,' he insisted, knowing that Tahitians aboard the *Endeavour* had been able to interpret as the ship sailed from island to island. Except when they got to New South Wales, which seemed to be inhabited by a different breed of men altogether.

As Elizabeth watched her son take his next backgammon move, she thought of her Quaker friends and their edict that all of God's creations, every plant, every animal and, especially, every human being, deserved the same loving attention. She attended the Church of England, in St Dunstan's, but she still carried the Quaker light in her heart. She would treat the islander with the same courtesy as she would any freeborn Englishman. Yet she had a curiosity about this creature from the other side of the world. He came from a place she had only ever imagined.

'Mama,' said Nat, 'are you distracted?'

'Why?' Elizabeth asked.

'Because you threw a three and a six, but you moved a four and a six.'

Elizabeth tracked her move, found that her son was right, and adjusted it accordingly.

A jet of steam escaped from the kettle. Elizabeth removed the kettle from the fire in case it burnt dry. She had not seen Mr Banks since the business with the *Resolution* more than two years ago. He had not made reference to the matter when he sent word, asking, in the politest manner possible, if he could bring Omai to meet her.

Several coaches went by on the increasingly busy road, and finally the one they were listening for stopped. Elizabeth abandoned the game, put the kettle back on the fire, smoothed down her skirts, and waited.

Gates came into the parlour saying that Mr Banks, his sister Sophia, and a . . . gentleman were calling. Gates had been told who to expect, but still she announced the guests with a flurry and a twisting of her apron.

None of her imaginings prepared Elizabeth for the creature that stood between Mr Banks and Sophia. She heard Banks say, 'This is Omai.'

'Oh my,' said Elizabeth, taken aback.

'O-may,' Banks corrected what he thought was her pronunciation of the Tahitian's name.

Omai, dressed in velvet with white sateen and lace ruffles, and grey breeches, bowed low and said, 'How do you do, Mrs Toot. I hope very well.'

Mrs Toot? She remembered that when he had been introduced to King George the islander had said, 'How do you do, King Tosh. I hope very well.' There were sounds in the English language that he could not get his tongue around, just as there were sounds in the French language that Elizabeth found very difficult. Banks explained that the islanders lacked certain letters in their alphabet, the 'c' or the 'k', and the 's', so that Omai called Dr Solander 'Tolano'.

Ten year old Nat was the perfect little gentleman, shaking the stranger's hand vigorously and welcoming him to their house.

He was beautiful, that was the only word Elizabeth could find for him. He had a flat negroid nose with a hint around the eyes of the Orient. The combination was most pleasing. His hair was long and flowing, and he wore no wig or powder. His lips were curvy, resembling bird's wings ready for flight. His chocolate-coloured skin was smooth and had a sheen to it. Elizabeth took care not to feel that skin, to keep her hands to herself. Omai was not an exhibit in the waxworks museum. But Elizabeth couldn't help staring at this creature from beyond the horizon, though she tried her best not to make it too obvious.

'Ah,' he said, looking at the game on the table.

'It's backgammon, sir,' said Nat.

'Yes, yes,' said Omai.

Elizabeth remembered hearing that, at the Thrales' in Streatham, the islander had quickly learnt to play chess and backgammon. 'Perhaps Mr Omai would like to play,' suggested Elizabeth.

Nat sat at the table, the islander opposite him picking up the game where Elizabeth had left off. He shook the dice and watched them roll out of the container.

Whilst Nat and Omai played, Banks explained that Omai had been inoculated against smallpox, speaking of him in his presence the way a parent might speak of a small child. Elizabeth remembered the Eskimos who arrived in London in January 1773. Major George Cartwright, a fur trapper and trader, had brought them from Labrador. Large numbers of people had come to look at them, and the party seemed to enjoy their visit, but on their homeward journey, before they had even left Plymouth, they fell ill with smallpox and all but one had died.

'Yes,' continued Mr Banks, 'we took him to Dr Dimsdale's Institute at Hertford. He seemed quite affected by it, but we looked after him well—myself, Dr Solander, and my servant, James.'

'He appears to be perfectly recovered now,' said Elizabeth, falling into speaking of him in the same way. She seemed not to be able to avoid it and still carry on polite conversation with Banks.

'Tea, marm,' said Gates, bringing the cups and saucers, teapot, sugar and milk. It was the best crockery, and Elizabeth watched Omai as he accepted his tea, bowing to Gates, who blushed and began twisting her apron. Guests usually didn't bow to her. The islander had obviously been schooled in the art of drinking tea, and picked up his cup, holding it between long slender fingers.

'What a lovely set,' commented Sophia. 'Staffordshire, isn't it?' Elizabeth nodded. 'So refreshing to see blue and white china that is not willow pattern.'

Elizabeth smiled but said nothing. She was aware that Mr Banks was speaking to Omai in the islander's native tongue. It was only a few words but she fancied she could hear the sea and the wind in them. She put down her cup and offered her guests little cakes from the china plate.

She had almost bought the willow pattern, which depicted the story of two young lovers who are turned into bluebirds, but James's revelation that the story was a Wedgwood invention, no older than the plates themselves, had put her off. In the end they had purchased a dinner service made by John and William Ridgeway, from Staffordshire. It had scalloped edges and was decorated with flowers, blue on white.

Nat disappeared and returned with some of the knick-knacks James had brought back from the *Endeavour* voyage. He showed their visitor the hatchet. 'Togee,' said Omai. Then when Nat brought out the fish hooks: 'Ba.' Omai made the motion of a fish with his hand. Nat and Omai talked for what seemed hours, with inventive gestures and Omai's exotic words.

Elizabeth turned her attention to her other guests, complimenting Sophia on her rather dashing dress and pert little hat. Like her brother, Sophia remained unmarried. She was quite pretty, although there would be those who'd say her shoulders were too broad. She and her brother shared a house at 32 Soho Square, a large house with a now prodigious herbarium which Elizabeth had visited after the *Endeavour* voyage, as had half of London, to see the botanical specimens he'd collected. Elizabeth's favourite was a plant from Botany Bay whose flower resembled a bottle brush. Its dull green leaves were thin and pointy but the crimson brush itself was feathery and soft.

'*Callistemon rigidus*,' Sophia told her the botanical name. She helped catalogue her brother's specimens, and was also a collector in her own right. Apart from objects of natural history, she collected tokens that shops gave out, coins, visiting cards, books and newspaper cuttings. In particular, she kept the weather reports, and could tell you what the weather had been like on any day of the year.

Sophia could also recite over fifty different expressions for being drunk, having clipped out and memorised the list she'd found in the December 1770 issue of *Gentleman's Magazine*. 'Drunk?' she'd begin. 'The fellow is more than drunk. He's intoxicated, fuddled, flustered, rocky, tipsy, merry, as great as a lord, in for it, happy, boozy, top-heavy, chuck full, hiccius, cropsick, cup-stricken, cup-sprung, hot-headed, pot-valiant, maudlin, a little how came ye so?, groggy, in drink, in his cups, in his beer, crank, cut, cheery, cherry-merry, overtaken, elevated, forward, crooked, castaway, concerned, bosky, in his altitudes, tipperary, exhilarated, on a merry pin, half-cocked, a little in the suds, as wise as Solomon, business on both sides of the street, got his little hat on, got a drop in the eye, been in the sun, soaked his face, come home by the village, clips the King's English, keels, heels and sets.' Elizabeth was not surprised to find nautical expressions on that list.

Elizabeth collected a few newspaper clippings of her own. She went to fetch the one for Thursday 14 July 1774, concerning Captain Furneaux's return. 'Captain Furneaux brought with him a native of Otaheite, who was desirous of seeing the great king,' she read, taking pains to clearly pronounce each word for Omai, who grinned broadly.

They drank a second cup of tea, and Omai said something to Banks, who leant towards the islander, the better to hear him. Mr Banks nodded, then said: 'Omai expresses a wish to see the Cook family's *marai*. Your sacred place,' Banks explained.

'Our sacred place?' said Elizabeth.

'I expect a visit to St Dunstan's would satisfy the request,' said Sophia.

It took quite a while to walk to the church as Omai was much caressed and touched and looked at by every passer-by. He did not seem to mind in the smallest degree, and welcomed the attention as if he were born to it. Omai and Mr Banks walked in front with Nat, who pointed out to the visitor features of interest—the green where he and Jamie played cricket, or the place on the road where the stagecoach had been recently held up by highwaymen.

Sophia and Elizabeth walked behind. 'My brother deeply regrets his behaviour prior to the departure of the *Resolution*,' Sophia began. 'He's not directly expressed those regrets this afternoon, but his sincere desire is that there be no ill will between himself and your husband. And indeed yourself, Mrs Cook.'

'Mr Cook holds him in the highest regard,' Elizabeth assured Sophia. 'I believe he's written to your brother, and I dare say he misses his genial company.'

The air lightened. 'What do you think of our illustrious islander?'

Elizabeth felt an unexpected blush rise to her cheeks. 'Polite and personable,' she managed to say.

The women paused to let a horseman pass by. Up ahead Banks and Omai walked side by side. Apart from the flowing hair of Omai, from the back it was hard to tell which was the islander and which the English gentleman.

'Joseph took Omai to Yorkshire, a month or so ago. With the party was George Colman, the playwright, and his son. Young George was full of excitement when he came back, and hardly knew where to begin when I asked how he'd enjoyed the journey. At Scarborough, he not only saw the sea for the first time, but took a dip in it, from a bathing machine. Omai waded out into the tide, much colder I expect than his home waters. George waxed on about it, describing Omai as being made of mahogany, his body varnished by the gloss of the water, and "curiously veneered" the boy said.'

'Veneered?'

'Tattooed,' said Sophia. Elizabeth knew of this South Seas practice—patterns and designs fixed into the skin by means of a sharp shell, or a fish's tooth, imbued with an indelible dye. 'From the small of his back downwards with striped arches, broad and black,' Sophia elaborated.

Elizabeth could not help but look at Omai walking up ahead and imagine his indelibly decorated body beneath those fine English breeches.

Elizabeth was as naked as the day she was born. Unlike other dreams in which she found herself in such a state, she was neither embarrassed nor ashamed. She was Eve, before partaking of the apple. As completely unaware of her nakedness as the animals of the field. In her Garden of Eden trees dripped honey-scented flowers, creamy cupped pendulous flowers, with stamens thick with pollen. Brightly coloured birds adorned the trees, blue and yellow macaws. Butterflies and fireflies rose from her hair like a shower of fireworks.

A light balmy breeze moved Elizabeth through the garden to a lagoon etched in moonlight, her toes caressed by tiny lapping waves and the soft nibbling mouths of fish.

Elizabeth did not find it odd that a man appeared, clothed in English finery while she was naked. He danced to the rhythm of a drum, and with each beat took off a piece of clothing, throwing item after item into the sea where the flickering fish ate them till there was no trace of clothes at all. Elizabeth admired the line of his chest, the muscles of his arms, the buttons of dark brown nipples, his legs firmly planted in the sand, drops of water glistening on his thighs. He turned to show her his buttocks tattooed in striped arches, like the wings of birds on the willow pattern plates.

Her bones felt loose in her body, no hard or rigid parts to her, languid as the breath of warm wind which moved the coconut palms. The man was close, and now they were both in the water, lapped by its teasing ripple. Desire drenched Elizabeth, every pore of her body open to it. The man reached out his arms and enfolded her, a flash at the point of contact, but there was no sudden sensation, merely the languid desire rippling into the water. His lips parted, full generous lips, like the wings of a great bird preparing for flight. She was ready. Ready to receive his mouth, to be engulfed, like Leda, by his great wings.

When he was a hair's breadth from her, when she was about to dissolve into him, into the sea, Elizabeth woke up. Her hair was sticking to her cheeks, her heart racing. The pillow, which she was holding to her breast, was damp with sweat. She could smell James, the yeasty gamey smell of his passion, yet he was nowhere in the room. She had been dreaming. Of birds, and fish and the sea. A man. All quickly fading from her memory. Elizabeth rose and padded to the window—perhaps James was returning this very minute. She looked up and down the street, but all she saw was the soupy fog of a London morning.

In June 1775, when Elizabeth had run out of *Endeavour* letters to reread, she received a fresh one. James was in Cape Town, homeward bound. All his brave *Resolution* boys were in excellent health, and James said to tell cousin Charles that 'Mr Kendall's watch had exceeded the expectations of its most zealous advocate.'

The letter was like the first bird of spring, a sign of return. Now Elizabeth began counting the days. The Cape was thousands of miles away but it felt as if he were almost home.

With the letter James had enclosed a poem, which he 'very much valued', composed by one of the crew, Thomas Perry. A poem Elizabeth would keep with her always.

THE ANTARCTIC MUSE

It is now my brave boys we are clear of the Ice
And keep a good heart if you'll take my advice
We are out of the cold my brave Boys do not fear
For the Cape of Good Hope with good hearts we do steer

Thank God we have ranged the Globe all around
And we have likewise the south Continent found
But it being too late in the year as they say
We could stay there no longer the land to survey

So we leave it alone for we give a good reason
For the next ship that comes to survey in right season
The great fields of ice among them we were bothered
We were forced to alter our course to the northward

So we have done our utmost as any men born
To discover a land so far south of Cape Horn
So now my brave boys we no longer will stay
For we leave it alone for the next ship to survey

It was when we got into the cold frosty air
We was obliged our mittens and Magdalen caps to wear
We are out of the cold my brave boys and perhaps
We will pull off our mittens and Magdalen caps

We are hearty and well and of good constitution
And have ranged the globe round in the brave Resolution
Brave Captain Cook he was our commander
Has conducted the ship from all eminent danger

We were all hearty seamen no cold did we fear
And we have from all sickness entirely kept clear
Thanks be to the Captain he has proved so good
Amongst all the islands to give us fresh food

And when to old England my brave boys we arrive
We will tip off a bottle to make us alive
We will toast Captain Cook with a loud song all around
Because that he has the South Continent found

Blessed be to his wife and his family too
God prosper them all and well for to do
Bless'd be unto them so long as they shall live
And that is the wish to them I do give.

A Letter from Dr Solander
to Joseph Banks

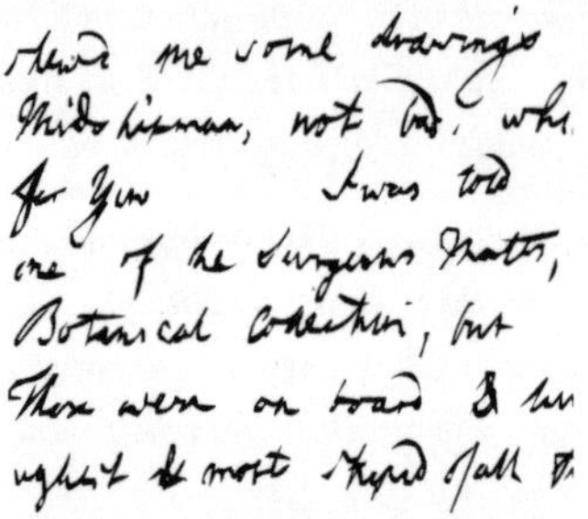

[handwritten text, partially illegible:]
...sent me some drawings... Midshipman, not Dr. who... for you... I was told one of the surgeons Mates, Botanical Collection, but those were on board & he ought to be most styped Jall D.

Two o'clock Monday—This morning Capt. Cook is arrived. I have not yet had an opertunity of conversing with him, as he is still in the board-room—giving an account of himself & Co. He looks as well as ever. By and by, I shall be able to say a little more—Give my Compliments to Miss Ray and tell her I have made a Visitation to her Birds and found them all well.

Capt. Cook desires his best Compliments to You, he expressed himself in the most friendly manner towards you, that could be; he said: nothing could have added to the satisfaction he has had, in making this tour but having had your company. He has some Birds, in Sp. V. for you &c &c that he would have write to you himself about, if he had not been kept too long at the Admiralty and at the same time wishing to see his wife.

James was back. After three years and eighteen days, after sailing more than twenty thousand miles, discovering new islands, new plant and animal species. He had gone further than any man before him, making a snail's trail across the oceans of the globe, back and forward he had swept in the icy southern latitudes, and had proved that the Great South Land, the one of riches beyond compare, existed only in the minds of men. All this. But James's proudest achievement was that of one hundred and eighteen men, he had lost only one to illness. Captain James Cook could keep his brave boys alive for months, years, and bring them safely home again.

Elizabeth had given Gates the day off so that she and James would have the house to themselves. Jamie and Nat had already seen their father in Portsmouth and would not be coming to London till Christmas. Though Elizabeth was full of excitement at the thought of seeing James again, of having him home, she told herself that after such a long voyage, after the hours spent reporting to the Admiralty, he may be exhausted. For her it would have been enough simply to be in his presence once again, to gaze upon him, embrace him tenderly, sleep by his side. But although she could see signs of strain in is face, his eyes glittered. In his urgent love-making he buried himself in her, again and again, as if he could never have enough of her.

In the days following his triumphant return, he was presented to the King at St James's Palace, then received his appointment as Fourth Captain at Greenwich Hospital, effectively a pension for distinguished service, with £230 per annum, free quarters, fire and light, and 1s 2d per diem table money. He was also given a promise of employment should he ask for it.

Captain Cook had become an influential person, a man about town, seen not only at the Mitre Tavern, frequented by the Royal Society, but at Jack's, Will's, and other coffee houses where men of science and art gathered. His advice was sought on practically any naval matter, and he was to shortly become a Fellow of the Royal Society, receiving twenty-three nominations for membership instead of the usual four or five. Cook was, as Banks had been before him, the talk of London, but he was wise and old enough not to have his head turned by it.

Another South Seas voyage was planned for the *Resolution*, to take Omai home, but this time with Charles Clerke in command, not James. Elizabeth was ecstatic. Her sailor was home from the seas, for good it seemed.

Elizabeth was approaching her thirty-fourth birthday, James his forty-seventh. They had an assured income for life, Jamie and Nat were on the way to becoming naval officers, and like a sweet ripe peach, Elizabeth was with child once again. But as the leaves changed colour, and the summer of 1775 turned into autumn, the days of Elizabeth and James's summer grew shorter too. Imperceptibly at first, as it always is with the shortening of days, and in the smooth favourable winds that carried her along, Elizabeth did not at first notice the occasional fitful rustle of leaves, nor ripples on the surface of the water, as she and James walked into the slowly growing momentum of a wave that would tear them asunder.

'A few months ago', James wrote to John Walker, in Whitby, 'the whole Southern hemisphere was hardly big enough for me and now I am going to be confined within the limits of Greenwich Hospital, which are far too small for an active mind like mine, I must however confess it is a fine retreat and a pretty income, but whether I can bring myself to like ease and retirement, time will shew. Mrs Cook joins with me in best respects to you and all your family . . . '

Elizabeth watched her husband at the Spanish mahogany folding table, saw the quill moving through the air as the pen shaped letters. James was almost fifty, his pace must slow soon. He could not spend the rest of his life circumnavigating the globe. Banks, a younger man than James, no longer felt the need to go discovering. Others brought the world, especially its botanical

specimens, to him. Several of the *Resolution* men had gone to
Mr Banks's house to offer him their curiosities, and James himself
had sent up to Solander at the museum four casks for Banks,
containing birds, fish and plants.

Elizabeth knew her husband's active mind. If he kept it
occupied he would settle to land life. She looked at the feather—
the instrument, as James had pointed out, of both flight and
writing—saw the movement of it as he worked. Surely if he were
using his feathers for writing about voyaging instead of doing it,
that would suffice.

Though preparing his *Resolution* journals for publication was
arduous, James had been so mortified by Hawkesworth's account
of the *Endeavour* voyage that he had determined to write this
one himself. A copy of Hawkesworth's 'brew', as Mr Boswell
described it, published in 1773, had been waiting for James at
Cape Town on his homeward-bound journey. The scribe had been
paid the handsome sum of £6000 to write an account of the
South Sea voyages of Commodore Byron, Captain Wallis,
Captain Carteret and Captain Cook. He had written each in the
first person so that it appeared that his own opinions, his turns
of phrase, were those of the various commanders.

James scowled at the way the fellow described a group of
Maori women using their toes to feel for shellfish as if they were
Diana and her nymphs, although Elizabeth found the classical
image pretty. 'The man has written to amuse, not to inform,'
thundered James. 'He knows nothing about seamanship, appears
to care little for geography, and has made so-called observations
that are just plain fanciful. Imagine my embarrassment, dear
Elizabeth, when I arrived at St Helena, looking forward to dining
with Mr Skottowe's son, John, governor of that island, to find
a number of carts and wheelbarrows outside my lodgings.
"No wheeled vehicles on our island?" Mrs Skottowe reproached
me with gentle raillery. "Cruelty to our slaves?" Of course they

knew by then that they were not my words or observations. Nevertheless I am determined that such a thing will not happen again.'

'It was an unhappy affair for Hawkesworth too, James,' said Elizabeth. 'The reviewers' pens were sharp as swords, society tittered, and the fellow died a few months after publication. Of chagrin, it was said.'

Though James had now set his course on preparing the account of the second voyage himself, it was by no means plain sailing. Mr Forster was proving to be as pesky on land as he had been at sea. Though annoying as a march fly, on board the *Resolution* Mr Forster had made a sacrifice that had saved James's life. James himself glossed over the illness. It was Isaac who revealed how close to death James had come and how the whole ship's company had feared for their captain.

'We were near Easter Island when he was overcome with bilious colic,' said Isaac. 'He had suffered the complaint earlier, which abated as we pushed towards colder climes. On our return to warmer latitudes, he had an attack so severe it forced him to bed.' Elizabeth knew how bad it must have been to confine James to bed. 'Aye,' continued Isaac. 'At first he tried to conceal it, to carry on in the usual manner, but the malady got the better of him. He even consented to taking medicines, opiates and glysters, but couldn't keep them down. Then he developed dreadful hiccoughs that went on ceaselessly for more than a day. Finally, a broth of fresh meat was prepared. It was the broth that nourished and gave him strength.'

Isaac appeared to have finished the story.

'And what part did Mr Forster play?'

'The broth was made from Mr Forster's favourite dog.'

Against her will, Elizabeth gulped. The mere thought of eating dog made her feel sick, as it would anyone. She did not know if the animal had been taken or offered, yet it had nourished her husband, and she was grateful to Mr Forster for that.

Elizabeth had met him, in the days before the *Resolution*'s departure. He appeared to be genial enough, bowing with a great flourish on being introduced to the captain's wife, kissing her hand in the Continental manner. When he rose from the bow, she saw a face with hollow cheeks beneath heavy-lidded eyes. The lines which ran from his nose to the corners of his mouth formed a pair of brackets of the unfortunate type that gave him a permanent sneer.

Elizabeth peered out at her husband from between the arms of Gates, who was fixing Elizabeth's taffeta bonnet. She noticed that James's land clothes were a few years out of fashion. Understandable, with him being away for those years, but she made a note to get him to the tailor at the soonest opportunity. She missed these small everyday tasks when James was away, took pleasure in them when he was home. Elizabeth, mindful of unnecessary expenditure, especially as it was she who did the household accounts, had brought her own dress up to date by trimming the front edges of the overskirt with the same material as the flounces of the sleeves, and by taking up the hem, as skirts were worn short enough this season to show the shoes and ankles. It was easier to get about without having to constantly lift skirts to avoid mud and effluent, but it meant increased care of shoes and stockings as they were now always on show.

'Hold still, marm,' said Gates. Though Elizabeth loved outings, preparing for them was such a chore. At least an outing to the Pleasure Gardens did not necessarily require full dress, otherwise Elizabeth and Gates would be hours arranging the hair over a wire frame, adding false locks and filling in the gaps with wool.

Elizabeth now took heed of Gates and sat up straight, observing her husband in the looking glass.

'Forster has no idea. In the islands the men would buy curiosities from the natives for a trifle and resell them to him for a considerably larger sum without him noticing.' James adjusted his kerchief, giving it a firm crisp edge close to the neck, despite the hot August day. 'Now he is complaining that £4000 for expenses was not enough.'

Through the window, open to catch any little thread of breeze, they heard a carriage pull up. 'The Dyalls,' said James, looking down into the street. 'Are you ready, my dear?'

Elizabeth looked at Gates. 'Almost,' she said.

Mr and Mrs James Cook, and Mr and Mrs Thomas Dyall, their good friends from Mile End, paid a shilling each at the turnstile then entered into the Grand Quadrangle of the Pleasure Gardens at Vauxhall, south of the Thames. This was Elizabeth's first visit to the gardens, although they had been a place of popular entertainment since the reign of Charles II, and she thrilled at the prospect. When Mama was a girl, the gardens were not respectable. They were whispered of as a place where young bucks loitered and, if they had coins in their pockets, might find accommodating women of the town in the lesser avenues such as Dark Walk, Druid Walk or Lovers' Walk. They would even force kisses and other unwelcome attentions on young ladies. Sometimes young bloods took out newspaper advertisements trying to trace a lady to whom they'd taken a fancy. These days, though, the gardens were more genteel, an urban pastoral with concerts in the Music Room and wandering minstrels, and all manner of fine entertainments. This evening's concert, with an orchestra of fifty-four musicians, was to be Mr Handel's *Water Music Suite*.

Elizabeth felt such joy as she strolled along the tree-lined South Walk on her husband's arm. So long she had waited for a moment like this, to be in a public place with her husband, instead of going about without him, and answering the inevitable question with: 'They don't have the penny post in the South Seas but I'm sure Mr Cook is safe and sound.'

The foursome walked towards the Music Room. It was more than the suggestion of it that brought music to Elizabeth's ears, because up ahead, coming their way, was a fiddler ducking and weaving through the trees. He circled Elizabeth's party, Mr Dyall gave him a penny and he was away again, disappearing as quickly as he had appeared.

The Music Room resembled a grand cockle shell. It was full of light, grand columns, high ornate windows and, best of all, a ceiling which was fluted and reached so high into the sky it made Lilliputians of all who entered it. The ceiling was decorated with huge painted ribbons and flowers growing towards the sun.

'It is like a giant skirt,' Elizabeth exclaimed.

'And where does that place us?' Mr Dyall teased.

They strolled towards a column, to have a closer look at the decoration. There was a pattern of leaves at the base, each leaf identical, and spiralling through was a kind of staircase with figures on it, their arms outstretched and joined like a series of paper dolls, a procession to heaven.

They headed towards a bench being vacated by a lady and gentleman. Elizabeth and Mrs Dyall sat, while their husbands stood.

'Captain Cook!' a voice resounded through the hall. James turned and saw Jem Burney, lieutenant on the *Adventure*, approaching with his sister Fanny. It was Jem who'd led the search party for the men massacred at Grass Cove.

'Jem!' said James, vigorously shaking the young man's hand. 'Good to see you.'

'And excellent to see you too, sir, safely returned.'

James made the introductions. Elizabeth was pleased to meet young Jem, for whom everyone seemed to have such a fondness. He had a pleasant open face, a quick wit, and was as voluble as his sister was shy. She was small in stature, no taller than Elizabeth herself. Lightly powdered hair curled onto her shoulders and framed a face that seemed to have a perpetual blush. Though shy, awkward almost, her eyes showed intelligence and a quickness of observation. The beauty of her smile was so unexpected it was like a peacock raising its jewelled feathers.

Elizabeth would remember this meeting, later, in 1778, when the young woman's first novel, *Evelina*, burst upon the scene and pushed its author forward into public acclaim and curiosity. Even this very day, before coming to Vauxhall, she may have written some words, the novel taking shape in secret as surely as the new baby growing in Elizabeth's womb.

' 'Tis a sad scrape poor Mr Clerke is in,' Elizabeth heard Jem Burney say to her husband.

'Yes,' James sympathised. 'He went guarantor for his brother, Sir John, in the East Indies,' James explained to the Dyalls, 'and barely we sail up the Thames than he's nabbed and thrown in debtors' prison. A fine welcome home.'

'But he has friends,' said Jem. 'Mr Banks and other influential gentlemen. He'll soon be out of that wretched place and setting sail for the South Seas. I hope to be considered for such a voyage,' added Jem, 'though regret it will not be with you, sir.'

'My regrets too, Jem.'

Quite a crowd was gathering in the auditorium, with many glances in their direction. In this room built to carry sound, Elizabeth heard whispers of 'Captain James Cook' lapping from one side to the other. It was a name that all London now knew, but unlike Omai, James did not enjoy being the centre of attention, an object of curiosity. James himself was aware of the thickening around him, and though they were well-wishers—those who wanted to know about such things as the preserved New Zealand head Pickersgill had shown to Solander, which had made the ladies in his party sick, especially when they discovered that the missing portion had been broiled and eaten by the Maoris, or those who wanted simply to congratulate and touch him—he thought it timely to make a departure. 'Will you join us for supper, Jem, Miss Burney?'

'We're meeting Father,' said Jem. 'Perhaps we'll see you at the concert.'

The Cooks and the Dyalls made their escape past pavilions and temples, towards the colonnades and alcoves which housed the supper boxes. They declined the arak for which Vauxhall was famous and settled instead for one of its excellent wines while waiting for supper.

On an outside bench sat a merry foursome, one of the men thrusting his face so close to the woman beside him that he cast her hat askew. She responded by wiggling his ears. The other couple was younger, but no less merry. The young man was facing his lady friend, booted legs stretched either side of the bench, and she practically sitting in his lap. It looked like she was riding him side-saddle. A waiter stood at the head of the table, attempting to open a bottle of wine held between his thighs, while a tray of mustard and condiments waited patiently at his feet. Cockneys danced a lively jig, zigzagging around the trees and the outside supper tables.

Though here the avenues were tree-lined, life ebbed and flowed along them as it did on the streets of London. The metropolis was a stew of high and low, of commerce and culture, beggars, sailors, gentlemen with fine clothes and money, an endless round of pleasures, a town in which you could gamble on anything, from a cockfight to the price of corn, and lose a fortune in a night. Foreigners always commented on the energy of London, its hubbub. Church bells vied with postmen's bells, the cries of street vendors, of 'Stop, thief!', the clattering of feet on cobblestones, the clang of buckets and clink of glasses, all players in the orchestra of the city. To some observers it was boisterousness to be feared. A well-dressed foreigner, rather than be admired, was as like to have a dead dog or cat thrown at him, or at the least to be spattered with mud. Other observers called this boisterousness a love of liberty. 'Paris is the City of the Great King, London of the Great People.' Wasn't that what poet Samuel Rogers said? The elegant in their drawing rooms, the fashionable, affected shock or tedium at life on the streets, yet it possessed an allure for them, a titillation, the way talk of South Sea cannibalism did.

More characters came on stage — two dandies, one young, one older, standing at close quarters to a girl with a sash and pretty bows at her waist. She was on the arm of one, an uncle perhaps, but giving her attention to the other, who had his hands casually in his pockets. The 'uncle' was leaning in to hear the flatteries the young woman so readily accepted from the other man. The trio moved on, exposing to Elizabeth's view a solitary man in fluffy wig, a napkin tucked under his multiple chins, devouring chicken legs, one in each hand, his mouth on them as if they were two beauties, kissing first one then the other, unable to decide which was his favourite till he had consumed them both.

'Every bit as thin as it's reputed to be.' Mrs Dyall was holding up a meagre slice of Vauxhall ham for which they'd paid a pretty penny.

Supper had arrived.

'Such a beautiful day,' said Elizabeth when they finally got home that night. 'I didn't realise how tired I was.' Although the baby was still small inside her this was Elizabeth's sixth pregnancy, and at thirty-three she was no longer a young woman. 'My legs,' she added, lying down on the bed. 'All that walking.'

'Perhaps I can be of service,' said James. He lifted her night-gown and began stroking her legs, long gentle sweeps as well as applying pressure in some places.

Elizabeth looked at him enquiringly. It was most pleasurable, and it did seem to relieve the tiredness, but he had never done such a thing before.

'It is "rumi", a Tahitian form of flesh brushing. If you appear tired or languid they will immediately begin "rumi" upon your legs. I have always found it to have an exceedingly good effect.'

'The Tahitians have done it to you?' asked Elizabeth sitting up.

'I had complained of a rheumatic pain in my leg, from the hip to the foot.' James drew his finger down Elizabeth's leg to demonstrate. 'Several women, eight or nine of them, came on board,' he said, continuing all the while to perform the treatment on Elizabeth. 'They desired me to lay down in the midst of them, then began to squeeze me with both hands from head to foot but more especially the parts where the pain was, till they made my bones crack.' James laughed at the memory of it. 'After a quarter of an hour I was glad to get away from them. However I found immediate relief from the operation. How are your legs feeling now, my dear?'

Elizabeth was astonished, and she didn't know what she found the most astonishing—that such an operation worked, that her husband had submitted to it, or the fact that he was now telling her about it. She had asked for detail so that she could imagine her husband in the places he visited but this was an oversupply. She knew that in his mind he was merely making a scientific observation but the last thing she wanted to do was picture her

Introduction to *A Voyage towards the South Pole, and Round the World*, written by James Cook, Commander of the Resolution

It is a work for information not for amusement, written by a man, who has not the advantage of Education, acquired, nor Natural abilities for writing; but by one who has been constantly at sea from his youth, and who, with the Assistance of a few good friends gone through all the Stations belonging to a Seaman, from a prentice boy in the Coal Trade to a Commander in the Navy. After such a candid confession he hopes the Public will not consider him as an author, but a man Zealously employed in the Service of his Country and obliged to give the best account he is able of proceedings.

James undertook the account of the voyage not because he had any special talents for writing, but to give the public what they did not get with Hawkesworth—a truthful and accurate history, with observations based on fact, not fancy, in the plain-speaking language promoted by the Royal Society's men of science.

By Guy Fawkes night, 5 November, when effigies of the Catholic traitor were burnt throughout the realm and fireworks set off, and the sky above London was thick with smoke and gunpowder, James was in the South Seas once more, carried along by a feathery quill this time instead of a sail, retracing the route of the second voyage, a task that would occupy him all of the winter and into the summer of 1776.

It was as well the boys were in Portsmouth, because the manuscript, the charts, loose papers, letters received and letters written, blotting paper, pencils, pens and inks spread over the house like lava. Every so often Elizabeth would raise her head from her embroidery and glance at her husband in the middle of it all, see his determined air, the furrowing of the brow, the look of focused concentration that Nathaniel Dance would so aptly capture in his portrait of her husband. She caught sight of the Newfoundland scar, the end of it disappearing into James's cuff, rolled up to keep it out of the way of ink.

The journals were no longer simply an extended report for the Admiralty but for all of England, for all of the world. When published, in May 1777, nearly a thousand pages and sixty-three plates—charts and drawings—in two volumes, they would sell out immediately and go on to become one of the great accounts of Pacific exploration.

In her Mile End home Elizabeth watched the masterpiece grow, a meshing of threads in James's sloped handwriting, additions, deletions, insertions between the lines, in the margins, at the foot of the page, wherever its author could find space, till the entire voyage had been caught in the web of narrative.

Elizabeth was in a boat, a tub, and she was surrounded by water. Not on the sea but in her own house, in front of the fire. Unlike her husband's vessels which were designed to keep the water out, Elizabeth's vessel kept the water in.

'A bath, marm, in the middle of winter?' Gates had protested.

Though James was a stickler for cleanliness, Elizabeth's ablutions were most frequently done at the washbasin. A bath, in a tub that was big enough to sit in, was more of a luxury than a necessity.

'Why not?' Elizabeth countered. She did not allow herself luxuries very often. They had, courtesy of James's pension, free light and heat. James was dining with Lord Sandwich, Sir Hugh and Mr Stephens, the Admiralty secretary, so it seemed appropriate that the Admiralty should pay for Elizabeth's little luxury.

'But the baby, marm.' Gates was a spinster and had had little to do with birthing, or even assisting a midwife.

Elizabeth judged herself to be three or four months gone. 'In my belly the little one is surrounded by water,' explained Elizabeth. 'A little more will do no harm. In fact, if the water is allowed to get neither too hot nor too cold, it will be beneficial.'

Gates had brought one big kettle then another off the fire and poured steaming water into the tub. Cold water had been added till Elizabeth had felt it with her elbow and deemed it to be just right. Towels were waiting on a stool near the tub, and the heat of the fire ensured that the bath would not cool too rapidly. Elizabeth could always call Gates to top it up with more hot water. She stepped into the tub, first her big toe penetrating the warmth, then the rest of her body following suit, sinking into it.

Perhaps the best thing about a bath, thought Elizabeth, was getting out of her clothes, the corsetry and stays, the stomacher, releasing her body from its confinement. She could breathe. The tightness of clothes, before the Empire style which would arrive from Paris in the next century and shock everyone, was between the breasts and the navel. Below that, between the navel and the stocking tops, no undergarment was worn, which created an airy space between body and clothes. Only when women were in their rags and folded cloth was slung between the legs and attached to the bottom of stays, or to a cord around the waist, was anything worn close to this part of the body. But Elizabeth's folded cloths would be tucked away in a drawer for a year at least. No blood came while she was pregnant, it being used instead to grow the baby.

James had been gone an hour perhaps. It was four o'clock in the afternoon and already night was falling. Soon Gates would be lighting the candles. As well as the voyage recently completed, James was busy taking a hand in the voyage soon to begin. The *Resolution*, due to return to the South Seas under Clerke's command, was currently at Deptford being refitted, and James, at the Admiralty's request, was on the lookout for a vessel to accompany her. By 4 January 1776, less than a month after James and Elizabeth's thirteenth wedding anniversary, and the arrival of Jamie and Nat from Portsmouth to spend Christmas at home, James had found yet another Whitby collier to accompany the *Resolution*. His advice on this South Sea voyage was much sought after, everything from navigational matters to details such as how many barrels of vinegar to take on board. It seemed to Elizabeth that her husband was busier in retirement than he had ever been in active service.

She wriggled her toes and sent a gentle wave of water up over her body, a ripple that soon subsided, to be replaced by the tiny undulations caused by her breath. How soothing water was in the container of this tub, how wild and wilful, turbulent, it could become outside. At night, when James was away and Elizabeth heard a high angry wind she, like every sailor's wife, tossed and turned, knowing how the wind whipped up water, how the two worked together with a potency capable of destroying whatever small barque they found in their path. Sometimes even without wind, water wreaked its havoc, the sea threw itself upon rocks, upon wild coastlines, again and again. Receding momentarily then returning to renew the assault, unmindful of the ships, the lives, it might take with it.

Elizabeth drew in a deeper breath, smelled the sprig of dried lavender softening in the water, then sighed it out. She would no longer worry on nights of high wind because James would be sleeping safely by her side. Lilliputian waves splashed gently on the sides of the tub. Elizabeth idled the time away, eyes closed, watching thoughts wing their way across her mind like migratory birds.

She felt as if she were on the verge of a new life, a life with James as a landman. She was a young bride and this baby she carried inside her was their first. Elizabeth dreamt of all the things she and James would do together once the voyage preparations were over and the *Resolution* had sailed. They would go to plays, visit the Pleasure Gardens again, stroll along the green with the new baby. This one he would see grow up. James would be here for each new tooth, the first steps, the first day at school. But even if a boy, the child would not go off to naval college as his brothers had done, Elizabeth would see to that. This new baby would be a landman's son.

The bath was growing cool. Elizabeth opened her eyes, saw her water-wrinkled fingers and decided against a top-up. Where was Gates at any rate? Why hadn't she lit the candles? Night had gathered outside and the only thing keeping it from overtaking the room was the dull glow of the fire, and its burnished reflection on the tub.

'Gates?' Elizabeth called. Gates appeared so quickly that she must have been just outside the door. She came in, took a twig from the fire and lit the candles. They had sulphur matches, flat, thin things, but as Elizabeth said, there was no point lighting one piece of wood when there were already plenty alight in the fireplace.

'Sorry, marm, not to have done it earlier,' Gates apologised. 'I looked in but you were so peaceful there in your bath I thought it would only disturb you.'

'We must always keep a candle lit,' said Elizabeth. 'To welcome home our sailors.'

Gates looked at her mistress, standing by the fire with the towel cloth around her, like a figure from antiquity. She knew it from her childhood, sailors' families keeping a candle in the window, a bright flicker of faith for the men at sea. But the master, as far as she knew, had not gone to sea, only to dinner with the sea lords.

It was late, time for bed, and still James was not home. At every carriage approach Elizabeth pricked her ears, but none stopped outside 8 Assembly Row. James would undoubtedly be returned in Sandwich's vehicle, but what if there had been an accident? There were so many, what with the state of the roads, the slip of winter ice, and the drivers drunk more often than not. Worse was the possibility of highway robbery, and although her husband had survived all kinds of dangers when he had sailed into the unknown, and could no doubt get the better of any highwayman, still Elizabeth worried.

She climbed the stairs. It was not that late, she told herself, it was simply the early fall of winter night that made it appear so. Elizabeth said her prayers, a special one at the end to bring James home safely that night, the prayer she said when he was away at sea. Then she parted the bed curtains and stepped into the cocoon.

Not long after she heard the front door open, then footsteps. But they did not come immediately up the stairs, instead pacing up and down. 'James?' Elizabeth called.

'Yes, my dear,' she heard his reassuring voice, 'sorry to wake you.'

'I was not asleep,' she replied, the whole exchange carried out in a loud whisper so as not to disturb Gates, despite Gates having said nothing disturbed her, the proof being that she had slept through the earth tremors that had rocked London in the fifties, and only when her mother grabbed her from her bed had she awakened.

Through the gauze of bed curtain, Elizabeth saw the play of candlelight rising up the staircase, the shadows it cast on the wall. It flickered as it entered the room, announcing the looming form of her husband. She propped herself up on her elbows, watched him place the candle on the bedside table. 'It was a good dinner?' she asked.

'Yes, my dear.'

Something was wrong. He had answered her question but the words were merely small bubbles which had risen to the surface. He was almost bursting with intensity, with fire. He made no attempt to disrobe and get ready for bed. If Elizabeth did not know her husband so well, she would have suspected by his behaviour that he had a mistress and that he had been with her. She pulled the bed curtain aside. Light glittered in his eyes.

'A fruitful discussion?' she pressed.

'Yes, my dear.' His eyes were fever bright.

'James, what is it?'

He paced around the room, came up to Elizabeth, walked away again.

He took a breath, then expelled the words in one gust. 'I am to command the voyage.'

Elizabeth caught hold of the words, felt their barbs. 'Command the voyage?' she repeated, the words tasting bitter in her mouth. Elizabeth searched for antidotes. 'But you are retired. How can they order you to do this? Surely Clerke . . .'

'Clerke will command the second barque.' James remained where he stood, as if the bed curtain were made of iron.

'Simply to return Omai to his home, you and Clerke both must go?'

Now James shifted, walked to the window then returned to the exact same spot, as if he were already at sea, already on the quarterdeck, already the captain. 'That is the public reason for the voyage,' he said. His voice lowered but retained its passion nevertheless. 'The true direction of the enterprise is to seek out the north-west passage.'

She understood now. The sea lords had not inveigled her husband into this, he had volunteered. The warm dreamy atmosphere induced by the bath turned to ice, an ice so cold and hard it was cracking her bones. She made an effort to breathe, but the cold was suffocating her. Fifty or so attempts had already been made to find a passage in the high latitudes of the Arctic Circle, a faster route from one ocean to the other, to the riches of China, the East Indies. But so far none had been found.

'You are prepared to set out on what might be a wild goose chase, to leave your wife, your sons, for something that may not exist, just as the Great South Land did not exist?'

'There is £20 000 in it,' said James. 'For whoever finds the passage. We will be comfortable for life.'

'We are already comfortable. I can do with less comfort and more of my husband. In the last seven years we have been together little more than a year. In all thirteen years of our marriage, if you add up the months, the weeks, the days, we have spent little more than four years together. When are you going to be a husband to me, a father to your sons?' Elizabeth demanded. 'Have you forgotten the words you spoke in St Margaret's, "till death us do part"? When we are apart, death comes. The children are born and die, and I bear it alone. They die in my arms, not yours. You hear about it, after the event. I know it disturbs you but it's not the same as watching it happen. I feel so helpless, nothing I do can stop it.'

James came and sat on the bed. 'It will be my last voyage, Elizabeth, I promise you.'

'You think you are the only one to voyage? I have made discoveries I didn't wish to make. Three children dead. Do you know to which bleak shore that takes me? You said your tribulations started on that long reef of New Holland, but the reef of grief is endless and the coral sharp as knives. So many times I have been stranded there, alone, James, without you. I doubt I can survive another voyage,' she said, her voice barely audible.

James reached out to his wife but she pulled away. So much she wanted to lie in his arms, to dissolve in his embrace, to have the pain soothed. But it would be a barbed embrace by the one who had caused that pain.

'Elizabeth, you are the only woman I have ever loved. I swear this by Almighty God. And I swear that I am, and have always been your faithful husband. At home and in parts beyond the seas, you are my constant companion, my succour and my desire, you are as much a part of me as my own flesh.'

'But not enough to keep you by my side,' Elizabeth threw his loving words back in his face. 'I've had to be mother and father to the children, struggle to learn about your precious instruments, navigation, astronomy, your precious South Seas, so that I can try to explain to Jamie and Nat what it is that keeps their father away from them.'

She saw him flinch, the muscles in his jaw tighten. 'Be patient, dear Elizabeth, for one more time.'

'I have been patient! I have waited two years, three. Before we married I waited seven years.' The waiting years rose out of Elizabeth like a tidal wave and came crashing down.

James looked on, wanting to help her but not knowing how. There was no rope he could throw to reel her in to safety. 'I must undertake the enterprise, it is my duty to my country.'

'Duty? It's more than duty that drives you. Is it not enough to be the celebrated circumnavigator Captain Cook, do you want to be *Sir* James Cook? Certainly your gentlemen friends love and admire you, but you're a curiosity to them, a farm boy from Yorkshire, a curiosity like Omai.'

'And they are a curiosity to me!' James lashed out. 'Sandwich, Banks, even the king himself!'

Elizabeth was shocked. 'You put yourself above the king?' It was close to blasphemy.

'Not above. Outside. He is the king of this island, but the world is full of islands. I have touched noses with Maori chiefs, shared their breath. Exchanged clothes, names, with the kings of Tahiti, and become their brother.'

'King Toot? Is that it? Perhaps you've voyaged too far already, James.'

By the time the darkness of night turned to a dirty grey, Elizabeth had exhausted herself. James had remained in the room but an ocean away from the bed, passing the last shreds of night in a chair, fully clothed. Neither slept, each wrapped quietly in their own pain. The vigilant Gates knew better than to knock on the door, to bring master and mistress their morning cup of tea.

Although Elizabeth lay still, James knew perfectly well that she was awake.

'Can I bring you anything?' he said quietly, his voice strained from the night.

'No thank you,' she replied sharply.

Elizabeth felt the icy breeze as James got out of the chair. 'I have business in town,' he said, and left the room, the house. Dressed just as he was, as he had been the night before.

Elizabeth heard a murmured query from Gates downstairs, then the brusque tone of James's reply. The door opening, the life of the street, vendors' cries, horses' hoofs and carriage wheels, all becoming muted as the door shut firmly.

They had argued, said terrible things. Elizabeth had uttered death's name, and it had all coursed through her blood to the unborn one. She took a deep breath, saw the mound of her stomach rise and fall. The anguish must stop here, she must draw a curtain on it. What had been said must never leave this room. Elizabeth wondered how much the sound sleeper Gates had heard. She had no reason to doubt her servant's loyalty, yet it had never before been tested in this way.

Elizabeth curved her hands upon her belly, making a net of her fingers. James's pronouncement was still there, a piece of grit in her heart. She must not let it grow, because then every time she took a breath she would feel the lump of it, black and hard as coal, till it grew so big she would not be able to draw breath at all, and the little one would suffocate.

Her dream of James as a landman would never become reality. She had married a seaman and a seaman's wife she would remain. With a big heave, Elizabeth pushed away the reminder that Mr Blackburn, also a seaman, had retired well before the age James was now, and had settled to land life. But Mr Blackburn was hardly in the same fish kettle as James.

Elizabeth cradled the unborn child in her interlaced fingers. She would like to hold her husband like this, in her belly, nurturing him, keeping him safe, surrounding him with her warm sea of protection. She carried James's seed inside her, and she must let the little one be nurtured in calm waters, not the tempest that had erupted last night. Elizabeth imagined her breath as wind, a gentle breeze that floated the clouds away. A sky of uninterrupted blue as far as the eye could see, a great empty sky, the weather at rest. A seabird, white as snow, flew into her imagined sky, bowed its wings then hovered in the uplift of wind before soaring into the blue. James must go, must sail, as surely as this bird must fly.

Elizabeth's husband did have a mistress—the Pacific Ocean—and he wanted no other man to have her. She had had other lovers before James, but he was her best. None caressed her the way he did, charted and mapped her every feature. None had penetrated her the way he had, found her most secret places. To no other had she yielded them. He loved her in all her moods, when she was calm and pleasant, when she teased, when she was fitful and sultry. He was alert to her every move, to her sighs, to the way she carried him along. He fought against her fury, a match of master and mistress. He rode out her lashings, never retreated from her. He loved her people and they took him into their family. He would sail to the moon for her. She had enchanted him, her juices flowed in his veins. When her sirens called to his blood, he had no choice but to answer, even if he was dashed against the rocks. He must go to her. Elizabeth did not seek out these thoughts, they came uninvited, the moist whisperings of her husband's mistress. They flooded into her ears and she was powerless to stop them. Against an ocean she could do nothing else but pray.

They were hard days that followed, the weather bitterly cold. The world had turned upside down—the sky the colour of dirt, and the earth covered in clouds of snow. Elizabeth's heart also was covered in cold hard snow. She had spent her life waiting; how wasted those years seemed now. She had dreams of James lying in the embrace of his ocean, its waves stroking him like the hands of the Tahitian women. After, she lay awake so as not to dream again.

The days grew longer and winter drew to a close. Her heart could not remain frozen forever. As she lay beside the sleeping storm of her husband Elizabeth felt the ice beginning to melt, the flow of love returning. She had only to wait one more time. This would be his last voyage, he had promised.

Elizabeth watched the slow rise of her body, felt the small increments of the days getting longer, and knew that the hibernating creatures of the fields behind her Mile End home, the moles and voles, would soon waken, that snowdrops would push up through the softening earth, their crisp white skirts hemmed in festive green spots, like sprigged muslin, then the daffodils, their yellow trumpets heralding spring, when the new baby would be born.

BOSWELL'S
AN ACCOUNT OF CORSICA

'It was curious to see Cook, a grave steady man, and his wife, a decent plump Englishwoman, and think that he was preparing to sail around the world,' Boswell wrote in his *Private Papers*.

English she was, decent she hoped, but plump? Mr Boswell obviously had trouble discerning plumpness from pregnancy. Elizabeth was resting after the dinner at Sir John Pringle's. It was early April but unseasonably warm. She was lying on the bed, her stays loosened, the big dinner and the unborn baby stretching her stomach to the edge of its capacity. So much so that when Gates appeared with a soothing chamomile infusion, Elizabeth doubted she had room for even one small drop of it. Nevertheless, talking about the meal did not make her feel in the least bit nauseous, rather, she enjoyed revisiting the scene. It was probably her last outing before confinement. Soon, very soon, Elizabeth reflected, surveying the outcrops and hills of her body, the baby would be so big that she would have to go without stays, and no support for her uncomfortable, heavy breasts.

Gates had wanted a full description of the dinner, every detail. Was there anything marm liked in particular that Gates might prepare?

Elizabeth saw them all seated for dinner, the women fanning out around Lady Pringle at the head of the table; the men around Sir John, with his bushy eyebrows and prominent chin, at the lower end. She saw Mr Wedgwood's cream-coloured Queensware, named after the approval given it by Queen Charlotte; the tureens and plates, the silver serving platters laden with food, the crystal wine glasses ready to be filled from decanters on a sideboard. All of this around a splendid centrepiece of porcelain Neptunes triumphantly riding in cockle shells, on an ocean of silver tissue. Between the dishes, plates and glasses, Elizabeth caught glimpses of a brilliantly white damask tablecloth, with long sides reaching almost to the floor, which the diners could rest on their laps and lift to wipe their mouths upon, an English custom that often horrified visitors from across the Channel, who were more accustomed to napkins.

'But, marm, what did they serve?' asked Gates.

Elizabeth listed the first course dishes—a remove of green pea soup, fricassee of chicken, neck of mutton boiled with caper sauce, hare collops, boiled tongue, currant jelly, paupiettes of veal. 'So beautifully arranged,' she told Gates, mapping out the placement of each dish, the suitability of some to the sides of the table, others to the corners.

After describing the first course, Elizabeth found that she did have room for a few sips of the infusion. Then she went on to the second course—roast turkey, preserved codlins, ragout of mushrooms, potted beef, collared pig, artichokes (at which Gates gasped, 'Oh, marm!'), roasted wheat ears, apricot compote, and blancmange. By the end of it all, Gates was practically swooning. It was almost as if she had eaten the dinner herself.

Elizabeth drank the rest of the infusion.

'Are you feeling more refreshed, marm?' enquired Gates, gathering up the cup and saucer.

'Thank you. Yes.'

'Anything further, marm?'

Instead of saying, 'That will be all,' Elizabeth felt a smile creep to her lips. 'After dessert they served pineapple and fresh peaches.'

'Oh, marm,' exclaimed Gates, delighted with this finishing touch when she thought the meal was over. 'In April. Well I never.'

Sir John Pringle, as well as being the king's physician, was also President of the Royal Society, and in both capacities paid great attention to the paper which James had presented to the Society the month before, 'A Discourse on the Means of Preserving the Health of Mariners'. Elizabeth was seated next to Sophia Banks, and at the end of the meal, when the servants had disappeared and the ladies took a glass of wine at the table before retiring to the drawing room, allowing the men's conversation to roam high and low—mostly low, to toast their mistresses and discuss politics—the ladies picked up the threads of the conversations that had wafted down from the men's end of the table.

News of events in the American colonies was so fresh that it couldn't help but be talked about. All had hoped that the incident in 1773 during which colonists disguised as Indians boarded a ship in Boston and threw three hundred and forty-two chests of tea into the harbour would be an isolated one. But unfortunately there was more to come. Open rebellion throughout Massachusetts, battles in Lexington and Concord in April 1775. By August of that year, at the time James made his triumphant return, a mere seven months ago though it seemed like years, a general proclamation of rebellion had been issued.

'The colonists are nothing but convicts, pirates and rogues, Dr Johnson avows,' said Mr Boswell over dinner, 'but I beg to differ.' After the first course of the American revolt, the second course had focused on the exotic topic of the impending voyage, with the men all leaning towards James.

'Are you not fearful for your husband sailing at such a time?' one of the ladies directed a question towards the celebrated circumnavigator's wife.

Elizabeth was watching Mr Boswell's double chins disappear then reappear as he nodded encouragement to her husband. She wondered what of this evening would end up in print. Mr Boswell had a remarkable memory for detail and, without notebook or pencil in sight, was able to record observations and whole conversations word for word. She watched as the man excused himself and made his way to the sideboard and one of the chamber pots. Excitement over the conversation must have gotten the better of him. Normally the chamber pots weren't sought out till the ladies had left the room and the men had begun drinking in earnest. Elizabeth turned back to her companions.

'I have a greater fear for our cousins in America,' said Elizabeth, sparing a thought for Cousin Frances and Mr Lieber. She hoped that fighting hadn't broken out in Philadelphia. 'Mr Cook has come home from two voyages to the South Seas, he will return from the third, God willing.' She dabbed at the corners of her mouth, not so much because she suspected a crumb or a sliver of meat to be lurking there, but to hide any slight quivering of her lip. Elizabeth was pleased with the way she conducted herself. At the table she had noted no sideways glances in her direction, no whisperings. The last thing she wanted from this gathering of James's friends was pity.

There was more talk of it in the drawing room to which the ladies retired. 'It is unimaginable,' exclaimed one young woman, with at least as much eagerness as Mr Boswell had displayed. 'Around the world. It's as fanciful as flying to the moon.'

'Yet it has been done,' said Sophia Banks, with a smile for Elizabeth.

'Is it true,' said the young woman, turning the conversation to more usual topics, 'that Lord Sandwich is openly living with Martha Ray?' It seemed she was directing her conversation to Elizabeth once again, although Elizabeth felt that Sophia Banks could address the question with more aplomb. Not only did Elizabeth draw a curtain on her own private sentiments in public gatherings, but on those of others.

It was true that Sandwich was by this time cohabiting with Miss Ray. Open cohabitation with a mistress was the least of Sandwich's dissoluteness. He was also an inveterate gambler, often staying at the card tables all night, not even leaving to have supper, instead holding meat between pieces of bread with one hand while playing cards with the other.

'It is true. All of London knows.' The question had been answered by an older woman, who had the longest neck Elizabeth had ever seen on a human being. It seemed to extend right down to the beginnings of her crinkled bosoms. Nevertheless, the long-necked woman had relieved her of the task of phrasing a diplomatic answer.

'Your brother has still not found a wife, Miss Banks?' the same woman asked.

'My brother is quite settled, thank you.'

Elizabeth smiled at the poise of Sophia's answer. Mr Banks maintained that he'd eaten his way further into the animal kingdom than any man, but he had also probably made his way further into the female kingdom. He'd sampled all the South Sea morsels, as well as the Dutch in Cape Town. There had been a first course of a fiancée, one Harriet Blosset, before the *Endeavour* voyage, whom he'd later disengaged to the tune of £5000. Then there was the side dish of Mrs Burnett, the woman waiting for him at Madeira. After another meal, so the talk went, there was fruit—a child. As if the mere thought had conveyed itself to her belly, Elizabeth felt the kick of her unborn child quicken her breath.

The sound of the gentlemen approaching the drawing room quelled any further questions. Tea and coffee were served, and the dinner came to its natural conclusion.

A few weeks later Mr Boswell came to tea, bringing with him an account of his own travels in Corsica. It was the third edition, printed for Edward Dilly in the Poultry, 1769, with a new and accurate map of that island, dense with place names such as Talano and Grevellina, and surrounded by a jigsaw of coastline. The brown cover was smooth and shiny, gilt on the spine, the outline of stars in between a pattern of diamonds.

Elizabeth allowed Mr Boswell to pay his respects then she went upstairs, heaving herself up the banister. She felt so enormous in these last days of April that she was no longer comfortable sitting on a chair. Words of the conversation her husband was having with Mr Boswell wafted up with the twittering of birds in the apple trees and bees buzzing in and out of the blossoms. She heard her husband confess that his observations on matters of religion and government in the South Sea islands might be quite erroneous. Scant knowledge of the language made room for misinterpretation, and in that great ocean even truth was fluid. On occasion it was hard to discern whether the information being given was accurate in the first place, and there were gaps through which understanding might fall.

If James was not actually voyaging he was talking about it, Elizabeth reflected as she fanned herself. At least, she consoled herself, this time he would be here for the birth of the new baby.

After several cups of tea, and much voyaging, Mr Boswell departed, and James brought the book upstairs to show Elizabeth the dedication. On the frontispiece, in a clear, sloped, smallish hand, with the crossbars of the 't's joined if there happened to be more than one in a word, Mr Boswell had written: 'Presented to Captain Cooke by the Authour, as a small memorial of his admiration of that Gentleman's most renowned merit as a Navigator, of the esteem of the Captain's good sense and worth, and of the grateful sense which he shall ever entertain of the civil and communicative manner in which the Captain was pleased to treat him. James Boswell'.

It had been a pleasant afternoon in the garden for James, a pause in the busy round in which he found himself, and it more than made up for the remark Mr Boswell had made at the Mitre a few days earlier. Upstairs in Assembly Row, James relayed the witticism to Elizabeth. 'I have had a feast,' Boswell had told Sir John, Banks, Solander and other members of the Royal Society as they rose from dinner to take coffee at Brown's before proceeding to the meeting rooms for presentation of papers. 'I have had a good dinner,' he said, pointing to James, 'for I have had a good Cook.'

THE PORTRAIT OF CAPTAIN COOK BY NATHANIEL DANCE

'An excellent likeness,' Elizabeth pronounced after she'd studied Nathaniel Dance's portrait of her husband.

In the painting James was seated at a table, holding a map, his right hand resting on it, index finger outstretched, pointing. To what, it was difficult to tell. Perhaps to the hoped-for entrance to the north-west passage. In any case James was looking away from it, his gaze fixed on something beyond the picture frame. He was wearing navy dress uniform, appropriate for the rank of post-captain. White breeches, white waistcoat with brass buttons, a few of which were undone, white neck-cloth; a dark blue jacket with gold braid trim around the collar, down the edges and along the length of the cuffs, which finished with a modest display of lace from the shirt beneath. The squaring of the pose, the upright torso, everything about him suggested a man of strength and determination. The concentrated focus of the furrowed brow, the intent look in the eyes, the straight nose over the curve of mouth and the set of the chin. A master of men and, it would appear, of his own destiny.

There were other portraits but Elizabeth deemed Dance's to be the truest. When her husband passed into history, it would become the definitive one.

It was a wonder James had even found time to sit for the portrait commissioned by Banks. When he sat down at all, which, it appeared to Elizabeth, was not very often these days, it was to put finishing touches on the voyage narrative. But it was the new voyage that sucked everything into its vortex. James was writing letters of requisition to the various boards, other letters to associates and friends, studying the details of his proposed route. He was often out—at the Admiralty, discussing matters with his officers, seeking news of Clerke, who was still in prison, meeting with the supernumeraries—astronomers, botanists, artists. Elizabeth had resigned herself to waiting one more time. In a way the voyage had already started, but at least this leg of it, the preparations, she could share with him.

Omai would be going of course, to be returned to his home. Just as voyagers to the South Seas had brought back curios, so Omai was taking home his—gunpowder, wine, a globe of the world, tin soldiers, a hand organ, crockery, fancy goods and, heavens know why, a complete suit of armour were going on board the *Resolution* as Omai's luggage.

With slightly less paraphernalia was John Webber, the young artist whose work in the recent Royal Academy exhibition had been noticed by Solander. Mr Bayly, the astronomer who had sailed on the second voyage, was this time to go aboard the *Discovery*, and Banks had sent David Nelson, gardener at Kew, to collect botanical specimens. Then there was the crew—ignorant, drunken, blockheaded English tars who had such a bad reputation abroad for fighting and creating a disturbance that ports such as Cape Town would not let them ashore unless

accompanied by an officer. The men were distrustful of inno-
vation, but they knew the reputation of the captain, some of them
having sailed with him before, and were prepared to eat sauerkraut,
wash their clothing, swab the decks, fumigate and do whatever
else the captain deemed necessary to keep them alive and healthy.

James was taking marines aboard as well. Elizabeth remembered the name of one of them—Corporal Ledyard, an American,
who was so determined to make the voyage that he walked from
Portsmouth to London. She would later hear how the former
missionary from Groton, Connecticut, had walked across Siberia,
and, later, that he died in Africa looking for the source of the
Niger. Sailing towards their places in history were midshipman
George Vancouver, and ship's master William Bligh, a talented
navigator and surveyor, but known to be an 'awkward fellow'.
Clerke, captain of the *Discovery*, was to eventually meet up with
the *Resolution* in Cape Town, having either escaped from prison
or bribed his way out.

James dined with Banks and Solander, frequented Will's and
other coffee houses to read the newspapers and catch up with
the talk when he could. Mostly it was of the war in America.

In the midst of all this came the birth of another son. On that
bright day in May, James avowed he was the happiest man alive,
and held the wee thing with such tenderness Elizabeth thought
she would melt at the sight of it. 'We shall call you Hugh,' James
whispered over the newborn's head, 'and Sir Hugh shall be your
godfather.' Elizabeth smiled and nodded, remembering the
morning Mr Palliser, as Sir Hugh was then, had come to the door
with news of James, how he had lent her his handkerchief and
lifted her spirits out of the ashes.

This new little Hugh lifted her spirits every time she looked
at him. He was the most beautiful child of all. At first Elizabeth
fretted at his fragility. He had the transparency of an angel. Soft-
eyed, cherub-lipped. But there was a light in him that had been

lacking in baby Joseph and even baby George. This child would survive. The Almighty had already taken more than His tithe from Elizabeth. God willing, this one would be spared.

The birth of Hugh was a short respite in the bosom of the family, and soon James was once more dashing hither and thither. One piece of business, and a vital one at that, to which he was not giving enough attention was overseeing the work being done at the Deptford yards on the *Resolution*. The river from Wapping, through Limehouse Reach to Deptford where the city wharves tailed out and the ship-building facilities began, was always crowded, and thick with odours, miasmas, curses, shrieks and cries, but this spring and summer of 1776, it was worse than Bedlam.

First there were the prison hulks, pensioned-off navy vessels no longer fit for service, their wings clipped, their sails dismantled, where prisoners passed the night in fetters, to be awoken at dawn and rowed to labour in the dockyards. If the smell of the river itself wasn't enough, there was effluent and refuse from the hulks, the stench of rotting ropes, of rotting hulks, rotting lives. A visitor to the yards had to row through all of this, past the hulks festooned with clothing and bedding hung out to air, like a sad parody of fairground pennants. With the American colonies no longer accepting English convicts, the prisoners' lives were in limbo. The American revolt was also responsible for the sheer volume of work in the dockyards. For thirteen years England had been at peace, the dockyards at an ebb, and now they were suddenly a hive of activity. So much so that often a lick and a polish replaced actual structural work.

At the best of times the dockyard workers had to be watched, and these were not the best of times. The mission of the *Resolution* and her sister ship, the aptly named *Discovery*, was above and beyond war and politics, yet was dragged down into it. No ship had priority in the Deptford yards unless someone made it so. James Cook was not shying away from the stench of the hulls, the chaos in the yards, it was simply that he was already stretched to the limit.

James had sailed to the extremes of heat and cold, and Elizabeth imagined that he had no boundaries, that he could perform whatever task was set before him. Several tasks. He was a big strong man but a man nevertheless. He had personally supervised preparations for the first and second voyages, every detail of the refitting and overhauling of his vessels, but then he had not been stretched in so many different directions. Now he was. Visiting the dockyards was but one of many tasks, instead of being the overriding one. He simply did not have time.

Elizabeth remembered when the boys were young, how excitable they were for adventure, for staying up late, for fireworks, for special occasions, and how they would say no, they did not want to go to bed, even though Elizabeth could see their eyelids drooping with fatigue. In those months before departure, James was like that. Eager, wanting to do everything, unaware of his own fatigue. Sometimes he winced and put his hand on his stomach. When Elizabeth asked he would say: 'Nothing, my dear.' And in these summer months of 1776 she would remember Cousin Isaac saying that the bilious colic returned in the warmer latitudes. The hottest day of an English summer was nothing compared to the tropical heat of the low latitudes.

Though Elizabeth could not help but be swept along, uplifted in the zephyr that surrounded her husband's voyage, she was also grounded by the presence of baby Hugh. She would rise in the night, glancing at her sleeping husband, and tend to the baby. Hugh's eyes were bright with the candlelight, his cherub lips already searching for her nipple. The milk of love poured out of her, and as she fed the newborn, she tried not to think about her husband's hazardous journey. She was feeding succour, nourishment into baby Hugh, she did not wish to brew anxiety into it.

THE WILL OF JAMES COOK

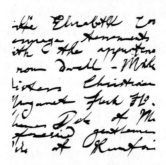

To my dear father, Mr James Cook — one annuity or clear yearly
sum of ten pounds ten shillings. I give to my dear and loving
wife Elizabeth Cook all my leasehold messuage tenement and
premises with the appurtenances wherein I now dwell — Mile End
old Town. Sisters Christiana Cocker and Margaret Fleck £10.
Good friends Thomas Dyall of Mile End old Town aforesaid
gentleman, and Richard Wise of Rumford, Essex gentleman £10
a piece as a mark of the great regard I have of them. Rest of
estate 1/3 to Elizabeth Cook, 2/3 to Elizabeth Cook, Thomas
Dyall and Richard Wise in trust for the children (all and every).

Witnessed by Mr Bussett, Nath Austen, Joseph Neeld, 14 June,
1776

Elizabeth rubbed Hugh's little back and when he produced a burp, put the milk-drowsy baby in the crib. James had a few more formal occasions to attend, then he would close the door and spend the remaining days, and precious nights, with Elizabeth. The *Resolution* was ready and would soon set sail.

On Saturday 8 June, to a seventeen-gun salute and three cheers from the yard workers, Sandwich, Palliser and other notables came aboard for a farewell dinner of turbot, trout, lobsters, shrimps, chickens, raggove mellie, stewed mushrooms, peas, beans, spinage toasts, cauliflowers, petit patties, venison, a tart, sweetbreads, biscuits, currant jelly, sauces and twenty-four French rolls, all of it victualled by Messrs Birch, Birch and Co of Cornhill near Wapping, for a cost of £12 2s.

By evening of the following Monday, the sounds of oinking, clucking, mooing and baaing filled the ship. Not only did the animals provide a living larder for the people, but also the king was intent on making Tahiti an antipodean English pastoral, with rabbits, sheep, horses, hogs, cows, bulls and chickens. To top it all was a pair of peacocks. James frowned as he told Elizabeth about it, thinking of the space King George's 'gifts' were taking up, and the discomfort that would result. 'Ah well,' he said, 'it is only till Tahiti,' as if Tahiti was a few stops down the river instead of the other side of the world.

When Elizabeth went to put her accounts book back in the drawer of the Chippendale chest in which they kept their marriage certificate, deeds to the house and other important documents, she discovered a new addition.

'A will, James?'

'It is a matter of course,' he tried to assure her. 'A mere formality.'

He may have written wills before his previous voyages but Elizabeth was unaware of it. Thus, on finding it in the place where he knew she would look should that dreadful need arise, of course Elizabeth asked. She would have liked to dismiss her anxiety and unease about the impending voyage as merely the concerns of her sex, but when she saw those ephemeralities transformed into masculine substance, into his last will and testament, as if James wasn't long for this world, she could not help but give voice to them.

The will was the least of it. Never before had James prepared so thoroughly for the prospect of his not returning. When Elizabeth urged her husband to add her best respects to the letter he was writing to Commodore Wilson on 22 June, she noticed he described his imminent journey as 'hazardous, and must be made with great caution'.

Elizabeth was not to know till later that in Plymouth, while waiting for the tide and the wind, James wrote other letters dealing with arrangements he had made for Elizabeth and the boys. To Lord Sandwich:

> *I cannot leave England without taking some method to thank your Lordship for the many favors confered upon me, and in particular for the very liberal allowance made to Mrs Cook during my absence. This, by enabling my family to live at ease and removing from them every fear of indigency, has set my heart at rest and filled it with gratitude to my Noble benefactor. If a faithfull discharge of that duty which your Lordship has intrusted to my care, be any return, it shall be my first and principal object.*

To Reverend Dr Richard Kaye, chaplain to the King, who had supplied James with Maundy money to be put in bottles on newly discovered islands, he wrote:

> *I cannot leave England without answering your very obliging favor of the 12th of last Month, and thanking you for the kind tender of your service to Mrs Cook in my absence. I shall most*

certainly make an acknowledgment in the way you wish, if it
please God to spare me till I reach the place for Discoveries.

Having written his last letter from Mile End, the one to Commodore
Wilson, James put away his pen and papers. He and Elizabeth
played with baby Hugh in the blossoming garden, laughed as
they watched him watching the movement of hens amongst the
greenery.

On Sunday 23 June they went to church. It was the first time
Elizabeth had left the house since the birthing. The vicar of St
Dunstan's led the congregation in prayer for the voyage and the
safe return of those aboard the *Resolution* and the *Discovery*.
Elizabeth's head remained bowed, her heart full of fervent prayer
even after the hymn was announced and the choir members lifted
their voices to the rafters.

'You must sleep,' James whispered to his wife that short summer
night.

'I will sleep in the coming years.' Elizabeth felt the same
urgency James had when he returned from the previous voyage.
She initiated the intimacies, pleasuring him with her lips, her
hands, till he was ready for her. Again and again. She wanted to
hold him inside her forever, for this union to be seared into his
soul so that when he was in the embrace of his ocean he would
hunger for his wife and know that this was the greater love.

They were still awake at first light. Elizabeth felt a pang in
her heart as she caught sight of James's valise waiting by the chair.
The bulk of his luggage was already aboard. Gates knocked softly
at the door, with tea and toast.

After breakfast James rose and attended to his toiletries.
Elizabeth must rise too and get dressed because soon Sandwich's
carriage, with Omai aboard, would be here. A short ride to the
river then a boat to the Nore where the *Resolution* waited. But
Elizabeth did not want to leave the bed which held her husband's

warmth, his smell, the indentation of his body. She watched him button his waistcoat, tie his neck-cloth, arrange his cuffs so that the gold braid was parallel to the line of his arm and just the right amount of lace was visible.

When everything was ready he turned to her. 'Elizabeth?' He was presenting himself to her, the celebrated navigator in the prime of his life. Every step he had taken had led him to this very place, to this very moment. They had been husband and wife for almost fourteen years, yet behind the splendid uniform, behind the lines of maturity, the lines that sea and wind had etched on his face, Elizabeth saw the young seaman who had just joined the navy, to whom she had opened her door. 'Yes, my dearest,' she said. 'Yes.'

A carriage pulled up. An exchange of greetings, a quick kiss, and James was gone.

THE COPLEY MEDAL

'Such a crowd at Plymouth to see the *Resolution* off,' Jamie and Nat wrote. 'You would have loved it, Mama, it was like a fair, so many people, vendors selling sausages and oysters, oranges, pots and pans, and whatever else they could think of. Everyone craning their necks to catch a glimpse of Omai, as if all of London hadn't already seen him. He remembered me,' Nat went on, 'and said if ever I go to Otaheite we shall play backgammon. Sailors danced, musicians played, and Papa and Omai were piped aboard by the highlanders in their kilts, accompanied by cheers, and men throwing their hats up into the air. So many marines going on board in their splendid red coats, and so many warships in Plymouth Sound.'

Bound for North America, thought Elizabeth, the same as her husband on a more peaceable mission. Elizabeth read her sons' words while rocking their baby brother. Except for Hugh, she was alone again. She did not know which was worse—having said goodbye to her husband, yet knowing he was still in England and not seeing him, or the long years after he had sailed over the rim of the horizon and there was no news at all.

She had tried to quell feelings of bitterness and resentment in front of her husband but now that he was gone, those thoughts batted their black wings at her. Perhaps if she pinned them down they would not flap about so. She placed sleeping Hugh in the cradle and took out pen and paper. So often when she did this it was to write a letter to James, and this time also she found herself addressing him.

Mostly her letters to him were buoyant with hope and encouragement, telling him how much she looked forward to seeing him again, her feelings of love for him, as well as news of what was happening at 8 Assembly Row, always glossing over anything that might give him cause to worry. What was the use when he was so far away and could do nought about it? She never wrote when she was feeling low, or of her anxieties for him, the devastation of the children's deaths.

'Dear James.' She saw these marks on the page. But it was a letter she would never send him so she did not have to gloss over what was in the dark side of her heart. 'It was so unnecessary for you to embark on this voyage and to cause such pain to your wife. No man before you has made three such voyages and as well as the anxiety I always feel, this time I have fears that have never manifested before.' Elizabeth put down the pen. These fears she dared not give shape to, dared not put into writing—that James was challenging the Almighty Himself. He had successfully pitted himself against the elements once, twice. But tempting fate a third time, and without such painstaking preparations? It was almost an act of reckless defiance.

She picked up the pen again. 'Clerke was appointed to command the voyage but you actively sought to take his place. Do you know how it makes me feel to realise that you willingly chose more years of absence from me? Perhaps if you could fulfil your marriage vows for only a small fraction of the time you should never have married at all.' As soon as these words were on paper Elizabeth immediately crossed them out. 'Perhaps I should not have been guided by my heart in the first place, should have chosen a man who wanted to be more of a husband to me.' Elizabeth crossed these words out too. In fact, when she saw what a mawkish black crow mess her words and the crossings-out had made, she tore the letter up and threw it in the fire. Nevertheless she felt much better watching those words turn into smoke and curl their way up the chimney and out of her house.

The *Resolution* sailed from Plymouth on 12 July, four years to the day that it had set sail the first time. The coincidence would have been auspicious had the news been better. The ship leaked when it rained, and at the first sign of bad weather. By the time they got to Tenerife it was not only rain but the sea itself coming in. In his letter home, James was caustic about Deptford, saying that he had stressed to the officers of the yard the importance of securing the sail room and other vulnerable parts of the ship, 'But it did not appear to me that anything had been done that could answer that end.' The Deptford neglect had already started to show. This was just the beginning of the voyage, when the ship should have been at its best.

Elizabeth turned her attention to baby Hugh to prevent worrisome thoughts from going any further. These were summer days of cloudy mornings, bright afternoons and frosty nights. Elizabeth stood at the window with Hugh, after the crowing cock had woken him. 'Is it a garden day?' she whispered into her son's silky dark hair. 'Look. Look at the billowing clouds,' she said as they moved across their pale blue sea. 'Just like the sails of Papa's ship.' She held their child up to see, focusing on a particular cloud till it had moved past the window frame, out of sight. 'God made the sky and the clouds, and the sea and the stars, and God will bring Papa back safely to us.'

She whispered stories of Papa to Hugh, even though he was far too young to understand the words; but nestled in her arms, he would have felt the rhythm of her heart, the vibration of her breast as she spoke, and would take it into himself, in the same way that Elizabeth felt the vibrations of her husband's voice in his chest when he told her South Seas stories, taking her on a sea of words to faraway places.

They were glorious days spent in the summer garden with Hugh, Gates shooing the clucking hens away from the crib where he slept and sighed and made sucking noises beneath the veil of net protecting him from bees and gnats, and any possible dangers. 'He is the most beautiful child, marm,' Gates would say over and over. So said the neighbours, the Curtises and Honeychurches, the Blades and the Witherspoons when they came to see him. Elizabeth smiled proudly. They had all been beautiful babies, Jamie and Nat now on the verge of manhood; but for Elizabeth, Hugh was the treasure of her heart.

Sometimes in the garden Elizabeth read the newspaper to Gates. Often it was some instance of a criminal nature, to which Gates would listen avidly. 'A countryman having bought some linen at a shop in Holburn offered in payment a light guinea,' read Elizabeth brushing away a bee, 'which the master of the shop instantly clipped in two. The countryman stared first at the guinea and then at the man who clipped it, and snatching up the scissors made a chop at the shopkeeper's hand. He cut off the first joint of the finger and ran away.'

She paused to allow Gates her 'oohs' and 'ahs' before going on to the next item. 'A woman was whipped through Fleet Street to Temple Bar, for decoying children from their parents, and putting out their eyes, in order to beg with them.'

After rounding her eyes in astonishment, and putting her hand to her cheek, Gates would always want more—for instance, what happened to the shopkeeper's finger, was the man apprehended; who was the woman who put the children's eyes out, what age was she, where did she come from, how many lashes did she get, was there a big crowd watching, did they jeer and throw eggs?

Elizabeth often said that she knew no more than what was in the paper, but Gates seemed to take no notice, as if the printed words were windows on the events. If her mistress were to look through the window again, perhaps a bit to the right or left, she would see everything there was to see and all of Gates's questions would have an answer.

Sometimes, to keep Gates happy, Elizabeth would make up the missing parts of the story. The countryman came, like so many, to London, hoping to make his fortune. He had fallen into hard times or bad company. He had tried to pass the light guinea, panicked when discovered, and fled. The shopkeeper's finger mended, and when the missing joint was remarked upon by customers, he said: 'A counterfeiter did that, but I ran after him, the top of my finger lying on this very counter. He is now in the prison hulks in Deptford. How many yards of linen was that, sir?'

As for the woman who put out the children's eyes, Elizabeth could not find a story.

One afternoon in August, when James was anchored off Tenerife, Elizabeth opened the newspaper and read to Gates the Declaration of the Representatives of the United States of America, dated 4 July 1776. It was a long declaration, and although Elizabeth knew that Gates much preferred an account of a good whipping to events in the American colonies, she insisted on reading it in full. 'It is much more important than a whipping, Gates,' Elizabeth said. 'One of the signatories is Benjamin Franklin, a scientific man of Mr Cook's acquaintance, a fellow member of the Royal Society. He used a kite to show that lightning is electricity. Did you know that, Gates?'

In the garden of the Mile End House, close to the kitchen door, Gates sat up as straight as she could, understanding long ago that her duties in this household were not just domestic, and that to a mistress whose husband was away so much, she was also companion.

'Another is Thomas Jefferson, the son of my dear Mama's friend from Shadwell,' Elizabeth added, to pique Gates's interest. 'Jane Randolph went to America and married Mr Jefferson and their son Thomas was born two years after me. They called their estate in Virginia, Shadwell,' Elizabeth told Gates.

While Elizabeth read in full the American Declaration of Independence, Gates remained silent, and Elizabeth was so taken up with it she did not notice whether the silence was due to lack of understanding, lack of interest or, as for Elizabeth herself, the sheer eloquence of the document. Apart from the 'right to bear arms', the whole thing had a Quaker essence—equality, freedom of speech, of religion, of everything.

Elizabeth thought fondly of the Sheppards in Essex and the Walkers in Whitby, 'the Friends' as Quakers called each other, and she was glad that both she and James had felt the warmth of the Quaker candle burning in their hearts. Now, though it may not have seemed obvious to anyone else, it was the declaration of a nation.

At Sir John Pringle's dinner that afternoon in April before James went away, Mr Boswell had conveyed Dr Johnson's opinion that the Americans were a nation of convicts, or worse, pirates. But neither Elizabeth nor James were of that opinion. Most of London, certainly the merchants and tradespeople that Elizabeth dealt with, and her friends in Mile End, sympathised with the colonists and thought that the government had treated them unfairly. That night as Elizabeth knelt beside her bed, she prayed for Cousin Frances, and all those caught up in the 'course of human events'. Especially, as always, she prayed for James.

⌒

Shortly after 30 November 1776, the anniversary meeting of the Royal Society, Elizabeth received an official visit from Sir John Pringle. She sat waiting in the parlour, hat arranged on her carefully coiffed hair, hands neatly folded in her lap. Into these hands she would shortly receive the Copley Medal. On that windy, blustery day Elizabeth gazed at the milky, finely textured skin stretching over her knuckles. She had rubbed goose fat into her hands, then washed it off in warm, lavender-scented water.

Gates had prepared sugar cakes, which were waiting under a muslin cover. The Staffordshire china, from which Omai had drunk his tea so delicately, was also set out. Such a formal honour as receiving the Copley Medal would not be done lightly, there would be some sort of ceremony, but cakes and tea were ready should Sir John wish to stay.

Sitting in the wintry afternoon, her hands quietly in place, her back straight, the soft sleeping breath of six month old Hugh marking time, Elizabeth imagined James in the illustrious premises of the Royal Society. She saw Sir John, Sir Joseph Banks, and all the other gentlemen gathered in their best breeches, wigs and hats to hear Sir John's presidential address and comments on James's prize-winning paper, the gentlemen having enjoyed a good dinner at the Mitre beforehand, and drunk to each other's health and then drunk a little more against the chill of the day.

Elizabeth would read the speech later in its entirety, published in the Society's *Philosophical Transactions*:

Allow me then, gentlemen, to deliver this medal, with his unperishing name engraved upon it, into the hands of one who will be happy to receive that trust, and to know that this respectable Body, never more cordially nor meritoriously bestowed that faithful symbol of their esteem and affection. For if Rome decreed the civic crown to him who saved the life of a single citizen, what wreathes are due to that man, who, having himself saved many, perpetuates now in your transactions the means by which Britain may herself preserve numbers of her intrepid sons, her mariners; who braving every danger, have so liberally contributed to the fame, to the opulence, and to the maritime empire of their country.

Elizabeth already knew the gist of her husband's paper, having seen him working on it. Preserving the health of mariners was not only a matter of getting them to eat sauerkraut and fresh vegetables. James ensured his men got more sleep by introducing three watches instead of two—four hours on and eight hours off. Then there was the regime of cleanliness. Once a week the men had to change their linen. Cleanliness made them more sober, James wrote, more orderly and attentive to duty. Bedding and hammocks were dried and aired. Fires were lit to drive out foul air; the acid steam of the burning wood dried up moisture from human and animal sweat, dispersed the stench of bilge water, and acted as an antiseptic. 'It promotes not only health of the body but of the mind,' James had told Elizabeth.

Elizabeth was immensely proud of her husband's achievements and pleased that they had been recognised with the prestigious award. But where was the medal for being the wife of such a man? What award recognised the hardships and efforts of running the household on her own, bringing up his children largely without his assistance, the heartache of watching their babies die?

She listened for the coach bringing the medal, difficult to distinguish one coach amid the many, although above the noise of traffic Elizabeth was always able to single out the barely audible murmurings of baby Hugh. He was sleeping soundly. London had spread out to Mile End and had over half a million inhabitants with more and more people arriving from the provinces, seeking work, looking for the same fabled fortunes that Dick Whittington had sought. Not all of them would end up becoming mayor as he did; they would find disease and heartache instead of gold.

Although her back was perfectly erect, Elizabeth straightened up even further when she heard the firm knock at the door, then Sir John announcing himself to Gates. Gates brought the visitors in, Sir John and a footman dressed in livery, who was holding a velvet cushion on which lay the medal.

It was the end of a long day, most of which Elizabeth had spent waiting. But waiting was how she had spent much of her life. Not in the everyday detail of it, where there was much to do, but in the great long sweeps of night after the chores were done, in the constant yearning and anxiety pinned to her like a shadow.

Sir John stayed for tea and cakes, and of course they talked of James. She was not to worry about his safety, Sir John admonished. If ever a man could hold his own on the oceans of the world, it was Captain Cook. Yes, she nodded, while the great unspoken thought tugged at her skirts like a child—her husband, the celebrated circumnavigator, had done more than any man in his field, yet no man could pit himself against the Almighty.

Hugh woke eventually and amid his soft cooing and searching for her breast, Elizabeth showed him the gold medal, with the

Society's coat of arms, the engraving of Science seated, and read to him the motto: *Nullius in verba*. She dangled it in front of him and he reached up for the shining thing as if it were a plaything. 'Your father has saved the lives of hundreds of seamen,' Elizabeth whispered into the baby's ear. 'And the lives of those yet to sail, if his good example will be followed.'

When Elizabeth finally drew the curtains on the day, and snuffed out the candle, she held the medal between her hands. There were no stars visible in the cold dark sky, so she imagined them in the firmament and stitched her prayers onto them so that wherever James was he could see them. She climbed into bed and lay on her side, her arm reaching to the cold empty place of James's absence. She held his pillow as if it were his body and fell asleep in its feathers.

Elizabeth sat bolt upright. Baby Hugh was crying. She did not know if her own screams had woken him or the howling wind rattling at the window. She gathered the baby up in her arms and held him tightly. 'There, there,' she said, trying to soothe both him and her thumping heart. 'It is only the wind.' Elizabeth relit the candle. The medal glowed as if it had a life of its own. She grasped hold of it, comforted by the solidity of metal. It was only a dream, the wind had caused it. Sir John and his footman had entered the house, but instead of a medal on the velvet cushion, there lay James's bloody heart.

Hugh's cries dissolved in Elizabeth's milk. The little one suckled, and though the wind continued to howl as if it wanted to rip the window out of its frame, it did not succeed. Nevertheless, Elizabeth felt wisps of wind snake their way into the room.

'Just a dream,' she said, her breath rippling the fine dark hairs on the baby's head. 'Papa is well. Probably at the Cape of Good Hope. Letters will be coming any day now.'

Through the howling wind outside, Elizabeth imagined Cape Town and the Cape of Good Hope, saw it in the details that James and Isaac had given and that she had seen in paintings by James's artists. She whispered to the contented baby in her arms about the remarkable mountain whose top was as flat as a table. 'Then the creases and folds like giant elephant's feet run down to the town. The bay is as full of ships as our Thames,' she continued, looking down to find the baby's eyes closed. She covered her breast, but kept the baby there, feeling his tiny streams of breath on her skin.

'Ships from all over the world stop at Cape Town—Dutch on their way to Batavia, French to Mauritius, Portuguese to the Indies, and of course our own British ships.' Elizabeth closed her eyes too, thinking of the homeward-bound ships which would bring news of James. She let her mind sail into Table Bay and saw the huge Castle of Good Hope, which held stores for the Dutch East India Company. Her mind flew to the top of Table Mountain and had a splendid view of the town, the whitewashed houses under thatched roofs, arranged in precise Dutch geometrical lines, so unlike the chaotic growth of London. It all seemed to gleam like sunlight on salt. Elizabeth saw zebras, elephants, tigers, ostriches and great horned beasts circling the town. 'It is a windy cape,' James had told Elizabeth, 'jutting into a windy sea.'

Wind. Elizabeth opened her eyes. The howling and rattling had stopped. Everything was still. Still as death. Elizabeth wanted to live somewhere in the middle, in the soft breeze between howling wind and complete stillness. She tried to imagine a world without wind. Even a perfect summer's day, everything in blossom, would seem dead without some slight breeze. Perhaps birds would not sing if there was no wind, bees cease buzzing. It was the wind that brought the scent of pollen to them. It was the wind that carried James around the world and though Elizabeth hoped for an always steady breeze, she knew that was only part of its ever-changing nature.

With as little disturbance as possible, Elizabeth put Hugh back in his crib, the same crib that all her babies had slept in. She blew out the candle and watched its vapour trail away. Elizabeth picked up the medal once again, held it to her breast as if it were a pendant.

She had sat this afternoon waiting for the coach, waiting for the knock on the door. Perhaps one day a coach would come, delivering the news she dreaded most. But she must not dwell on this, she must think only of the wind. She prayed that the breath of God would blow cleanly through her heart, that she would have the strength to stand in the face of both its turbulence and stillness, that her heart would remain an open place, and that the wind that blew bitter sorrow and grief into her heart would also take them away.

THE UNFINISHED VEST

February 14 1779. It was St Valentine's Day, the day on which birds chose their mate for the year.

Although James was always Elizabeth's invisible companion, for a moment she felt his presence so strongly that she immediately looked towards the door, as if he might be standing on the other side of it. Though there had been no knock, not even the rattle of the wind, Elizabeth put her embroidery aside, opened the door, looked up and down the street.

Puzzled, she came back to the piece she was working on — a vest for her husband to wear to court on his return. The silk thread was of the finest quality, and had the sheen of freshly washed hair, combed so that each strand was separate. It was smooth to the touch, as Elizabeth imagined the hair of South Seas women to be. Smooth also was the cloth from which she would fashion the vest, once the embroidery was finished. It was not linen or English wool, but exotic tapa cloth from Tahiti. Elizabeth imagined the women beating the fibrous inner bark of the paper mulberry tree to make it the smooth durable cloth she was now holding. She saw the rhythm of their work, their arms lifting clubs, and the arc and sway of their breasts. The tapa cloth had been a gift to James from Queen Obadia. In the way of the South Seas, James had given the Tahitian queen reciprocal gifts, including, he said, 'a child's doll which I made her understand was a picture of my wife'. Queen Obadia fastened the doll to her breast and paraded it around.

There had been no letters from James for two years. Both Jamie and Nat had sailed to America; the war which had been declared in 1776 continued, and the French had joined forces with the colonists, becoming once again England's enemy. Elizabeth's constant fear for her boys was lightened by the thought that in American waters they might meet up with their father. But no, they said. Nor was there any news of him. 'He is in the Pacific Ocean, Mama,' they said with assuring grown-up tones, Jamie nearly sixteen and Nat not far behind, 'on the other side of America.'

The stitches were smaller than ants, each exactly the same size as its sisters. She employed greens soft as the English countryside, to remind James, after the bright colours of the world, that this was his home. The stitches formed undulating lines, to resemble vines, an inch or two in from the edge of the cloth. For the core of the vine Elizabeth chose a paler green and either side of the core, a darker olive green. The vine also bore flowers—some tipped in blue, some red—and was decorated with red sequins.

Elizabeth brought her attention back to her embroidery.

As the days grew warmer Elizabeth embroidered in the garden, looking up every now and then to see Hugh chasing the hens. Though he still had the same soft transparent baby skin, Hugh was thriving. Everyone loved him. Cousin Charles smothered him in kisses which the two year old accepted, wrinkling up his nose.

Charles even got down on the floor and rolled balls to Hugh. When Jamie and Nat, now young midshipmen, came home, they let him play with their shoe buckles, or put their hats on his head. He would look up, the hat coming down over his eyes, and laugh with delight. 'Another sailor, Mama,' Nat said, and Elizabeth smiled but in her mind she whispered: 'No. The sea shall not have this one.'

Hugh loved going to church, to St Dunstan's. 'Go to God's house, Mama?' he asked, and Elizabeth took him, even when there were no services. He loved gazing at the stained-glass saints, letting their light play on his face.

Sometimes she embroidered with Gates, or with neighbours who dropped in. Of course they were all taken with the cloth and watched the slow progress of the embroidery as it began to take the shape of the eventual vest. 'It is exquisite,' exclaimed Mrs Honeychurch. 'I hope Queen Charlotte sees it, as well as the King.'

In April, Mr Curtis brought in a copy of the *Historical Chronicle*. 'Have you seen this, Mrs Cook?'

M. Sartine, secretary of the marine department at Paris, issued the following letter, which he has caused to be circulated through the entire marine of France. 'Captain Cook, who sailed from Plymouth in July, 1776, on board the Resolution, in company with the Discovery, Captain Clerke, in order to make some discoveries on the coasts, islands and seas of Japan and California, being on the point of returning to Europe and as such discoveries are of general utility to all nations and it is the King's pleasure, that Captain Cook shall be treated as a Commander of a neutral and allied power, and that all captains of armed vessels, etc, whom may meet the famous navigator, shall make him acquainted with the King's orders on this behalf, but at the

*same time let him know that on his part he must refrain from
all hostilities'.*

James was on the point of returning, that was the news that made
Elizabeth's heart leap. She read it over and over.

'Our enemies will not fire upon him,' announced Mr Curtis.
'Your husband is held in such high esteem he is above the concerns
of war.'

'Yes,' said Elizabeth, holding back tears. 'Yes.' Her heart was
so full of pride and relief, she thought it would burst.

In the following months, Benjamin Franklin made a similar
declaration on behalf of the Americans. James could sail anywhere in the world and he would be safe.

Each stitch brought the day of James's return closer. When
Elizabeth worked in the sequins she pictured her husband surrounded by sunlight, the sea bright with flecks of it, the light
flashing off the sleek bodies of porpoises. As she stitched the red
tips of the English flowers, she imagined exotic Tahitian flowers.

She was working on a red-tipped flower in January 1780 when
Sir Hugh Palliser came. It was a cold dark day and night had
already fallen. Elizabeth had just stoked the fire, breathing in the
smoky smell of coal. Dinner was over, the dishes washed. The
cloths were hanging by the fire. Elizabeth caught the shine of the
blue and white china in the sideboard. She remembered seeing a
cobweb on the door sill and thinking that she must get Gates to
wipe it away. Elizabeth fastened a red sequin into the embroidery,
penetrating the tapa cloth with her needle. There were murmured
voices at the door as Gates opened it. Elizabeth remembered the
last time he had come, with the news that had lifted her heart
out of the ashes.

Gates announced him. Elizabeth watched him enter the room,
hat under his arm. Though it was only a few steps it seemed to
take forever, as if he were walking down a long dark corridor.

She saw the look in his eyes. And in all the remembered detail she could not recall his exact words. Instead it was the faltering gaps in between. News had been received from Russia, a letter to the Admiralty. Elizabeth remembered saying: 'Was it in the ice? Did the ship founder? Was it frozen in the Artic waters?' It was none of these.

'Oh, marm,' whimpered Gates after Sir Hugh had left. 'The master.'

'It is all right,' said Elizabeth stiffly. 'Dry your eyes, Gates.'

'Marm . . .' Gates implored.

'There have been rumours before,' Elizabeth said briskly. 'Remember the report about the *Endeavour*?'

'But, marm, Sir Hugh said there was a letter from Captain Clerke.'

Elizabeth looked at the letter Sir Hugh had given her. It was not from Captain Clerke, but from Lord Sandwich. 'Dear Madam, what is uppermost in our minds allways must come first, poor captain Cooke is no more . . .'

'It is not my husband, it is another captain, who spells his name with an "e".'

'Marm,' said Gates, wringing her apron, 'you must . . .' But Gates did not know what her mistress must do. Nor what to do for her mistress.

Elizabeth returned to her embroidery but did not have the strength to push needle through cloth. 'I am going to bed,' she said.

'But, marm, it is only—'

'Thank you, Gates, nothing further is required.'

The bed curtains encased Elizabeth like a shroud. Though it was the coldest January night, Elizabeth felt a fever start at her heart and spread to the tips of her fingers, her toes, to the very ends of the hairs on her head. How could her body react like this to mere words? Yet she was so feverish she could not bear the touch of even the sheets. Elizabeth lay on the bed while her mind hovered close to the ceiling, a bird looking down on the restless body below. She had endured more than this. Such a fuss over nothing. Rumour, rumour, she repeated, trying to quell the tide rising in her. She must not succumb. She must remain a bird buffered on the warm air of faith. She would not be dragged down into the mire.

Little Hugh woke up in the middle of that long night and Elizabeth took him into bed with her. 'It is nothing,' she cooed to him.

Late the next day Mr Curtis came, newspaper under his arm as he had come before. But this time there were tears in his eyes. Mrs Curtis dawdled behind her husband, using him as a shield. 'Mrs Cook,' Mr Curtis began.

'You will have tea?' Elizabeth asked them.

They did not want tea.

The Curtises exchanged a quick glance. 'You have heard . . . ? You have seen . . . ?'

'The rumour?' asked Elizabeth archly.

'But,' said Mr Curtis, 'the newspaper says—'

'What nonsense are they printing now?' said Elizabeth grabbing hold of it.

Admiralty Office—Captain Clerke of his Majesty's sloop the Resolution, in a letter to Mr Stephens, dated 8 June, 1779, in the harbour of St Peter and St Paul, Kampschatka, gives the melancholy account of the celebrated Captain Cooke, late commander of that sloop with four of his mariners having been killed 14 February last, at the island of O'whihe, one of a group of new-discovered islands in 22 degrees of north latitude, in an affray with a numerous and tumultuous body of the natives.

Elizabeth's hands trembled. The words rose from the page like a tidal wave, looming menacingly overhead. She must not let it crash down on her.

'They say the king cried on hearing the news, Mrs Cook,' said Mrs Curtis. 'All of London is mourning.' Her voice sounded as if it were coming from a long way off, though she was standing less than an arm's length from Elizabeth.

'My deepest sympathies,' Mr Curtis said, 'for the loss of your husband and our dear friend.'

Everybody believed the news, but Elizabeth would not. Could not. Her faith alone would bring James home.

The will was proved on 24 January, such haste, but Mr Dyall had called in and collected Elizabeth to go to the lawyer. She went with him so as not to cause a fuss. As the will was read, she murmured words of her own. 'Bring him home safely, oh Lord, bring him home.' The nations of the earth had given him immunity, the Almighty would do so too. January 24. It was Elizabeth's thirty-eighth birthday.

At home she rocked little Hugh so hard that he began to cry and she did not know the reason for it. She lit candles in all the windows and stoked the fire up. 'It is winter,' she told herself. 'He can feel the cold of winter, that is all.'

'It is like a furnace in here, marm,' said Gates, beads of sweat forming on her forehead.

'Nevertheless,' said Elizabeth, 'we will keep it good and hot. It is for Hugh,' she reasoned.

So many letters of condolence. It was nice of people to send their esteemed thoughts. But no-one, except Elizabeth, kept faith.

Faith was a weapon, faith was a directive of life. Faith was the sea that surrounded Elizabeth.

When she fitfully dropped into sleep, bad dreams sailed her ocean of faith, sails hanging down like shrouds.

One hot night in June, shouts and cries and the stamping of feet entered Elizabeth's dreams. Numerous and tumultuous natives, with clubs, sticks and daggers, were bearing down on her.

Elizabeth gasped herself out of the dream, sat bolt upright in her bed, eyes wide open as could be. But still the dream continued, only Hugh was in it now. 'Mama,' he said, 'lots of men running.' Elizabeth could hear them. Then she smelled fire, and looked wildly around.

She went downstairs searching for the fire, and found Gates crouched in a corner.

'What is the matter?' Elizabeth asked.

'It's the anti-Papists, marm. Burning and looting. I don't dare to put my head out. It's terrible, marm. So many of them.'

Elizabeth went to the window, opened the curtains a fraction. Fires blazed everywhere, angry rioters silhouetted against the flames. Men armed with sticks were throwing chairs, tables, pictures, whatever they could find, onto a huge bonfire. Some of them were dancing and waving their hats. Further back from the fire she saw others brandishing banners which proclaimed: 'No Popery'.

Elizabeth held Hugh close to her and got down on her knees and prayed to Almighty God. While she prayed, the mob continued on its path of destruction, and reached into the West End, to St Martin's Street, right to the door of Dr Burney, who shouted out to the mob: 'No Popery!' to save the house from being attacked.

The newspapers were full of the riots in defiance of Parliament's Catholic Relief Act repealing some of the existing anti-Catholic laws. Fifty thousand men led by Lord George Gordon. It started, as many riots did, in the East End, but quickly spread. The thirst of the mob for Catholic blood seemed unquenchable. Everyone was afraid, Papist and non-Papist alike. Even the Lord Mayor of London seemed powerless to stop them, saying: 'I must be cautious what I do lest I bring the mob to my house.'

On 8 June the Riot Act was read but the rioters continued, freeing the prisoners from Newgate then burning the jail and throwing the keys into the fountain in St James's Square. They torched other jails, the Blackfriars Bridge tollgates. They tried to storm the Bank of England but armed clerks and volunteers routed them. Eventually the twelve thousand troops summoned by the king quelled the riots, with seven hundred rioters dead, four hundred and fifty arrested and twenty-five executed. For days after, the fires continued to burn into the hot summer haze. Gordon was tried for high treason but acquitted, and the Lord Mayor fined £1000 for criminal negligence.

It was a hard summer. Elizabeth read the papers from beginning to end, yet found not one word of the news she was searching for.

THE DITTY BOX

In October 1780, the *Resolution* limped into Deptford. Elizabeth waited. Earlier in the year the king had ordered her a pension of £200. James would be proud of her. She had invested the money and managed their financial affairs admirably. The house was spick and span, not a cobweb in sight. Her eye perused the interior of her house as she waited.

Elizabeth heard the stories that snaked their way up the river, that Captain Clerke had succumbed to tuberculosis, a legacy of his time in prison. There were no great fanfares or trumpeting this time. The newspapers remained subdued on the matter. Days passed and still James did not come. Elizabeth found that her ocean of faith had dwindled to a thin, muddy estuary.

When she heard a coach stop, then the knock on the door, Elizabeth's heart raced. It swelled even further when she heard the sound of heavy boxes being unloaded. Gates was about to open the door but Elizabeth said no, she would go herself.

On the threshold were James's sea chests, but James was nowhere to be seen. In his place stood Jem Burney. He looked grave, much older than he'd looked that bright summer's day at Vauxhall.

'Mrs Cook,' he greeted her. 'My deepest sympathies,' he said. 'We have lost our great captain.' Elizabeth bowed her head. She could not speak. She knew now that her dear husband was dead. 'The crew of the *Resolution* would like you to have this.' He handed Elizabeth a small package.

Elizabeth held the package for a long time after Jem Burney had gone. Eventually she untied the familiar knots. The package contained a box, a ditty box of smooth dark brown timber, shaped like a coffin, small enough to rest in the palm of her hand. Inset into the lid were two silver plates. Onto one was engraved: 'Lono and the Seaman's Idol'. On the other: 'Quebec, Newfoundland, Greenwich, Australis'. Stars and circles were worked into the timber and around the edge, chiselled into the wood itself an inscription: 'Made of *Resolution* oak for Mrs Cook by crew'. The bottom side of the box had a plate engraved: 'James Cook, slain at Owhynee, 14 February, 1779'.

As Elizabeth opened the box, its lid swivelling outwards, she could not help but think of another box, long ago, in which was written: 'Elizabeth, marry me'. Instead of words, in this one was a painting, a watercolour, the wash of blue water, green trees, a hilly mound jutting into the painted sky. Near the shore was a boat, a man in naval uniform, too small and indistinct to be James. On the other side of the boat was a group of brown figures and behind, a thatched roof. In the foreground, as if floating in the water, was a lock of James's hair, secured in a figure of eight with a thread. Elizabeth could not bring her eyes away from those dark strands, all that had come back of James.

'Marm?' Elizabeth heard Gates's voice. Soft, tentative.

'What is it?' asked Elizabeth.

'The sea chests. They are still at the door.'

Elizabeth sat there in a trance, as if mesmerised.

'Marm,' said Gates, looking with concern at her mistress, 'shall I fetch them in? Someone might steal them.'

Elizabeth rose, clutching the ditty box. The pain in her heart was so immense she felt as if her ribcage, every bone of it, had cracked. 'Thank you, Gates. I will attend to it,' she heard herself say.

On 22 January 1780 Fanny Burney wrote to Samuel Crisp:

I am sure you must have grieved for poor Captain Cook. How hard, after so many dangers, so much toil, to die in so shocking a manner, in an island he had himself discovered—among savages he had himself in his first visit to them civilized, and rendered kind and hospitable, and in pursuit of obtaining justice in a cause which he had himself no interest but zeal for his other captain. He was besides the most moderate, humane and gentle circumnavigator who ever went out upon discoveries; agreed the best with all the indians, and till this fatal time, never failed, however hostile they met, to leave them friends.

Dr Huntery, who called here lately, said he doubted not but Capt. Cook had trusted them too unguardedly; for, as he always had declared his opinion that savages never committed murder without provocation, he boldly went among them without precautions for safety, and paid for his incautious intrepidy with his very valuable life.

Sir Hugh Palliser's
Monument to Captain Cook

TO THE MEMORY OF
CAPTAIN JAMES COOK

Elizabeth Cook was a widow, but the Almighty was not done with her yet. Death came in waves, swept her out to sea only to gather force to dash her against the rocks again. Time after time. A few short months after delivery of the ditty box, death took Nat.

Jamie brought the news on that cold crestfallen day. He entered the house, and for a moment Elizabeth felt the breath catch in her throat, so like his father was he. 'Mama,' he said, his eyes brimming with tears. It was a moment before he could speak the words. Elizabeth gathered Hugh up into her arms, instinctively knowing there would be a need. Jamie took in a deep breath, enough to draw out of him the leaden words. 'Nat has drowned, Mama. There was a dreadful hurricane in the West Indies. The *Thunderer* went down. Along with all hands.'

The three remaining members of the Cook family held each other for a long time, the tears of one mingling with the tears of the others.

As it was with Nat, so it was with James. Elizabeth had to keep telling herself he was dead, that he would never be coming back to Mile End, that he was not simply on a long voyage.

Once, in a dream, James did come back. 'Is it really you?' Elizabeth whispered.

'Yes, my dearest.'

Elizabeth marvelled at how beautiful he looked. His seaweed hair rippled across his shoulders, his eyes had the lustre of black pearls, his face a radiance that filled the whole room. Elizabeth was not the least bit surprised at the sight of him. In the dream she had no memory that he'd died.

'I am exceedingly well,' he told her.

When his features faded the radiance remained. Elizabeth carried it with her to the moment of waking but when she opened her eyes to the cold empty bed the weight of grief returned. How she wanted to prolong that dreaming state, to sleep for the rest of her life and dream only of radiance. Yet she could not let herself be so seduced. She could not abandon Jamie and Hugh. She must rise from the bed of dreams, rise to the pain of the real, bear the ache in her bones, her heart, her soul.

While Elizabeth carried on daily life as best she could, Captain James Cook, RN passed into history. In the years to come there were medals to commemorate him, crockery bearing his likeness, wallpaper, paintings representing his apotheosis, plays and pantomimes depicting his death, not only in England but also the Continent. He was the hero of the age, a self-made man who brought agricultural arts and tools to the Pacific. He was likened to Ulysses, guiding his men not through Scylla and Charybdis, but through coral shoals and the underworld of Antarctica.

Among the monuments erected to James's memory was a globe fixed to a square block in the grounds of Sir Hugh Palliser's estate in Buckinghamshire, with the inscription:

> *To the memory of Captain James Cook, the ablest and most renowned Navigator this or any country hath produced . . . Traveller! Contemplate, admire, revere, and emulate this great master in his profession; whose skill and labours have enlarged natural philosophy; have extended nautical science; and have disclosed the long concealed and admirable arrangements of the Almighty in the formation of this globe, and, at the same time, the arrogance of mortals, in presuming to account, by their speculations, for the law by which he was pleased to create it.*

Nothing would compensate for the loss of James, but Elizabeth wanted to make sure that his family shared in the fruits of his labours, as they would have done had he lived. On 13 June 1781 Elizabeth sat at the Spanish mahogany table and wrote to Lord Sandwich.

> *I hope your Lordship will pardon my troubling you with this adress, I have avoided all application, as much as possible, that might call for your smallest Attention, but upon the presumption that the History of the Voyage in which my dear Husband lost his Life will soon be laide before the Public by which through your Lordships favour my self and Family may be benifetted, I humble hope from your Lordships usual goodness to us you will be pleased to consider us for compensation as you may deem us deserving of by his merit and for the part he acted in the course of the Voyage, untill his unfortunate Death put a period to his Labours whereby we became great sufferers from his not returning safe home, I therefore most humbly implore Your*

*Lordships favour and protection to myself and Family which will
ever be retained in gratefull remembrance.*

When the *Voyage to the Pacific Ocean . . . for Making Discoveries
in the Northern Hemisphere* finally appeared in June 1784, it sold
out in three days. Elizabeth, Jamie and Hugh received, in the
following year, half of the profits—the interest being assigned to
Elizabeth, the principal divided equally between Jamie and Hugh.

Also in 1784, Elizabeth received from Sir Joseph Banks, now
President of the Royal Society, the society's gold medal which
Lewis Pingo, engraver to the Royal Mint, had struck in commemor-
ation of her husband. She wrote a letter of thanks to Sir Joseph,
adding: 'My greatest pleasure now remaining is in my sons, who,
I hope, will ever strive to copy after so good an example, and,
animated by the honours bestowed on their father's memory, be
ambitious of attaining by their own merits your notice and
approbation.'

In September of the following year, the Cook family was
granted a coat of arms. Elizabeth did not have a carriage on
which to display it but she was grateful that the family should
be honoured in this way. On the shield were two polar stars, and
between them, a map of the Pacific with longitude and latitude
marked. The red track of James's voyage ended at Hawaii. The
crest was an arm, in the uniform of a captain of the Royal Navy.

Elizabeth also had her own commemorations, notably a
memorial ring decorated with her husband's hair in the shape of
a vase surrounded by a sprig of leaves. The ring box bore the
seal of the coat of arms, but the ring remained constantly on
Elizabeth's finger.

A doctor had once told Elizabeth that the human heart was roughly the size of a clenched fist. Elizabeth felt that instead of a heart in her ribcage she had such a clenched fist. She prayed for the breath of God to uncurl and relax it but relief never came. She went through the motions of daily life, attending to the chores, instructing Gates, nodding a curt greeting to neighbours in the street. Gates made her mistress little sugar cakes and other treats, but Elizabeth seemed to find delight in none of these things. Only Jamie and Hugh brought a smile to her face.

Elizabeth took Hugh to see the hot air balloon which lifted off from Stepney Green. A big crowd stood gasping at the size of it, and the impossible thought that it would rise into the air, but rise it did, and all eyes followed, accompanied by 'oohs' and 'ahs' and applause. Hugh was ten years old when he saw the balloon and said that he would like to fly away in such a machine.

'Then we might never see you again.'

'I could fly to the stars and see Papa and Nat. I could be the first man on the moon.'

Though he was growing tall, almost as high as his mother's shoulder, Elizabeth held him closer to her skirts, and thought of James. If such a contraption had been invented ten years earlier, James would probably propose voyaging in it. Back when James had set out on his first voyage, the idea that a balloon could float from one country to another would have been considered laughably impossible. But the preceding year, 1785, the first hot air balloon crossed the Channel.

Elizabeth watched the balloon rise higher and higher into the summer sky. She felt as if everything in her life was pulling away from her, stretched so hard that she would rupture.

She brought her attention back to the ground. The fashionable women in the crowd were wearing huge flounced hats—Lunardis after balloonist Vincenzo Lunardi and his daring exploits. Elizabeth looked up to the brim of her own hat, outmoded despite the new

A Letter from Elizabeth
Cook to Frances McAllister
(nee Wardale)

Dear Cousin

I received y[our]
was glad to hear you we[re]
comfortably indeed you[r]
deal of trouble.
America — War. I beg
you upon your man[?]

Jamie had finally persuaded Elizabeth to leave 8 Assembly Row. It had become such a dark little house, full of the cobwebs of death hanging everywhere no matter how much Elizabeth dusted and polished.

Clapham was a pleasant respectable village, with handsome villas and mansions surrounding the Common, the whole planted with trees and shrubs, and crisscrossed with carriage drives. Some days the breeze blew the scent of lavender from the fields on nearby Lavender Hill to the village. At four miles south it was far enough away from London for the air to have health-restoring properties, yet it was very well connected to the metropolis by road. The post arrived four times a day from London and could be received at Mr Batten's, Clapham Common; Mr Taylor's, Park Road; or from Mr Oldie's, Clapham Rise.

She had chosen Clapham because of its convenience for Jamie when he returned from Portsmouth. The large three-storeyed red-brick house she bought in 1788 was on the section of the London road which would later be known as Clapham High Street. As well as several bedrooms the house had a parlour front and back, dining room, scullery, laundry and cellar. The ceilings were intricately decorated with soft pastel plasterwork in the style of Robert Adams. In the dining room Elizabeth put up heavy velvet curtains, and in the study the folding mahogany table.

As she sat arranging the ink and pen on the honey-coloured surface of the table she remembered how she had lovingly polished it before the *Endeavour* voyage. Though this was a new house, a new beginning, she had brought everything of her husband with her, maps and charts, journals, the unfinished vest, the ditty box, James's South Sea relics, the medals and the coat of arms. His letters, of course, which she read till the pain in her heart got too much to bear.

Elizabeth took a fresh sheet of paper from the drawer and dipped the pen into the ink. She continued her weekly letters to James, even after Sir Hugh had brought the news and Jem the ditty box. She wrote to him of the new house in Clapham, how she had started a garden in the back, how there was a place for Jamie's horse, that Jamie had been made lieutenant on 4 May 1782, and that Hugh was doing well at the Merchant Taylors' school in Charterhouse Square.

The letter for which she was now preparing was not to James, but Cousin Frances in Philadelphia. Mr Lieber had died, and Frances was remarried. Elizabeth could not imagine herself being married to anyone but James.

Clapham, April, 1792

Dear Cousin,

I receiv'd yours by Col Oswald, was glad to hear you was well and settled so comfortably indeed you must have had a deal of trouble. I often thought of you in the American War.

Elizabeth looked up from the page. Hardly had that war ended than troubles had started brewing in France. To begin with, in 1789, the reforms across the Channel—the cries of liberty, equality, fraternity—had been greeted with approval in London, but by 1792 the reforms had turned to terror. King George had already issued a royal proclamation against seditious activity and Elizabeth felt sure that England would once more go to war with France. She prayed it would not come to that. Jamie would have to fight on the seas and the French would not grant him the same immunity they had bestowed on his father.

Elizabeth looked at the few lines she had written and took up the pen once again.

I beg leave to congratulate you upon your marriage with so good a man. Col Oswald gives him the highest character. I am very glad to hear you have such fine children. My sons are oblig'd to you for your present.

Elizabeth knew that cousin Frances corresponded with the old neighbours in Mile End, but she wondered if Frances had had news of her Cook relatives, if she knew that James senior had died, a few months after James himself.

She dipped the pen into the ink once more.

Your Uncle died about thirteen years ago. Mrs Fleck lives at Redcar. She has got six children. They were all well when I heard last.

Elizabeth remembered the good times she and the boys had had with Frances, how fond they were of her, and she of them. Hugh of course knew cousin Frances only through letters, but Jamie remembered her well.

*My son will take another opportunity to write to you, he joins
with me in love to you and family.*

It was all she could manage. Elizabeth put the pen down, folded
the letter and sealed it. She looked at the clock. 'Gates,' she called.
Gates appeared. 'Will you take this letter to Mr Batten's? If you
hurry you shall make the post.'

In the spring of 1793 Hugh was entered into Christ's College at
Cambridge, destined to become a clergyman. Elizabeth arranged
with Reverend Kaye, the King's chaplain, that Hugh be considered for a favourable position on completion of his studies. She'd
not yet told her son of the arrangement, did not want him to
consider his time at Cambridge an easy ride.

Elizabeth and Gates waited that fine spring day while Hugh's
luggage was loaded onto the coach. What a fine tall youth Hugh
was, and how calm. Nothing ever ruffled him. He seemed to take
his departure to Cambridge in his stride, as if he'd been destined
for it all his life. Elizabeth remembered seeing Jamie off all those
years ago. How anxious she was for him, how much she had fussed,
or so it seemed in her memory. Now her youngest was leaving
home. She still felt the knot in her chest but Elizabeth worried
less for Hugh's safety than she had for young Jamie's. Hugh was
entering into the service of the Lord, he would be protected.

He embraced first Gates then Elizabeth. She felt the warmth
of his cheek against hers. 'I'll be home for Christmas,' he said,
kissing his mother gently on the forehead.

The two women watched and waved till the coach was a small
speck on the London Road.

'For heaven's sake, Gates,' said Elizabeth as they walked back to the house. 'Stop blubbering or you'll have me doing it too. It's not as if he's going to the South Seas or America,' she said, trying to assure herself as well as Gates. 'Cambridge is only a coach journey away.' And not nearly as fraught with risk as being at sea, war or no.

But there was no place safe from the hand of the Almighty. In December Elizabeth received news, by the post that was delivered four times a day, that Hugh had contracted scarlet fever. He was in mortal danger. She packed her bag, donned her hat and set forth on the second coach journey of her life.

'Not Hugh, do not take my youngest,' she prayed silently through the cold bumpy countryside. This child was dedicated to the church, surely the Almighty would spare him. Huddled in a corner of the coach, Elizabeth prayed so hard that her fingernails dug into her hands.

Elizabeth stayed inside the coach when it made its stop in London, barely aware of new passengers coming aboard, their luggage being loaded. She kept her eyes closed, wanting to see nothing but the face of her beloved Hugh. She shut them tightly to keep out the panic threatening to engulf her. He would survive, he had to. The Lord would not take the child already dedicated to Him. Elizabeth saw nothing of the snow-covered fields and brown brick buildings as the coach came into the winding streets of Cambridge.

The coach dropped her at the grooved timber doors, the Great Gate of Christ's College, where she was escorted to Hugh's room.

At the top of the stairs a black-coated gentleman, a physician, said: 'Mrs Cook?' Perhaps he introduced himself, told her his name, Elizabeth no longer recollected. 'The young gentleman died but an hour ago.'

Elizabeth flew into the room, her skirts black and shiny as ravens' wings. One hour. Perhaps he had not yet begun the journey, perhaps his soul was still here. Her son was as still as a portrait. His face was an oval above the covers of the narrow bed, his hair damp on the pillow, his hands placed one on top of the other on his breast.

There was another young man in the room, the same age as Hugh, a fellow student. 'I'm sorry,' he said gravely.

Elizabeth nodded an acknowledgment, then knelt beside her son, touched his cheek. It was still warm. 'Hugh,' she breathed his name like a sigh. The warm breath of his mother travelled into Hugh's ear but he did not hear. The fellow student, tears in his eyes, turned away and gazed out of the window. Elizabeth stroked her son's forehead, trying to coax a response, any sign of life at all, but there was nothing. He was seventeen. It was 21 December, Elizabeth and James's thirty-second wedding anniversary, and their youngest son was dead.

Hugh was buried in Great St Andrew's Church, across the road from the college. In a dull dream Elizabeth received the condolences of her son's friends, of his masters. She remembered nothing of the journey back to London, nothing of Christmas or New Year, except the cold suffocation of snow and ice.

Of six children, there remained only Jamie. A bare month later, a day or two after Elizabeth's fifty-second birthday, she received news that Jamie had drowned in a fierce storm off the Isle of Wight while attempting to join the man of war *Spitfire*, of which he was commander.

The letter shook like a wind-blown leaf in her hand. There was darkness all around and Elizabeth was falling.

A Letter from Mrs Honeychurch to Frances McAllister

London, Sept. 12th, 1794

Mrs McAllister,

I received yrs dated June, 25th, and am very glad to hear that you and your family escaped the dreadful calamity [yellow fever] that threatened you, indeed the newspapers gave very terrible accounts of it and I was afraid that you or yours might have fallen victims to it, and you have great reason to be thankful to the Almighty that the dreadful scourge passed over you. I saw Mrs Cook a short time since, she has been very ill ever since the death of her oldest son which was a month and a day after the death of her youngest, who was a very promising youth who, designed for the Church, had been at the University of Cambridge a few months, where he died of a violent fever. She had not been out but once after his decease when she heard of her eldest son's being drowned, which quite overcame her, and she has not been able to come downstairs or eat a bit of bread since, within these few weeks she has eat a small bit of veal or lamb or a little fish, since which she has thought herself better tho she has two fits every day, night and morning and they hold her an hour, and I am afraid they will never leave her, it is a long time to be in such a state as James was drowned about Christmas as he was going aboard his ship, it was a very stormy night and his friends with whom he had spent the day would have persuaded him not to have gone, but he said it was his duty to be on board his ship and nothing should hinder him, seven men share the same fate with him. His body was found at the Isle of Wight and taken to Cambridge to be buried with his brother.

I have been fourteen weeks with Mrs Shanks at Packham, she has been in a very poor state of health, sometimes subject to spasms in her breath, which has been more frequently this summer than they used to be at that season of the year.

As for myself I am but very indifferent, being very short breath'd, and my walking days are not what they used to be, half a mile is quite walk enough for me.

Elizabeth was in a deep wide sea, she was drowning, her lungs bursting. When she finally took a breath she felt slime oozing down her throat. The thick black sea covered all the world, and Elizabeth was no bigger than a pea. She felt the touch of slippery fish on her skin and saw sharks coming at her, their teeth like bright little daggers. Far below, wraiths were reaching up for her, trying to pull her down to them. Dead sirens, mouths as big as sharks, their lamentations full of dread. Their floating cobweb hair threatened to strangle her. She was day and night in this sea from which she found no respite. Warm hands rubbed her cold ones but she thrashed them away. Elizabeth saw amongst the wraiths all her beloved dead, her whole family drowning in the cobweb hair weaving its way around gravestones: James Cook, 1779; Joseph Cook, 1768; George Cook, 1772; Elizabeth Cook, 1771; and the boys—Nathaniel Cook, 1780; Hugh Cook, 1793, and James Cook, 1794.

She wanted to drown with them but the wraiths pulled her another way, offering her food that she tightened her mouth against as if their offerings were poison.

There were periods when she remembered nothing. She must have slept but awoke again into the drowning sea. Sometimes she caught glimpses of a room, a woman in bed, with people surrounding her. Elizabeth saw Gates among them. Downstairs she heard Mrs Honeychurch's voice, other neighbours from Mile End, and wondered what they were doing there and who the wretched creature in the bed was. Then the wraiths would call to her again.

The opiates put her in a deathly dream but when they wore off Elizabeth raged. 'You've taken my husband!' she shouted at the Almighty. 'All my children. Take their mother, I am ready to die.' She flung the bedclothes away, offering herself.

Elizabeth flailed about, shoving away the doctor, Gates, whoever else was trying to calm her.

'Hush, marm. The neighbours will hear you.'

'Damn the blasted neighbours. And damn the Almighty!'

'Marm,' said Gates, shocked. 'You'll go to hell.'

'I am in hell!' Elizabeth shrieked.

They managed to hold her down. Elizabeth saw the little cup with slimy brown liquid being put to her mouth. She struggled against it but they forced it down. She tasted its bitterness on her lips, and a trickle of the mixture trailed a long way down her throat, as if her body were a large empty tunnel. She lay back on the pillows, her eyelids closing heavily.

Eventually, there were cracks of daylight, a wind lifting the curtain, but it was too bright for her to bear. Elizabeth had no idea how much time had passed—hours, weeks, months. She sank back.

She found herself in the dark brown dream of the alehouse. 'Mama,' she called, 'I've lost Sam Bird.' There was no response. The alehouse, usually so full of noise and smell and busyness, was deserted. Elizabeth climbed the stairs which seemed enormous; she had to lift her legs up to them. When she got to the top, she was surprised to find yet another set of stairs. Everything was still as the grave. 'Mama?' But the whole place was silent; Elizabeth couldn't even hear her own footsteps. The second set of steps got narrower and narrower, and she had to press with her hands to stop the walls caving in on her.

She hadn't seen a door, it was as if a section of the wall had opened, and she found herself in a long attic. It was full of treasures—maps and charts, crockery, furniture, medals. Framed in the light from a small window, sitting on a high-backed chair, was an old lady as wizened as a walnut. She had a tiny little fan and as she waved it to and fro Elizabeth saw the glint of rings on her fingers. In the wrinkled old face were the bluest eyes Elizabeth had ever seen. She sat as erect as anybody the size of a walnut could sit. She did not open her mouth but Elizabeth quite distinctly heard her say: 'I have been waiting all my life for you.'

It was a perplexing thing to hear. Elizabeth did not understand, but she suddenly felt completely overwhelmed by darkness; it was coming in through the window, through the floorboards, she could feel it cold and sticky like treacle. Elizabeth started to climb up the leg of the chair to get away from it. The walnut woman stretched out her hands, and when Elizabeth finally reached the safety of her lap, the old lady put her arms around her.

'What would they think, seeing you suffering so?' she whispered into Elizabeth's hair, rocking her as if she were a baby, fluttering the fan so that Elizabeth could feel its gentle breeze. 'You have travelled beyond the horizon. It is not always easy, but it is bearable.'

From out of the air, the walnut woman produced a little bird and gave it to Elizabeth. It was battered and worn, the green and red paint chipped, but she recognised it straightaway. How good to see Sam Bird once again, to know he'd been here all the time. The old woman started humming a little song, a lullaby that Elizabeth herself had sung to the children when they were babies. Just before Elizabeth felt herself drift off to sleep the old lady whispered, 'It is time for us to change places.'

Elizabeth's eyes opened abruptly. 'Change places?'

'You stay here and I'll go down into the house. You won't be lonely, all the things of your loved ones are here to play with and we can visit each other as often as we like. But I need your help.' She said it in such a way that it sounded like a game.

'What must I do?' said Elizabeth.

'I have been waiting in the attic for so long, I'm not sure I can move my legs. I would just like you to be here, in case I fall.' It was an easy thing for Elizabeth to do. She could pick the little woman up and place her on the floor, or put her in her pocket. 'No, I must do it myself.' She moved herself to the edge of the chair and Elizabeth saw tiny legs appear. The walnut woman wiggled them a bit as if she had just put them on and was trying them out.

In no time she was standing on the floor, steadying herself by resting her hand on Elizabeth's shoulder. Now that she was off the chair she seemed to have grown to normal size. At first she shuffled, as if she did not know the proper movements for walking. But soon she was gliding effortlessly. Elizabeth skipped beside her, right till the moment that the old woman disappeared down the stairs.

Embroidery on Silk of Captain Cook's Voyages by Mrs Elizabeth Cook

OWHYHEE

Such a celebration to see the new century—1800! There were those who thought the world would end, who stood on street corners loudly proclaiming it, but others held hopes for a more enlightened future. In the closing years of the eighteenth century there began in earnest a campaign to abolish the slave trade, with Elizabeth's Clapham neighbours forming the nub of the crusade—banker John Thornton who lived on the south side of the Common, his brother Henry on the west side near Battersea Rise, and their friend William Wilberforce. It was in the oval library of Henry Thornton's house that the campaign was planned, with Zachary Macaulay, James Stephen and others.

London was the city of progress, of newness and an unshakeable belief in its own glory. It was the grandest city in all of Europe, none other could match it. Experiments were being done with gas lighting and some envisaged the whole of London being lit by gas, although Sir Humphry Davy declared that: 'it would be as easy to bring down a bit of the moon to light London, as to succeed in doing so with gas.' Above it all, above the palaces and prisons, banks and hospitals, parks and squares, the docks and the riverside's steam-powered industries, hovered the city's thick belching breath. Elizabeth was glad of the fresh, genteel air of Clapham.

Elizabeth joined her neighbours to watch the fireworks on the Common on that cold frosty night of 31 December, 1799. Cousin Charles and his wife Mary, who had bought a very nice property at Merton, Dr Elliotson and his family, the Ravenhills and other Clapham neighbours had persuaded Elizabeth to come out.

It was six years since Jamie and Hugh had passed away but December and January were still difficult months for Elizabeth. She felt even more keenly their loss in the midst of the festive season which families held so dear.

In that terrible winter the crazed china she was had shattered completely. She'd thrashed about, damning the Almighty, challenging Him to take her. But He had not. He had taken her whole family and left her stranded in this life. 'It is not always easy but it is bearable.' The words of the old woman in her dream echoed back to her. She had mended but there were too many cracks in Elizabeth for her to go back to unblemished joy, to the weightless happiness she'd felt as a young bride when she had embarked upon her journey with James. Grief was ever a part of her now. But she prayed that the load would lighten, that she would not crumple under the weight of it. For the sake of her celebrated husband and her dear children, it must not affect her dealings with others. She prayed that, in public at least, what Mr Banks and others called her 'excellent character' would be maintained.

On the anniversaries of the deaths of James, Nat, Jamie and Hugh, Elizabeth fasted and meditated, using as a guide her Book of Common Prayer, or the big Bible that had accompanied James

on his voyages. She submitted herself to the pain of praying to
God the Father, who had bid Abraham sacrifice his child as a
test of faith. In the Lord's Prayer Elizabeth had to summon all
her strength to say, 'Thy will be done on earth.' Often she faltered, felt the words stick in her throat.

Sometimes on the anniversary of Hugh's death Elizabeth took
the coach to Cambridge. The service was faster and the roads
much improved since that time long ago when she and James had
journeyed to Yorkshire. On her visits to Cambridge she knelt and
prayed in Great St Andrew's Church, where Hugh and Jamie were
buried. She also sat alone in the grounds of Christ's College. She
imagined spring in those gardens, pansies and daffodils, crocuses,
but on the anniversaries of the deaths it was always winter.

After silent prayer, Elizabeth walked in the college grounds.
Souvent me souvient. I often remember. The coat of arms was
on the oriel window above the master's lodge. Upholding the
banner were two white carved yales with gilt antlers. These were
the arms, badges and motto of Lady Margaret Beaufort, mother
of King Henry VII, foundress of Christ's College. Elizabeth knew
the story of the illustrious foundress of the college into which
Hugh had been accepted, of her piety and great political influence, but when she gazed at the portrait, it was not the mother
of the king that Elizabeth saw, but the girl she once was, pregnant
and widowed at the age of thirteen.

Sometimes Elizabeth walked the curved streets of that brown-
brick town, the voices of choir boys floating like feathers over
the buildings, floating upward to heaven. As her black silk skirts
swished along the cobbled streets, she moved in the midst of boys
the same age as Hugh had been. Young men full of the promise
of youth, some self-important, others engaged in horseplay, but
all of them ardent, and in passionate conversation about mathematics, poetry, botany, music and, no doubt, young ladies.

Elizabeth walked among them, invisible to them in her old age, and she gazed at their unmarked faces, belief in their immortality wrapped around them like a gown. Each year she was older, but the faces in the street were always young.

How hard it must have been for Jamie to lose his only remaining brother to the fever, to be the only Cook child left. Elizabeth often wondered if that was part of his determination not to be dissuaded by his friends, to brave the terrible storm that night. Was he foolhardy? Jamie's body had been found on the shore of the Isle of Wight, with a head wound and his pockets emptied of valuables. No trace of the boat's crew had ever been found.

Elizabeth made enquiries through Cousin Isaac regarding these puzzling circumstances but no further information came to light. Finally she put the mystery to rest in her own mind—Jamie had drowned while attempting to join his ship, his body had washed ashore, and his corpse had been robbed. Such indignity was not uncommon.

Elizabeth had three extra servants, including a footman, by the turn of the century, but old Gates was still with her and swore she would remain for the rest of her life. Gates responded well to the additional help and took on the role of housekeeper, making sure her underlings were fulfilling their duties. 'Too much parsley on the anchovy toasts,' she'd say to Mary. Or, 'Marm likes the bread cut half an inch thick.' She was getting too old to perform active duties, although the last person to realise this was Gates herself. The young servants probably considered her a nuisance, but Elizabeth kept her on. She and Gates had grown old together, knew each other's ways.

At the dawn of the new century Elizabeth decided to embark on the work of her life. Whilst she admired Fanny Burney, Hannah More and Ann Radcliffe, she did not have the inclination herself to take up the pen to tell a story. Rather, she took heed of the words addressed to Madam Melpomeme Metaphor, the central character in a play Elizabeth had seen called *The Female Dramatist*. Madam Metaphor had been told to 'turn her pen into a needle, and her tragedies into thread papers'. It was intended as a slight but Elizabeth found needle and thread an excellent medium.

Elizabeth and Gates took the carriage into London. How busy and crowded the town was, almost a million inhabitants according to the census of 1801. They crossed Westminster Bridge and entered Pall Mall. Elizabeth and Gates, in their old-style goffered hats, looked at the young women walking arm in arm. Despite the war with Napoleon, French fashions—Empire style, it was called—had traversed the Channel. Young women had thrown off their whalebones, corsets and stays, and adopted high-waisted dresses with long flowing trains. As they stopped to peruse the windows of the Pall Mall shops, they resembled classical statues. Elizabeth reasoned that the style allowed for more mobility than her hooped skirts, but she was sure she would never expose her bosoms in that way, or go about with naked arms. It was as if the young women had come out in their nightgowns. They wore no hats and instead of the extravagant bouffant hairstyles of Elizabeth's youth, the Pall Mall women wore cropped hair, with curls sticking to their cheeks. 'They look as if they are ready for the guillotine, marm,' remarked Gates.

One fashion that Elizabeth was willing to engage in was map embroidering, which had arisen largely, Elizabeth reflected, through her husband's bringing back to London the shape of the world. When Elizabeth was a girl, they used to put their own maps onto linen or silk, drawing the outline first on tissue paper and pinpricking around it. They laid the paper on the fabric, sprinkled on powder, then marked in pencil where the powder fell through the pinpricks. These days maps were printed directly onto the fabric, and the outlines of continents and countries simply had to be followed in stem or cross-stitch. It was such a printed map that Elizabeth Cook was intending to purchase.

For the new work, Elizabeth decided to buy new tools, so she and Gates went into Deards and looked at all the pretty needle-cases and scissors, as well as the purely decorative baubles that Deards sold. There were chatelaines, a kind of handbag in which to carry small tools, which hung on delicate chains attached to a clasp at the waist. But Elizabeth judged the chatelaine to be cumbersome and had instead made herself a folding case with compartments in which to carry her embroidery tools when she was going about. At home she had the oriental box.

'Oh, marm, look at this!' Gates exclaimed.

Elizabeth made her way over to the item her servant was pointing out—a beautiful white satin case lined with pink, containing pencils for drawing, scissors, compass, and bodkin in gold and mother of pearl. The scissors had elaborately carved handles. Elizabeth much preferred her own folding scissors. 'Do you like it, Gates?'

'Oh, very much, marm. It would do you proud.'

'And you,' said Elizabeth.

'Oh, marm,' said Gates. 'I couldn't.'

'Nonsense, Gates. Of course you could.' Elizabeth was pleased to see that though her servant was the same age as herself, an old woman in her sixties, she could still flush like a girl. 'Sir,' Elizabeth called to the shopkeeper. He looked up. Elizabeth suspected that he was reading a novel held furtively under the counter. So many ladies came to admire the items in his shop but few made a purchase. 'We will have this folding case.'

'Certainly, madam,' he said, invigorated by the promise of a sale. 'Shall you take it with you or will I have it sent?'

It could easily fit into Gates's pocket, there was no need to go to the extravagance of having it sent.

Every Thursday, promptly at 3 pm Elizabeth Cook held dinners. She invited her many Smith relatives, or new friends and neighbours such as the Ravenhills and the Elliotsons, Mrs Hook, Miss Bower, Mr Stark, the Warrens, Miss Davies, Miss Williams.

Dinner today was with old friends—Sir Joseph Banks, his sister Sophia, and his wife Dorothea. Yes, Sir Joseph had finally married. In March 1779, at the age of thirty-six. Sometimes Elizabeth smiled at the memory of that pompous young whippersnapper full of himself, now eclipsed by the man of influence and prestige who was consulted, as James had once been, on every aspect of South Seas exploration.

He had been elected President of the Royal Society when Sir John Pringle had retired, the year after James received the Copley Medal. He maintained contact with scientific men of all nations, even France, despite England being at war with Napoleon. Sir Joseph had been involved in organising George Vancouver's voyage to survey the north-west coast of America, and was a patron of William Bligh, proposing him for command of the ill-fated breadfruit expedition on the *Bounty*. When the shame of the mutiny had died down, Banks had recommended Bligh for the position of governor of New South Wales. Elizabeth heard that a mutiny of sorts had occurred again, this time with the New South Wales Corps. Bligh was an excellent officer, but not always a likeable man.

It was Sir Joseph who'd advocated the establishment of a colony in New South Wales. Elizabeth wondered whether James would have approved. He came and went, but the colonists stayed, exposing the natives to convicts. James had found the natives of New South Wales 'an inoffensive race. All they seemed to want was for us to go.' Of the South Seas people in general he wrote: 'We introduce among them wants and perhaps diseases which they never before knew and which serves only to disturb that happy tranquillity they and their forefathers enjoyed ... If anyone denies the truth of this assertion let him tell me what the natives of the whole extent of America have gained by the commerce they have had with Europeans.'

Over the years, Sir Joseph, Sophia and Dorothea had all grown enormously fat. When Sir Joseph wasn't troubled with the gout, he enjoyed his food and wine with the same enthusiasm he had for botany, or any of his other pursuits. As Elizabeth watched Gates setting out the new pearl-ware Wedgwood, she couldn't help but recall once again Banks's boast that he had 'eaten his way further into the animal kingdom than any man'.

Nothing so challenging as penguin or armadillo would be served this Thursday. Elizabeth's few remaining teeth had a hard time chewing great lumps of meat, and for the dinner with the Banks she had organised an onion soup, followed by a fricando of veal garnished with lemon and barberries. A syllabub for dessert and, when the Banks arrived, to whet their appetites, anchovy toasts. This was a dish Elizabeth was fond of, and often had by itself for supper. Gates would cut slices of bread, fry them in butter then place half an anchovy on each piece. A good sprinkle of grated cheese mixed with parsley from the garden, and the dish was ready to place under the salamander to brown. It had to be browned in the dish which would come to the table, to keep it nice and hot.

'The Banks, marm,' announced Gates.

They entered the room like three round tumblers. Despite his obesity, Sir Joseph still had a great deal of flourish. 'I trust you are keeping well, Mrs Cook,' he said.

'Very well, thank you,' she replied. It was a politeness to answer in this way. Elizabeth often was not very well; the fits which had attacked her when Hugh and Jamie died threatened to return, she became feverish and could not sleep without the assistance of powders, especially on nights of high wind when she tossed and turned, and no amount of prayers could settle her.

The Banks were not frequent visitors but Elizabeth was always glad to see them. Sophia, who still continued collecting things, noticed any new relics and curiosities Elizabeth had, and Mr Banks always brought news of London and the world, of the men, like Bligh and Vancouver, who had sailed with James. What officers they were! 'You men of Captain Cook,' Sir Joseph repeated the words of politician William Windham, 'you rise upon us in every trial.'

The last time the Banks had come to dinner the talk was of the then recently published *Lyrical Tales*, by Mr Samuel Taylor Coleridge, now secretary to the governor of Malta. The poem which had most caught the public's imagination was *The Rime of the Ancient Mariner*, which told a dreadful tale. In that first 1798 edition, the precis read thus: 'How a ship having passed the Line was driven by storms to the cold country towards the South Pole, and how from thence she made her course to the tropical latitude of the Great Pacific Ocean; and of the strange things that befell; and in what manner the Ancyent Marinere came back to his own country.'

'Why, it's James's voyage on the *Resolution*!' Elizabeth had exclaimed to Isaac when it first came to their attention. The matter elicited quite a bit of discussion, Elizabeth remembering exact words from the *Voyage* which had found their way into the poem, and Isaac remembering incidents aboard.

The matter had been taken up again at dinner with the Banks. Sir Joseph listened to what Elizabeth and Isaac had to say.

'Isaac, let's not forget Mr Wales, may he rest in peace. Do you remember him, Mrs Cook? Astronomer aboard the *Resolution*, a Fellow of the Royal Society, elected 1776.' Elizabeth admired the way the man could refer so smoothly to that second voyage, the preparations for which had caused him to become a laughing stock. It all seemed so long ago. 'On his return, Mr Wales was appointed Master of the Mathematical School at Christ's Hospital, where Coleridge was a pupil.' Sir Joseph explained. 'It was the most dreadful school till Wales took command, the boys a terror to all around them. He reined them in, with strict discipline as well as a kind heart and a sense of humour. My guess is that a little storytelling wouldn't have gone astray. Nothing boys like so much as a good story of adventuring, Wales no doubt blending a little science in with the wonders of the sea and the ice, the strange phenomena of our world.' Banks laughed. 'Perhaps Mr Coleridge saw Wales as the ancient mariner. He was forty-odd when he commenced teaching, closer to fifty by the time he had Coleridge in his charge.'

Then began a kind of a game, with Elizabeth, Isaac and Sir Joseph looking for all the correspondences between the poem and the voyage, using James's account and Isaac's memories. 'And now there came both mist and snow, And it grew wondrous cold: And ice, mast-high, came floating by, As green as emerald.' In James's journal they found: 'The weather became hazy . . . the haze increased so much, that we did not see an island of ice, which we were steering directly for, till we were less than a mile from it. I judged it to be about fifty feet high.' As high as a mast.

The poem made mention of a phenomenon Elizabeth had heard of—the eerie sound of cracking ice, as if the whole earth was being rent asunder. All who had been to the high latitudes spoke of it. Mr Coleridge described how the ice 'cracked and growled, and roared and howled'.

There were many other correspondences, and though Elizabeth thought it was a very fine poem, the one closer to her heart was *The Antarctic Muse*, which James had enclosed in one of his letters to her. It had a much more positive ring to it.

After the dinner, with her head full of the voyage and the poem, Elizabeth had thought of the albatross. They were rather magnificent birds, judging by the paintings. Whether it was bad luck, as the poem suggested, to shoot an albatross, Elizabeth did not know. James noted in his journal the shooting of albatrosses, particularly by Mr Forster. But he would have none of the superstition. Perhaps part of Mr Forster's peskiness came from this, Elizabeth had mused before she'd drifted off to sleep. That night she had dreamt of white birds on great airborne voyages around the globe, a pair of them dancing their courtship in the sky high above the ice.

After the syllabub of the present dinner, over port and coffee, Elizabeth took up her embroidery.

'What a splendid idea, Mrs Cook,' said Sophia. 'All the ladies are embroidering maps, but no-one is more suited to it than you.'

'Where are you up to?' asked Dorothea.

'Approaching Botany Bay.'

Dorothea leant over for a closer look, careful not to spill anything on Mrs Cook's precious work.

'Ah, Botany Bay,' sighed Sir Joseph. 'So long ago yet my picture of it is still vivid. It was May when we were there, the creeks full of water from the autumn rains and the grass green. Flocks of lorikeets and cockatoos. Curious kookaburras giving out great guffaws of laughter that echoed through the trees. Stingrays in the bay weighing nearly four hundred pounds— without the guts. So much botanising to be done! You know,' he said, shifting in his chair, 'when we arrived your husband said: "Isaac, you shall go first". What a thrill for a boy of his age, the first European to step onto that pristine shore.' Sir Joseph paused, thinking perhaps of the shore no longer pristine, of the struggles the fledgling New South Wales colony had endured.

When Captain Arthur Phillip had arrived on that January day in 1788, the middle of the antipodean summer, the creeks had been but a trickle and the grass brown. They had all nearly starved. Yet the natives had been living there for some considerable time and had not starved, thought Elizabeth. She smiled at the memory of young Isaac. It was a well-loved family story, Isaac being the first to step ashore. And now he was a post-captain, commander of the *Perseverance* under Commander Cornwallis of the East India Station.

Elizabeth spent the winters in Clapham and summers at Cousin Charles's estate at Merton Abbey, also known as the Gatehouse, further south in the county of Surrey. In 1807 she was joined by Isaac, who had become ill with the yellow jaundice and had to retire, having obtained the rank of rear admiral.

In both houses Elizabeth embroidered and the work elicited interest whenever anyone saw it. Even little Horatia, product of the union between Charles's neighbours, Nelson and Lady Hamilton, was curious, mesmerised by the shiny thread Elizabeth was pulling in and out of the cloth. Elizabeth gave the child a piece of silk to play with, as she had once done with her own dear little Eliza.

Elizabeth stitched her way across the world and chequered it with the firm dark lines of longitude and latitude. James had told her that the Polynesian navigators of the South Seas made 'maps' of their ocean that resembled skewed lines of longitude and latitude, maps made of string with shells knotted into them, which were used to teach their apprentices, the lines representing the direction of currents, and the shells islands. Now Elizabeth was nearing Hawaii, about to stitch her way into Kealekekua Bay, where James's voyage, and his precious life, ended.

Kealekekua Bay. Elizabeth looked again at the watercolour of it in the ditty box and imagined James there. A turquoise bay with coral and brightly coloured fish, the water so clear the white sand could be seen on the bottom. Behind the bay ran a rocky cliff. Further away still was a massive snow-capped mountain. All around the bay was black volcanic rock, and at one end, a stream of fresh water.

Elizabeth will stitch only once into Kealekekua Bay but James went twice. The first time he was revered as a god. Over eight hundred canoes came to greet him, as well as a multitude of swimming natives. James's diary entry for 17 January 1779 read: 'I have no where in this Sea seen such a number of people assembled in one place, besides those in the Canoes all the Shore of the bay was covered with people and hundreds were swimming about the Ships like shoals of fish.'

An old priest came on board and presented James with coconuts and a pig. When James went ashore that afternoon the natives prostrated themselves before him. Echoing from the cliffs was their chant of 'Lono, Lono'. He was escorted to a sacred place which was bedecked in skulls and carved images. The priests wrapped a red ceremonial cloth around James and bade him prostrate himself in front of one of the images, then the islanders lined up and made offerings to him, all the while chanting 'Lono, Lono'. In return, James distributed trinkets and pieces of iron.

James King, second lieutenant, described the proceedings as a 'long, and rather tiresome ceremony, of which we can only guess at its Object and Meaning, only that it was highly respect-ful'. Later they would learn that the appearance of the *Resolution* on the horizon, a floating island with white banners secured by crossbars, matched exactly the predicted return of Lono, the Hawaiian god of abundance and peace. As well, the ships happened to arrive in the middle of *makahiki*, the season celebrating the god, in which warfare was suspended, and sport and entertainments took its place.

So began days of mutual friendship, reverence and gift-giving, including daggers and more pieces of the iron which the islanders so prized. As the days turned to weeks, Kalei'opu'u and the chiefs 'became inquisitive as to the time of our departure and seem'd well-pleas'd that it was to be soon', wrote King. Even in this season of abundance there were only so many offerings the people could make to their god. They had already provided all they could spare.

The *Resolution* and *Discovery* departed on 4 February. But on the night of the seventh strong gales blew up and damaged *Resolution*'s foremast. A sheltered harbour in which to make repairs was needed.

They returned to Kealekekua Bay, to a very different reception. As Jem Burney noted, the islanders 'appeared much dissatisfied'. The mood darkened even further, and thievery, which had been in abeyance during the first visit, now became rife. The blacksmith's tongs, tools which helped fashion the daggers, were stolen, not once but twice. Vancouver and others who tried to apprehend the thief had stones thrown at them. Reverence had turned to contempt.

That night, James called a meeting of his officers. 'The Capt expressed his sorrow,' wrote Lieutenant King, 'that the behaviour of the Indians would at last oblige him to use force, for that they must not he said, imagine they have gained an advantage over us.'

In the early hours of the morning, Sunday 14 February, Jem Burney noticed, on his rounds, that the *Discovery*'s cutter was missing, the boat having been stolen from under the very noses of the men on night watch.

On hearing of the theft James immediately ordered a blockade of the bay. Any canoe attempting to leave was to be driven back to shore. He gave an order for the marines to load their muskets with ball, which would kill, rather than shot, which merely caused superficial damage. James loaded his own gun, one barrel with shot, the other with ball. He went ashore in the pinnace with Lieutenant Molesworth Phillips and nine armed marines.

They landed on the black volcanic rockshelf and made their way towards the village, James intending to invite King Kalei'opu'u to visit the *Resolution*, and keep him there till the cutter was returned, this 'kidnapping' having worked on other occasions. The king had just woken up but was happy to go, as were his two sons, one of whom ran ahead and climbed into the pinnace.

Then came the sound of musket fire from the south end of the beach, and soon a ripple spread through the gathering crowd that a chief trying to leave the bay had been shot. More islanders gathered, some wearing protective war mats, others carrying clubs. And the iron daggers. A great humming arose and the trumpet of conch shells. One of the king's wives rushed forward and tried to persuade her husband not to go. The king sat down, confused. With the crowd teetering on the edge of war James could not compel the king to accompany him without bloodshed.

Several of the islanders threw rocks at the marines, knocking one of them to the ground. Another islander came from behind, aiming a spear at James. James turned and fired shot but it did not penetrate the thick war mat. When a marine told James he'd fired shot at the wrong man, James ordered him to shoot the right one. Which the marine did. The islanders momentarily fell back, but then began the scene of 'utmost horror and confusion'.

The natives showered the shore party with rocks. Four marines were killed. Phillips was knocked down then stabbed in the shoulder. He managed to shoot his assailant before swimming to the pinnace. As James waved for the boats to come closer, an islander armed with a club struck James a blow to the back of the head. James fell to one knee, his musket under him. As he rose again, another islander ran at him, drew an iron dagger from his feathered cloak and plunged it into the back of James's neck. James staggered into the water, and fell face down. The islanders held him under, snatching daggers out of each other's hands and plunging them into James's body long after it had become a corpse, swept along in the surge of destruction, just as the Gordon rioters had been, in which all humanity and reason is lost.

There was shocked silence on both sides. Then began the aftermath. Many on board the two ships, Bligh included, wanted to bombard the village, raze it to the ground. Captain Clerke took command, and ordered restraint.

It was a week before James's remains, or parts of them, were returned—his hands, one bearing the signature scar from Newfoundland, the long bones, the scalp. The rest, it was explained, had been divided among the chiefs of the island, as was the custom with the death of a grand personage. The returned remains were buried at sea, 'committed to the deep', Clerke wrote, 'with all the attention and honour we could possibly pay it in this part of the world'. Captain James Cook was in the embrace of his beloved ocean. Before the ceremony, someone was thoughtful enough to cut a lock of hair from his scalp, to be returned to his wife in the ditty box.

Elizabeth sat for a long time looking at Hawaii, such a small scatter of islands on the blue ocean that had so seduced her husband. She drew her focus away from Hawaii to see the world as a whole, the embroidered coastlines, the letters marking the Southern Ocean, Great South Sea, the Pacific Ocean and the Western Atlantic Ocean. Across all the oceans and seas were Elizabeth's fine antlike stitches, the traces of Captain James Cook's voyages.

THE BOOKPLATE

The wind goeth toward the south, and turneth about unto the north; it whirleth about continually, and the wind returneth again according to his circuits.

All the rivers run into the sea . . .

Ecclesiastes 1: 6–7

'Into the blue?' repeated Isaac. 'What do you mean?'

Elizabeth dabbed paste on the inside cover of the Bible and carefully placed the bookplate, smoothing it down with a cloth to make it adhere. The bookplate bore the Cook family coat of arms with the two polar stars and map of the Pacific. 'I mean I want to depart, on a ship. A supernumerary like Banks, and the others.'

'You want to sail to Botany Bay?' Surely Elizabeth couldn't be serious. Never in her entire life had she expressed a wish to sail. Isaac eyed his cousin carefully. Was she finally losing her faculties?

'Of course not to Botany Bay,' she said impatiently. 'The blue water must start sooner than that. I want to see the brown river turn ocean blue.'

'But you get seasick,' Isaac protested lamely.

'I feel queasy on a boat,' Elizabeth corrected him. 'Unlike Nelson, who vomited his way to Trafalgar, I have never actually been ill. I've survived many things, queasiness is not going to kill me.' Elizabeth watched her cousin's mouth, on the verge of saying something, his eyes flickering, searching for more excuses. 'It's not a whim,' she continued. 'A short passage to Portsmouth should be easy for a rear admiral such as yourself to arrange. A sailing ship that goes with the wind, not one of those new steam-powered things belching smoke into the air. No special arrangements need be made. I'll not be bringing a suite of servants, horn players and dogs, or any paraphernalia. Just myself, and one small valise.'

Mrs Elizabeth Cook and Rear Admiral Isaac Smith were piped aboard a sloop bound for the East India Station, with all the pomp and ceremony that Elizabeth had heard of years earlier through the excited voices of her sons. She was not interested in the carry-on, but Isaac had said that the widow of the celebrated Captain Cook could hardly come on board unnoticed. So Elizabeth steeled herself. She proceeded up the gangway, black mourning garment billowing about her. The officers waiting at the top of the gangway bowed as if she were the queen.

Elizabeth stood still amid the flurry of departure, the thwack of ropes, the flap of canvas, squawking of seagulls, and the bark of commands—'Jib the mizzens!', 'Up the foresheet!', 'Port the helm!'

The pilot guided the sloop past Limehouse and Greenwich, the marshy edges of Bugby's Hole, Purfleet, Gravesend and Tilbury. How well the sailors harnessed the wind, adjusting the sails to suit its moods, working always with it, as James had done, never against it. The further they went the more the brown river widened. By the time they reached Sheerness, the place of James's terrible storm that last season in Newfoundland, night had fallen.

Elizabeth did not see the point at which the brown turned to blue. Though she rose early the next morning, she found herself already surrounded by it. 'That's Dover,' Isaac said, indicating the chalky white cliffs. But Elizabeth was not interested in the land with its affairs and preoccupations. She wanted only to be in the emptiness of blue.

She stood at the bow in her billowing black, and watched the sloop slice through the water beneath her, giving the vessel a lacy white edge, and blue ripples that fanned out and away. Behind her was a wake of white water, then the waters came together again, leaving no trace of the ship's passing. She closed her eyes and felt the sea wind on her face, the wind that moved the waters around the globe. Elizabeth imagined the wind to be like the water, closing up behind her, so that her passing, too, left no trace. How exhilarating to be away from the refuse and garbage that sullied the waters of the Thames. She imagined its pure source, a gurgling baby spring that fed a bubbling brook and became the immense slow river on which she had grown up and passed her life. She saw the flow of water find its way around rocks and other hindrances in its path, watched it fill the deep dark cracks that grief had worn into her, move on and finally dissolve into the ocean.

Standing at the bow of the ship, with harlequins of light sweeping across the water, Elizabeth felt the clenched fist of her heart relax and open out. Blood flowed freely through it, pulsing life into the rivers of her veins. It would continue to pulse in the darkness of winter, the season in which Elizabeth prayed for her dead. Her time of remembrance beginning in October with Nathaniel, then the day of longest darkness, the winter solstice devoted to Hugh. January was the time for Jamie, and finally, on 14 February, the day on which birds chose their mate, James.

Portrait of Elizabeth Cook
by an Unknown Artist

When Elizabeth was somewhere in her eighties, Charles and Isaac persuaded her to have her portrait painted. 'Then we can put the portrait in the window to satisfy the curious,' said Charles, 'and you can go about the house in peace.'

They employed a young artist known to the sculptor William Wyatt, who was distantly related by marriage to Isaac's great-niece, Caroline Cragg. Elizabeth no longer remembered the name of the artist but she recalled very well dressing in her best goffered hat, wearing it even though she was at home in her own house in Clapham. She sat very still, something she did well, for long periods at a time, while the young man circled around her, looking at her this way and that. Her steady immobility made quite a contrast to the way James flew off in a carriage to Nathaniel Dance's studio to have his famous portrait painted.

The young man made a couple of visits; Gates served him tea, and while drinking it, he asked Elizabeth about the old days.

Elizabeth loved telling young people the stories and showing them the curiosities James had brought back from his voyages—the fish hooks and tapa cloths, feathered helmets and capes, carved wooden figures. A favourite story, especially when the man himself was present, was 'Isaac, you shall go first', and the young ones—Elizabeth's goddaughter, or John Leach Bennet from Merton, would imagine themselves there and the captain saying it to them. Elizabeth had endless patience for those who wanted to hear the stories, but found her temper growing short with people who stood outside her house trying to look in the windows to catch a glimpse of her, as if she herself were a monument, a living relic.

'This is my husband's dress sword,' she said, pointing out the silver handle and silver trim on the scabbard. 'And these are the shoe buckles he wore to court.'

'What of yourself, Mrs Cook?'

'Myself?'

'Do you have stories of yourself? Your rings, for example,' the young man searched for a way in. 'This one on your right hand.'

'Oh,' she said. 'That is the memorial ring for my husband. The vase motif on it is made of his hair. All that came back from Hawaii.' Elizabeth was silent for a moment, travelling back to that place.

The artist then switched to her left hand, to happier memories.

'My wedding ring,' she smiled. 'We walked across the fields to St Margaret's. I wore a cream silk dress,' she said, looking down at her widow's dress of black satin, 'with matching hat.'

Elizabeth showed him the oriental box. 'This was Mr Cook's first present to me. It didn't have embroidery tools in it then.' But she didn't tell him what the box first contained, it seemed too . . . personal.

The tea and the stories finished, the artist went to his easel, and Elizabeth to the high-backed chair. It was a pleasant drowsy experience being painted, like having her hair combed.

When the portrait was finally completed Elizabeth was so surprised. She looked exactly like the old woman she had seen in her dream, the one who reminded her of a walnut, grown erect and tall. She saw an old woman's face, the softly wrinkled skin, lips thinned by the absence of teeth, a hint of crepeyness at the neck. The hands were quietly folded one on top of the other, and revealed Elizabeth's rings. Best of all were the eyes. In that old-age face the eyes were still the deep limpid blue eyes she had had when a child, a girl, a young wife and mother. Elizabeth considered the artist's work a gift, that he portrayed her as a venerable old lady yet brought into the eyes the whole span of her life.

'Wait one moment,' she said to him. She knew that Charles and Isaac had commissioned the work, but Elizabeth was so pleased she wanted to give the artist something herself. 'It is a page from my husband's log,' she said, handing him the sheet. Elizabeth often gave such pages as gifts. People collected Cook memorabilia, and Mrs Elizabeth Cook had the best collection of all, which was obvious to anyone who came to the house and had to thread their way through it. Once she gave her servant, Charles Doswell, a gilt button from James's dress uniform. He seemed to treasure it much more than the book she'd given him as a birthday present—William Wilberforce's *A Practical View of the Prevailing Religious Systems of Professed Christians, in the higher and middle classes in this country, contrasted with real Christianity*.

How could she recall the lengthy title of Mr Wilberforce's book but not the name of the young man who'd painted her portrait? After he'd gone Elizabeth opened up the fan of time. How odd to have found it amongst James's papers when she went to get the log page. She couldn't remember placing it there, one of the servants must have. The fan was almost as old as

Elizabeth herself. She could see signs of wear in the silk, the embroidered numbers beginning to fade. She remembered how the half-circle of the outstretched fan looked like the sun rising up from the horizon. Now she saw that it was the same shape as the setting sun.

How excited she'd been when she made the fan, at all its possibilities, how she could open and close it, could find her birthday in the fan of time, make it show years yet to come. She swept her hand across the fan, feeling the soft smoothness of the silk, the ridges of the bone struts. Eighteen hundred had been so far in the future then, but it was now more than twenty years ago. She manipulated the fan and found the happy times of her life—1762 when she married James, 1763 when Jamie was born, the birth dates of Nat, Eliza, Joseph, George, and darling Hugh, the dates of James's returns from Newfoundland and the voyages. She smiled looking back on those happy times, the years of grief hidden in the folds.

A Letter from Isaac Smith to Edward Hawke Locker

Merton Abbey 8 Oct 1830

My dear Sir,

I am sorry Mrs Cook had not returned to Clapham when you favoured her with a call on Wednesday last but she intends to do so next week & desires me say that she has not in her possession any letter or even a paper of any sort of her husband's writing nor do I believe that there is now left a single paper with his signature in the house, so many applications having been made for it and as to any communication she could make was much better made when Dr Keppis wrote the Life as then Mr Banks, & Hugh Palliser & other of his friends did their utmost to select information & had several conferences with her on the subject but she feels herself hurt by the idea that the Captain was severe & says he was a most affectionate husband & a good father to his children whom he dearly loved & she always found *fault with the picture for that stern look which it has otherwise a good likeness. As for myself that was with him the first two voyages as a petty officer & youngster, I never thought him severe & he was both loved & properly feared by the ship's company & when he was very ill on the second voyage the first question ask'd both by the officers & men on the relief of the watch at night was how does the Captain do, is he better, but Capt. Clerke & King, who have given their opinion of him is of much more consequence & later than mine, not having seen him after the year 1775. The publication you mention I hope will equal your most sanguin wishes & Mrs Cook thanks you for preference you have given to her deceased husband & hopes you & your family are well, and I propose returning to Clapham with Mrs Cook for the winter, a great invalid from a severe illness*

*and am Dear Sir with respect
yours most faithfully*

I.S.

It was a most mellow autumn in that year of 1830 and Elizabeth had stayed on in Merton. Isaac was ill, and Elizabeth did not want to take the journey till he was improved. Nevertheless, it would be better for him to spend the winter in Clapham, where Dr Elliotson could administer to him.

As for the visit from Mr Locker . . . He was writing a book, or setting up a gallery at Greenwich Hospital, something or other. Elizabeth was sure he was a man of good intention but she no longer cared. She disapproved of the portrait he'd made mention of by William Hodges. It made James look stern, ill even, with sunken eyes. It was not the way history should remember Captain James Cook.

Elizabeth had dictated the letter to Isaac, with her cousin adding his own opinion.

'Read it back to me,' she instructed. Though her mind remained sharp, her eyesight had softened and blurred, laying a permanent veil over everything. Elizabeth could no longer thread a needle, and certainly could not have written a letter.

She remained silent during Isaac's reading, and for a long time after.

'Is everything all right, Cousin?'

'Why do you say that Clerke's and King's opinion of James is of much more consequence than your own?'

'Well, because I can only speak of the first two voyages. I was in America on the *Weazle* by the time of the third.'

'Would your opinion be different had you sailed with James on his final voyage?'

Isaac started fiddling with the gold braid on his sleeve.

'Isaac, I asked you a question. Was he "loved and properly feared" on the third voyage?' she asked more directly.

'I wasn't there,' he mumbled into his kerchief.

'But you know, don't you?' Though King, Burney, even Isaac, put a shield around their captain's widow, the odd rumour got through. 'Did his temper get the better of him?'

Isaac sighed. 'That, among other things. A common saying amongst both officers and the people was: "The old boy has been tipping a *heiva* to me". Or, "I had a *heiva* of the old boy".'

'And what, pray, is a *heiva*?'

'A South Seas dance.'

'A dance? Surely a dance does not denote temper.'

Isaac cleared his throat. 'A war dance. A lot of stamping on the ground. Yelling, and fearsome facial expressions.'

'I see.' Elizabeth fingered her mourning ring. 'They called him the old boy?'

Isaac shifted in his chair. 'I believe so.'

Elizabeth was silent for a moment, the portrait of which she disapproved fixing itself into her mind. She saw the severe lines around his mouth, the almost demented look in his eyes. 'Did he turn into a monster?'

'Oh no,' he tried to laugh it off. 'I wouldn't say that.'

'What would you say?'

'He was erratic. There were incidents.'

'What kind of incidents?' Elizabeth set sail on her husband's final voyage.

'Well, for example,' Isaac began, adjusting himself once again, as if he couldn't find a comfortable position, 'in the Arctic they came across a colony of walruses, and the captain ordered them to be butchered, thinking that the fresh meat would preserve the people's health. Despite being hung to let the oil drain off, boiled for four hours then fried, the meat was disgusting. Midshipman Trevenen said it tasted like train oil. The people couldn't keep it down and refused to eat any more of it. The captain flew into a rage and called them "damn'd mutinous scoundrels who will not face novelty". If they'd not eat walrus then they'd eat nothing but ship's biscuits. He came close to mutiny. The men started collapsing at their work stations through malnourishment, and the captain had to lift the ban.

'He made navigational errors, changed course suddenly, and several times in the ice put the ship in imminent danger. This was not the man we revered as our great captain and father. He lost his patience with the South Seas thievery, on one occasion threatening to burn canoes if a stolen goat wasn't returned. A Tahitian they were transporting from one island to another stole something and the captain ordered not only that his head be shaved but his ears cut off as well. The barber had completed the first part and was beginning on the ears when an officer, King, I believe, sent him to the captain to have the order verified. The rage had passed, and the islander swam ashore with only one ear lobe missing.'

Elizabeth could not believe her husband capable of such cruelty.

It was a blighted voyage from the beginning, before the *Resolution* even left Deptford yards, workers' negligence bringing the ship undone time and time again. Clerke had succumbed to tuberculosis, as had Surgeon Anderson. At one stage, even Mr Kendall's clock stopped—dirt in the mechanism.

Dirt had somehow found its way into James's mechanism. He had gone not only as far as it was possible to go, but too far. Elizabeth remembered the captain of the second voyage, who, in *The Antarctic Muse*, 'conducted the ship from all eminent danger', whom the 'brave boys' held in high esteem, and would 'toast with a loud song all around', the captain 'who had proved so good'.

Then she thought of the other poem inspired by the second voyage, the one in which Elizabeth and Isaac and Banks had found correspondences and made a game of it. 'A grey-beard loon with glittering eyes, and skinny hand so brown.' Had the Pacific Ocean become for James a 'rotting sea' on which he wandered aimlessly? Had Captain James Cook become the Ancient Mariner?

Was it the illness Isaac referred to in the letter that transmogrified him? Elizabeth recalled those final days before the third voyage, James wincing and putting his hand to his stomach.

The next time Dr Elliotson came, which was fairly frequently with Isaac being so poorly, she asked him about it. He told her that bilious colic was perhaps caused by a parasitic infection of the intestine, which could produce digestive disturbances, irritability, and even change of personality. James had exhibited all of these.

Elizabeth needed to know the man of the third voyage, but knowledge is one thing, memory another. Not just Elizabeth's memories but those of others, including the South Seas people. From subsequent travellers Elizabeth heard the memories of Te Horeta, who had been a small boy when the *Endeavour* came to

New Zealand. The Maoris assumed the English were creatures from another world, had eyes in the back of their heads because they rowed their boats facing the opposite direction to where they were heading. Te Horeta recollected that 'there was one supreme being in that ship. We knew that he was lord of the whole by his perfect gentlemanly and noble demeanour. This man did not utter many words; all that he did was to handle our mats and hold our spears, and touch the hair of our heads. He was a very good man, and came to us—the children—and patted our cheeks, and gently touched our heads.'

Elizabeth recalled how James had held their first-born, lifted little Eliza into the air when she took her first steps, how tender he was with Elizabeth herself. She could not reconcile the husband of her memories with the mariner of the third voyage.

'Isaac, was James faithful to me in the South Seas?' It was a question she'd hardly dared ask herself, let alone her husband, even when he performed the Tahitian flesh brushing on her.

'Yes, of course,' said Isaac without the slightest hesitation or shock that Elizabeth should ask such a thing.

'You can vouch for his behaviour on the third voyage also?'

'There would have been talk. Especially as he had never previously indulged in such behaviour. Unlike Mr Banks. Quite the opposite. There were occasions when he had to decline the invitation of amorous young ladies, and do it deftly enough not to cause insult. Quite amusing, really,' Isaac's voice trailed off.

Elizabeth wondered how life might have been had she not married James but instead taken a safer, less adventurous path with someone like Frederick, Reverend Downing's son. Her childhood friend would certainly not have died in the way James did, killed by numerous and tumultuous natives. But Death was ever inventive and may have found its way to Elizabeth's loved ones no matter which path she had taken.

Perhaps it would be better never to have been born at all. What decision would Elizabeth have made if the Almighty had revealed His plan for her? I will send you a great man and you will love each other profoundly. But he will die, and so will all of your children. Your well of grief will be so immense you'll think you can't bear it, but you will survive, living out the missing years of your loved ones' lives. Would Elizabeth have said no, I want a husband and children and grandchildren who'll remain with me into old age.

She looked at Cousin Issac, the only one who had remained with her. James would have preferred the quick sudden death, violent though it had been, to the slow death nibbling away at Isaac, a once proud rear admiral shrunken inside the uniform he still insisted on wearing, even at home. Would Isaac have said yes to this, to a long life of voyaging, in which he never found love, never married and had children? What would anyone say if they held in their unborn hands a map of their life?

'Marm, can I help you?' It was Sarah, one of the servants, sounding a little alarmed at finding Elizabeth bending over the fire so early in the morning, throwing sheets of paper in, one at a time, watching them curl and burn in the flame.

'Thank you, Sarah, it is a task I must do myself.'

Despite the words that had been written to Mr Locker, Elizabeth still did have papers with James's signature in the house. But fire could easily turn that lie into a truth.

Isaac coughed as he entered the living room, a blanket around him as he felt the cold so terribly nowadays. 'Are you feeding the fire, Elizabeth? Surely, one of the servants . . .'

Elizabeth suddenly felt exasperated. Would they ever leave her alone? 'I am burning letters, Isaac, what do you think I am doing?'

'Letters?' said Isaac. 'But . . .'

'They are private correspondence between me and my husband,' Elizabeth said curtly. Elizabeth was burning all the letters James had written to her, and she to him. There were hundreds, maybe thousands, of them. She could recall each and every word without even glancing at the page. Nevertheless, she had spent the entire night beforehand leafing through them one last time. 'Too personal to be printed in a book for the public to gawp at,' she added, more to herself than to anyone else in the room. 'It is only paper, Isaac,' she said softly.

Occasionally, a coloured flame, blue or green, appeared as the letters burnt, a stain or pigment in the ink. The wax which had once sealed the letters melted and ran over the burning letters, concealing them from prying eyes forever.

ELIZABETH COOK'S MONUMENTS

Charles died in 1827, Isaac in 1831. Dear Gates, who had been with Elizabeth for more than fifty years, died in 1833. Lord Sandwich was dead, Sir Joseph, Sir Hugh, Cousin Frances. Everyone.

Elizabeth remembered the games of bullet pudding played at Christmases long ago. She was now the only one left in the game. Soon, the bullet would fall to her. But Elizabeth had to make sure the living would remember the dead before she could finally lay herself down.

Lawyers drew up a long and complicated will for Elizabeth Cook. She remembered everyone. James's relations and her own, all the Smith descendants. Her friends, neighbours, her doctor. She bequeathed bank interest from her investments as well as specific items—the Copley Medal to the British Museum, the contents of her kitchen, wash house and scullery to one servant, and bedroom furniture to another. She made bequeaths to the

School of the Indigent Blind, the Royal Maternity Charity, to widows and poor aged women. She also left money to continue the family monument in Great St Andrew's Church, the church in which she wished to be buried, in the middle aisle as close to her sons, James and Hugh, as may be.

Elizabeth had a headstone made for Gates in the church grounds at Clapham, which read simply: 'Elizabeth Gates, of this parish, died 30 July, 1833'. Then she commissioned William Wyatt to sculpt a memorial in St Mary's at Merton, to the Smiths. Charles and Isaac, their nephew Isaac Cragg Smith, Caroline Cragg Smith who died in childbirth, and her infant. 'Sacred to the memory of those whose names are here recorded,' the inscription read, 'and whose remains are deposited in the family vault adjoining the chancel of this church. This monument was erected by Mrs Elizabeth Cook, widow of Captain James Cook the circumnavigator in affectionate remembrance of the many estimable qualities of her departed relatives.'

The sculpture featured a kneeling woman looking upwards to memorial plaques. Carved into the stone beneath her were the words 'THY WILL BE DONE ON EARTH'.

May 13 1835. Elizabeth chose a fine spring day to slough off her worn old coat.

'Mrs Cook?' enquired Sarah when she came in to open the curtains and attend to her mistress. Elizabeth was very still and quiet. Sarah was alarmed. She crept over to the bed, bringing her cheek close to her mistress's nose, and was relieved to feel the warm dampness of breath.

'Gates?' said Elizabeth, her voice barely a whisper.

'It is Sarah, Mrs Cook. Sarah Westlake.'

'Where is Gates?'

Sarah hesitated. The mistress knew Gates was dead. She visited the stone in the churchyard the first Friday of the month. It was not like Mrs Cook to let her mind wander so. 'Shall I plump the pillows? Are you feeling all right?'

'Bring me the embroidery.'

'Which embroidery would that be, marm?' There were so many.

'My husband's voyages.'

Sarah looked about at all the paraphernalia that crowded this room but which Mrs Cook would not have stored away in cupboards. The embroidery hung on a wall, beside the coat of arms and Captain Cook's medals. Sarah carefully lifted the embroidery down and laid it on the bed. Her mistress felt around for it. Gently Sarah guided her hand, such a cold hand, till it found the embroidery. Something was terribly wrong. 'I shall get Charles to fetch Dr Elliotson.' She pulled the tasselled cord which would bring a servant to the room.

'Is Cousin Charles here?'

'No, Mrs Cook. Charles Doswell, your servant.'

He came to the door and Sarah signalled him to get the doctor.

'Please open the window.'

'But Mrs Cook, it is cold, you'll catch your . . .' Sarah was going to say 'death' but stopped herself. Her eyes may have deceived her, but it appeared to Sarah that her mistress smiled.

'Open the window, the bird wants to fly out.'

'There is no bird in here, marm.'

'Open the window.' Sarah heard the determination in her mistress's thin small voice, and opened the window a crack. 'More. It is a big bird.'

'But Mrs Cook—'

'Do as I ask.'

Sarah sighed and opened the window fully, letting the crisp breeze carry in the morning song of birds, although Sarah was sure there were none in the house.

'Thank you, you may go.'

'I will stay, if you don't mind, marm. Till Dr Elliotson comes.'

'If we are having visitors you must make tea.'

Sarah reached her hand out to touch her mistress's forehead but withdrew it. She quietly went to a stool in the corner and sat down.

Elizabeth's eyes were closed but she saw everything as her hands glided over the embroidery of the world. The great continents, the equator and all the latitudes. The tips of her fingers traced James's voyages across the oceans. She felt the breeze of the world through the window, and it occurred to her that with such a breeze blowing in there was no longer any need to breathe. She could finally let out the breath she'd been holding all her life. Breeze flowed effortlessly through her.

The white bird, as large as the room itself, started to lift its great wings. Elizabeth heard voices, felt her clothes being loosened, the coldness of a stethoscope on her breast. But she was already lifting into the air on great white wings.

She saw the house in Clapham, heard sobbing, such a small sound in the greatness of the world. 'Elizabeth.' Sequins danced in the breeze. Elizabeth was ready, she would fly with the bird wherever he took her. She nestled in the soft downy feathers of his bosom, high above everything.

Down below was a river of ice. Elizabeth saw all the stalls and amusements of the Frost Fair before she was born, boys playing skittles, food sellers, jugglers. She saw her mother and father walking arm in arm towards the printer who would print their names in the ice, the great dome of St Paul's, and all the buildings of the city. How small the hustle and bustle of life appeared.

'Elizabeth,' the bird called once more. How her heart thrilled to hear that voice. Up, up they went, over the whiteness of ice. The bird no longer needed to flap his wings, he had found the tides of wind and sailed with them. Below was the continent of ice, yet Elizabeth felt warm and safe in the feathery bosom. She saw all the peoples of the world as the bird rode on the winds circling the globe. Eskimos, Tahitians, English, Chinese. Higher and higher he went, towards the stars that were her babies, and higher and higher, to the bright star, whose light would guide her into the Great Ocean.

WHERE ARE THEY NOW?

Mrs Cook was a great accumulator of objects, her house in Clapham 'crowded and crammed in every room with relics, curiosities, drawings, maps and collections' as Canon Frederick Bennett, son of John Leach Bennett, executor and residuary legatee of Mrs Cook's will, remarked. Frederick was twelve years old at the time of her death.

It seemed in character to structure her story thus. More generally, we reconstruct the past through the artefacts left behind.

The Frost Fair Print
The print described bears the name Mr Edward Hurley, and was 'Printed on the river of Thames when Frozen over, January 18, 1739 (from Nichola Johnson, *Eighteenth Century London*, Museum of London, 1991, page 42).

The Quill
The method of making a quill pen, pupils with marks against their names, spelling and arithmetical problems from Dan O'Sullivan,

The Education of Captain Cook, Captain Cook Schoolroom Museum booklet, Great Ayton, England.

The Bell Alehouse
The building was probably redeveloped during the early nineteenth century, in common with the rest of Wapping, where the expansion of trade resulted in a demand for warehouses. That warehouse has been subsequently demolished and the site stands empty, being used for car parking.

The Great Tree
A cedar of Lebanon flourishes near the site of James Cook's birth. It may have been there during his time but more likely was planted by Henry Bolckow when he bought the Marton estate in 1858.

A Box of Letter Tiles
A popular eighteenth century educational toy.

John Walker's House
Now a museum dedicated to Cook. A little poetic licence has been taken here, as Walker did not move to this house till after James had finished his apprenticeship.

Execution Dock Stairs
This is the old name for King George Stairs, the set of steps closest to where the Bell alehouse once stood.

The Fan of Time
The fan as a fashion accessory reached its height of popularity in the eighteenth century. They were made of silk, paper, chicken-skin parchment and other materials. England adopted the Gregorian calendar in 1752. For practical purposes almanacs

were used. The Book of Common Prayer contains a church calendar with a table of lessons.

The Porcelain Teapot
National Maritime Museum, London. Mrs Cook's teapot is c.1750, from the Ch'ien Lung Period. Tea, silks and porcelain were the main imports from China to Britain.

The Oriental Box
State Library of New South Wales, Sydney. It is said to have been Cook's first present to Elizabeth.

The Marriage Certificate
National Library of Australia, Canberra.

A Plan of St John's
State Library of New South Wales, Sydney. Measurements: 20 x 26 cm. Original ink MS, hand coloured, showing soundings, sand banks, coastline, buildings, wharf, batteries.

The Telescopic Quadrant
State Library of New South Wales, Sydney.

The Endeavour
The *Endeavour* became a transport which during the American War of Independence was deliberately sunk, along with other ships, to protect the harbour at Newport, Rhode Island. Marine archaeologist, Dr Kathy Abbass, heads a team currently trying to locate it.

The Folding Table
State Library of New South Wales, Sydney. An elegant piece of furniture used by Captain Cook during his three voyages.

Mrs Cook bequeathed it to her servant, Charles Doswell, who married Sarah Westlake, another of Mrs Cook's servants.

The Book of Common Prayer
State Library of New South Wales, Sydney. Frances (nee Wardale) Lieber took the Book of Common Prayer to America with her. She married John McAllister on 28 August 1783. The inscription on the flyleaf reads: 'presented by Capt. James Cook to Frances Wardale in the year 1769' (an error here? In 1769 Cook was already in the South Seas).

The Telescope
State Library of New South Wales, Sydney.

Bingley's Journal
The quote is from JC Beaglehole, *The Life of Captain Cook*, Stanford University Press, 1974, Stanford, California, page 269.

Portrait of Sir Hugh Palliser by George Dance
National Maritime Museum, London.

A Pair of Shoe Buckles
State Library of New South Wales, Sydney. Diamanté-covered buckles used for court wear, as opposed to leather-covered ones for everyday wear, also in the State Library.

A Damask Serviette
State Library of New South Wales, Sydney. Measurements: c. 72 x 84.5 cm. Described as a tablecloth in the Dixson Library Realia Collection, but according to staff member Margot Riley is probably a large serviette, the reasoning being that it is too small even for a teacloth of the period, but big enough to cover the large skirts worn by the women. The embroidery 'EC' with a number

'9' centred below the initials is in very fine cross-stitch in blue/grey thread in one corner. The cloth was number 9 in a set.

Cook Cottage
Fitzroy Gardens, Melbourne. Purchased in 1933 by Victorian businessman Mr (later Sir) Russell Grimwade and donated to the state. The bricks of the cottage, along with slips of ivy from the walls, were shipped to Melbourne from Hull, in 253 cases and 40 barrels.

Mr Kendall's Clock
National Maritime Museum, London.

The Glass Tumbler
State Library of New South Wales, Sydney. Engraved: RESOLUTION, Capt. Cook, 1772.

The Staffordshire China
Captain Cook Schoolhouse Museum, Great Ayton, England. Blue and white china was fashionable during the period. Three plates and a dish from the service are on display.

A Letter from Solander to Banks
State Library of New South Wales, Sydney.

Introduction to a Voyage towards the South Pole and Round the World . . .
Copies in several libraries including the State Library of New South Wales, Sydney.

Boswell's An Account of Corsica
The journal of a tour of that island, and memoirs of Pascal Paoli, 3rd edition, E & C Dilly, London, 1769. State Library of New

South Wales, Sydney. Boswell's presentation copy to Captain Cook has the signature, 'J. Cook' on the back of the frontispiece.

The Portrait of Captain Cook by Nathaniel Dance
National Maritime Museum, London.

The Will of James Cook
The original is in the Public Records Office, London. The will was proved 24 January 1780 by Elizabeth Cook and Thomas Dyall.

The Copley Medal
British Museum, London.

The Unfinished Vest
State Library of New South Wales, Sydney. Of tapa cloth, embroidered by Elizabeth Cook for her husband to wear to court, had he returned from the third voyage.

The Ditty Box
State Library of New South Wales, Sydney. Ditty boxes were used by seamen to hold their smaller possessions.

Sir Hugh Palliser's Monument to Captain Cook
The monument is in Vache Park, Buckinghamshire; copies of the inscription are held in the State Library of New South Wales, Sydney.

A Letter from Elizabeth Cook to Frances McAllister (nee Wardale)
Copies are held in the National Library of Australia, Canberra, and the State Library of New South Wales, Sydney.

A Letter from Mrs Honeychurch to Frances McAllister
Copies are held in the National Library of Australia, Canberra, and the State Library of New South Wales, Sydney.

Embroidery on Silk of Captain Cook's Voyages by Mrs Elizabeth Cook
National Maritime Museum, Sydney.

The Bookplate
State Library of New South Wales, Sydney. The Bible was printed by M. Baskett, Oxford, 1765. On Elizabeth's death it passed to John Leach Bennett of Merton, Surrey. The bookplate bears the coat of arms and the name Cpt. Cook.

Portrait of Elizabeth Cook
State Library of New South Wales, Sydney.

A Letter from Isaac Smith to Edward Hawke Locker
State Library of New South Wales, Sydney.

Elizabeth Cook's Monuments
The monument to her Smith relatives is in St Mary's Church, Merton, London.

Most of the other objects mentioned in the text are also in library or museum collections.

All the churches are still in existence in one form or another. Another St John's was built close by the original which suffered subsidence because of the marshy ground. Great St Andrew's is now a community church.

On 27 February 1971 the Elizabeth Cook Memorial Fountain was switched on in the EG Waterhouse Gardens, Sutherland Shire, Sydney. It is believed to be the only memorial dedicated solely to Elizabeth Cook. The fountain feeds a waterfall edged with tree ferns, ivy growing up the trunks of some. Near the memorial plaque itself grows a *strelitzia*—bird of paradise.

Elizabeth Cook's image also graces a matchbox label, one of a set of forty-two issued by the Federal Match Company, Australia, in 1970 to mark the bicentenary of Cook's landing at Botany Bay.

OBITUARY: MRS COOK
—FROM GENTLEMAN'S
MAGAZINE, JULY 1835

May 13. At Clapham, in her 94th year, Elizabeth, widow of Capt. James Cook, RN, the celebrated navigator.

This venerable lady, remarkable alike from the eminence of her husband, and for the length of time she had survived him, as well as estimable for her private virtues, was married in the year 1762. She was a Miss Batts, of Barking in Essex; and Cook was then a Master in the Navy, thirty-four years of age. To the last she was generally accustomed to speak of him as 'Mr Cook', which was the style by which he had been chiefly known to her during his residence at home, as he was not appointed to the rank of Commander until 1771, nor to that of Post Captain till 1776. His death at Owhyhee took place on the 14th of Feb. 1779, having then been absent from England for more than two years and a half. Mrs Cook had, after his departure, received from the Royal Society, the Copley gold medal, which had been voted to him for a paper explaining the means he had employed for preserving his crew in his previous voyages, and this, with many other interesting memorials, she treasured with faithful care.

When the tidings of Captain Cook's death were communicated to King George the Third, his Majesty immediately directed pensions to be settled on the widow and three remaining sons. But Mrs Cook had the grievous misfortune to lose them all within a few years after. Nathaniel, the second, who had embraced the naval profession from hereditary emulation of his father's name, not without affectionate apprehensions on the part of his mother, was lost in 1780, at the age of sixteen, with Commodore Walsingham, in the *Thunderer*, which foundered at sea.

Hugh, who was considerably the youngest, died in 1793, at the age of seventeen, whilst a student in Christ's College, Cambridge. His mother had purchased the advowson of a living, with a view to his preferment; but he died unacquainted with a circumstance which might, if prematurely announced, have damped his personal exertions. James, the eldest, at the age of thirty-one, was drowned with his boat's crew, while Commander of the *Spitfire* sloop of war, off the Isle of Wight, in 1794. A daughter had previously died of dropsy, when about twelve year of age. The memory of these lamentable bereavements were never effaced from her mind, and there were some melancholy anniversaries which to the end of her days she devoted to seclusion and pious observance.

Mrs Cook selected Clapham as her place of residence, many years since, on account of its convenience for her eldest when coming to town by the Portsmouth coach. There her latter days were spent in intercourse with her friends and in the conscientious discharge of those duties which her benevolent and kindly feelings dictated to her. Her amiable conduct in all social occasions, her pious acquiescence and resignation under extraordinary family trials and deprivations, and her consistent demeanour throughout a long life, secured her universal esteem and respect.

The body of Mrs Cook was buried on 22nd May, in a vault in the church of St Andrew the Great, in Cambridge, near those of her children, to whose memory there is already a monument. Mrs Cook has munificently left £1000 three per cents, to that parish, under the following conditions:—The monument is to be maintained in perfect repair out of the interest, the Minister for the time being to receive £2 per ann. for his trouble in attending the execution of this trust; and the remainder is to be equally divided, every year on St. Thomas's Day, between five aged women belonging to and residing in the parish of Great St Andrew's, who do not receive parochial relief. The appointment is to be made each year by the Minister, Churchwardens, and Overseers. She has also bequeathed £750 to the poor of Clapham; and has left many handsome legacies to her friends; to her three servants, besides legacies, she has bestowed all the furniture in their respective rooms. She has bequeathed the Copley gold medal, before mentioned, and the medal struck in honour of her husband by order of George III (of which there were but five) to the British Museum. The Schools for the Indigent Blind and the Royal Maternity Charity, are benefited to the amount of nearly £1000 consols, besides various other public and private charities. Her will has been proved in the Prerogative Court of Canterbury by her relation, J.L. Bennett, esq. of Merton, and J.D. Blake, esq., the executors, and her property sworn under £60,000.